A SPELL OF TROUBLE

I. C. PATTERSON

Cover Design by James, GoOnWrite.com

To my husband Matt,
this book wouldn't have been possible without you.

MAP OF NEWLANDS

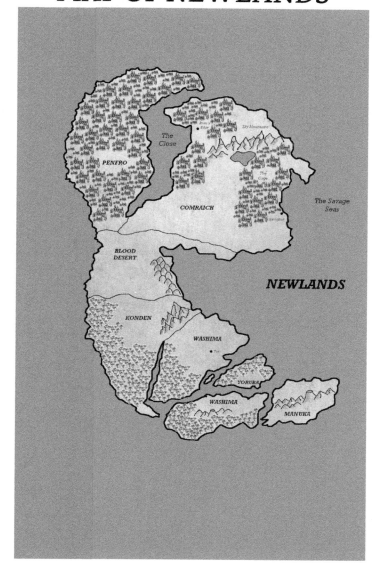

CHAPTER 1

Faylinn

"Well, show me, you dimwit." My aunt's shrill voice made me jump in my seat. "Quick, now!" Head bent over I got up, making a show to readjust my skirt as I smoothed the frown on my face. It was at times like these I resented the mask I put on; my temper wasn't one easy to tame. I let her words flow over me as she was a force to be reckoned with. Although not intelligent, the queen took pleasure in tormenting people below her eminence. Suffice to say, I have been one of her favourite targets since I moved into the Castle.

I placed the threadwork in her waiting hand then glanced at my cousin Gwynn, small and frail looking, working with quick expertise. She used a spelled needle of course. The queen prodded my work with a dainty manicured hand.

"I suppose this is acceptable for someone like you. You do have rather thick fingers for a girl." Her brown eyes were intent on me, waiting for a reaction.

I gave her none.

She reminded me of a Sabre-toothed tiger poking, playing with its prey before the kill. She liked making snide remarks, the ones about my family abandoning me hurt the most. I grew a thick skin with time, yet some scars ran deep within my soul. It was frustrating not to be able to give her a piece of my mind, but that didn't mean I couldn't retaliate in my own creative way. I used the one thing I knew she hated: cocking my head to the side, mouth slightly open, I gazed at her through vacant eyes. It was even more satisfying seeing her infuriated face knowing she was the one who accidentally gave me the idea of playing the slow-witted cousin.

My aunt huffed and thrust the lace in my hands. "That will be all, silly girl. The seamstress will be here shortly to see to Gwynn." *As though she needed a new dress.*

"You may retire until dinner."

I squared my shoulders as a burst of joy rushed into my veins. If she had any inkling how pleased I was, she'd make sure to find me some dreadful chore to do. "Thank you, my Queen."

I made a cursory curtsy and went out of the room before she could change her mind. Time to myself was few and far between, and I planned to use it to my advantage, which meant lurking. The guards on both sides of the door didn't even blink when I thrust it open. Fiona, my handmaid, got up as soon as I walked out the doorway – the queen did not approve of servants staying for long periods in her private sitting room – then followed behind me. As a lady I was forbidden under any circumstances to go anywhere by myself, not that I could leave the Castle's grounds like the others. More than the tormenting, this was what drove me insane.

I pursed my lips at the opulence surrounding me. My sequined slippers sank into a green carpet as deep and soft as I imagined the sand dunes of the Blood Desert to be. Vivid paintings and the most beautiful, handcrafted tapestries I'd ever seen adorned the grey stone walls of every main room and hallway. These represented a portion of the royal wealth gathered over hundreds of years. It all came from the annual boat that sold goods from the Closed Lands to the South. At an exorbitant price, of course, and paid with the sweat and blood of Comraich's poorer subjects. Pain shot down my jaw I ground my teeth so hard.

Fiona's voice cut my mental outrage short. "Me Lady, am I needed?"

I looked up surprised to be by my chamber's door. Stepping inside, I said, "That will be all, thank you."

Weeks had flown by filled with preparation for Gwynn's coming of age ceremony. Mine was only two months away. For ten years I'd been living in the viper's den, almost half of my life. The celebration of a young person's twenty-first birthday was an important event in every family, be it poor or rich. Until that age, the magic within us was shifting, growing in tune with our body. It was as much a period of discovery as one of caution. If a person was lucky, or perhaps unlucky, to have rare powerful magic, it was imperative they seek help from a tutor or enrol in school to learn how to prevent it from running amok. Every boy and girl knew the tale of the boy, too poor to pay for either, whose gift had gone out of control and erased a whole village. The story was so tragic and heart-breaking, that everyone under the age of twenty-one did not dare forget the signs of an imminent magical blast.

As a general rule, nobles used tutors to teach their children the essentials, then at the age of sixteen their paths converged. Girls stayed in the seclusion of their homes and were encouraged to use their magical gifts towards tasks befitting female arts, beautification and sewing, while the boys were sent to the Kingdom's University where they could learn to enhance and master their gifts for the betterment of the Kingdom, until they reached their twenty-first birthday. My two older brothers had.

I threw the cloth on my bed. How I longed to see my whole family. Maybe the king would send for them, or even better let me go home to celebrate. I flopped down on the bed, my shoulders slumping. *Right, and the Savage Sea made for a tranquil voyage.*

The sound of Fiona's footsteps retreating, I got up to turn the key in the door before rushing to the back of the room. I stood in front of the secret that had kept me sane for the past six years. That, and occasional reunions with my brother Haelan when he attended court. One afternoon, out of boredom I had scrutinised the beautiful oak panels furnishing my bedroom's walls. I loved wood; it made my skin tingle with life. I had been running my hands on the intricate carvings of a forest scene, when the tingle turned into sudden heat. Precisely over one petal.

Excitement fluttered in my chest as my fingers found the familiar ridged shape. With a practised touch I pushed and turned it, my mood soared in anticipation. A section of the woodcarvings, big enough for a person to bend through, opened inward with a creak. The mixture of musty air and dust assaulted my nose; a smell I came to associate with freedom. I gathered the skirt of my morning dress with one hand while the other held a candle. When lit up, the red mesh glowed through the wax, the only indication it had been spelled to increase its lifespan. The flame caught at spider webs as I stepped through the doorway, leaving an acrid smell in the air.

To my left the passage would lead deeper into the Castle before terminating at the solarium, built by my great grandfather as a present to his wife. It was an oasis of rare and foreign plants which was rarely used nowadays, and therefore another good escape. Today though, I needed fresh air on my face. I headed to the right. The corridor was narrow and small forcing my head at an awkward angle. Not for the first time I wondered about its size and history. Yet curiosity hadn't been incentive enough to look for answers, I only willingly touched books to read novels. That left me wondering and making up silly speculations during my walks. Had the people who'd built the castle been very small? At five foot ten, an average male size, I was towering over the other women, and I doubted they had made this passage.

A scuttling sound neared me. I froze then relaxed as I spotted two rats, they usually ignored me if I did them. As I continued the slow walk, parts of the skirts slipped from my hand and got caught on the damp and dusty wall. *Rotten stars!* I would need to pay for a cleaner now. I loved Fiona dearly, but I couldn't be sure she wasn't coerced into reporting my every move. If there was one thing I had learnt at court, it was to trust no one.

Reaching the point where the passage branched off into two, I headed for the one to the left towards the back of the Castle. I'd found two outward openings so far. I headed to the one emerging in the walled garden at the farthest point in the Castle's gardens, used for growing vegetables and herbs; not a place I would encounter unwelcome faces. The other one was special. Like an assassin's hidden blades, it was my mental weapon, my reassurance that if things went awry, I would be able to run away. My throat constricted as the memory of the day I'd nearly gone through it caught me in its grasp.

"You heard me well, dimwit." The king looked down his red bulbous nose at me. "From now on, you'll spend the summer at the Northern Castle with the Court as you should be. I have been generous so far, don't you think? A companion to the royal princess should not go frolicking with commoners."

The murmur of assent from the nobles mingling in the Throne room reached me. I bit my tongue hard, the trickle of blood in my mouth washing away words of fury, of despair. Unable to constrain tears, they dripped down my hot cheeks taking with them fond memories of a family I would scarcely see, leaving me empty. I was trapped for good. That very night I packed a bag, intent on walking out of it all. I didn't know where the other door led, but I didn't care. My fingers resting on the panel, my father's words as I left home swept over me and knocked me back. "Stay strong", he'd said, "your presence at the Castle is vital". To this day I didn't know why. I went back to my room. Sometimes, I wished I'd gone regardless.

* * *

As I neared my cousin Quentin's quarters, I slowed my steps. With years of exploring under my belt, I had memorised the layout of secret corridors. It had obviously been built for the Royals to flee undetected in the event the Keep was under attack or siege. Few rooms held a secret panel, all Royal quarters had one, including Quentin's which was round the corner. I despised many people, but none so as him. There was something truly evil about him, something that would raise the hair at the back of my neck every time he was near.

His loud voice resonated as I approached; I cursed under my breath that he was in his room. Knowing, through unpleasant experiences, people on the other side of the panel could hear me as well as I did, I stepped on the tip of my toes.

"If I may, your Highness? I don't understand why you are so infatuated with the girl." Talk about people I despised. I pursed my lips hearing Roldan's voice, suspicion stopping me in my track. I'd rarely seen him address my cousin with anything but the barest courtesy. As the High Mage, the supposed most powerful mage in our Kingdom – I knew better – his contempt for people was as strong as his magic.

"We have more pressing matters at hand that need discussing, if you please." he added. The deference in his tone, his obsequious manners were so out of character, curiosity caught me in its sticky web.

"Is the potion ready?" Obviously, Quentin didn't care for his opinion. Clothes rustled and a chair creaked to my left.

"Here, your Highness." Was that a hint of exasperation? "At midnight," he went on, "on the next dark moon, which will be in a fortnight, mix a drop of her blood and yours with this. As you recite the spell on this paper, you need to put precisely five drops of the mixture onto the doll's hair. Too little, the spell would break after a season. But be warned, too much and the devoted love you're seeking would turn into pure hatred. This is critical."

The stale air felt heavy in my lungs; I forced small breaths through my parted lips. Their conversation made me uneasy, something sinister was going on.

"If I may overstep my position," Roldan said in a smooth voice. I didn't like the familiarity between them. Nothing good could come out of their association, and why the duplicity in front of everyone? "I am acquainted with two young women of good noble lineage who would befit your future position in every way without these forced undertakings."

"I'm well aware of your opinion on this matter, Roldan. I want her, only her, as my wife." Quentin's voice was cutting. "I'll tame her. I'll have those disdainful eyes of hers regard me with adoration, and I'll savour my victory every night."

My blood travelled from head to stomach in a nauseous wave. The past year, I'd caught him watching me with a lecherous flicker in his eyes, the hold on my revulsion and hatred slipping at times. *Curse his soul, he's talking about me!* Resting a hand on the cold stone, I willed my legs to stop shaking. I had to flee far away from here, but Roldan's next words rooted me on the spot.

"Using the Black Arts can have unfortunate consequences, your Highness. Take heed on this."

My head was pounding through the crush of these revelations. To my knowledge, Myrddin had banned the Black Arts, more commonly known as the Leechings, centuries ago. Manuscripts and books on the subject had been burned, disciples either imprisoned or executed. The realisation that Roldan, a mage as powerful as he was egocentric, practised them made my blood curdle. My feet started back towards the way I had come. I'd heard too much; the stars knew what they would do to me if they found me. Before I could take more than three steps, the word "Coward" throbbed through my mind over and over again.

No! I unclenched my white-knuckled fists, small, rounded lines marked my palms. I traced them over one hand, focusing on the stinging sensation. I'd never shied away from trouble before and today wouldn't be any different. I wouldn't let fear scare me away. I stayed put, body shivering. My father needed to hear about this. Although the king had banished him to the province of Highlands in the North, he'd made sure to keep informed of the political goings-on. My eldest brother Haelan, I knew, was required at the Castle next week. I could pass on the information then.

"Enough, I've made up my mind." Quentin's raised voice brought me back to the conversation. "You came for another reason if I'm not mistaken."

"Yes, I found a more effective... avenue to our plan. However, it will take me at least three full moon cycles to brew it. I understand your need to make haste your Highness, but I must beg for your complete trust on this account. The potion I have in mind is entirely untraceable. It will pass as an unknown ailment that will tragically prove fatal. You will be king without anyone having the slightest suspicion."

This revelation elicited a gasp I failed to catch in time. Belated, I covered my mouth listening for any indication they had heard me.

Nothing.

Exhaling a shaky breath, I made to turn away only to realise my legs weren't responding. In fact, I couldn't feel any part of my body. *What has he done to me?* Sheer panic shot down my spine as I heard a chair being dragged along the wooden floor.

"It would seem, your Highness, we have unanticipated company. Now, if I'm not mistaken," Fingers were tapping along the wall until a hollow sound resounded on the wood panel. Seconds dragged like mage years. The creaking sound of rusted hinges resonated in my small cage, the sound as chilling as mourning bells. I closed my eyes in dawning realisation.

They were going to kill me.

CHAPTER 2

Faylinn

Bright light and fresh air invaded my hiding place. I stared in front of me, eyes blinking hard until they adjusted to the luminosity. Both men were looming by the doorway, faces in shadow. Although only a couple of inches taller than I was they were much stronger. The passing observation this panel was man-sized penetrated my sluggish mind.

The High Mage flicked his hand towards the room. Of their own volition, my legs directed me to a chair; the air erupted from my lungs as I sat down hard. He muttered an incomprehensible spell that caused the air around me to shift, then a dizzying tightness slammed into my head. All at once, sensations that would normally go unnoticed came crashing into my body and overwhelmed my already befuddled mind. If it hadn't been for my thoughts, I could have sworn I'd been dead one minute and alive the next.

Quentin appeared suddenly before me, red tainted his pale face, the colour clashing with his ginger hair. He slapped me before I could react. The violence of his blow sent my head sprawling to the side as a high shriek filled the room.

Mine.

Black shadows dotted my vision, but I sat back holding my head high.

"How dare you spy on me! You filthy shrew?" he pointed a large finger at my face. "I should have known. Is this why your father was so amenable to your staying here? Don't think I didn't see through your stupid act."

My playing a simple-minded girl had started as a young girl's sulky reaction upon my arrival, which developed as a sort of instinctual self-preservation. Now it was a role I played to survive in this insipid world, my own armour of sort. Within a week of my arrival, the whole court assumed Myrddin's blessing had not been kind to me. They left the simpleton to herself. Whispers of mother dropping me as a babe followed me for a time, disgusted or mocking stares soon after. I was the new entertainment in their monotonous and rigid routine. Thankfully, the news Lady Anne, a window of two years, was with child put a stop to it all. I could have been under an invisibility spell for all the attention I got from the nobles after that. I didn't care as long as they left me alone. Unfortunately, my little plan backfired. The queen and her sons insulted me on a constant basis. Sometimes I wondered if they had made an agenda in order to take turns, as I couldn't recall a day when I hadn't been mocked on my looks or wits. The king watched all this with amusement, some days taking part in it when he was in good spirits. Gwynn left me alone. It was neither out of compassion nor kindness though, as I caught her many times watching me with her lips curved in disdain. Probably too scared to be near me in case my stupidity was infectious. But when had Quentin figured it out?

Words escaped me. Nothing came to mind that would sound plausible, and anyway Quentin wasn't so dupe he would be inclined to believe me. Bleak acceptance sank into my soul; I'd heard too much.

"Your Highness, would you like me to attend to this little complication? It would be quick." Was this how I would die?

Would my family ever know the truth?

Not taking his gaze off me, Quentin replied, "No, you may go. I'll handle this my way." Nothing good for me, I was sure.

Like an injured animal waiting for the predator's fatal strike, I couldn't bring myself to look away. The door closed behind Roldan leaving the room in ominous silence. I waited for my fate. Terror must have slipped from the brave mask I was trying to put on because his mouth twisted, giving him a demented look. My head shot back. I'd heard accounts of his violence and brutality, of his severing fingers of people unable to pay the heavy taxes the King had imposed, of good citizens, who in a fit of madness had criticised the monarchy, put to death under his sword. And although he'd been anything but abominable to me, that look, that blood thirsty look, had never been cast upon me until today.

"I much prefer this look on you, little cousin. Fear me, for your life is at last in my hands. I have a perfect place to keep you, and no one will be the wiser." His face was too close for comfort, his rancid breath made my stomach turn in a sickening upheaval. "I will tell my father you had to rush to your poor sick mother. Being the gentleman that I am, I kindly provided you with my carriage. That will give me plenty of time to hide you and brew the potion that will make you mine for as long as I see fit." My top lip curved in distaste. He scrutinised my face. "Heard that part too, have you? Shame, I was hoping for a better reaction." He straightened. "But first," he grabbed a handful of my hair and forced me up. "I've enough time for a little diversion."

I struggled in his grasp as he steered me to his four-poster bed. Understanding washed over me like the freezing water of the Spire River. The stars be damned, I wouldn't go down without a fight. Survival instinct kicked in. The heel of my hand extended, I hit him as hard as I could on the solar plexus. One of the perks of growing up with two big brothers was I had learnt a trick or two on how to defend myself. Sunlark, the second oldest, was the one who had been adamant to teach my sister Mara and I self-defence moves since we were six. The blow had the desired effect; Quentin bent over, letting me go as he struggled to catch his breath. I ran to the door only to be pulled back by my hair. My neck cracked in excruciating pain as one large hand encircled my throat while the other retracted to hit me. A loud knock at the door made us both jump.

"What?" barked Quentin, not letting his grip loosen.

"Your Highness, I have an important message from the King." The king's valet.

Quentin squeezed my neck and whispered, "Not a word from you, do you understand?"

I stared at the door. It might be my sole chance; I could cry for help. Then what? I clenched my jaw. No doubt Quentin would threaten the servant or worse, kill him before my eyes. He pressed harder. I nodded with reluctance.

"Out with it you gimp," he shouted through the door. "I'm occupied." I grimaced at his rudeness. He treated his hunting dogs better than the servants, and as this one had a limp...

"I'm sorry your Highness, but the King requires your presence at once." The valet pressed on, the clearing of his throat the only indication of his being scared.

Quentin swore then told him he would be there shortly. Dragging me with him, he took a leather belt and raiments out of a chest of drawers then forced me to sit next to a bedpost. With a false air of equanimity, I let him handle me. A growing river of expletives clustered on my lips when he gagged me and bound my hands around the post. A flame of hope ignited in my heart despite the leather digging in my skin as this was my chance of escape. The difficulty being how.

Done with his deed, he took my face in his hand and squeezed hard. I flinched.

"I'm not done with you," he leered down at me. "I'll show you what else I can do with a belt."

I shuddered in spite of myself, a sight I was all too glad he missed for he crossed the room in three big strides then slammed the door shut behind him.

With no time to spare, I wiggled my fingers upwards to reach the piece of the belt overlapping the other, however, my wrists were tied too tight to move. I shook and pulled my body forward with pent-up frustration and fear. Nothing shifted. Canting my head to the side of the post, I looked up and noticed the wood was thinner near the tester, which was draped in a glorious green velvet reminding me of a canopy of pine trees. An idea came to mind. Gathering my legs in a crouching position, I heaved myself up on the bed, the skin on my forearms smarting against the leather and polished wood. Then, I grabbed the post in as strong a grip as I could manage, lifted my legs up and kicked at the joint a few times. The wood was unbending under my feet. Catching my breath while I turned around, I spotted a knife on the bedside table. No point stretching my legs, it was too far. Once again, I moved my body to try and dislodge the post, but to no avail.

My shoulders slumped; fists clenched. My forearms, pressed against the wood, were tingling as though an army of insects was marching on my skin. It was almost painful. Haelan had so much power he could flatten an entire mountain with the click of his fingers, a fact our family kept carefully hushed from the King. Even the delicate Mara could cast fire.

Me? I had an affinity with wood, with trees to be precise. It was the strangest sensation; with a simple touch it became an extension of myself. I focused on the wood resting against my skin, an image of a cherry tree dressed in beautiful white flowers bloomed in my mind: its former lifetime. A lovely thing to know to be sure, and I loved my connection with living trees, but it was quite unhelpful in my predicament.

Haelan speculated my skills at whittling and making bows and arrows were due to this strange ability. On my part I was dubious, hard work alone had honed my bow-making skills. My first one had been a pure disaster; it seemed so long ago. Closing my eyes, I recalled the smooth grains of ash under my palms, the heady scent of sawdust. Unskilled, I'd ended up cutting too much wood resulting in its breakage. The surprise and following anger of my first failure still felt raw in my mind. I had not been an easy child to say the least, my temper taking over me many times. I had screamed and stamped my feet to channel the frustration. To my side, Mara had looked, eyes as wide as our dinner plates, at the broken bow, which had missed her by a hair's breadth. A moment passed before it burst into flames. Her gift seldom materialised, strong and violent emotions the only precursors. I had been so severely reprimanded at scaring my sister I could still taste the bitterness on my tongue.

Heat against my skin tore me from my daydream. As I was about to inspect, a noise as loud as a thousand branches cracking at once deafened me. I yelped, the sound dulled by the cloth in my mouth, as pain radiated down my arms. Next thing I knew I was falling on the ground headfirst. On instinct my body twisted, head tucked in; a move which, I was sure, saved my life.

Standing up with tied hands turned out to be difficult in my stupor, but not impossible. I looked in a daze at the damage around me. Wood fragments of different shapes and sizes littered the bedspread and floor; the top of the bed was hanging down at an odd angle. The feeling something important had just happened nagged at my mind, but I couldn't focus, too many emotions were clashing for superiority. Wood crackling in the fireplace snapped me out of it; now was not the time to be stunned. I went straight for the knife. The belt proved tough to cut. I chanted encouragement in a soothing murmur to stave off the mounting panic. Any moment I was expecting Quentin to walk through the door and do his worst.

My restraints on the floor, I placed a hand over my heart to send a blessing to Myrddin, amazed I was free. Not yet. The thought induced shivers all over my body as I walked across the room. Reaching for a candle I stopped mid-motion at the sight of my arm. The upper part of my sleeve was shredded, red lacerations forming uneven patterns down to my wrist;

the other arm hadn't faired any better. Now that surprise had receded, their throbbing was hard to ignore, especially the big splinter protruding from my left forearm. Refusing to give it much thought I pulled it out, flinching at the pain. Good thing I wasn't squeamish; my blood was glistening on its sharp end. I shoved it in my pocket, then rushed back to the bed and collected any shards of wood with even the slightest trace of blood. My knowledge in the Leechings was limited, however, even a ten year old could tell you blood was an essential part of its practises. We'd all heard the tales of the Leech Emperor.

As I headed towards the secret panel, a vial and what looked like a doll made of hay caught my attention. Roldan's earlier words sprang back to mind. I grabbed both and closed the panel behind me with one thought predominant: I had to flee home.

Back in my room, I hid everything under the bed and took the painstaking task to clean my arms. My ears were drumming as the water in the delicate porcelain dish turned a dull pink. Next, I cut one of my undergarments up and used strips of cloth on the deepest wounds. Satisfied with my administrations I changed into my nightdress and threw the water away. A glance into the mirror confirmed my suspicion: my cheek had doubled in size, its colour already a dark purple. My index grazed a cut at its centre. Quentin's ring had caused it no doubt. I tempered the unwelcome jumble of emotions rising within me. This was nothing, I sighed through clenched teeth, it could have been much worse. I'd had a close escape, but I wasn't yet out of the woods.

Time to think.

Glancing at the secret panel, I decided to slide the chest of drawers in front of it. It wasn't heavy enough to stop Quentin, but it would give me time to run away; he wouldn't dare abduct me in front of servants. I hoped. After setting the room to my satisfaction, I settled in bed. The burning wood in the grate creaked in a semblance of approval. In a clear voice

I pronounced, "Fiona, I request your assistance immediately." All personal servants were bound by a spell to the nobles they served under. This exuberant spell, with a price which could feed a commoner's family for a year, was the rage amongst aristocracy. The old-fashioned system of bells would have sufficed, but nobles with too much money in their pockets generally were inclined to waste it in extravagant spells and trinkets.

A knock at the door roused me from an unexpected doze. Limbs felt heavy while a mild throbbing pulsed in my brain. I wouldn't need to pretend feeling unwell. I cleared my throat, "Come in."

As she stepped through the doorway, Fiona stopped short, a hand at her throat while she took in the sight in front of her: closed curtains, dim light and me, her charge, in bed. Concern took over surprise in her homely round face. Putting back a stray lock of golden hair in her bonnet, she placed herself next to the bed. I kept the sheet up to my nose, the injured side away from her. If she noticed, she would make a fuss, send for a healer and soon enough the whole castle would know of it. I was in no mind to make up some silly explanation, and therefore kept my face turned as far away from her as possible without looking suspicious. The glim of the candle by my bedside table was strategically placed on my good side, casting the other in shadow.

"Me Lady, clearly you're unwell. Whatever can I do for you?" She was wringing her fingers in her neat apron. Hers was one of the few friendly faces I'd come to like in this place. In fact all of them were servants. I would miss her good-natured temperament and handy gossip.

"Please forward the King my apologies for I will be unable to attend supper. I have a terrible migraine, I'm certain it will be gone after some rest." That way, she won't insist on staying with me.

"Oh, no need to worry yourself me Lady," she placed a jug and glass of water on the bedside table. "His Majesty, the

Crown Prince and Prince Quentin are gone away."

I took a shaky breath. "Are you sure?"

"Aye, Little Tom saddled them horses. Some important goings-on of sorts in the South borders. It's got to be bad though, if the King took both princes and the High Mage with him. Cook says it's a rebellion. How she knows?" she shrugged, then chuckled, "Prince Quentin was furious, said he'd to get something in his rooms. The King wouldn't have none of it, told him to quit fussing like a Lady. Turned bright red Little Tom said." I bet he was. Her shaking head stopped at my silence, which she misinterpreted. "Beg your pardon, me Lady. My tongue ran away with it again."

I smiled gratefully at the woman who had been kind to me all those years, sorry this was the last time I would see her. A part of me wanted to tell her everything, ask her to come with me, but I'd heard rumours the King had spelled his servants into forced loyalty. Whether this was true or not I couldn't tempt it.

"You don't need to apologise Fiona. You provided me some much needed peace of mind. I shall rest well now. And I don't need a healer." I added, before the question left her lips.

After requesting for supper to be brought up to my room, Fiona slipped away silently leaving me with clashing thoughts. Seconds, minutes passed as I lay down, my mind a blurry haze, unable to comprehend what I was feeling. Then, it hit me. The King had saved my life. The irony I'd been saved by the very man who'd shattered my life in the first place wasn't lost on me.

Ten years ago, King Filius, ruler of Comraich, requested of my father, his youngest brother, he send my older sister Mara to live in the Royal castle to be a companion to our cousin Gwynn the Royal princess. Worried for her sensitive nature, my parents sent me, the unruly tomboy, in her stead. So, at the tender age of eleven, my days of freedom and innocence had ended the moment I'd stepped through the Keep's doors. Feeling betrayed and heartbroken, I was convinced my parents loved me less than Mara. Yet, despite my misery it took me little time to realise they had made the right decision. She would have been eaten alive.

Here, women fluttered about like vicious black wasps, if you got in their way, they would sting. The younger generations were more approachable but reminded me of prettily dressed and made up puppets, their brains as equally empty. I had yet to find a lady I appreciated. The so-called gentlemen weren't much better, eyeing us, the fairer sex, like future breeding mares. I went from a life filled with laughter, independence and nature to this. Clarity came with renewed energy. *I will get it all back.* I threw the covers away, now far more determined, then slipped out of bed to get dressed.

Nothing would stop me from going home this time.

CHAPTER 3

Selena

"**M**ummy!" The word slips from my mouth as I wake with a start. The bedroom is pitch black. The cracking sound of wood makes me pause before I call once more, my tiny voice quivering. I don't like the dark. Why isn't the hallway's light on? Holding Timmy tightly to my chest, I get out of bed and make my way to daddy and mummy's room.

It's empty.

They don't like it when I go downstairs after bedtime, but I feel sick to my tummy for some reason. The house is gloomy and silent, outside lights cast shadows around me and I don't like that. I shuffle on my bum on the steep stairs, the carpet muting my movements. As I'm halfway down I hear shouting and sobbing. Why is mummy crying? My legs quicken, soon I'm walking quickly towards the noise in the sitting room. The room is dark there too, apart from mummy's beautiful necklace. I've never seen it do that before. There's a big shape on the floor. Mummy puts her arms up and says something as a strange man gestures towards her. She falls to her knees, eyes wide open with fear when she glances at me.

"Se–" she gasps before falling on her side.

"Mummy?" I squeak. The strange man faces me, eyes cold. But he is no stranger.

Granddad!

His face startled me awake. Eyes wide in shock, I pressed a shaking hand over the wild beatings of my heart. Dim light was escaping through the blackout curtains. My pjs were stuck to my clammy skin. I sat up and rested the back of my head on the metal frame, taking in every detail of my bedroom: the clock emitting its comforting tic toc, the fireplace with its mantelpiece full of trinkets, the furniture. The familiar rumbling of cars droned up to my bedroom on the third floor; I could even smell a waft of freshly baked bread from the bakery down the road. All this normality helped me ground myself to reality, to the present.

In time, my breathing went back to normal; only then did I let the remnants of the nightmare unravel once more. I normally did everything in my power to forget about it, but this time something had left me apprehensive. It had started as expected, the dark room and creaking sounds, mum and the body on the floor, whom I could only assume was dad, but then granddad had appeared instead of the usual shadowed presence. I shivered remembering his face. He'd looked much younger; the way his eyes looked at me, even how he'd held himself had been different, yet I knew with an iron certainty it'd been him.

I rubbed both hands over my face. Nothing to be concerned about, I was sure. It was normal for the mind to bring up unrelated titbits of experiences and information through strange dreams, sort of a way to store up what it has processed throughout one's life. And let's face it, granddad was the closest person I had. It made sense, right? I shouldn't put too much importance on the nightmare anyway, that horrible night had happened very differently. One fact was true though.

Mum and dad were murdered that night.

A mere three days after my fourth birthday, granddad, who'd lived with us in a spare bedroom downstairs, had found them when he'd woken up from the gathering smoke. After he'd gotten me out of the house and phoned the fire brigade and police, the murderer was long gone, never to be found.

So, why was I having the same dream over and over again? What bugged me was it felt too real to be a figment of my imagination, so much so the only person I had ever spoken to about it was my doctor. Of course, he'd blamed it on the trauma of losing both parents. But after so many years? And no change until now? Is it possible I'd actually found the bodies and granddad had lied in order to protect me? *That's it!* I breathed easier now. He probably found me in the sitting room with their bodies, and that would explain why he had been in my dream. Maybe my mind was at last remembering some of my life before their deaths.

I suffered from dissociative amnesia, which were pretty words for memory loss caused by emotional shock. After the incident, the police recommended I see a child's psychologist as a precaution. It soon transpired I had needed the help. What had really baffled my therapist though, was that I couldn't remember anything before the incident except my parents: their voices, their smell, even the way they'd sandwich me in a family hug. But try as I may, I could not picture my old house or bedroom, not even granddad.

My eyes fell on mum's favourite necklace, the one from the dream. She used to wear it every day. Attached to a thin silver chain was a tree, its branches delicately reaching out to the thick rope-like circle encompassing it. Or was it a root? I loved it, yet resented it for what it reminded me of: a sad memento of things lost to nightmares. It hung there against the only photo I had of my parents; all the others had burnt in the fire. I'd never gotten the nerve to wear it, feeling unworthy for some stupid reason, but also afraid if I did, a tsunami of anguish would drown me for good, and take me under. On impulse, I inhaled deeply, got up and took the pendant in a gentle grip.

It felt cold and heavy against the palm of my hand, yet right. Turning it this way and that, I scrutinised every inch. Just normal silver. No way it could shine. Once more, I questioned the meaning of my dream. One minute I was sure it was real, the next – with evidence such as this – I very much doubted it.

"Granddad keeps telling me I have an overactive imagination," I mumbled rubbing the sleep from my eyes. "And I'm starting to agree with him."

An idea sprang to mind. I read a book once on how being positive, seeing things in a positive angle could alter your state of mind for the better. *That's what I should do, see the necklace as a memory of mum's love for me, of her smile.* The thought immediately brought one to my lips. With sweaty hands, I lifted it and placed it around my neck. In the same manner as an anti-climactic ending, nothing extraordinary happened. I reflected on why I had expected something. *Must be that overactive imagination!* Yet despite no life changing moment, I was confident I had crossed a huge mountain. *Every little helps.* I snorted. Now I sounded like a walking advert. The alarm ringing by my bedside called me to task. I had a shop to open.

Every Saturday, I was up by 7am, had breakfast then headed to work downstairs; a routine that would make most twenty-six-year-olds cringe, but not me. As soon as I opened the door separating our flat to the shop, the distinct smell of old books welcomed me into granddad's secondhand bookshop. How I loved that smell. It was like a drug invading my soul, sentencing it to a life lost forever to stories and daydreams. This was where I felt most at ease, among books. Every day I would spend hours alone reading in a corner and travel to faraway places, some real, others the incredible imaginings of vivid minds. Wasting my youth away, my best friend Anna kept moaning.

From the outside the building appeared to be rather small; however, like most period houses the facade was deceptive. The shop, though narrow, was deep and laid out over three floors. Quirky stairs that appeared out of nowhere directed avid readers to small rooms where you least expected them. Towers of perfectly organised bookshelves were filled up to the ceiling and corridors, with piles upon piles of books to be shelved, formed this organised chaos that was Magnum Opus Secondhand Bookshop. After checking everything was in its place, I unlocked the front door and flipped the sign to open. No sooner had I placed myself behind the counter than my first customer came through the door. He called a good morning then headed downstairs where we'd put crime books. Two more people came in then and I flicked a look at the book I'd placed next to my cup of coffee. Sadly, for my reading addiction but a good thing for our bank account, the morning was really busy.

In the afternoon, the cheery jingle of the door announced Anna's entrance. She greeted me with her usual "Hiya, Se-chan!" while putting a stray lock of blond hair behind her ear. I'd met her nearly two years ago at the start of our first year of Japanese BA. After passing my A-levels with good enough grades, I had decided to keep on working full time at the bookstore despite granddad insisting I get a higher education. I couldn't imagine a better place to work, surrounded by what was in my eyes a treasure for the soul. I felt content, days passing by pleasantly until one day I chanced upon the original version of a Japanese anime online. It was love at first sight; within a short time, I'd become as obsessed with everything Japanese as I was with reading. I started Uni the following year without much thoughts of my advanced age, and it came as a bit of a shock and embarrassment that I was one of the oldest in my class. Anna and I sat next to each other in the first class and hit it off straight away, which surprised many people as we were as different as a paperback and a kindle: me, quiet veering on the introvert and Anna, bubbly, outgoing and popular with our peers.

Anna lifted a book from the shelf I was filing, gave it a cursory glance and put it back. In a casual tone she said, "Remember we're going out tonight?"

I hid a heavy sigh behind the cover of a book on modern art, then said brows raised. "Fine by me if that "we" doesn't include me,' I gave her a pointed look. "And yes, I'm sure." I added, anticipating her reply. "I've a backlog of new books to categorise today, and to be frank I don't feel like being around loud music and drunken people, again." I slapped the book shut, my way to end the subject.

I was rewarded with an eye roll. "Yeah, I forgot Miss who won't date anyone that's not like Mr Darcy. You know if you keep going like this, you're never going to taste real men and will end up as a crazy old cat lady." She wrapped her arms around herself and mock shuddered.

I narrowed my eyes. "At least I won't be lonely."

Anna decided to ignore my sarcasm and said, "Please!" holding her hands in prayer. "Some fourth-year guys have been nagging me to get you out with us for ages." Making a face, she added. "Unfortunately, the one I was aiming for was one of them." Her teeth were playing with her bottom lip, a gesture I was all too used to reading, melancholy. This wasn't the first time she had set her eyes on someone interested in me, but in spite of her heartbreaks, she never resented me, and I liked her all the more for it. I didn't get why she was still single; she was so much fun and kind, but she did have a crazy sense of fashion that could scare men a mile away. Only last week she wore a bright pink ball gown and there were the cat-eared hats she'd bought on a Japanese website. Today she was more subdued with a green dress and tall Doc Martens boots.

"Well, he's got bad taste! You're prettier than I am." And I meant it.

Anna dropped her arms. "Alright, I give up," she sighed. "You're a lost cause anyway. A beauty in vain! What's the point in having good looks if you're not using them?" she shook her head, walking away. "I'm going to make us some coffee."

We chatted for a while in-between serving customers until granddad joined us downstairs at the usual time. My heart did a funny beat when I saw him approaching. After mentally telling myself to get a grip – it was only a dream – I went round the counter and kissed him on the cheek. Saturday being his day off, he was usually out the house before I got up. After a short but pleasant conversation, Anna bowed to us (a habit we both took from our Japanese teachers) and exited the shop. Granddad, amused as always by this gesture, watched her go.

"She's such a cheerful girl, that one." he chuckled. "I'm glad you'll both attend the same university in Japan. I was worried you'd feel lonely on your own."

I took his warm hand in mine. "I know you won't believe it, but I can cope well on my own now. I'm tougher than you think." For a furtive second, something akin to fear reflected in his eyes when he glanced down, it was long gone before I could be sure. *What was that?* I shook my head, feeling silly. With a smile, I directed him to the front door.

"See? I can keep a shop all by myself without any problems. Now go and enjoy your evening with your friends, ok?" I kissed his wrinkled cheek while he laughed in a good natured way and closed the door behind him.

Must have been my imagination.

The rest of the afternoon went by in a mad flow of tourists. The only benefit to a rainy day was it usually brought customers to our shop. After locking up, I went into the storage room situated right at the back and unpacked a box full of books donated by an old man yesterday. A cloud of dust tickled my nose. I was a firm believer the genre of books a person read was a window into their soul. I took a handful out eager to find out what jewels I would uncover.

"I doubt he read these." I giggled. They all adorned covers of a couple embracing each other, women in long flamboyant dresses, and men's shirts half revealing hairless and muscular pectorals. *Must have belonged to his wife.* A sharp pain throbbed in my chest at the thought she might have died, leaving behind her lonely husband.

After reading the blurb at the back I made a pile of the books I wanted to read. This was the best part of owning a bookshop, I could read the newly acquired books before placing them on the shelves. I wasn't a fussy reader and loved all sorts of fiction depending on what mood I was in, but historical romance was my absolute favourite. The idea of elegant dresses and gentlemen, real ones, had kept me up many nights fantasising.

The sound of my ring tone across the room brought me back to reality. As I hurried to pick up my mobile I tripped over a box. My hip knocked into the bottom part of the bookcase containing the rarest books in the shop, kept here in the only locked room. Books toppled to the floor in consecutive thuds. When the bookcase jerked forward, I sprang up in time to catch it, arms and feet wide apart, before it could crush me. Death by books was so not my thing. After being sure the bookcase would not budge anymore, I allowed myself to look at the mess I'd made. Books had fallen on top of each other, some their pages open. *Damn it!* Granddad was going to kill me.

He had forbidden me to touch any of these books for as long as I could remember. They were far too old and precious for my dirty little hands; he'd said when I was a child. I had seen new covers come and go throughout the years, but out of respect for him and, of course, the books, I decided to withstand the niggling urge to look them up. With time, the curiosity faded to a mild occasional interest. Even now, he was the only one dealing with the rare books. Which was a tad odd now that I really thought about it.

Dust gathered for years was floating in a thick cloud around me. Nose itching, I opened the door to let fresher air in. My phone was still going, but I ignored it and crouched down to pick the open books up to verify the damage. I cringed. Ugly creases stared at me. I carefully smoothed page after page with my hand, shut each book then set them in a pile before placing two heavy tomes on top. *That should do the trick.* Next, I shuffled closer to a large encyclopedia that had landed on the edges of its hard cover like an upside-down V. I frowned. The pages didn't look right. I ran a finger along its length; it felt hard and ridged, giving the illusion of closed pages. Wood, not paper. *Oh! What do we have here?* Intrigued, I sat down in front of it, opened it wide, then smiled to myself. A secret storage book. I'd always wanted one, not that I had anything to hide. I just like the idea of it. I removed the smooth cloth tucked inside the hidden compartment and stared not quite believing my eyes.

A small book nestled deep in its hollow. The beautiful dark brown leather imprinted with long-leaved flowers would make any book lover salivate with envy, but it wasn't the craftsmanship that had me hold my breath. Not one bit. Attached to the front cover and glinting in the overhead lamp was a silver jewel, a silver tree to be precise. I stared down at my mum's pendant, then back to the book. They looked just the same. Ignoring granddad's voice in my head warning me to keep my hands off his treasured books, I extracted the book with gentle hands and held it beside the necklace. *Amazing.* Their likeness was too much to be a coincidence: the tree's delicate features, even the roots were identical. Maybe the pendant had come with the book as a set. Maybe it had belonged to mum.

Goose bumps rose with the excitement of my discovery. Could it be mum's old diary? Or possibly just a blank notebook with the same design as the pendant? Maybe granddad had kept it as a graduation present. Too many maybes. Catching a breath, I opened the book reverently. Yellow pages of a soft texture felt smooth under my fingertips. I flicked through the first pages then frowned, checked the last pages, but sure enough, it was filled with column after column of beautifully handwritten Japanese. With luck, I'd worked on a paper about the old version of hiragana only last month and recognised their cursive forms amongst kanji. The book had to be hundreds of years old. *Odd.* The ink was as black and sharp as the kanji I'd written for my calligraphy class only yesterday.

I went back to look at the first written page in the book: it contained two large symbols, brushed exquisitely. I paused a moment musing on its meaning. I could read them just fine, but I couldn't figure out why the author would use them in the first place.

"Normally at the beginning you'd find the title," I mumbled. "Or if it's a diary the name of the author, or a date maybe. Why write these symbols which mean "open!"? Could it be an invitation to read further?" I pursed my lips. "No, it doesn't make sense. Maybe the kanji's got another meaning I don't know about." While mentally writing a note to myself to ask one of my teachers, I traced the symbols with a finger. "Why write *ake*?" My thoughts were cut short as a blinding light emerged from the pages and enveloped me. I put a hand in front of my eyes to stave off the sharp pain in my head while a pressure like the air had become a thick, condensed mass pulled me forward. A sickening dizziness took over me before I fell into darkness.

I came to, body curled in a foetal position and pain searing through my right arm. Licking dried lips, I tasted a mixture of blood and grit. I grimaced, sick and disoriented, while a pounding headache played drums in my skull. I groaned. What did Anna put in my drink? Something hard was digging into my side, I tried to move and winced at the sharp pain. Past my foggy brain a warm breeze, carrying a flowery fragrance and the sound of birds, floated to my senses. Opening my eyes an iota, I squinted at blinding daylight.

Not a hangover.

I was laying down on a dirt path outdoors, a book clutched in my left hand. *That book!* It all came back in an explosion: the storage room, the book, the light then nothing. No, not nothing anymore as I moved my head up. What the hell had happened? My mind felt as dense as thick wool, slow and unable to concentrate well. Was it me or the ground was vibrating a bit? And was that distant rumbling real? I couldn't be sure with the ringing in my ears.

Gritting my teeth, I used my left arm to shuffle to a sitting position whilst holding the other against my chest. A wave of dizziness caught me off guard, and I rested my head on bent knees until it passed. In spite of myself I glanced at the injured arm and regretted it at once. A moan of distress escaped me. The forearm was swollen and at a funny angle, the skin already bruising.

Tears of panic came out all of a sudden, I let them flow for some time. What was I going to do? I was lost, hurt and confused at what had happened to me. My thoughts and emotions were a jumbled mess, but the panic attack ebbed. I sniffled and blew my nose. *Trust me to carry a damn handkerchief, but not a phone.* I laughed ruefully, then took a good long breath before letting it out. *Crying won't help. I need to calm down and think.*

I considered staying right there and wait for someone to come however, my instincts kept pulling at my mind: hide yourself, run away, they kept saying. Or it could have been my sluggish brain. I struggled onto my feet and wobbled to the edge of the dirt road, the middle of which was furrowed with foot and hooves prints. Hopefully I was close to stables and people. The sun's heat was blazing down, too bright, too hot. An unwanted voice pointed out the English weather was never this hot in March.

My eyes teared up once more. Where was I? The question on how I got there came and went, round and round like a kitten chasing its own tail. What scared me the most wasn't the broken arm to my side, or that I was standing someplace I didn't know. What petrified me was the huge blank after I'd seen the light coming out of the book. If it was what I really saw. Was all this mess something to do with my amnesia? Did I get here by myself and just forgot? Was I abducted? I ran a hand over my face. *Get a grip!* It didn't make any sense for anyone to abduct me and just leave me on my own. Abductions often ended in a dark room, not a well-used track. Thinking hurt too much and didn't help one bit. My eyelids felt heavy with sleep. I swallowed with difficulty; my mouth parched. I needed to find water. Dehydration would explain the nausea and blurriness at the edges of my vision.

I squinted to take in what was in front of me. Beautiful was too mild a word: semi-circular rows after rows of dark green bushes, their tops neatly trimmed into a rounded finish, sloped down and away from me, the vista resembled an organic roman amphitheatre. The rows ended into a cluster of trees as its centre stage.

My mouth curved into a smile: fields meant people. And people meant water and food. And directions. I tucked the book in my jeans' waist and was deciding which way to go when, from far away down the track, the thunder of hooves, following by yelling and swearing voices headed my way. Tremors darted from the ground to my body. On a weird impulse and a good bit of panic I slid down into the deep ditch separating the road from the field.

This was madness, I thought, arm cradled to my body. Of all the rotten luck! The noise was deafening; someone shouted something I didn't understand, horses neighed and grunted. Trying to ignore my injury, I leaned against the side of the ditch. The heavy clunks of galloping horseshoes reverberated in my throbbing head. Good thing I'd moved in time, I would have been as flat as a trodden pancake had I hesitated two seconds more.

My eyes closed. I took deep, slow breaths to calm the fear consuming my heart. As the sounds receded, I swivelled my head with much care to glance up at the road to make sure they had gone. To my utter shock, a young man was looking at me with inquisitive eyes.

"You're not from around here, are you?" he smiled looking at me up and down. "I've never seen such peculiar attire." *Peculiar? What is he talking about?* I shook my head to take the fogginess away, I needed to concentrate. Taking my eyes off his face, I saw a long blue garment covering his thin frame. Funny shaped strings secured it closed from the high collar to its hem, which fell just above his sandals. Slits on each side revealed a pair of white loose trousers underneath. My mind struggled to take this in. Why would a Caucasian man be wearing traditional Chinese clothes?

In one agile movement he jumped down to me. As I backed off on unsteady feet, he caught me by the shoulder.

"I don't know where you're from, but you shouldn't tarry by yourself. It's not safe to be alone around here." He pointed at the opposite side of the track. I followed his finger in a daze and blinked, a deep forest bordered the path. *How did I miss that?*

"There are dangerous creatures in there. I could..." My surroundings started to fade away, his mouth was moving, but his words seemed to be swallowed by the drumming in my ears. My legs failed to hold me, and I slid down the bank, my breathing coming out in irregular pants. Once more, oblivion edged around my vision and engulfed me in its painless grip.

CHAPTER 4

Faylinn

After a light supper, my stomach was a turmoil of apprehension and anticipation. Procrastination had never borne fruit, so rammed mother every time I'd put off doing boring chores. So, I planned to leave the Castle's grounds at first light; meaning, I needed to get to that special opening in the night. That didn't leave much time to do what I needed: pack essentials, get food and a map. Preparations were the easy part all in all, the walk home on the other hand... I shied away from thoughts of defeat. No need to start with a pessimistic outlook, I had coins and wits enough to make it work.

A draining fatigue enveloped me in a hazy cocoon, I forced a stretch as I needed to get up. Fiona might have said they'd be gone for days, but I couldn't rely on hearsay. For all I knew they'd be back the next day. I'd feel better by putting more distance between us as soon as possible.

My body and head screamed at me for moving, but rest would be for another day. Rummaging through my closet, I chose a change of clothes and the plainest and most comfortable dress I owned to wear: a dark grey cotton overdress embroidered with delicate scarlet roses covering the bodice and petals scattered on the left side of the skirt, as if they'd got blown away in the wind. The vibrant colours could easily be concealed with my black cloak.

Leaving my shoes behind, I traipsed through the hidden corridors to reach the library. The panel opened unto an obscured corner and besides rarely used bookcases full of hundred years old tomes on taxes. After checking for any noise or unwanted presence, I stretched my back and looked around me. It never ceased to amaze me. It was a magnificent room. Every wall was mounted with bookshelves, two sets of stairs cut into them on opposite sides. A balcony separated the first two stories while a third one was only accessible with ladders, which craned up to the top of the room where an arched ceiling, made from unbreakable glass, let in the wonders of a starry sky. Although women were not allowed to use it (our study books were chosen by our male tutors) I'd spent many hours here reading novels at night. Eyes looking left and right and unsure where to start, I wished I had been more inquisitive about what I classified as the boring arts. No scholar blood in me.

The better part of the night ended in searching throughout the room for a recent map of the Kingdom. Fists tight by my sides, I gritted my teeth in anger and a dose of dread. There had to be a place where they needed maps, like when they discussed all things war. I tapped my forehead in exasperation and hurried back to the panel to head to the king's study in record time. Even though I knew for sure he wouldn't be in, I waited a moment before pushing the panel door open. This was my first time in here. I made a face, disgusted. It smelled like him, of alcohol and sweat.

A large table, opposite his desk, had large maps spread out; the corners pinned to the wood. At a quick glance I saw it was exactly what I needed, but even I wouldn't be so reckless as to steal one in plain sight. I went to a bookcase to my right and found one discarded amongst books and rolls of parchments. It was of the finest quality, smooth under my fingers and a crisp smell of fresh ink. The different colours, representing the amazing variety of Comraich's topography, jumped at me when I opened it wide. This was no ordinary map. The details were too accurate to be a simple drawing. Hand hesitant, I stroked the lines of vivid hues representing the Castle gardens, then stopped, finger firmly pressed on the map. I blinked once and stared in awe. In front of my very eyes floated an image of the exact place in the gardens my finger was resting on. Although it was night-time, I could discern the main fountain, encircled by Mage lights casting a dim halo around its imposing shape. This was amazing. It was a wonder this map had been left unprotected; it must have cost a small fortune to make. I grinned at my luck. Something told me it would end up being one of my best weapons. Lifting my finger, the image blurred into nothingness. I traced the way back home with my eyes.

Due to the rise of rebellions amongst the commoners, the king had built more garrisons to keep them under control, they were strategically placed on the borders between provinces. I needed to stay well clear of them. Thoroughfares, too, would be well guarded; I wouldn't last a day after Quentin gave his orders to find me. The journey seemed straightforward enough: I would cut through the deep forest skirting the Castle's gardens, then head North making sure to bypass the Forest of torments. I bit my lips. It would take me weeks on foot, months. Could I really pull this off? Home was to the far North of Comraich in the coldest and less populated province. I'd done the journey between home and the Sky mountains as a child, accompanying father and my brothers for business, and I was confident I could find rivers and places to hide when I'd get there, but the first part of the journey was unknown to me. What if Quentin put up a reward to find me? As soon as the thought crossed my mind, I rejected it. Too risky, my family would come to hear of it. But he would send guards to find me. So, inns were out of the question. I was sorely tempted to steal a horse, it'd cut down this insane journey to bearable, but I couldn't risk the exposure on the roads and doubted the forest had trails wide enough to accommodate large animals.

On foot it was then. My back straightened with hope. Small farms skirted the forests, that will do for food, and sleep outside won't be so hard as the weather should keep warm for the next month or so. The idea of falling asleep under a sky full of stars was appealing to the romantic part of me. I could do this. I would do this.

I put the parchment in my satchel, watched the room for any tell-tale signs of my presence, then retreated through the passageway. Time to get rations in the kitchen. The only secret doorway on the ground floor was in the male servants dormitory, too risky. Which meant getting out in the drawing room situated in the same wing, one level up. Mentally I visualised the necessary route through the main corridors in the castle, making notes of hidden nooks in the event of unwelcome company, which consisted of two pairs of guards on duty prowling through the corridors at night. This proved more time consuming than I anticipated.

No sooner had I closed the drawing room door than the clacking sounds of footsteps echoed in the silent night. I darted down the corridor and slid behind a well-placed marble sculpture, a huge and grotesque portrayal of the king. After a minute, I dared a peek round the stone. They were facing away from me. The glimmering lights, set into the walls, revealed the roaring red dragon, its wings wide open in a fighting stance, emblazoned on their immaculate black tunics. Long swords brushed the royal red of their trousers, not their only weapon. Each royal guard was carefully selected for his gift as much as his fighting skills. As long as the gift could be beneficial for military reasons, a soldier was guaranteed to be promoted to the royal guard. Anything went. Even if the guard could only conjure a small burst of wind or turn metal into wood for a second, it was more than enough to distract the enemy. And unfortunately, the guards proved to be quite creative on how to use them for harm. Every other spring, the king held a tournament where the strongest men showed off their strength and courage. The event was divided in two groups: one for male commoners who aspired to be soldiers in the strongest army in all of Newlands, or so the king liked to indoctrinate us. As for the second and most favoured tournament amongst the populace, soldiers avid for a promotion or recognition travelled from every part of the Kingdom to take part in one or all categories ranging from unarmed hand to hand combat, weapons mastery to duels on a horse. Many times, I had seen proof of their violence and cruelty, so I kept still, as quiet as the slow breeze on a summer's night.

After they passed me by and all sound died down, I scurried down the corridor to the servants' stairs hidden behind a tapestry of the first king standing proudly with his boot on a servant's head. I scowled. As though they needed to be reminded every day of their place in the Kingdom. Although I was confident all servants were sleeping deeply, I tiptoed down each step into the kitchen. One of the serving boys was asleep, curled up in front of a dying fire. Poor boy, he was probably too exhausted to drag himself to the attic where women and children slept. It wasn't the first time I'd stolen food in the middle of the night, so I knew my way around. Taking a kitchen knife carelessly left on a surface, I went into the pantry at the back of the room. A Mage light, dangling from the ceiling, lit up in a blink of an eye, illuminating the multitude of succulent food. Wasting no time, I cut portions of cheese, dried meat and leftover bread, wrapping them in clean linen cloths, then grabbed two water-skins hanging by the door, kept there for the hunters. As I was dropping handfuls of dried fruit and nuts in a pouch, I heard the boy coughing. Opening the door, I peeped in his direction; the shadowy contours of his slight body hadn't moved. I let a short breath out and glanced behind me. This would have to do. I couldn't risk meeting any of the guards during their shift change, which would be soon. Sometimes they came down here to brew themselves coffee before starting their watch. Bag on my shoulder, I retraced my steps back to the safety of my chamber.

* * *

I didn't let myself go to sleep. I paced, repacked my satchel and checked my route on the map, twice. Everything was ready. Time was slipping, the moon was creeping up the sky, yet all I could do was pace some more. After another turn of the room, I stopped in front of the panel, my stomach in twined knots. I was scared. I'd waited for this moment for years. I'd imagined running down the passage and opening the door to freedom. Never in any of my daydreams I'd had felt so anxious. *That's because you didn't imagine yourself walking the whole way home, silly girl.* This was the most insane idea I'd ever had, by far. However, insane or not, it was the only way I could run away. My only hope. Before I could second guess my sanity, I put my cloak on, grabbed the satchel and candle and went through the panel.

By the time I reached the intersection that led to the outside world, the pressure on my chest had eased, the headache gone. I sighed with relief at the higher ceiling, then stopped to stretch the stiffness out of both back and neck. While taking sips of water, I inspected my surroundings. Damp moss covered the walls, spider webs long as tapestries – their inhabitants either hidden or long gone – hung down a rounded ceiling. The air was saturated with moisture which held a mustiness I knew would cling to my clothes for days. I must have been underground, probably under the gardens. I was the only person to venture in these parts in many moons. An unpleasant thought struck me. Roldan and Quentin knew about the passages now. Guards would invade a space I'd always considered my own. *It doesn't matter.* I would need to be fairly addled to come back here. They could use it to their fancy for all I cared. It was strange, though, that its existence had faded away from people's knowledge until I'd found them. Maybe father or Haelan would know about the Castle's history. I smiled, elated with the knowledge I would see my family soon.

The abrupt change of the walls took me by surprise. I hadn't noticed it last I walked here. I cast the light on the ceiling. As with the walls, it was formed by natural rocks. Irregular lines showed where it had been chipped into a rounded shape. Everything felt closer, the space around me compact. Here and there, I spotted roots, most no thicker than a hair with the occasional clumps of thick ones dangling. When at last I arrived in front of the time-worn oaken door, the weariness of the sleepless night vanished. *This is it.* I placed the palm of my hand on the last hurdle of my escape. The worm-eaten wood felt coarse under my skin. A flash of a beautiful oak being cut with an axe made me falter with sadness; it had been an ancient tree. I couldn't help but fear it was a foreboding of what was to come. "As if a crumbling door is a dratted omen." I shook my head, chasing away the pessimistic train of thought. Once more, I thanked the stars for finding this secret way out. I didn't dare think of how I would have escaped otherwise.

I wouldn't have, I thought grimly.

From a hole where the door frame had rotted through, I squeezed a hand, tore at the leaves blocking my view, and waited until the first rays of the sun touched the green carpet of clover skirting the woods. Heart afire, I pressed on the rusted latch and pushed. The door didn't budge. Anchoring my feet in the dirt floor, I shoved at the door with all my might. Green leaves scattered all over me as it cracked open just wide enough for me to inch through. I threw my satchel first, sucked my stomach in, then squeezed through, my cloak scrapping against the rough frame. It was a tight fit. Breathing hard I stared at a green cascade of thick ivy covering the lower part of a small bluff and the entryway. I heaved the door back into place, making sure the ivy didn't get caught. It took precious minutes I didn't want to spare, but I didn't want to leave even the slightest evidence of my whereabouts. I looked at the result. *No wonder it had stood undiscovered all these years.* The door, which was covered in a yellow and green moss, now stood inconspicuously amongst the foliage, some of the branches as thick as my arm.

Satisfied, I slung the satchel on my back while turning away, took a couple of steps forward then stopped. Chestnut trees, oaks and silver birches formed the welcoming entrance to the awakened forest. Ignoring the small voice at the back of my head yelling to make haste, a strong urge to listen to and feel my surroundings overtook my better judgement. The fresh smell of wild flowers just kissed by the sun as well as the melodious chorus of chirping birds worked to soothe my tumble of nerves. I opened my eyes feeling refreshed, determined. Looking back over my shoulder, I bid goodbye to this part of my life, to the few people who had been kind to me, then I placed a hand on the first tree I encountered. "May you and your friends protect me on my endeavours." My smile faltered, and tears built up in my eyes as a gentle tingling sensation swept throughout my body. How I'd missed touching wild old trees. The ones in the Castle's gardens had been subdued or silent as if they, too, had felt imprisoned. Warmth filled my heart with a familiar feeling: love. Grey fur and yellow eyes invaded our connection and I frowned at the confusing image, my hand slipping to my side. Maybe an animal had paced close to it, I shrugged. I loved this personal link with trees even though it proved a bit of a puzzle at times, yet some days I wished my gift was more useful. Today was one of those.

I set a fast pace, intent on putting as much distance between me and the castle as possible. Leaf mulch amassed through many seasons squished under my footsteps. The first hours were spent enjoying my re-acquaintance with the wild. My senses were overwhelmed by its life, everything felt new and exciting. I felt at home, and I could finally breathe. It was hard not to touch every single tree as I passed or pick wild flowers with the most beautiful colours. Even though my shoes were unfit for long walks, I made good speed and many hours passed by before a slow growl coming from my stomach reminded me I'd had no breakfast this morning. It was high time for noon break. I sat under the shelter of a large oak tree. Careful of my injured cheek, I took small bites of the portion of bread, cheese and dried fruits I'd rationed. Though it didn't feel sufficient after all those lavish meals I was used to, I had to ration. What I brought wouldn't be enough to last more than a few days, let alone the whole journey. I set the map down while nibbling at my food. The village of Lowspring was along the way; I would stop at a farm close-by. If my calculations were right, I'd reach it in about two days' time. And tomorrow I would start work on a bow and arrows to hunt game. I hoped I wasn't too rusty.

The clouds were getting heavier over my head, a sign of approaching rain. I picked at my bread, a sudden gloom pressing on my chest. Sighing, I stretched my already sore and aching body. Time to make a move. I grimaced as I started walking, each step smarting. Sitting down once more, I removed shoes and stockings to reveal ugly blisters on both feet. With quick hands I took the clean strips of linen in the satchel, bandaged them then put on the thick pair of socks I'd brought for cold nights. It was awkward to walk at first but at least it stopped the pain.

A drop of rain caught me on the nose before the clouds let loose. No matter. I put my hood up and walked on. My mind, influenced by the gloominess of the sky, went in an unpleasant direction. I started regretting my hasty decision of fleeing. I should have sent a message to father before I left, telling him what I was planning to do. And then what? If Quentin returned to the castle tomorrow and started a search party, my family would have no means of finding me before them. I clenched my fists hard. I had no doubt he would use any means in his grasp to search for me. I knew too much. But he and the High Mage would never presume I'd walk all the way back home. They would most likely check every inn and thoroughfare going up North, using the usual slow process of halting all passing travellers and carriages. It would give me time aplenty to disappear unnoticed. Like most men at Court, they considered a woman's intellect far below their own. Sadly, it was true for most of the Ladies I'd met. They were brought up as immaculate and submissive diversions to please the Lords whenever they felt the need to be amused. Undoubtedly, we women, were kept in the dark on important matters of the Kingdom, matters I for one would love to know. The queen who had the power and ability to be informed chose not to, satisfied in her riches. A smile broke out on my lips as I envisioned how my dear old aunt would react to my disappearance.

✻ ✻ ✻

That first night, I stayed in the hollow of a rock formation sticking out of a hillside. The moss covering the rocks as well as the ground was saturated with water. No chance of fire. Sitting here by myself with nothing to do but eat, the feeling of loneliness finally sank in. It felt strange, being alone. This freedom to decide what or when I wanted to do something was a novel thing for me. I felt empowered by it, yet I wasn't sure how well this lonely adventure would fare on my nerves. Cocooned in my warm cloak, the calls of a hooting owl hunting in a tree close by, of a distant wolf howling to its pack, and dreams of being a hunted deer kept me up half the night. I watched with gratitude dawn work its magic on the living creatures inhabiting my surroundings.

That day was spent in a similar pattern to the one before: trail walking and short breaks ending in a long sleepless night under a precarious shelter, which drew up an unappealing picture of what my forthcoming future would be like. By the morning after, body as heavy as a trunk, the elation of being free in the wilderness abated. With a slighted pride I slowed right down, afraid my energy wouldn't last until night time. My feet were sore, and a fatigue throbbed deep within my bones. My brothers would laugh at such a weak body. I deplored it but my resolve was strong. I was yet to give up.

The animal trail I'd found earlier in the day ran parallel to a narrow river. I knelt next to it and drank my fill of fresh water, then refilled the waterskins. Cold water dripping down my chin, the nagging question that had gone round in circles in my head most of the day, resurfaced. It was all well and good relaying what I'd heard to my family, but to what avail? What would happen next? My father's fighting force was on the small side, the king had made sure of that. Representatives to the provinces, like father was, were allowed no more than twenty guards, other nobles five guards at the most, and each garrison contained the king's men-at-arms to keep their designated area under subdued control. Soon after his coronation he had implemented a rule that if in need, nobles could request the use of his guards at his discretion, so they didn't need to worry about their own security. Now I understood the consequences of this edict. Even if all nobles were to join and rebel against him, they'd never rival his army. Last I'd heard it was ten thousand strong. I sat back and let the warmth of the sun burn away my unpleasant reflections. From its position in the sky, I guessed I had an hour or two before it would sink too low to penetrate the thick canopy of the forest. The night would be soon upon me after that. I kept to the river hoping to find a reasonably dry place close by.

Some time later, a flicker of movement caught my attention out of the corner of one eye. I stopped short and looked in that direction. Only then did I realise how silent my surroundings had become, as though the forest had taken a deep breath and was holding it in expectation. This did not bode well. I scanned the green foliage, thick with brush and brambles covering the hillside to my right. Then I saw it, looking straight at me.

Breath caught in my throat, my heart started hammering in my ribcage, its rhythm roaring in my ears as loud as a gush of water.

A wolf.

Nothing unusual about that. I'd seen plenty in our family woods and knew how to be rid of them, but the stars have pity on me, I'd never seen one like this. Its fur was the striking white of fresh snow on a winter's dawn, but what rooted me on the spot in complete shock was its size: nine feet long, maybe more. It ambled on silent paws and stopped fifty yards in front of me. His penetrating eyes held a tinge of glee and anticipation, as if it was thrilled to have caught me unaware. I cursed words a lady of my standing should not even be aware of. Terror must have addled my mind for I swore its muzzle opened in a smile, revealing long, sharp teeth. The wolf then lifted its head high and gave a chilling howl. The sound triggered the memory of a similar one I had dismissed on the first day. It had sounded so far away... The hair at the back of my neck rose. Had it been following me all that time? And here I was, all complacent and confident I could hide from guards, I'd never even considered wild animals. What a fool! I heard growling to my right and stared in dismay at the pack of wolves that had crept up on me. Apart from the occasional brown or black, they all had dense grey fur. Although smaller than the white one, which I assumed was their leader, their size was considerably bigger than normal wolves. I couldn't help reflecting how magnificent they all looked.

I cussed my stupidity once more. Why in Myrddin's curly beard did I forget to take a weapon with me? The castle was brimming with old, historical daggers and swords. I slowed my breathing trying to smother the increasing panic while surveying the ground around me for anything I could use to protect myself. A big lump of wood was protruding from the river, it didn't seem too heavy. *This will do.* I just had to get it without them noticing. *And I've about as much chance of this as growing wings.* Not taking my gaze off their leader, I shuffled sideways in the direction of the prospective club. In the seconds I looked away to pick it up, the impossible happened. An animal's whimper broke the silence, and to my amazement the white wolf slumped dead on the grass, an arrow sticking out of its head. I dropped down on all fours looking for the bowman, when another three sank into the skulls of the wolves nearer to me. Beyond the corpses, the grass was now empty, the pack's departure as eerie as its arrival. Euphoria filled me from head to toe.

I was safe.

Laughter died on my lips as dawning realisation sank to my stomach, and a chill wreaked havoc upon my heart. I wasn't in the least safe. Quentin must have found out I escaped through his valet and sent a direct order to his men to find me. With a shaky breath I crawled to hide by the roots of a tree, not sure why I took the trouble as I was surely surrounded. A wolf, its tongue limp in its open mouth, lay down right in front of me. The arrow sticking out did not belong to the Royal guards; I had been around them long enough to recognise their fletchings. I dismissed the dim light of hope. That didn't mean anything, they could have bought those at any bowyer's shop. I looked over the river, the terrain sloped at a sharp angle on the opposite bank, thick shrubs and bushes covered its expanse and prevented a fast escape. That option out, I considered the only one left. Maybe I could lose them if I ran fast enough.

Only one way to find out.

CHAPTER 5

Faylinn

"Please don't be scared." I jumped at the voice behind me, then turned towards its owner. An old man appeared to the side of the tree, his hands palm down in front of him like he was attempting to placate some wild animal. Well, I did feel like running away like a frightened rabbit. Long white hair fell on a slim frame, he wore a dark brown cloak that had seen better days.

"We mean you no harm." He gestured behind him. Men and women, a dozen or so, were standing amongst the trees and undergrowth. I hadn't heard any noise, not a single crack or rustle that didn't belong to the forest. The panic from earlier had by now subsided and my mind felt numb as exhaustion threatened to take over me. I sat there staring up at him, a jumble of questions clashing with one another, yet I could articulate none of them.

His gentle eyes grew concerned. "Are you hurt, child?"

I swallowed the bile lodged at the back of my throat.

"No, I'm well enough." I croaked. "Who are you?"

He smiled down at me. "We are wanderers living in these woods." He didn't sound like one with his sophisticated voice.

I looked over the man's shoulder, his companions wore similar clothes of soft leather and rough cloaks, various hunting weapons about their bodies. My head thumped gently against the trunk in heartfelt relief.

I had met people like them back home. No more than nine years old, I was on my way to the village when I came across them setting camp in our woods. Curiosity giving me wings, I ran the rest of the way to ask Mrs Pots, the innkeeper's wife and local gossip, who they were. She exclaimed in a distraught voice they were outlaws, calling themselves wanderers. Putting a hand on her large bosom, she moaned. "My dear girl, I've asked good old Alistair to put a protection spell around my inn. I can barely sleep at night knowing they're so near our village. But every year..." her voice trailed; her attention caught by a customer. I remembered being both fascinated and petrified at the time.

Heading back home the long way round – for I was unsure about these strange people – I rushed to tell father the news. He gave me that warm smile I missed so much. "There is no need to worry Faylinn. Indeed, the king considers them outlaws, but they will do you no harm or anyone else for that matter. I have granted them access to our woods."

"But father, how could you trust outlaws? Won't they steal from the villagers, or worse, kill someone?" How I'd felt like an adult talking about serious matters with father.

"I see. Perhaps you have spoken to Mrs Pots about this by any chance?" He enquired, amusement dancing in his eyes. I hesitantly nodded. "You see, dear girl, wanderers are nomads. That means they live for a short time in the same place, they travel all over the Kingdom. And I know from first-hand experience that the king proclaimed them outlaws solely because they refuse to pay any taxes for the right of living in his Kingdom. Before his reign the old kings thought quite differently, they had been allowed to live as they wished with the understanding they would respect the lands and its people wherever they decided to settle. They are not outlaws in my eyes sweetling; and shouldn't be in yours. It's the third time they've stayed here, and they have never caused any trouble."

"Does it mean I can go and talk to them?"

Father threw his head back he laughed so hard. "As long as you don't pester them with too many questions. Now, off with you child."

The next day I went to greet them with Sunlark, both of us intent on adventure. For weeks, one of their leaders, a woman named Mira, showed us what we could eat in the woods and which berries, mushrooms and plants were poisonous. Although I learnt countless names and techniques from hunting to cooking in the wilds, I had never felt bored as I did with my old tutor Mrs Spratt, who only taught subjects befitting a young noble lady, insipid subjects like Arts and Etiquette. The wanderers had lived in our woods for two full seasons while the weather was warm. That time had been one of the best of my life.

A deep voice drew me out of my reminiscence. "Dwennon, we cannot linger much longer. The light's almost gone." Piercing pale blue eyes under frowning eyebrows met mine, I couldn't help flush at their scrutiny. "I don't know yer history lass, but ye'd better come with us. These woods aren't safe at night as ye've probably guessed." He jutted his chin in the direction of his companions carrying the wolves on their backs, then he spun and proceeded to give various orders. The old man, Dwennon he'd called him, looked on with satisfaction. His son? I rejected the idea as quickly as it crossed my mind; they looked nothing alike, yet I sensed a strong relationship between them.

"Sawyer's right, child. Do you feel rested enough to walk?"

"Yes, I will be fine." I wasn't, but I'd do anything to be among friendly company tonight. Taking the hand he offered, I got up on unsteady legs, and in the same manner as a perfect gentleman he held me until they stopped quivering. Before I could stop myself, I brushed my clothes and arranged them properly. As if they cared about the state of my outfit. But some habits were far too ingrained to let go quickly. I was reaching down for my satchel when a large hand grabbed it before I could; the man called Sawyer put it on his shoulder, then stepped past me before I could so much as form any words of refusal. I frowned at his fast-retreating frame; I didn't care for my belongings in somebody else's hands. I started walking with Dwennon by my side.

"Please accept my belated gratitude. I dare not think what would have happened if not for your help." I shuddered at the thought.

"It's the least a fellow human being can do. We need to help one another in times like these." I looked at him startled by this statement. Times like what? "Besides, you don't need to thank me. Keltor and Sawyer were the ones that scared the wolves away. As you can see," he pointed at the two men at the top of the next rise. "They move much quicker than the rest of us, they got to you in time. Good shots too, if I might add." I couldn't agree more.

The walk back to their camp went in a haze of tiredness, the surroundings morphing into dark shadows as the sun set low upon the horizon. After tripping a couple of times, I kept my gaze fixed on what I could see of the floor, taking small careful steps. Dwennon was thankfully silent all the way because I had neither strength nor wit to make conversation. Even a small part of me was grateful I didn't have to carry my heavy satchel.

By the time we arrived at their encampment, the first stars were showing in a cloudless sky and a gentle breeze was chasing away the heaviness in the air. I followed Dwennon between tents lit up by small cooking fires and scattered between trees and foliage; the uneven path leading us to a huge bonfire which I assumed was the communal fire. Its light was casting fluttering shadows along the sides of the big tents positioned in a circle around it. Sawyer and Keltor were standing by it, my satchel at their feet.

I hesitated a moment but squared my shoulders and stopped in front of them, then cleared my throat to get their attention as they were talking to each other. Two equally unreadable faces looked down at me, I blinked, lost for words for a moment. They were huge, well over six feet tall. Even I had to strain my neck to look them in the eye. They had removed their cloaks and in the flickering blaze, I could discern tight fitted clothing that accentuated big, solid shoulders and long limbs covered in hard muscles. Their supple leather vests, belts and even vambraces were adorned with an assortment of blades. The darkness playing on their faces accentuated their hostile countenance. I quivered inside but pressed on.

"I apologise for interrupting your conversation, but I would like to thank you both for saving my life today. It was very brave; I wouldn't have stood a chance against those wolves." I shook my head remembering the size of them. "If there is anything I could do to repay you, I feel indebted to do so." I resented the shakiness in my voice.

The dark haired one, Keltor, chuckled. "Today ye say," he scrubbed a hand over his jaw. "Ye planning on needing rescuing again? If in need, call me anytime." The smile on his face and mischief in his eyes made him at once more approachable. "As for repayment..." he said looking me up and down. "I've a good idea on how ye could...help... a lonely soul like me." I froze in place. Had I misunderstood? Was he propositioning me? A big shadow by his feet moved. I glanced down and took a step back. Two yellow eyes were staring at me.

"Enough, Kel." Sawyer's low voice rumbled. "Can't ye tell ye're scaring her?" That and the wolf now sitting up.

Kel sighed deeply. "Apologies my Lady." He bowed flamboyantly. "I was but jesting. Ye seemed a bit stiff you see, and I couldn't help teasing ye a wee bit. But worry not,' he grinned. "If I were to ever lay an uninvited finger on yer delicate self, I would be chased through these woods by fierce female creatures armed with cooking pans." My mouth twitched, but I couldn't help casting a glance at the wolf. Kel, noticing the direction of my gaze, hunkered down next to the wolf and gave it a good rub round the ears like I would a dog. "And don't worry about Blaith, she's the sweetest thing." Just to prove his point, the wolf went down and let him rub her belly, tongue lolling to one side of her mouth. "She only bites bad people. Don't ye? Baby girl."

The incongruity of his demeanour so at odds with his appearance, added to an infectious grin, got the best of me. In spite of myself, a smile slipped onto my lips, and I hastily covered my mouth with a hand. On the rare occasions the queen had caught me smiling, she took extreme pleasure likening me to a starved horse. I'd been aware of my big teeth as a child, no more than that, until her words had struck a self-conscious chord. As a young woman, it was a barb I hadn't been able to ignore. Sawyer was staring at me, an emotion I couldn't quite catch, fleeting across his eyes.

"Apologies accepted. I'm sorry for my, er..., stiffness too. You both look quite imposing, and –"

"Ye should stop talking right about now or their pretty ankles won't be able to fit their boots no more, for that ye can be sure." I looked up to see a beautiful young woman standing by Sawyer, Dwennon was chuckling at her side. Her pale hair, arranged in a long plait resting on her shoulder, was reflecting the flames, giving it an orange hue. She was dressed in a short-sleeved homespun dress, tight around the waist, which then flowed to her ankles. I couldn't help considering how she would be prominent at Court: a small constitution with well-defined curves, and a very pretty face would set more than the queen into raging jealousy. Though her appearance seemed frail, she had a confident air about her, and although she was staring at me with cautious eyes, there was something I quite liked about her.

"Myrddin's blessings. I'm Luela." She said as she raised her hand, palm facing me. I stared at a loss for a moment. I'd forgotten about this greeting between females, the Court never used commoner's ways. Ladies inclined their heads to greet one another, touching someone else was considered distasteful.

I placed the palm of my hand on her small one then removed it. "Myrddin's blessings. My name is Faylinn."

"I see you've met Sawyer and Keltor." Luela said waving a hand at the two men standing as still as boulders. "Don't be fooled by their muscles, it's all for show."

I doubted that very much, I thought my gaze lingering on the sharp blades. Her tone was light and playful, yet it didn't reach her eyes; there was an air of anxiety in them. The others were all contemplating me as well: the outsider.

I forced a smile unsure on how to react. "Thank you for your hospitality." I said to no one in particular. I had the impression Dwennon was one of the leaders, but one could never be sure.

Sawyer crossed his arms on his chest and said his voice heavy with criticism. "Ye're fortunate we came upon ye, lass. By the look of this," he pointed at my belongings. "Ye've not packed enough to survive more than a couple of days out there." Heat rose to my face. It was a fair observation, of course, but that didn't give him the right to humiliate me in front of his people. Some time passed before I looked him in the eye.

"I...Circumstances were such, I couldn't take any more than I did." His eyebrows raised a little, his eyes still intent on me as if trying to coerce more out of me. *You will have to be satisfied with that.* I didn't look away. I'd had a lifetime worth of forced subservience. Right then, I decided it was high time I showed some gumption, or I wouldn't live for very long. I almost smiled when he broke contact first, then remembered I was long past my adolescent self. I didn't like the way he frowned at my clothes, I crossed my arms over my chest and waited for his next rebuke.

A loud clap made me flinch, breaking the uncomfortable silence. "Right, I'm sure everyone's tired and hungry." Luela said, "Let's leave important talk for the morrow after some well-deserved rest."

I'll be on my way as soon as possible tomorrow, talk or no talk.
Everyone scattered away as Luela took me by the elbow and
directed me to a log, its top as flat and smooth as a bench,
right by the fire. I sat down with as much grace as the wooden
guards Sunlark used to love playing with. The animal fur flung
over it was to my surprise soft and thick. I stretched myself
out. How I longed for a hot bath.

Unawares, my gaze strayed to the flames, reds and yellows
licking at the logs like hungry beasts, their tumultuous
swaying keeping me trapped in a hypnotic state. A minute or
an hour could have passed for all I knew; by the time I managed
to tear my eyes away from the fire, I felt calm yet aware.
Taking in my surroundings, I enjoyed listening to the people
mingling around me. Apart from Dwennon, a detail I would
have to ponder at another time, they all had to some degree
what the queen would call, the vagrants' tongue. Vowels were
stretched longer, consonants omitted here and there, but it
was the way they pronounced some of the "r" at the back of
the throat that threw me. It changed a word so much that my
brain struggled to associate it with the correct pronunciation.
My earlier conversation had been easy enough but some of the
voices around me sounded as foreign as any extinct languages.

Thankfully, everybody left me to my contemplations. Many
curious stares tried to get my attention, but I looked down
fast, feeling a coward for refusing their silent invitations. They
seemed nice enough, however I appreciated the time to reflect
on how my life was turning out.

Supper, brought by a young girl, consisted of rabbit and
vegetable stew with wild rice, a simple meal, yet the combined
aroma of herbs and meat was simply delicious. In an untoward
manner that would have brought deep frowns by my peers,
I ate fast and emptied the wooden bowl clean, a warm and
content feeling spreading throughout my body. None of the
meals at the castle had ever affected me this way; the rigidity of
protocol and never-ending tedious conversations contributed
to spoil the food.

As silent as a shadow, Sawyer appeared before me, his palm outstretched with a pot at its centre. "For the swelling." he said, looking at my cheek. What with the wolves and exhaustion, I'd forgotten all about it. I stared at the pot, astonished, before taking it. A dark green congealed-looking substance felt cool and soothing when I spread it gingerly on my wound. I looked up to thank him only to realise he was already gone, the pot the only proof I hadn't dreamt the whole thing. To say I was confused by this man was an understatement.

"Was the food to yer liking?" Luela sat next to me, and I shook my head to clear it.

"The best I've had in a long time." I replied truthfully.

"I'm glad," she said grinning, "I made it myself. Now, am I right ye'd like to sleep?" Seeing me nod, she added. "Follow me then."

She took me to a red tent right behind one of the big ones. Candles, ensconced in glass bowls, lit up upon our arrival. It was modest in size. The main part was shaped like a dome supported by a wooden framework reaching up to two feet above me, this then dropped at the back to form a low and wide extension. All of it was covered in a red-dyed wool felt I knew from that summer time with wanderers, was both insulating and waterproof. The place was sparse but homely. Two chests of drawers, their wood pattern so unusual my fingers twitched to feel it, were placed to my left. A small table which was low to the floor had been placed to my right, big comfortable looking pillows at each side. No chairs. Luela pointed to a pallet covered in brown and grey furs in the extension, a long sheet had been draped on the poles separating it to what I assumed was the rest of the sleeping area. It was to my surprise quiet; a faint murmur of voices could barely be heard. Luela placed a gentle hand on my shoulder, this time the smile reaching her eyes.

"I thought you'd like privacy. Somlin, my lifemate, and I sleep on the other side." Something must have shown on my face for she added mistaking my thoughts. "It's rather big for two people but," she stroked her tummy and smiled. "A little one is on the way." Luela didn't look much older than I was, and she was with child. I lowered my eyes, not wanting her to read the swirl of feelings I couldn't control. I knew commoners started having children young, but seeing it was very different to learning about it. "We want at least three children. That should fill this tent nicely. Normally newly bonded couples live in a small tent at the furthest edge of our settlement in respect to our elders, and as they grow older and have more children, they move closer in the circle. But being Sawyer's sister has got its privileges." She winked at me. I stared bemused, wondering what had changed her attitude towards me. So, Sawyer was her big brother, now that I looked closely, the similarities between the two of them were obvious: fair hair and the same straight nose.

"Is he one of the leaders then?" I couldn't help asking, remembering how everyone had waited for his orders when they'd found me.

Luela grew serious at once. "Yes, since he came of age nine years ago. Then he became an elder last year." My eyebrows rose at the unexpected news. Noticing my reaction, she asked if I knew about the wanderers' hierarchic system.

"A little. I was fortunate to spend some time in a wanderer's group as a child." A warm smile spread on her lips. "I'm afraid I've forgotten quite a bit about the hierarchy." I admitted, it hadn't been my favourite topic. "Am I right in thinking only the wisest and most competent mages can become elders?"

"Ye're not far off. Leaders help the elders maintain peace and security within our group, each have a set number of families to look after. But the elders' duties are quite broad, although mentally for the most part. A wise mind is more in need than power in this case. Whether it's leader or elder, he's far too young for such responsibilities if you ask me." Her right hand was twisting and untwisting her dress. "He never got the chance to be selfish and enjoy life for himself. He's always been burdened with one thing or another, always had to put our people before himself. I just wish...." she shook her head. "I'm sorry, I shouldn't speak of such things." To a stranger, no less. She gave a dry smile and added, "As you can see it's a subject close to my heart." Curiosity pulled at me, but the moment was gone.

All of a sudden, Luela's back straightened. "Sorry to blabber when ye're dead on yer feet, I'll let ye sleep now. I've plenty of preparations for the ceremony. May your dreams bring ye peace." She then turned around and left me alone with a mountain of questions. Weary to the bone, I stripped down to my shifts and covered myself in the soft furs. It felt like true decadence, cold silk had never felt this good. As I lay in this unexpected place, I became aware of the subtle presence of nature. The melodic rhythm of crickets, the rustling sounds of the wind caught in the trees soon lulled me into a dreamless sleep.

CHAPTER 6

Selena

Whispering voices, words floated to my slumbering self. "Wish...stop...strays, Zen." I wished they would shut up; they didn't make sense and I was trying to sleep here. I focused on my breathing for a moment to do just that before an uncomfortable feeling pooled in my stomach. Why were people in my bedroom? Wait, this was not how my bed felt. Opening my eyelids a tinge, I took in the people at the end of the room and lowered them down immediately. I kept my eyes shut, face expressionless, to hide my incredulity.

A very petite east Asian woman was talking with two men in hushed voices, nothing weird about this picture except one of them was the young man I'd seen in my dream and the other... *It's not possible, I'm still dreaming.* I mentally joked at my wild imagination, but memories of the dream, memories far too vivid and unbroken, quashed my certitude. I flicked my eyes open for a second. Yep, they were still there, and the other man had, no doubt about it, shining eyes: they were blue this time, but they'd been orange a minute ago. No real person had eyes like those my sensible self said. My mind, my rational mind to be precise, was clashing with my sensations – not real, no way it said – my imaginative one on the other hand was clapping, dancing in glee. I smothered it as it had obviously run amok during the night. Maybe I ate something dodgy last night. *God, let me get out of this freaky dream, or better yet, let me sleep, I feel so exhausted.* Ruffling sounds approached me, and the air shifted. I could feel the hair on my arms standing guard in response.

"How are you feeling?" A lovely nasal and somewhat creamy voice asked. Even asleep I had a thing for voices, I sighed inwardly. I didn't move waiting for the dream to move on.

"I know you are awake." A pause. "I saw you frown." *Did I?*

Now it was my turn to pause, this all felt far too interactive and real for a dream. I could smell flowers, some were roses if I wasn't mistaken and every sense screamed reality. Biting my top lip, I opened my eyes to two sets of curious eyes and a very strange pointy hat with a veil at the front hiding, what I could only assume, that man's strange eyes. Interesting.

"Ha, there you are girl." Clucked the old woman, clearly unimpressed at my slowness.

"Shina," the one with the hat and lovely voice admonished her.

She bowed from her seated position. Now that I looked properly, they were all sitting on cushions, legs tucked under them in a very Japanese manner. "My apologies, master."

Ugh, master? I stared confused at the room. My bed was laid on tatami mats, the walls were formed of wood and thin sheets of rice paper with breathtaking drawings of dragons and flora. An icy chill woke every nerve ending down my spine and settled in my guts.

Something was wrong here, very wrong.

Was I on my university placement in Japan? I forced myself to recall my last memories. I remembered seeing the young man sitting in front of me, but only vaguely. Maybe he was a friend? Pieces of the dream resurfaced: there was that blinding light when I opened the book. No! It came after I said *"ake"*, and then I passed out or something. The sick feeling in my guts intensified, not once in my life had I dreamed something that felt so real, and the more I thought about what happened with the book in our bookshop, the more I started to wonder if I'd been propelled to Japan through some sort of magical portal. Magical, right I snorted. Eyebrows rose but I didn't care, no way magic was real. Then a thought struck, maybe I was in Japan after all, but hit my head or something and had amnesia? It wasn't far-fetched as I was still suffering from one and couldn't remember anything from before my parents' murder. My heart rate slowed down with the rational thought, the situation wasn't ideal, but I could live with that.

"Am I in Japan?" Their English was heavily accented, a firm clue, but it didn't hurt asking anyway.

"What's Japan?" said the young man for the first time, he gave me a reassuring smile. I frowned, not the answer I expected, and shifted to a sitting position. Without a word, the woman put an extra pillow behind me and gave me a beautiful handmade cup, the familiar aroma of green tea made my mouth water, and my stomach growled in due course. Heat rose to my cheeks as I took a sip to avoid looking at their expression. The warmth and flavour of the drink accomplished more than satiate my thirst. It was proof I was wide awake, no dream could be this intense, so the dream theory was discarded. I studied the man more closely. He looked European, with blond hair and brown eyes holding a mischievousness about them. Yep, definitely could be a friend taking the mickey out of me in spite of my predicament. My gaze swept the room again, what I saw reinforced my belief. I decided to play along, hopefully the memories would flow back soon enough. "Where are we then?"

The others looked at the man in the hat for guidance.

"Toa, in Washima." he said in a soft tone. The uncomfortable feeling came back full force.

Not a name I recognised, my throat constricted I whispered, "Which country?" His shoulders tensed a tad, the only sign my question had surprised him.

"Washima is the name of our domain."

Domain? Was there such a thing nowadays? I took another sip recreating the world's map in my head, no Washima to my knowledge. Out of the corner of my eye, I watched the hat turn to the other man. "Did she bump her head hard?" he asked as though I wasn't right next to him.

The young man shook his head, "No, I caught her before she could fall to the ground." A gasp broke out of my mouth, my arms splashing tea all over my hands and blanket as I remembered the pain that had caused me to faint. I looked down at my normal looking arm, ignoring the woman – Shina, was it? – fussing over the mess.

I lifted my arm at them, the words, "My arm…broken?" coming out slow and thick on my tongue.

"Ryu–, I mean Kondo, our master," he presented the hatted man with a polite gesture. "Mended it; he's the best healer in Washima." He added with a friendly smile.

I looked down at the undamaged limb with a frown, the skin was smooth and pale, no sign I'd had any injury, yet I could now recollect the intense pain, the swollen redness.

"How?" I asked in a quiet voice.

Again, uncomfortable shared looks passed between my strange hosts. At last, the young man looked at me, tentative. "With magic, of course. Injuries like those would take an age to heal without magic."

My mouth opened and closed in a loud snap. That's it, I decided in that moment, I'd gone mad, this was mad. Anna must have slipped something in my coffee, and I was on my back tripping. I set the cup down and buried my face on my raised knees.

"Maybe she's from the Northern Kingdoms?" The one without the hat said.

"She doesn't talk like them, and her clothes…" Shina said.

"Magic?" I interrupted, unable to keep the dismay out of my voice. "Are you kidding me?" I got up and stared blankly at the long cotton pyjamas I was wearing, my head felt light-headed, and I sat back down hard. I rubbed at my face with shaking hands. "I want to leave, now." I hated hearing the whine in my voice, I was twenty-six acting like a six year old. But damn it, I just wanted to be back home.

"You need to rest, child." The old lady's voice was kind. "Master's magic healed you, but your body needs to sleep it off."

"All the more so as it was so full of poisons." The master added, "I'd never seen the likes of it."

What was he on about? What poisons? I shook my head, it didn't matter. "Could you get me a phone? I'd like to call my granddad please." After a prolonged silence, I lifted my eyes to them all. They all shared perplexed expressions.

"What is this phone you're talking about?" The master asked at last.

My arms fell limp on my lap, did I go back in time? Was Japan called Washima at some point in history? I refuted the idea straight away, they were speaking English between themselves, not Japanese. My confusion or whatever feelings I felt in that moment must have shown on my face because the master got up and left the room. I watched numbly at the sliding door until he came back, sat down and spread a parchment – *a frigging parchment* – in front of me. This was no map I'd ever seen: one massive continent filled most of the paper with a smattering of islands in the South.

He placed a long and delicate finger on the biggest one of them. "This is where we are, and this," he went over brown lines. "Is the Domain of Washima." Newlands was written in big and elegant cursive writing at the bottom of the map. Was this how they called their planet? *Planet?* I was too scared to ask. I nodded my head dutifully, taking in the information while I stretched one arm out and pinched it hard. I hissed at the pain and stared numbly at the pink skin. The master jerked back. He rolled the map in a careful gesture and straightened to his feet.

"Shina, Zen," he said, "I think we need to let..." his voice trailed for a second.

"Selena." I provided.

"I believe we should let Selena rest for a while longer." I didn't blame him, he probably thought he'd helped a deranged woman.

Before they left, Shina brought a tray of food set in little bowls, placed it on my lap – the message was clear – and wished me a good meal. I stared at the food, so like the ones I'd received in Japanese restaurants in Soho. Tears splashed the wooden tray in irregular drops. Washima. Magic. A headache was throbbing in what felt like a very compressed skull, my stressometer right up there. Resting my head on the wall behind, I took deep and slow breaths. The aroma of hot food wafted to my nose. My mouth watered at once. I picked up the bowl with what smelled like miso soup and took a sip. *Delicious!* I lifted another bowl full of rice, suddenly famished. I'd eat first, then think after.

A satisfied sigh escaped from my lips as I set the chopsticks on the tray, which I then put on the ground next to the bed. Knees pressed close to my body; I rested my chin on them. Eating without thinking of my situation had been difficult. Tears had threatened more times than I cared for, but I'd managed to calm myself down and enjoy the meal in the end. I cupped my face with my hands and massaged my forehead while recalling everything that had happened. I couldn't sit here all day crying and complaining about my misfortune. The plain facts were, I was somewhere foreign, and I couldn't rely on my scientific beliefs or what I had considered normal. Magic was a bit out there, but that didn't mean it didn't exist. Maybe like in some of the books I'd read, I was on another planet or a parallel universe where magic was the norm. It was possible, right? Many old sci-fi books had predicted new technologies, which were far-fetched for their time, but normal to us. And besides, no other explanation came to mind.

This was mind-boggling though. Too much change, too fast. I'd have to take a day at a time and see where it led me. In a way this was my own adventure. I was like one of these characters suddenly swept through drama after drama until their happy ending. Well, I hoped there would be a happy ending. But first things first, I needed more information about where I was and where I could stay while figuring out how to get back home. If I could get back home. The true meaning of the whole situation sank in. All those times when I'd read a book and foolishly wished to be the heroin. I had all the ingredients for a good fantasy and all I could think was, why me? *Why can't this be a crazy dream?*

✳ ✳ ✳

Early afternoon, if the sun's direction was any indication, Shina and Zen came back to check up on me. I was still in bed, staring at the room, unable to find the effort to get up. I'd finally made peace with the fact I had landed – for lack of a better word – somewhere alien and mysterious.

"I'm Zen," He bowed, then sat down next to my futon. "Feeling better?"

I nodded, a small smile escaping in return to his one. "Although I fear I've lost my mind." I forced a laugh.

His back became more rigid if that was possible. "Don't you remember anything from before our encounter?" two lines between his eyes formed on his smooth forehead.

I looked at my lap, my mind in override setting. Maybe this was a better explanation than the "By the way, I think I'm from another world" speech I'd rehearsed the past hour or so. I'd have to be careful with what I said as they obviously had no electricity, no phones, nothing modern. But they had magic, I mused in awe. I couldn't wait to see what kind of magic they could use. Would it be like in Harry Potter? That would be so cool, the fantasy nerd in me squealed. Zen shifted, the movement reminding me of his question.

Taking a leap of faith – I hoped I was doing the right thing – I said, "I don't. It's just one big blur." I shrugged, the way I spoke would be difficult to change, hopefully they'd overlook it. I didn't know if going back home was an option, so I needed someplace to stay, and I really hoped to stay here. Even though I knew nothing about them their actions spoke for themselves, they'd been nothing but kind and welcoming.

"Well, no need to worry yourself, the Master said you could stay and work here as long as you wanted."

"Work?" Was it so easy?

He nodded, "Are you interested?"

"Yes." I replied so fast he jerked back in laughter.

"That's good. We'll leave you to get dressed and come back to get you."

"What kind of work will I..." I managed to ask before he interrupted me.

"It's easier to show you, the master asked us to give you a tour of the estate if you wanted to stay. We'll be back soon." he added sliding the door behind him and Shina, who'd watched our conversation with a thoughtful expression. My hand went unconsciously to mum's necklace peeking under my nightdress, searching for comfort. I was glad I hadn't lost it. With more effort than it should have taken, I got up. A neat pile of clothes was folded on a small cushion next to the bed. The room was sparse: a low table with cushions around it and a half-filled bookshelf, one book flat on its cover while the others were organised, were the only furniture, a large vase of lilies stood to the side of a different set of doors, which opened on to the outside, considering the bright light coming through.

My head spun back to the bookcase: that book. I rushed closer and took the book in my hands and opened it, revealing the familiar symbols. A short laugh escaped. Well, that blew away the last of my doubts. I had somehow travelled to another world thanks to this book. I flicked the pages absent-minded while considering the possibilities of having such a book. Was it some sort of portal? Maybe I could come and go as I pleased between the two worlds. *Wait until I tell Anna!* But could she travel with me? I didn't fancy another landing like last one, especially if there wasn't a magical healer to mend my injuries. A magical healer. Magic.

I opened the book to the first written page. Did I really want to leave right now? There was so much I wanted to see. Magic, for crying out loud. Anyway, if I left now, who knew where I'd land the next time I came here. It was a chance to learn about this world, and if I didn't like it, I could always go back.

A huge smile broke out on my face, my head was floating, giddy. I would stay. I had to stay. Nobody in their right mind would pass out on the opportunity to live in a world the likes of a fantasy novel. I closed the book and put it back where it was, resisting the impulse to always keep it on me. They probably couldn't read it. They spoke English, the map was in English, so it was safe to say it was the official language here. Nevertheless, I hoped they hadn't peeked inside, I wanted to avoid unwanted questions for as long as possible.

Hands shaking with a recklessness so unlike me, I took the foreign clothes and spread them on the bed. They consisted of beige baggy trousers, a fabric belt, and a sort of kimono, only half its size. *Simple enough.* I got dressed very fast, a giddy excitement filling me up at my luck of having a place to live while I could figure out where and why I was in this place.

"Are you ready?" Zen called. "May we come in?"

"Of course!" I looked about me, checking I had made the bed, and left the room clean. The door slipped open, and I realised they wore the same clothes I was given except Zen's tunic was of a dark blue. Shina's tongue clucked in her mouth at one look at me. In an instant she was right in front of me, undoing my belt. She was fast for someone with such short legs. And quiet.

"Now look carefully!" she barked, then wrapped the belt

twice around my waist, made a knot and hid the loose ends inside. It looked neat. I was about to thank her, but the words never got a chance to be said as she undid her handiwork, then placed the belt in my hand. "You try." Ugh!

Never one confident with people watching my every move, I recreated her movements with shaking hands. She had made it look so easy. It wasn't. Why couldn't a good old double-knot be enough? I thought when she asked me yet again to start over. On my sixth go, she huffed. "This will do." Obviously, she'd been bored watching my poor attempts. Raising my gaze from the not so bad looking belt, I caught Zen's snickering.

"Right," he said. "Now that you're finally ready," *Damn him.* "Prepare to be amazed." He gestured for me to follow Shina. I looked down at myself, then pulled the tunic down all the while wishing for a mirror. Catching Zen appraising me, I wished I looked as good as him. Yet, the clothes felt strange on me, surprisingly comfortable, but strange. Zen's brow rose. "Ready?"

I gave a sharp nod. I couldn't wait to discover where I was.

CHAPTER 7

Selena

The master's house sprawled almost the entire width of the Estate. It had, in many aspects, the look of a traditional Japanese house with a wooden structure and a tiled pitched roof, flying eaves raising to the welcoming blue sky. Yet, it was constructed in a kind of L shape. The shorter section, I was informed, belonged to the master. I was in no way allowed to enter uninvited, not even for cleaning: this duty belonged to Shina and Zen. After catching a short glimpse of those forbidden rooms, they brought me to the walkway which gave out to a breathtaking enclosed garden – again one I was not allowed in – with a large pond surrounded by aesthetically placed trees and plants. A gazebo, black and red limbs supporting a majestic roof in the shape of a dragon's head, sat – a silent sentinel – on an island right at its centre, accessible by a low wooden bridge.

The rest of the house was not much different from my current bedroom: the rooms were big, yet sparsely furnished. Not one speck of dust. The place felt as bereft of life as those show homes you see in house decor magazines. Shina made a point to show the closets on one side of each room, where unnecessary belongings could be stored. Out of view, out of mind, she'd said. Shame, I thought, looking at some of the vases and wooden boxes, they would put more personality in the place.

My favourite room had to be the kitchen, though they didn't call it that. It was the main room to them, and I could see why. The biggest, it was right in the middle of the building. A traditional sunken hearth, made from a darker wood than the flooring, was at its centre; a long metal rod hanging from a beam overlooked the pit filled with sand and various metal implements. Pristine cushions were placed at each side. I could easily imagine myself on one of those in the colder days basking in the fire's warmth. A low table was standing on one side of the room while another corner beheld everything necessary for cooking: a sink with a pump, surfaces and open cupboards overflowing with bowls, plates and odd-looking pans. This was a room well used.

A covered walkway wrapped around the house, a feature I'd always envied the Japanese. Big paper sliding doors opened to an exemplary manicured oriental garden to the back of the house and the rest of the complex to the front. It was huge. It was difficult not to gawk. I expected Shina to huff and hurry me along, but I couldn't have been more wrong. If pride could take on any form, it would be in the shape of how Shina stood right then: posture stiffly elegant, but eyes brimming with satisfaction and love as she gazed upon the complex. And no wonder. It was simply magnificent.

Different sized buildings, some made out of wood, others of the local stone, spanned along the eight-foot wall surrounding the compound. They were all interconnected by covered walkways with lovely mini roofs, flying eaves included. When I questioned their necessity, Zen replied in a barely suppressed chuckle to wait and see until the rainy season. One of the structures was a dormitory for single servants who had nowhere else to live. I wondered why I wasn't put there in the first place.

Shina and Zen guided me around every building, and

though the layout was simple enough in itself, by the end of our walk, I couldn't remember which was the laundry room, the main hall or where the food cellar was. Cutting the courtyard in two uneven parts was a structure with an inner gate. The master's private guards lived there. People had to go through it to go and visit him. The courtyards themselves were lush with bushes, flowers and a sprinkle of trees. The master obviously respected nature. At length, we reached the main gate; nobody could get into the complex from anywhere else. Two guards were placed by its side at all times.

Two gates to see the master. It seemed everywhere rich people had to take precautions. Throughout my exploration, and no doubt Shina's inspection, we met servants in their day-to-day tasks. I was pleased to see a variety of ages and ancestry, while East Asians were prominent, I saw many of African, West Asia or Caucasian descent. They wore different coloured sashes depending on which building they worked in. I had a vague memory of Shina informing me exactly which colour belonged to which job (not that I asked) but, at that point I was too busy goggling at the man waving his arms up and down, left and right over a boy's broken leg. The action was arresting, but it was the bright green and white lights coming out of his hands that did it for me. I forgot all about Shina and Zen's presence until he was finished. I did remember his sash was forest green.

As we left the room, Zen placed an arm around my shoulders and guided me to the courtyard. "I see you love a good show. And today you're in luck." he beamed. "Ryuu... the Master" he rectified at Shina's throat clearing. "Is the most powerful healer in Washima. Once a month, people from all over the Domain come to see him in the hope he'll choose them. And today's the day."

"You mean, they walk all this way and they're not even sure to be picked?" he bowed his head. "Why can't he heal them all if he's so powerful?" I crossed my arms. Then again, could Dumbledore perform such a feat at the hight of his magic? Gandalf? Should I worry that my only references were characters from books?

Zen eyed me for a minute, confusion and uncertainty plain on his face. "I forgot you've lost your memories. The best is for you to see it for yourself. Come!" he hurried across the courtyard to a building which, if I remembered correctly, the master used for assemblies and ceremonies. I half ran to catch up with him. As soon as we opened the door, sounds of people talking loudly over wailings battered our poor ears. It took me a moment to fully comprehend how we'd missed this ruckus from outside.

Magic.

Contrary to the chaotic noise, everyone was sitting down in perfect rows facing some sort of platform to the back of the room, even children held their backs straight next to their parents. Zen made a gesture to follow him, then led me to the side of the platform in front of a door. Now that I faced them, I realised the scale, the importance of this assembly. There was easily a hundred people. And only a few would benefit from the master's healing. Who would he choose? Rather, who would take his fancy? This man who held his arm close to his chest? Or the screaming babies? I counted six of them. Perhaps some of the people laying on makeshift beds. The smell of sickness and blood wafted to our corner. My stomach churned. Zen's hand patted mine.

"The first time Ryuu held a session there were so many people the queue extended to the village." They must have been in the thousands. "It took us hours to separate the ones with real sickness from those who came for a good look at the man in the hat." He shook his head, eyes glazed deep in the memory.

"So, the master started this gathering?"

"Ah no! It was the old mistress, Ryuu's grandmother, a grand woman." Sadness fell over him. "When it became clear Ryuu had these amazing healing abilities, she came up with the idea twenty years ago. At the time, the war with Konden was still raging, so she refused to take any payment from the people healed, but lots of them gave something to show their gratitude, usually food."

"And the master was happy with that decision?" It was his magic after all.

"Of course! He still doesn't make them pay." he looked at me in surprise. "Ryuu is as kind and fair as the mistress was. Every person who comes here to get healed is also fed for free." Admittedly I had spent little time in the master's presence, who had been withdrawn, aloof even, so I'd assumed he didn't like to socialise with a mere servant. The person Zen described didn't fit the same mould I had made up in my head, which resembled a fair part of the UK's richest politicians now that I thought about it. *Guess stereotyping comes too easily.*

As Zen clearly waited for some sort of response, I said. "That's very kind of them. These people are…" His past words suddenly sparked some understanding. "Wait, you said twenty years ago? How old are you?"

He grinned. "Thirty-three. I was thirteen for the first one." The howling that erupted when he saw my expression didn't put a dent to the cacophony already taking place. No way! I assumed he was younger than me. Before I could question him further, Shina came into the room from the door behind us and asked for silence. When this was achieved to her satisfaction – even the babies' cries seemed subdued – the master, all dressed in his splendour, shuffled on to the platform with small steps. And no wonder he did, with the ridiculous mass of clothing he sported. On top of a dark green silky kimono, he wore two or three types of jackets each of a different length and hue of green. Unfortunately, that weird hat put a stain on this walking piece of art. To my surprise, he bowed deeply to the people. Nobody reciprocated the respectful gesture. Then, he lifted his arms up above his hat, revealing deep sleeves, and brought them down in front of him in one slow and graceful sweep. He repeated the motion many times. *What the…?*

I raised my eyebrows inquiringly at Zen when he looked

at me. He brought his mouth to my ear and whispered. "He's gathering the magic to himself. Can't you feel it?" Now that he said that the air around us did feel warm and peaceful. "Before each session he meditates in his garden. He needs contact with the natural world in order to borrow its magic."

"The magic is not within a person?"

"Not really, our planet is imbued with magic. The way we can use it depends on each person."

"Why is that?"

He shrugged. "We don't know."

"No one has ever been curious as to why?"

"No. We just accept the way things are."

I shook my head.

"But I heard some scholars researched it in the Northern Kingdoms, not sure it's true though." What a strange culture. No, I shouldn't say that. The fact it was different in principals from mine didn't make it strange. Just…dissimilar. And maybe they were onto something. Maybe thriving to understand everything didn't warrant the stress it brought with it. Back home was a good example. We always wanted to know more, be greater than the other people. And look how that turned out. WW2 came to mind and the race to make the atomic bomb. With greater knowledge came terrible things.

The master gestured to Shina to come closer and spoke to her while pointing at people in the room. With a bow of her head, she went to talk to each one and had them gathered on the platform in a line within five minutes. Not considering parents and bed carriers, I counted ten people.

"Is that the only people he's going to heal?" I asked, facing Zen. The anger in his eyes could have bored a hole into Shina who, catching him looking, grimaced. What was going on?

Zen brought a hand to his face and sighed; his anger deflated. "Unlike your assumption, ten persons are one, possibly two, too many. What has got into him? He's usually reasonable." His body looked tense, his attention all on the master kneeling next to the man in the makeshift bed.

"Is there a problem?"

His eyes didn't leave the master who had, with lightning-strike speed, cured the man now walking off the platform, a huge grin directed at his tearful family. The next person's face was pinched tight as the master approached. I frowned as the woman recoiled at his touch. Was that fear on her face?

"Yes. No." Zen's voice made me lose my train of thoughts. "That depends on the healing he has to make and how much of his power it takes. Last time he attempted nine people he collapsed on the stage." *Oh!* I looked at the man who had cured me out of kindness as well as given me a job and a place to stay. I berated myself for focusing on his status, not his actions which spoke for themselves.

The master was fast in his healing. He was on the eighth person when Zen excused himself and strode next to Shina. The two of them were hovering like two overprotective bodyguards behind him. I wasn't mistaken the last time, every person either shook with fear or turned their head in disgust. Their reactions and what Zen had told me clashed. What was the story behind this?

After the last person was cured, Zen seemed to breathe again, but he still stuck close to the master who bowed to the room and left. Shina gestured for me to follow them. People had started talking once more, laughter joined with the grumbles of the ones not chosen. It was a relief to close the door to the noise. What awaited me though...

"Selena, please help me carry the silliest master I've ever known to his room.' Zen's face was as white as his tight fists. The master was slouched on a chair, head bent to his chest. "Of all the stupidest things to do." he growled. "You've healed Selena only a few days ago." My gaze shot to the ground, I did not like confrontations. Zen didn't mince his words; no servant would dare address his employer like that. Their relationship was more complex than I'd first thought.

"Be quiet Zen, my head hurts."

"Yes, your foolish highness. This is the last time, you hear me? What if you'd collapsed in front of them? Don't you remember the problems it created last time?"

"Fine, fine. I promise I won't do it again if you could just shut up." Both hands went behind the veil.

Zen flashed me a smile. "Oyo! The almighty master is feeling grouchy. Selena, can you take the other side?" he asked as he placed himself to the master's left and put an arm around his neck. Mimicking Zen's position I placed my arm around the master's waist to hold him up. It was a good thing I was short; an inch or two more and the hat would have hit me in the head. Under the layers of clothing was a thin and delicate frame.

Nobody interrupted our awkward walk towards the master's residence. The servants we happened to pass by bowed deeply, then rushed away to their tasks, eyes never leaving the ground. None of them ever attempted to ask what had happened or whether they could help, which I found peculiar; he was their boss after all. The polite thing to do would be to at least ask after his health.

By the time we made it to his bedroom, the master's feet were trailing, and my shoulder was aching from the weight which had increased step by step.

"Thank you, Selena," Zen whispered. "I'll do the rest on my own."

"Are you sure?" I glanced at the futon on the floor.

"No problem."

I removed the master's arm as gently as I could, afraid to wake him up, then helped Zen hold him up. "Go, now!'

I bowed then retreated to the sliding door. Peeking over my shoulder, I saw Zen rolling him down with expert hands. The hat went askew, and Zen's head shifted my way, so I spun round real sharp. Twice I'd found the nerve to tell Zen I'd seen those strange eyes, only to lose it at the last second. As I was sliding the door closed I finally understood what had stopped me. No matter how welcomed I felt, I still didn't know much about them.

＊ ＊ ＊

The next night after dinner, alone in my bedroom, candles flickering to the tune of my steps, I stopped in front of the bookcase. It wasn't my sore body from hours of menial work that made me reach for the book, nor the disappointment at not witnessing any magic during the day. The previous day's excitement had abated and although the cleaning jobs, I was expected to do every day, had been hard work, they had not prevented the self-doubts, the questions from popping out throughout the day.

Was granddad looking for me right this moment? Retracing my last steps in the bookshop, trying to make any sense of the clues left behind. Had he called the police? He and Anna must be worried sick right now, waiting to know what had happened to me. How could I be so selfish? Here I was, willingly staying in this world to fill my stupid curiosity, while they were hurting. Shaking my head, I went to sit on the bed gripping the book hard. I couldn't do that to them.

Now I had the book, I could come back here anytime. And who cares if I landed somewhere different next time, I could always find my way back. With Anna, if she wanted to. I snorted. Of course, she would. I looked around me and smiled, the only true smile I'd had today. This felt right. I just hoped Zen, Shina and the master would welcome me back next time. Because I was sure I would come back, no matter what granddad said.

Book opened to the right page, where the word *Ake* was written, I took a deep breath and said "*Ake*" while shutting my eyes hard in anticipation of the light and dizziness. My breath caught in my throat; my body was tense. When after two seconds I didn't feel any different, I opened them wide, heart pounding in my chest.

It hadn't worked.

I stared at the page. Did I say anything else last time? Ignoring the ringing in my ears, I relived in my head every moment, every detail that happened that day. Then it clicked. I took out my mum's necklace – I should really stop calling it that, it was mine now – from under my clothes where it rested over my heart and held it in my left hand as I had last time. After swallowing hard, I pronounced in a soft but clear voice, "*Ake*."

Nothing.

My hand's pressure on the pendant was painful. "*Ake*". I called, louder. And again, and again until my voice was shaking and coarse with fear. The book fell to the ground, the sound swallowed by the tatami mat. Why wasn't it working? I did everything in the same way. I pressed the palm of my hands over my eyes and wiped the tears away. I wouldn't crumble again. Not this time. There had to be an explanation. Maybe the magic that brought me here needed to recharge or something. Maybe in a couple of days, I'll be able to get back home. And in the meantime, I can learn as much as I can about how magic works; it might help me to find out how this whole portal thing was possible. And how to recreate it.

I had to keep my wits about me, no more meltdowns.

CHAPTER 8

Faylinn

The tantalising smell of bacon and fried eggs dragged me from a deep slumber. Half-awake I stretched my limbs, reviving aches and pains that brought the previous days' escapades vividly to mind. My determination faltered for a moment. I wished to stay in bed, hidden from the world, hidden from my task. How would I manage the long trek when a mere three days had left me so sore? Was I strong enough? Getting out of the comfortable covers with reluctance, I held back tears of frustration. *I can do it.* I whispered those words over and over as I put on the clothes someone had set at the end of the pallet, my own nowhere to be found. I whispered them until I believed them and made them my own. I fingered the pale green dress with a pretty pattern of violets at the hem, it was simple yet beautiful, and although it was made of inferior material to what I was used to, it felt comfortable and light, no heavy petticoat here. After making a sorry job of plaiting my hair – How I missed Fiona – I lifted the leather flap working as a front door and was met by four pairs of curious eyes.

"Kel's right, you're mighty pretty." said a girl of no more than eight. She appeared to be the oldest girl in the group and the bravest for she stood right in front of me, her stare taking in the stranger amid their tight group. The other girls, wearing similar expressions, kept their distance.

"Thank you." I said and felt my cheeks redden. Compliments were somewhat foreign to me. The girls, hair dishevelled and dresses covered in dirt, looked full of life. I envied their innocence and freedom; our ages might not be so far apart, yet in comparison I felt old and weary.

"Now ye had a good look, off with the lot of ye." chuckled Luela who was sitting by a small fire. "She needs to break her fast without being pestered by annoying younglings." A tune of giggles floated through the camp as they departed, their little legs sprinting around the tents gleefully. Luela patted the place next to her and set a plate of food on the ground as I sat down. Once more, I ate everything up, stopping only long enough to sip at the hot tea. Maybe there was something about eating in the outdoors that made food taste so good.

Luela waited until my plate was empty to start talking. "There's something I'd like to... discuss with you." She paused for a while, looking at her lap. This had to be serious. I shifted on the log but waited without pressing her. Her prolonged silence made me uneasy.

"First of all, I'd like a promise from ye, a promise ye won't interrupt my talking until I finished." She was wringing her hands, eyes still anywhere but on me.

The request was simple enough. "I promise. I'll listen until the end."

Luela nodded and stared right in front of her, taking a deep breath she said. "Ye see, my gift is one that makes people uneasy, so our elders have set rules I have to follow, and I've sworn on my life to do so. But in exceptional circumstances, when I feel we're in danger or if we come across strangers," her gaze fleeted to my hands for a brief second. "I'm allowed to use it." I nodded at the implication. I knew I wasn't a threat, but I understood from their point of view I could be a possible enemy; female Royal spies were not unheard of. Likewise,

I'd seen desperate or unscrupulous men and women sell the location of wanderers to the king. Of course, the king paid them scant money.

Luela looked up and met my eyes for the first time. "I read minds."

I gasped. I'd heard some strong mages in the Closed Lands had the ability, but never quite believed it. My first thought was the king would kill to get his hands on her, he'd see her as a weapon. Then a numb feeling of nakedness prevailed, how much had she read? Many questions rose at once, but I forbore the words slipping from my tongue, as promised. It was easy enough to guess what she was about to say. I held my clammy hands tight on my lap.

"One look at ye and it was clear ye didn't belong to the villages round here. Yer clothes, the way ye talk made me think of aristocracy, not I've seen many in my life, mind ye. Ye ken, nobles aren't...much...appreciated by wanderers." she straightened her back and squared her shoulders. "And for good reason, if ye ask me. Anyway, just wanted to make sure for myself. Ye seemed nice enough, but it's not every day we find a Lady walking the woods alone. Strange things have been happening of late and I'd to make sure ye weren't a threat to my people. I didn't want to take any chances." she shrugged. "I'm not sorry I did it, but it was without your knowledge, and for that I apologise."

I admired and appreciated her honesty. Court had been a slippery mess of lies and omissions. It was refreshing and for a moment I was at a loss for words by her outright frankness. An urge to ask how much she knew battled with caution. Welcoming they might be, I didn't know them well enough to give away my trust so soon. She'd told me not a minute ago they didn't like people like me. At least we agreed with one thing, I smiled dryly. But if they knew, would they force me back as a cruel vengeance? A small reprisal to the bloodsheds they'd suffered over the years. My hands balled into fists within my lap. I hated how I'd become so cynical. Enough of that, I was not the prey in a catch the mouse game any longer. My father had trusted their kind, and so would I.

"May I speak now?" At Luela's shy nod I added, a thought mostly present. "Were you the only one who made that decision?" I needed to know what kind of people I was dealing with. Luela looked up sharply.

"Ye've a good head on yer shoulders for a Lady." she sighed. "Very well, I owe ye the truth. Sawyer asked me to check if ye were trustworthy or not. If not, we'd oust ye where we found ye. His words, not mine." She added quickly seeing the look on my face.

Somehow, this piece of information didn't surprise me in the least. I'd felt his cold eyes on me most of dinner and I could sense he didn't like me amongst his people. Luela answered the question I was about to ask. "But I would have done it regardless. I did it while ye were eating, it doesn't take me long anymore."

I tried to recall if I had felt anything, surely it would have manifested in a spell of dizziness, a headache or nausea, yet my mind drew a blank. Maybe my state of exhaustion had made me an easy target. I watched her face, a face still so close to childhood and marvelled at a gift so powerful, so dangerous in the hands of someone so young. Mine felt ridiculous and insignificant compared to hers. Even though she had invaded my mind without consent, I felt neither anger nor fear towards her. Her reasons were unselfish, she didn't do so for the pleasure of it; she was protecting her people and I admired her for that.

"To tell the truth, I only stroked yer mind a wee bit to see its colour, but a whole lot of unpleasant memories came rushing into my head, like they were desperate to be shared with someone. I'm still sore from the experience."

I was thrown back to my younger self then. Quentin and his brother Brentley, the crown prince walking on each side of me. Brentley sniffed loudly. "What's that putrid smell, Quentin?"

Quentin bent down and smelled my hair and flung his head

back. "Eww, I think the dimwit mistook the pigs pen for the wash room again, brother."

Brentley burst out with laughter. "Can't be too hard on her, poor thing. She probably mistook the pigs for her family." The boys ran ahead howling while my fists clenched tight.

Luela hesitantly put a warm hand over mine bringing me back to the present. "They felt real to me in the moment, then dwindled away and I'm glad for it for there is too much sorrow in such a beautiful mind. Ye've lived a difficult life, my Lady. With all my heart I wish the rest of it be filled with joy and happiness."

Tears, I had kept from spilling over the years, came rushing unbidden at those gentle words. I bent my head down, and let them overflow in silent, wet trails down my cheeks. I waited until the flow subsided and wiped my eyes with a sleeve. Not proper behaviour crying in front of someone. A broken laugh slipped away, I wasn't at Court anymore, for a very long time I hoped. It was then I noticed Luela had an arm around my shoulders in another compassionate touch, one to a stranger that belonged to a social class that had caused the death of countless of her people. Though, with everything she had learnt about me, I could scarcely be called a stranger now.

"I'm sorry to do this so soon," she let me go when my cheeks were dry. "But I've called for a gathering with the Elders. Ye must tell them why ye ran away. I'm sure they'll want to help."

Eyes wide, I shook my head. "No, no, I'll be on my way as soon as possible. This is too dangerous. I couldn't possibly ask anyone to put their lives at risk for me."

"But don't ye see? This isn't just about ye or yer family. It's our cause as much as yers. The implications of what could happen are frightening, I scarce slept last night. The Elders will know what to do, trust me. This is a favour I'm asking as a friend, for I'm sure we will be."

Her last words surprised me so much so the reply I was about to give died on my lips. In the face of all the future struggles, it warmed my anxious mind. It was nice to know I wasn't the only one who felt a connection between us. I liked the idea of a true friend, the boys and girls I had played with as a child a distant memory. This female friendship was very foreign to me. I had been the centre of mockery and petty and vicious acts at Court. I couldn't help fear how the speed of this newly forming friendship might make it brittle. The rational part of me might not know enough about Luela to make a sound judgement, but my heart, however trampled it had been, was still willing to trust and love. I nodded, a seed of hope within me. Past sufferings would be replaced with joyful days. Now I finally grasped my life in my own hands, I would make sure of it.

Soon enough, I was standing in the largest tent, its colours similar to the bushes and trees surrounding us. The interior looked even bigger, I suspected, due to a lack of furniture of any kind. It was bare save for a scattering of cushions. Fifty people could easily fit in here. The young warrior, who had escorted me, led me to a dark green pillow in the centre. I lowered myself unto it.

Facing me was an imposing group of people with equally imposing faces. I'd met Dwennon and Sawyer out of the four people sitting on large red cushions. I pondered if the colours had any significance as I waited for the meeting to start. I made sure to avoid eye contact with Sawyer. I was apprehensive enough as it was, no need to make it worse by seeing the wariness and suspicion I would see in them. Luela was sitting behind to my right. Anxiety at talking to their Elders overwhelmed me. By acting simple-minded at Court for so long, I worried whether it had lessened my ability to express myself in a clear and intelligent manner. Had I become more stupid by faking it? Sweat was running down my spine, the heavy beating of my heart throbbing in my ears so loudly Dwennon had to repeat his question twice before I heard he was talking to me.

"You seem pale, child. Are you unwell?"

Like yesterday, his gaze and body language were true to his words. It struck me once more to see someone sincerely considerate of others; I had met so few these past years. Dropping my gaze to the soft fabric covering the floor, I said. "I must admit I am nervous. What you're asking me to tell you is of such importance, I'm worried I'll not be eloquent enough for you to understand the dire situation."

"Enough with this dawdle, girl. We've got others waiting to seek our counsel." I looked up at the rebuke, feeling like a youngling chastised before my aunt. A middle-aged woman of fair proportions was looking down her long narrow nose at me. Her dark hair streaked with grey was held in a long plait set on top of her head like a crown. She had a severe look about her that made me dislike her straight away. Obviously, it was reciprocated. Anger in me spiked at her unfair treatment, she didn't know me. Words I wasn't proud of were about to come out, as an old man, even older than Dwennon, frowned at the woman and said.

"Now Salma, there's no need to be unpleasant to the poor girl because she's from the nobility. We all know well enough yer view on the matter. However, she's but a pawn in a broken system. Yer venomous tongue is unwelcomed here. If ye can't keep a civilised conversation, be gone with ye."

Eyes ablaze on me, Salma pursed her lips and nodded. Apparently, there was a hierarchy among the Elders; this man was, I would guess, at the top of it, being the most weathered. His scrutinising blue eyes swept over my face. "Please collect yer thoughts as you must. Talk whenever ye're ready."

"Thank you." I mumbled, not knowing how to deal with all this kindness. I glanced back at Luela, her presence reassuring; she offered a firm nod and a smile when she saw me looking. I hoped I was doing the right thing.

After taking a deep breath I said, "I am Faylinn Wymer. Daughter of Albus Wymer, 3rd heir to the throne."

Astonishment spread among them, they probably wondered even more so now why I had been alone in the woods without an escort to accompany and guard me. "Since the age of eleven, I have been living with the king and queen as a companion to their daughter, my cousin Gwynn. By chance, many moon cycles ago I came upon a set of unused secret passages running throughout most of the summer castle grounds. There's even a way out into the forest at the back of it. No one knows..." I paused, recalling my mistake. "No, nobody knew about them except me. It has been for some time my only solace as I was forbidden to go anywhere outside by myself."

I took a sip of the tea placed to my right; its warmth soothed my shaky nerves. The tent was silent, even with my eyes averted I could feel their rapt gazes on me. I then proceeded to describe the events that had transpired the previous days: the conversation I'd overheard, my capture and what went on after that, omitting details of the assault by Quentin. There was no need to share this piece of information, I wasn't even sure this was something I could tell my family. Luela's stare felt heavy on the back of my head.

"I decided to leave at once. I couldn't risk Quentin or the High Mage catching me." I went on. "I gathered the barest essentials deep in the night and waited at the end of the passage until dawn to make my escape. You may think me foolish not to take a horse, but I didn't want to raise attention to myself for as long as I could. And no one would assume that I would – or could – undertake the long way back home on my own. It was a gamble." I shrugged, the action a stark opposite to what I felt.

This was the longest I'd ever talked, and a staggering weariness overtook me. My mouth felt parched, aches and pains from sitting on the floor for so long were shooting down my limbs, like they'd been lit on fire. The speech had been daunting to say the least; it had been hard to share events and feelings when I had enveloped myself in a protective bark for so long. Yet, retelling everything, seeing the different expressions on their faces – even the guarded Sawyer had let his mask slip once – had worked peculiarly like a soothing balm to my heart. I wasn't the sole keeper of this terrible secret anymore. As the words had flown, I'd realised I was doing the right thing, that I needed as many people rallied to my family's side as possible. Like a truth carved in my bones, I knew my father would not let this happen without retaliation. However, even as esteemed as my father was in Highlands, he would never gather enough fighting men by himself to fight against Quentin, if indeed he took the throne. I recoiled from the vision of Quentin as king with Roldan at his side.

I sipped the tea Luela had kindly refilled waiting for Myrddin knew what. Like a seer who'd just foretold chaos and death to their group, I felt contrite, unsure if they'd take my words and act upon them or run away to the farthest point of the continent. They were only wanderers after all, who felt no allegiance to the present king. Why would they risk their lives for a monarchy they didn't abide to? While they were whispering to each other in their tight circle, I started imagining what they were likely to say to me. Probably something along the lines of "our apologies, but please be on your way." That's why Dwennon's sudden question threw me off.

"What did the doll look like?" he repeated slowly. *Why is he asking about the doll?* He must have read my confusion for he added, "If my suspicions are correct, another evil might be unravelling at this very moment."

"Oh," I exclaimed both curious and terrified. "I have it here." He leaned forward, eyes bright, and nodded to my satchel. I took the doll out and placed it in the palm of his frail hand. In all my self-absorption, I'd failed to notice how sickly he looked. He turned it around taking his time, examining all its details.

Placing it gently on the floor, he said, "It is what I was afraid of, child. When you said the High Mage mentioned the Leechings... Faylinn," I straightened my back at the sound of my name on his lips; I understood from the tone in his voice I wasn't going to like what he was about to say.

"Before I can explain exactly what malicious powers this doll has, I must share a secret of my own. It's only fitting as you trusted yours with us, I'll trust mine with you." He cleared his throat. "Before I began my years as a wanderer, I lived in the very same castle as you did. In fact, I believe we have met before." I frowned, looking at him hard. His face didn't bring back any recollection. "You see, I was the High Mage to the old king."

"That can't be true," I exclaimed, shock and incredulity taking my manners in their stride. "He was executed in front of the whole Court for the highest treason possible. He killed my grandfather in his sleep." I added outraged, as though this wasn't common knowledge to all the populace.

Dwennon was looking at me, his gaze filled with pure sadness and guilt. "I got caught unawares in Filius's trap. My powers were diminished at the time due to a previous battle, which I found out much later had been of his doing. He killed King Cardian in front of my very eyes with my own weapon." His eyes glazed over; his mind trapped into the past.

"He had put an incriminating letter in my study to show what I'd planned to do. How he could forge my signature is above me, but it's of no importance anymore, the nobles were convinced. I barely escaped and he staged my death to save face in front of his subjects and instil sympathy."

I was shaking my head, yet I believed he was telling the truth. Why would he lie? And I could well imagine my uncle planning the murder of his own father to get power. *History is repeating itself, how ironic.* Maybe we should let it happen, he deserved it.

"My point in revealing my past," Dwennon went on. "Is I have a far greater knowledge than you probably attributed to me. I know what this doll can be used for. As a matter of fact, Roldan was one of my last apprentices. I saw early on he was drawn to the Black Arts, he never called it the Leechings like most people, and he asked odd questions about the afterlife, whether they could be used for good. I tried my best to explain to him the nefarious effects one would have to endure upon using them, and he stopped talking about it. I assumed he'd lost interest. But this doll proves how wrong I was." His voice finished in a whisper.

Everyone else was enraptured by his words, maybe it was the first time they'd heard this incredible tale. "But don't be alarmed, I know a way to destroy it without causing you any harm. Although I didn't care for the Black Arts, I learnt how to counter its magic." He waved his hand at me. "Come and sit closer, I'll show you what to look for."

Getting up on tingling legs, I placed my cushion in front of him. Out of the corner of my eye, I saw Sawyer taking a place next to me, the others moved closer forming a tighter circle. Dwennon put the doll in the middle of it and tapped its poorly made clothes. The seams and cuts were uneven as though a young child had sewn it. "You might not recognise it as it is, but this fabric comes from some old dress or clothing of yours."

I used to have so many different dresses and overdresses that I couldn't possibly tell. "The more personal effects you use on these dolls the more efficient they become. That's why," he placed a finger on the head, "They used your hair on it."

I stared dully at the light brown and reddish curl: the colour, the thickness, no doubt it was mine. How did they get a hold of it? In my sleep? The idea chilled me instantly. All those years, I had become complacent, so sure of myself that I was more knowledgeable than the other women when in truth I had been as ignorant and malleable as them, just a pawn indeed. This very doll, Dwennon went on, represented me, whatever was done to the doll would then be passed on to me. It could be spells and potions, even body harm.

"So, the prince could have controlled her without her knowledge?" Luela's sharp tone cut through my sorry state of mind.

Dwennon grimaced. "Yes, it's a disturbing thought.

Myrddin was with you child when you took it. Had you left it behind, he would have been able to find you and the stars know what else." He then explained the doll would need to be burnt on a pyre made of cherry wood; numerous plants and flowers, all unknown to me, had to be thrown into the fire at specific intervals whilst he cast a spell. I groaned inward, why couldn't a good old bonfire do the trick?

"This, of course," he added. "Must be done within magical grounds. The nearest one is short of a day's journey. This, plus the resources I need will add roughly two days to the preparations I'm afraid." He looked at me with an understanding someone I barely knew should not possess. "I'm aware you would like to be on your way as soon as possible." Seeing me acquiesce, he went on, "Therefore, I'll ask a favour of you. I would like you to wait until we, Elders, discuss the events you kindly shared with us."

My fists clenched as I tried to squash the rising anger down. Didn't he hear me? I needed to go now, and their little meeting wouldn't make any difference.

"Please Faylinn," the old man put a roughened hand on my shoulder. "We would like to help." Why? The word wanted to burst out of me, but I kept it in that safe place where I stored all my thoughts and feelings for when I was alone. Luela got up then, my cue I should leave too. Sagging a little I said, "Very well." I followed Luela to her fire unable to decide whether the meeting had gone better than expected.

CHAPTER 9

Dwennon

Dwennon had seen and experienced many things in his lifetime, some as delightful as a bird's melodious song early in the morning, others – savage beasts – haunting his nights. Although the pain of his downfall, of losing a dear friend and ruler had slowly abated to a robust scab, the guilt held a heavy hand upon his soul. So many late nights spent dwelling upon what happened, the what ifs, the shame of surviving. Dwennon and Cardian had both known Filius inherited the arrogance and violence of his ancestors. It was a testimony to them that Cardian, the youngest of five sons had been the sole survivor when his father King Richard, known for his cruelty and short temper, had met with his fate at the hand of his heir; his favourite and eldest son. A hardened soldier, he'd given as good as he got; both perished from their wounds. Cardian, a man as gentle and good as his mother, had found himself at the age of forty-three the new king of a frightened and broken-down Kingdom. It had taken years for the people to fully trust the goodness in the mild-mannered king, for a better king had never existed in Comraich. A long period of peace and prosperity flourished. In their complacence they'd failed to act upon Filius's faults and his reoccurring misdeeds bordering on depravity.

The guilt, this gnawing disease, reminded him day after day of his shortcomings, of what his incompetence and short-sightedness had caused the Kingdom. And there he was, undeserving of the role, a leader once more helping his people survive through the mess he'd created. Life had ironic twists like that. Maybe, he'd thought upon hearing the girl talk, this was his chance to make everything up to the old king, to the people. As the other elders were expressing their ideas on the matter, he felt like an impostor. What right did he have to make a vote on this matter? However, one thing he was sure of, fate seemed to repeat itself. Although in the last couple of years the wanderers' chases had been subdued and sparse, Filius was still feared in the Kingdom. And from what Faylinn had said, Prince Quentin would make for another ruthless and violent king. The apple didn't fall far from the tree. The Kingdom would drown in further darkness if he let the guilt rule him. He had the power to make it stop, to redeem his past faults and he would do anything, anything within his power to make things better. For it was time.

In the end, they all decided to help Faylinn, even Salma had seen the precariousness of the situation. "The hunts," she said when her turn to vote came. "Have become few and spread out as King Filius has lost interest, preferring wine and social gatherings in his old age. I fear for our people, we need to rid ourselves of our enemy before he stands out of our grasp. My vote is yes." Dwennon reflected upon her words. Ousting the present king and his sons seemed as dangerous as riding an untameable earth dragon, yet not impossible. As far as he knew, Prince Albus was their best bet, he'd vouch for his honesty and the short time he'd spent with Faylinn was enough to reassure Dwennon he hadn't changed throughout his years of banishment.

Adym, the oldest amongst them, shifted on his pillow to look at Sawyer. "Can we entrust ye with the journey?"

Sawyer bowed his head sharply. "Ye honour me, elder

Adym. I will do my best to bring the message to Prince Albus. May I take Keltor, Jolis and Veena to join me? It'll look less conspicuous if we go as a group."

"Wise decision." Dwennon said. "We don't know the extent of Roldan's powers; we have to expect anything from now on."

"Do ye think they know the girl's here?" Salma's face was turning an angry red. "She should go with them; we can't have her bring misfortune to our group."

"No, no Salma, it's a strenuous journey," Adym shook his head and added with a warning in his eyes. "We can't and we won't ask her to leave. Well, if she's set to go, we'll have to accept her decision of course," Dwennon watched grimly Sawyer frown at this revelation and his eyes narrow. "But I'd rather she stay with us, on safe ground. If they find her here, we'll do everything in our power to protect her." Dwennon had a feeling things would go a different path. The girl had her own plans if he'd read her well.

"With our best warriors gone?" Salma watched the set faces of her peers and sneered. "Ye might have just condemned us all." She stood up muttering about useless nobles before disappearing through the flap.

"Well, that was foreseeable." Dwennon said exasperated at the woman's narrow-mindedness. Her loyalty to their people held no bound; shame it couldn't extend to outsiders.

"I'm actually impressed at how long she kept that in.' Adym chuckled. "Her temper is tiring at best, but she does have our group at heart."

"She did raise an important point though." Sawyer spoke with care. "While we're gone ye'll need to be on yer guard. I'll put more scouts out day and night." At Adym's frown, he added. "To be sure."

"I'll also set another protection on the camp; you don't need to worry about us boy." Dwennon patted Sawyer on the head after getting up, the same way he'd done through his apprenticeship. "You'll have enough on your mind."

"Sawyer," Adym interjected, "There is someone I want to

add to yer party."

Dwennon marched to the flap, he suspected whom Adym was referring to and wanted to steer clear of the conversation. "I'll let Faylinn know the outcome of our meeting." Nobody took any notice; the other men were deep in conversation. "Although I have a feeling she'll have a say about it." He muttered as he left the tent.

* * *

A breeze rustled his long hair with its warm touch as he meandered around the camp. He found her at one end of the boundary, watching young women gathering flowers in their baskets for the next day's celebration. The wildflowers would adorn their hair and clothes, a superficial but nonetheless pleasing detail meant to enthral the ones they were enamoured with. His mood lifted at the sound of love songs and laughter. He loved that about the wanderers. No matter what adversity, what hardship they kept going full of life, full of love. As he approached Faylinn, she got up and started towards him. He stopped her with the lift of his hand. She sat back down with an innate grace. Although she favoured her mother more, he reflected, she had her father's nose and generous mouth. When she'd spoken at the meeting, he'd seen him in her gestures and expressions too.

"I hope you're enjoying your stay with us?" He placed a hand on the log and lowered himself, he had seen the endearment in her eyes.

"Yes, it is a different world to me, so simple." She covered her mouth with her hand. "That didn't sound right, I apologise. I didn't mean it in a rude manner."

"Be at ease," he nodded. "I know very well what you mean, I lived at court longer than you did, although I expect in my days it was tame in comparison. What you said is true, life among the wanderers is simple and peaceful. Mind you, there's plenty of menial work to do every day, but everything is straightforward, even the people." He saw the stiffness in her position relax and her gaze settle on young Melina picking flowers. He was impressed at her self-control, and broached the subject she, no doubt, was bursting to discuss.

"We've all agreed to help you in your cause, our cause." He rectified shaking his head in a morose movement. "Most of us felt you should stay here for your safety while we send some of our people to deliver a message to your father. However, we'll let you decide whether..."

"I'm going no matter what."

Dwennon fell silent, staring at the young women in front of them. That's how it should be, he thought, girls being insouciant, girls being selfish and foolish in their young age, their heads full of love. Too soon, time would bring the unrelenting worry. He looked at Faylinn's face, her brow was wrinkled and a flame of something, determination or maybe stubbornness, burnt in her eyes.

"I was afraid you'd say that." he sighed. "You seem to crave adventure after being shut in for so long." He broke his gaze and looked inward, dark memories resurfacing. "There will be danger, mark my word. Are you sure you are prepared for this?"

She pressed her lips hard, silent for a long time, lost within herself. He hoped she was re-evaluating things. With a sudden shift in her posture, he knew her answer before she spoke.

"Only time will tell."

In that instant he wished he'd known her better, in a day or two she might have valued his opinion a little more. She didn't trust them. In her eyes she was one, one determined to finish a task she had set her mind to. *Your father would be proud.*

"I see you've made up your mind. Only the stars know what will happen along the way. My only comfort is that you'll be in good hands." She raised an eyebrow at this. "We've chosen our best warriors to go with you on this mission. Tomorrow evening is our bonding ceremony, an important ceremony for our young people, hence the flower gathering." He waved at the young women. "So, you'll all be leaving at dawn on the following day.' He lifted a hand before she could argue. "The rest will be beneficial, take it while you can."

"What about the doll? Do I have to do anything?"

"Your presence isn't necessary. It should be burnt for good in a few days' time." Her lips pursed; her eyes narrowed. "In the event I can't destroy it, I will hide it where nobody can find it, rest assured." She watched him silently for a moment before she nodded her approval, or more likely begrudged trust. He couldn't blame her on this matter. He rose slowly. "Ah, I almost forgot. I would like to give you this." He lifted a chain hidden inside his robe and handed it to her. A gold pendant in the shape of a dragon laid on the palm of her hand. Two red rubies were in place of its eyes, scales had been delicately carved on its twisting body.

"I cannot accept this my Lord." Her stare didn't leave the pendant.

"I knew your father very well Faylinn." Her head shot up at his words. "Show him this pendant and he will have the proof I am still alive. You can give it back to me the next time we meet. Now rest, we'll provide for everything."

❊ ❊ ❊

Dwennon left Faylinn feeling dissatisfied. He would make a brew to keep her strength up, she was obviously not fit for this journey. He strode to the South boundary where Sawyer's magic pulsed with delicate threads. He was walking at a snail's pace head bent, whispering reinforcement spells when Dwennon came upon him. He was strong enough to do so with thought alone, yet Dwennon knew it was a habit hard to break. As he approached, Sawyer straightened up and looked at him with his usual gravity. When had he last seen him smile wholeheartedly? Oh, he smiled to women and laughed at Keltor's idiotic jokes, but his body language always felt restrained and sometimes forced as though his deepest emotions were bound in a tight vice. Seeing one's parents brutally murdered would scar anyone to the bone, especially a child.

Over the years, Sawyer had let a select few get closer to his heart, but even with him, his master and substitute father figure, Dwennon felt he'd raised a protective barrier. He should never have agreed to let him be elder after Willem had passed away. There had been older hopefuls, all worthy one way or another. Yet, despite Sawyer's young age, his maturity, confidence and intelligence had secured him as the fourth elder. He hadn't asked for it, indeed he was shocked when he heard his name being called by Adym in front of the congregation. The position could be refused without shame, the elders understood all too well the pressure of the responsibilities that came with it. Sawyer had stood up by the communal fire without hesitation and received the blessing, shoulders and head high, face not betraying what was deep in his heart. He understood the group needed him and was prepared to give his life for it. However, Dwennon couldn't help wonder what Sawyer himself truly needed.

"May I have a word?" Dwennon sat down on a well-placed log; his legs weren't as strong as they used to be, on days like these he didn't care for it.

"Anything the matter?"

Always straight to the point, Dwennon thought. He stalled for a second, unsure on how to break the news. Sawyer liked organised control, with Faylinn going with them... He too decided to be direct. "Faylinn will go with you."

Swayer let go a string of impressive cursing, sat down beside him, then stood up fast. "I'll go talk to her right now.

I'll make her change her mind. This is ridiculous." he was prowling back and forth. "The little fool doesn't know what she's getting herself into."

"No, it won't be necessary boy, I've already spoken to her, and she has set her heart on going. She won't change her mind for anything or anyone. In any case, I don't think you're exactly in the right temper to do so." he raised his eyebrows, his mouth breaking in a wry smile. Sawyer huffed and sat down hard, elbows on his knees. Dwennon suppressed a smile and said, "What I wanted to discuss with you is on another matter. I'm worried Prince Quentin and Roldan essentially, have other means to find her. I might be wrong, but one can't be too safe. I'll be gone most of the day tomorrow gathering herbs for a shadow spell, I'll make enough to last you until you're out of reach."

Sawyer nodded grimly. A shadow spell would keep the girl's essence shrouded in shadow, hence the name. It would keep their enemy at bay, yet it had possible unpleasant side effects for the one casting the spell: headaches, nausea and insomnia to name a few. Then, there was the added complication of the daily renewal, costing time and energy. Only Swayer could cast it.

Sawyer rubbed his face with both hands. "No chance to change her mind?"

"None." Dwennon watched his big shoulders sag with grudging resignation. "I'm sorry to add to your burden Sawyer, we've already asked too much of you. I just don't want anything happening to Faylinn. Her father was a good man, still is I'm sure, and I couldn't bear failing him as well."

Sawyer put his hand on Dwennon's frail one. Not many people knew he still blamed himself for the old king's murder and the following downfall of the Kingdom. This sense of guilt had brought them together more than their master-apprentice relationship had. Although Sawyer knew deep down he couldn't have helped his parents anymore than Dwennon could have saved the king, a part of him thrived in this guilt, which he moulded into helping their people. "I'll be fine. I promise to keep her safe."

Dwennon stood up. "I know you will, boy." he said with shining eyes and left Sawyer to his task.

CHAPTER 10

Faylinn

Rest I did. Luela and Somlin refused any of my attempts at helping, be it cleaning, preparing food or even the simple task of getting water at the stream. I never pushed, watching their harmonious routine so different from my old one. I refused to dwell on the future, it only caused a sickness in my stomach, a sickness I couldn't abide right now.

With my ears full of polite refusals, I made my way out and wandered around the camp. A gentle breeze was rustling in the branches while the sun, filtered from the trees, cast intermittent shadows on the colourful tents, which reminded me of a field of overgrown flowers. Traipsing aimlessly, I watched the people in their usual routine. I observed, stared even, but nobody took any notice of my presence. And if they did, they gave a slight nod then continued with whatever chore they were doing. Everyone was busy contributing to the wellbeing of their group. Money was obsolete, trade at the heart of all transitions: horseshoes exchanged for sturdy clothes with a few words and a pat on the back. It seemed everyone had a precise purpose based on their gift, which made me wonder if someone like me would fail to have a place amongst them. Somehow that thought made me sad.

Early morning the next day, Dwennon came to talk to me again. The band of warriors going with me had met the previous day to plan the journey. I did not voice my annoyance, it was of no matter if I wasn't welcome, going home was. And if I was left out by that petty lot, so be it; I could take it in stride. I let the irritation dissipate as best as I could, although the sympathetic look in Dwennon's eyes told me I didn't fool him.

We would follow the river Tathlay he said, and keep to forests whose names I didn't recognise. "It's unlikely you will travel close to the Cage," he added. "But they are considering the option in case of trouble, don't ..." He kept on talking, but my mind stayed frozen at the mention of the Cage, or the Forest of torments, its official name. Even though it was surrounded by a powerful barrier keeping its dangerous creatures trapped within, I was not comfortable going so close to it. Like all children from Comraich, I'd heard tales of dragons or two-headed snakes with fangs as long as a man's arm. However, I held my disquiet in, convinced they would leave me behind if I so much as complained. Dwennon assured me my companions were well trained in fighting and had travelled in its proximity many times with no trouble.

As terrifying as the Cage was, it paled in comparison to his next bit of revelation. Not only Sawyer was one of the wanderers travelling with me, but he would also be in charge. The little I had spoken to him didn't inspire any hope of getting along. I'd watched him from afar; he looked as competent as any elder should be, just a bit rigid and not particularly friendly. Then again, the hard looks he gave me whenever we crossed path might only be reserved for me. And there was this nagging feeling I would get whenever he was close, a feeling I couldn't quite decipher, something not quite right. Kel was a different tale altogether. Last supper he'd sat down next to me and regaled me with little snippets and comical stories about the people around the fire. I'd laughed so much I woke in the morning with sore cheeks. I was glad he was coming with us; he would be the light to Sawyer's darkness.

Sitting by the main fire after a walk around the magical boundary, which took a good part of the afternoon, I became aware of a group of men and women bent over a large piece of fabric, sewing, it seemed. Men sewing. I didn't know why the sight of this surprised me still, for during the past two days I'd seen women chopping wood, working metal into fine swords, men cooking and looking after babies. It felt as though I'd travelled to another Kingdom, not a couple of days away from the Castle. Were all wanderers' groups like this? I liked this equal footing. Women were not considered like frail flowers; they were recognised for their worth, their skills, and not solely on their ability to bear children. Men asked women advice with no shame on their face, only interest. They drank together, talked together, worked together and made a strong bond together. A bond not even King Filius had managed to destroy. This was how our Kingdom should be for all of us.

A gentle touch swept me away from my musings. Luela, head cocked to the side, was watching me, amusement clear on her pretty face. "You could stay, you know." She raised her hand in my direction. "I promise I didn't invade your mind, but it's plain on your face. I could see the longing."

"Things are so different for women, so open. Is it the same amongst commoners?"

"You don't know?"

"I went to our village many times, but I saw it through a child's eyes. And things might have changed, I wouldn't know." I shrugged.

"Guess being rich and part of nobility has its downfalls too. Meeting you made me realise how short-minded I was towards your kind. I guess it's the same for you."

I nodded my agreement, "I think that's what my father wanted me to see when he let me play with the wanderers all those years ago." I wondered how I'd have grown up if I'd stayed home. Would I feel more mature and knowledgeable? I felt like I'd been trapped in a minuscule box, whose lid had suddenly sprung open, letting me experience the real world.

"To answer your question, as far as I know only us wanderers do not make any differences between sexes. We're valued as a person, not by our gender. Although some women don't deserve it." She grumbled. Surprised by those unkind words, I followed her gaze to a group of young women a little away from us. A blond one at the front had her eyes intent on me.

"Word has spread you'd be travelling with Sawyer and his band. Some people are, let's say, unhappy with it."

"The blond one?" I couldn't resist asking. "Whatever for?"

"Laina is elder Adym's great grand-daughter. She's been besotted with my brother for as long as I can remember, but ever since she came of age, she's become overly pushy in her determination of becoming his lifemate. She's a good warrior in training but doesn't take orders as well as she should. She was supposed to go with them, elder Adym's orders. Sawyer was not happy." She chuckled. I took it that he didn't like the girl much. "I'm afraid she now has a tooth against you as the big dolt told the elders he couldn't take her as you insisted on going with them."

"He couldn't keep an eye on the two of us?" I whispered. Luela had the decency to look contrived.

"I'm sorry, I shouldn't have said it like that, that doesn't put a good light on Sawyer. He's a good man." At my scowl, she added, "Truly, you'll see… Ah, here comes trouble," she said, biting her bottom lip as Laina sauntered up to us, hips rolling in a smooth seductive movement I was in no way capable of executing, her group of followers right behind.

Hands on her hips, Laina stared, a sneer appeared on her thin lips as she said, "Mm, I wanted a look at ye, seeing all the fuss ye're causing around here." An eyebrow went up as she looked down at me, obviously she was enjoying her position. "Ye don't look much a lady, do ye?" Her words went high over my head, petty slander like these had no effect on me anymore. Haelan's voice sprang to mind. *Spiteful words are just that little one, words, not truths.* At my silence, Laina pressed on, "Well, maybe ye ain't one, just a sham and Luela, here, ain't as good as she claims to be." Her little group faithfully laughed with her but were giving wary glances at Luela. Interesting, maybe they were scared she'd read their minds. As much as I didn't care people talking badly about me, it was another matter entirely with my family and here, my new friend.

I rose to my feet and stretched my long body right in front of Lainy. A hand could barely fit between us. It was clear she had not been aware of my height as she looked up at me, eyes betraying her uncertainty and she took a nervous swallow. "You are right, I do not look like the beautiful and delicate ladies at court, but I assure you I am one of them. And I am well aware of people like you," my head bent down close to hers. "Words like venom, but no bite. You can say all you want about me, I don't give a damn, but my friends…" A strong grip on my shoulder made me pause, I looked down in surprise at Luela's hand. She was shaking her head at me. "Please, this isn't necessary, let's go." She pulled me by the arm, leading me away from trouble.

As we reached the safety of her tent, she let go. "I'm sorry Faylinn, I couldn't let ye fight my battle as well. I'm not like ye, I don't do well with confrontation.' Her fists were clenched by her side, her head lowered in shame.

This was unexpected, she appeared so confident around people. I wondered what had caused this. "I'm sorry too for letting my tongue run out on me. I've suppressed it for so long, it's like a wild animal on the loose with a will of its own." I shook my head in exaggeration. Luela burst out laughing and my whole being relaxed. When her outburst had subsided, she came and gave me a hug, my arms fell awkwardly on her thin frame. "You're a good friend Faylinn. I'm glad the stars brought ye our way."

"Me too," I croaked, eyes stinging. I blinked hard. "Please call me Fay. That's what my family calls me." She smiled at that and brushed her wet eyes.

"Right," she said clapping her hands. "The girls will be here soon to get ready for the celebration, let's make room."

"Oh, and I'm allowed to help with this?" I teased. Not a second after, a cushion landed right in my face.

We spent the next hour cleaning and tidying the tent. Furniture was moved to the sides and the back of the tent leaving the floors strewn with cushions and only a table with two looking glasses on top of it. As girl after girl swept through the flap, I understood the need for space; all unmarried girls and women gathered together. I found out soon that Luela had a talent for fashion, from colour coordination to adornments matching clothes, everyone vied for her opinion. To my dismay even Laina asked for her counsel, the earlier clash all forgotten in appearances at least. It was their favourite celebration and clearly no-one wanted to spoil the euphoric atmosphere. All resentment and anger were left at the door. Laina ignored me, which suited me just fine.

I sat on a pillow entertained by all the excitement and happiness emanating from everyone. Luela had explained two bonding ceremonies were held every year. The ceremony was the first step for two people to claim one another and become a couple, the same as being engaged: different words, same meaning I mused. I'd been shocked to hear they were free to bed whomever they pleased if they were unattached, and it was consensual. Wanderers were certainly forward and free-minded. I didn't know whether I approved of this; I couldn't imagine being so promiscuous, yet the idea of being able to choose whom I'd spend the rest of my life with was appealing.

The summer solstice ceremony, she'd said, was important to young women because it was their chance to express their feelings to the one they loved. It could be someone they'd been seeing or somebody they admired from afar. From the day they were born, all men and women wore a necklace crafted by their parents. On that night, the single women handed their necklace to the one they loved during a ceremonial dance.

Then, during the last dance of the festivities, the men either accepted the bonding by giving their own necklace or politely refused by returning the woman's necklace.

The concept was baffling. "Does it mean you can only start courting once a year?"

Luela laughed. "No, there's another bonding ceremony for the winter solstice, this one for the men. In our culture, men represent the moon, hence the shortest day of the year for their ceremony, and we represent the sun, so we get the longest. In the meantime, if two people are too impatient to wait for the ceremonies, they can appeal to the elders to be bonded beforehand."

"Then I don't understand the need for the ceremony."

She cocked her head. "Don't you? Not everybody is brave enough to pursue the one they love, and it's also a good way for the shy ones to express their feelings without words." This was peculiar, yet fascinating. In my world, the father chose whom his daughter would be engaged with. Marriage was seen as a political move, not a matter of love.

Someone placed a dark green dress with bow and arrows at the hems on my lap when I was putting my cup of tea down. I looked up into Luela's beaming face. "You don't think I'd let you off that one."

"It's beautiful," I exclaimed, I hadn't expected anything. "Did you make it?" She nodded. "In such a short time?"

"I had some help." She wiggled her fingers but didn't expand on the subject. I let my fingers run over the delicate fabric, it must have cost a pretty penny. This was the first time I'd received a gift from a friend, my throat felt constricted with emotion. I got up and embraced Luela. "Thank you so much, it's beautiful. I take it I have to attend tonight's festivities then?" I asked in pretend horror. To tell the truth, I was dying to see it.

Luela pushed me none too gently towards my bed. "Damn right ye are, now go and get changed so I can make ye even prettier." Then she closed the separation.

"Will see about that," I said under my breath but executed myself. The dress hugged comfortably on my hips; the top half was more revealing than I was used to though. When I came out heat suffused my face as Luela looked me up and down with the biggest smile on her face. "Gorgeous, I love it when I'm right." This was nice, this feeling of happiness. My hand went up to cover my smile. "And stop putting that hand over your mouth," she tutted while removing it. "Ye've a nice smile. It'd be a shame to keep on hiding it." She turned round when someone called her, leaving me speechless.

After what seemed like hours of brushing and fussing, of painting flowers on their necks to match their dresses, all the girls gathered around the communal fire. I stayed back next to a tent. From my viewpoint I could see everyone: the old preferred the comfort of logs while the young ones clustered in groups showing off their attributes; no sign of children. There were so many colours, it reminded me of a garden with its flowers moving, swaying in the waning light of the sun.

As Luela had explained, the beginning of the ritual started with a feast. Platters and bowls of mouth-watering food attracted hungry stomachs to men and women armed with ladles, ensuing an organised queue of people oohing and ahing at what they would soon feast on. My eyes fleeted to everyone's necks where I could peruse the object that held more meaning than I had first attributed. Each necklace was unique; the wealthiest had gold or silver ones, however the majority used my beloved wood, some even had crystals. I wondered if the shape had anything to do with family ties or the actual person, and made a mental note to ask Luela about it. Some looked incongruous, brawny men sporting delicate flowers, and even one old woman, no higher than my shoulder, adorned with a ferocious looking bear that hung heavily over her bosom.

Laughter and chatter filled the air, I counted myself lucky to experience such an important ritual. Kel came towards me, Blaith at his heels, accompanied by a shorter man with dark hair, whom he presented as Jolis, one of the people who would help me cross the Kingdom. Jolis gave me a quick smile, and an awkwardly executed bow. I was about to tell him to drop all formalities with me when Kel, in his good-natured way, put his arm through mine and led us to the back of the food queue where he pointed at a woman further ahead of us. "Her name's Veena, the last one of our lot." With that he left me alone with my new acquaintance, not giving me any chance to ask about our journey. I looked sideways at Jolis and considered asking him, but he seemed like the silent type, and anyway his attention was everywhere but on me. I sighed; I would ask Kel when he came back.

My plate overflowing with spiced meats and fermented or roasted vegetables – wanderers' traditional dishes – I sat on a log. People were assembled into little groups around the fire, their voices louder than the drums playing in the background. Some of them went from one group to the next like a bee flitting from flower to flower. Surprisingly Sawyer was one of them. Every gathering was happy to see him: men were clapping him on the back or shook his hands, women, especially young ones, seemed to drink his words in like the finest wine.

Mid-supper, Kel and Blaith joined me. I was so engrossed in observing Sawyer, I didn't feel his presence until he spoke.

"Tough to be an elder if ye ask me." he pointed his fork in Sawyer's direction. "Don't think he's had a bite yet." He handed a piece of meat to the wolf, who took it with delicate care in its jaws.

"Have you been asked?" At his confusion, I added, my stare falling momentarily on the silvery threads through his black hair. His face was unwrinkled, but that didn't mean a thing, the most powerful mages could stay in their prime for a hundred years. "To be an elder. You seem older than he is."

He laughed. "Don't be fooled by those," he gestured towards his hair and grinned. "We're of a same age. And anyhow, never been asked and don't want to be. Too much work for the likes of me." he waved his hand back and forth to reinforce his words. "Sawyer on the other hand is perfect. Ye don't seem convinced." he added in surprise at the scowl on my face.

"The few moments I've had with him haven't left me with the best impression."

"Is this why ye've been watching him all dinner?" A playful smile lit up his face.

Without thinking, I shoved him with my shoulder. "Watch it! No, seriously, I'm wondering why they all seem genuinely happy to speak to him. Every time I catch him watching me, it's with a scowl so deep I'm surprised his brow isn't cleaved in two. And from what Luela said, he had no qualms kicking me out, and … "

"But that was only if ye'd been up to no good, right?" he interrupted. I gave a reluctant nod. "See, once Luela had checked ye out, he let you stay, no problem. Sawyer takes his part as elder seriously, too seriously if ye ask me, but everyone recognises the work he puts in and thanks him for it. He's a good lad." I scrunched my nose. "But then again," he added hitting my leg with a light touch. "I might eat my own words soon enough. He's a real tyrant when we're on the move." Seeing my expression, he roared with laughter throwing his head back.

At that moment the drums stopped, and people gathered closer to the fire. Kel took my hand and got up, pulling me up in the process. My plate fell in a mess. As I made to pick it up, he put his hand around my waist, "Don't worry about it, Blaith will eat it." I glanced back at all the lovely food. *Such a waste!* He led me between two persons in what formed a huge circle around the fire. Oh no, I shook my head, but Kel held on tight to my hand.

"No worries me lady, this one's easy. Flap yer skirts a wee bit. Have fun while ye can is my motto." His white teeth were showing bright in the dimming light. A shiver spread through my veins; his words had felt like a bad omen. My apprehension was cut short by the coordinated thrumming of drums. The dance of life, Kel explained close to my heels while I was copying the slow tapping of feet around me, was to thank nature for everything it let them take. I caught Luela's eye a little way to our right, holding Somlin's hand, and she winked at me. A warmth enveloped me. This place, these people felt right and a part of me wished I'd belong with them. The music stopped. The other dances would be more intricate, and even though Kel assured me that he could teach me I refused, convinced I would make a fool of myself. My growling stomach led me to the buffet once more and I watched on a log, content.

The intensity of their enjoyment was contagious, my worries were blown away by the music, and I joined in the clapping, euphoric with their happiness. I recognised at once the dance of the Sun, where women offered their necklace to the ones they liked. All single men above the age of twenty-one had to be present, widowers and determined celibates included. Adym stepped amongst all the youth, scratching his cheek in embarrassment; Sawyer came next to him and tapped him amicably on the shoulder. The men formed a circle around the fire, the breadth of an arm's length separated them. Their silhouettes were casting long shadows over the people who were watching, curious of the outcome.

From what I'd gathered earlier from the giggling women in Luela's tent, it was a favourite amongst the wanderers. And no wonder, I thought soon after. At the first notes of a harp, the single women weaved their way between each man, their whole body moving in enticing and lascivious steps, hips sashaying languorously, arms waving in elegant movements. Some of the bold ones went as far as stroking a hand, a cheek. My own were burning at this forwardness. Everyone was watching as if entranced by fluttering butterflies. The air felt charged and heavy; the breeze had gone, replaced by a humid languor. However, nobody else paid heed to it. To my surprise, I saw one young woman give her necklace to another one. Decidedly, wanderers were full of wonder. Same sex relationships weren't displayed in plain sight in the Kingdom, let alone their bonding.

Many women stretched their arms to place their proof of love around Sawyer's neck while he bent down unsmiling, eyes cast to the ground. Kel received a few, Adym none and I could have sworn he sighed in relief at the last strum of the strings. Another happy tune started in the background, but weariness crept up over me then, as though the intensity of the evening had gorged on my very soul. I decided to retire, the morrow would be upon us far too soon.

The full moon cast its bright light among the treetops, creating a silver shroud over the camp. It was a magnificent night; one I would remember for the rest of my life. I placed the bowl on the ground and raised my arms to stretch only to be interrupted by Sawyer stopping in front of me. Powerless to ignore him I looked at his face, fighting the urge to stand up. I felt small and defenceless next to him.

Taking me by surprise Sawyer held out his hand to me, his piercing gaze held mine, inscrutable. "Dance with me." A man of few words.

I'd barely heard him speak since I'd met him. His voice had a deep timbre to it, which used with our Kingdom's vernacular, was oddly endearing. I'd caught him watching me many times this evening with serious eyes. I was convinced he wasn't impressed by what he saw.

That same look was cast upon me, and I heard myself ask, "Do you really have the intention of dancing? Because I was under the impression you've been dying to tell me something for a while." Though his facial expression didn't as much as flinch, a faint trace of what resembled as amusement sparked in his eyes.

He wrapped his hand around mine, obviously not expecting a refusal, and guided me to the fire before placing his big hands on my waist. The slow and delicate sound of a flute broke my discontentment with suspicion; around us couples of all ages were facing each other. Some of the men were placing their necklace around their dancing partner while others had their heads bowed deeply and placed a necklace on the palm of shaking hands. I looked at Sawyer in sudden realisation. The bonding dance!

"That's why you asked me to dance!" I exclaimed. "Can't you decide on one? Still need time to deliberate on the lucky one?" Sure enough, as I looked beyond the dancing lovers, a row of young women were throwing arrows at me with their stares. Thank Myrddin he didn't give me his necklace, or I'd have been struck dead on the spot. My gaze fell on the assortment of necklaces laced around his neck. I couldn't make my mind up whether he was a coward for not refusing them up front, or too kind and unwilling to humiliate them in front of the whole group. At his silence, I persisted. "What, couldn't you bring yourself to hurt all those women mooning after you? Oh, I know! You're planning to keep them all, start your private retinue, the perks of being an elder I take it." The tone of my voice came out harder than I'd meant to. *What is wrong with me?* I should not have drunk that sweet home-brewed wine.

He blinked once, face stony. "Ye got me there." The sudden ardour in his eyes reminded me of the blue flames of a fire, I wondered if I could get scorched from their heat. Confused, I looked away.

His aloof behaviour since I'd met him hadn't exactly enthralled me. That's right, I justified to myself, I had no obligations to be nice to him, making sure to suppress the reasonable voice reminding me why he'd acted so. I'd had about enough of people treating me like horse manure. I refused to look at him, that would let him know I wasn't one of those girls who were impressed by a sullen leader. But like an itch you should not scratch I ended up looking anyway and found him staring right back at me. I held my gaze. Maybe I could size him up, get a feel on who he was. I had a knack for reading people, at least among my peers. This man proved to be a conundrum.

After a while he sighed and looked over my head, childishly bringing a sense of victory. I took in the sight of his relaxed face: a strong chiselled jaw and although his nose was slightly crooked and his forehead too wide, all his features created a pleasant enough face. His eyes, though, could change his face from nice to menacing in an instant. Kel was more attractive in many ways, but Sawyer had this presence, this solidness that didn't leave him even in informal events and I could well understand why he had so many females longing after him.

Why hadn't he chosen anyone? Many were attractive and Luela had explained that although this bonding ritual was an engagement tied under the stars, either party could break it off at any time. The long-lasting lovers usually courted for two years before getting handfasted with a magical spell, a life bond. That one on the other hand was more difficult to break because the magical vows had to be read backwards to be severed. The person who'd created it clearly had a wayward sense of humour. I liked that. She'd also talked about one I had never heard of: a Mage bond. Apparently, the magic within the two people, recognising they were soul mates, tied them to one another from the moment they met without their awareness; that one was impossible to break, even in death or so Luela said. It sounded to me like a silly tale for hopeless romantics, one Mara would love.

"You could have chosen your sister you know; your little group of admirers are not exactly pleased with this set up." I waved a hand between us, a mischievous inner pull made me heave an exaggerated sigh to make a show of my dissatisfaction. I couldn't explain to myself this perverse need to annoy him. "I don't particularly like being looked astray because I'm going on a journey with you, and now you're throwing wood on an already roaring fire."

His body became rigid. "Have they caused ye trouble?" he glanced in their direction.

"No, no. It's nothing I can't handle." I regretted mentioning it at once, a part of me felt sorry for these girls desperately seeking this man's heart. "Having three brothers taught me a thing or two on how to defend myself." I added trying to lighten the mood. I didn't come here to raise trouble.

"It didn't sound like it from what Luela told me." his gaze focused on the almost inexistent cut on my face, the ointment he had given me no doubt the root of its speedy recovery. I squared my shoulders feeling hurt and worried by how much she had told him.

"If you're referring to my circumstances these past years, it could have been much worse. Yes, they hurt me, but with their words as they were aware I could hold my own in a fight." That last statement was false, but he didn't need to know that. "It was only in this last incident that I was unable to reciprocate." I was glaring at him now, daring him to contradict me.

To my surprise, he lowered his gaze and sighed. "I asked ye to dance to speak with ye in private without raising any eyebrows, but I've a fair idea of yer reply already." Bringing his head down close to my ear, he whispered. "Are ye certain ye want to come with us? It'll be long, tiring and tedious, little privacy or rest. We'll be sleeping rough; and the stars know what we'll encounter along the way," he paused for added effect. "Wild animals, robbers... Ye'd be safer here, I could take a letter to yer father. I'm sure –"

I pulled away interrupting his next words for I'd heard enough. Fighting hard to keep my voice low I leaned forward and said my fingernails digging into my palms. "This is my fight. My whole family is directly under threat, and you want me to sit here like a docile little girl?" My cheeks were radiating a heat as hot as the fire at my back.

Grabbing my elbow, he pulled me back against him; his other arm keeping me entrapped as he looked straight down at me. "Everyone is under threat, make no mistake. Who do ye think will be most affected if a king even more despicable than Filius were to be crowned?" His voice was raising. "Commoners, that's who, commoners who wouldn't have the means to pay for either food or protection if taxes were raised. Not nobles like ye and yer family, don't ye forget that. We must succeed in reaching yer father no matter what we'll be facing. Unlike ye, we've travelled through forests and mountains many times, and I don't want ye slowing us down because of some misguided sense of duty." He let go of me then, and I took a step back. We were both frowning at one another when the tune stopped in a cheerful note. The silent stare of people around us felt like an accusation.

"I won't." I said in a low voice then whirled around heading away from people, from furious whispers into the cover of a thick oak tree behind one of the tents. I placed my back to the trunk, fuming. That man was infuriating. How dare he imply I would be a burden to their almighty group? Sitting down, arms around my knees I looked at the bright starry sky; it always put into perspective how small and insignificant my grievances were in the hands of the stars. My head throbbed with the sting of his words in an incessant loop. It hurt because he was right.

Unbidden, the faces of my family came to mind and gave me strength. Yes, I had thought of my family's safety, not the future of thousands of others, but that wouldn't deter me. There was no shame in fighting for the people I loved and cared for. I could not claim to be this true empathic woman feeling strangers' pain as her own. However, my decisions came from good intentions. I wanted to save my small world first and foremost, and if my actions could save more people, all the better. Feeling more determined, I sat straighter and planned how to make myself useful to their group, an idea forming. *I'll show him what I'm made of.*

let the emotions roll off me a while longer, lost in the inky black of the sky. Satisfied my mind was at peace and focused, I went to Luela's tent, determination keeping my legs moving.

Luela was crouched by the fire pit, placing the wood with expert hands in a pile that would replenish itself throughout the night. "There you are." She exclaimed and went straight to me, worry shading her blue eyes, a blue similar to Sawyer's. "He did it again, didn't he? That big dolt! He's usually so good at talking to people." she made a face. "I saw yer altercation. That was my idea, not the argument mind ye, just the talk. I hoped he'd convince ye to stay here," Her fingers were threading through her hair in a nervous motion, eyes downcast. "I wanted to keep ye safe with me, but that's my selfish feelings. Of course, ye want to be with yer family." she looked up then. "I'm so sorry."

This was unexpected. I refused to believe he'd spoken to me solely on her account, yet I couldn't deny he'd withheld the information to protect her. The last of my anger was pulverised by her remorse, my mood sullen no more. *Big dolt, I like that.*

"I'm not angry with you, your brother..." I let the word drag.

She gave me a kiss on the cheek, a radiant smile on her pretty face. "Thank ye, and I hope yer forgiveness will be extended to my brother. At least try for me," At my hesitation she added, "Come on, ye're the better mannered out of ye two." She batted her eyelashes in a beseeching manner.

I sighed. "I'll try my best."

"Thanks, it means a lot." She gave me a quick hug then moved to the unlit fire.

Before my nerves took the better of me, I cried out. "Can I ask a favour of you?"

CHAPTER 11

Faylinn

A gentle shake on the shoulder roused me the next morning. Luela, a candle in hand and clad in her nightwear, sat on my pallet. "They will be here soon, Fay. I've made breakfast for ye all." I nodded to her retreating figure. My mind felt groggy and slow from lack of sleep as I spent a good part of the night trying, but failing, to find a solution to all this mess without starting a war. I'd tossed and turned, unable to get Sawyer's words out of my head, imagining starving children and women maltreated by the Royal Guards. Heaving myself off the warm pallet, I proceeded to clean up and get dressed as quickly as my tired body could move. I looked at the bed forlornly one last time; it would be a long while before I could get a comfortable night's sleep. Stepping outside into the pre-dawn crisp air I greeted everyone, ignoring their startled expressions. I sat down and took the plate Luela was handing me, then ate despite my protesting stomach. Blaith came to me, sniffed my hand, then lay down. I reached down to stroke her behind an ear, pleased she seemed to accept my presence.

Kel was the one to ask what they were all thinking. "Why did ye cut ... ?" he put a hand in his hair in lieu of words.

"I always thought Ladies would rather lose a limb than their hair."

I had to laugh at that for he wasn't far off. I could imagine the faces of the queen and Gwynn seeing me like this. "I wanted to look more like a wanderer." I shrugged, many of their female warriors had short hair, Veena, one of them, was staring at me with mocking eyes.

"Having short hair won't make ye act like a warrior." She sneered guessing my train of thoughts. The spoon stopped mid-way to my mouth. *Myrddin help me. Not another one.*

I sighed inside; this journey would be a testament to my patience. Good thing Keltor was there to lighten the mood, or we might all kill one another before day's end.

"Good idea." Sawyer's approval shocked me, Jolis and Kel were nodding their heads in unison. "Well thought of."

"Aye, and we'll have plenty time to teach ye a thing or two." Kel tapped me on the shoulder. I grinned back at him, maybe it wouldn't be so bad after all, and now I had something to look forward to. It'd been an age since I last practised self-defence moves with my brothers.

"I'd like that, thanks."

After teary embraces with Luela, the baby's fault she reassured me, we went on our way just as the camp was stirring to life. Its rousing inhabitants called out their farewells and good wishes to the tunes of awakening birds. To my disappointment, Dwennon was missing. This kind-hearted man had left a good impression on me, and I'd hoped to see him one last time. Elder Adym came to wish us good fortune on our endeavour, his troubled eyes lingering a moment longer on me. The sky had turned a lighter shade of blue, the horizon streaked with blushes of pinks by the time we crossed the magical barrier.

Without so much as a command, Kel ran out ahead of us – scouting, Jolis informed me – his wolf Blaith at his heels while the rest of us stayed together. The pace was fast, no time to take in my surroundings as my eyes were trained to the floor the entire time in order to avoid the numerous protruding roots and outreaching brambles. After seeing my hair this morning, they had given me a set of warrior's clothes: leather trousers and tunic which were lighter and easier to move around with than my usual dresses. My new boots made of deer skin – a present from Dwennon – had the softest fur; it felt like walking on cushions.

I kept up with them without any problem that day; it might have been the first time I was truly thankful for my long legs. Apart from a short noon break, nobody was talking, the only sounds that of nature and my noisy footsteps. My anxiety at going close to the Forest of torments was mounting with each step I took. Questions, lots of questions were bursting for answers.

Unable to stop myself, I approached Jolis. "May I ask you something?"

Veena pounced right next to me, eyes ablaze. "Shut up!" she snarled in a whisper, then retreated to her place ahead of us. Sawyer came by my side shortly afterwards. We were still too close to the Castle he said, we had to be vigilant. His thoughtfulness was a revelation. They had planned the whole journey without having me in mind, and I'd assumed because of our little altercation he'd be distant with me. Maybe I wouldn't feel so out of the loop as I'd feared. He fell back behind us, guarding our group from the rear. Glancing over my shoulder I wondered if Luela had been right after all.

By the time we set up camp for the night, tiredness had settled in my bones. *It's all right, nothing a good night's sleep can't fix.* The small clearing Kel had chosen was ensconced in the bowing limbs of ashes and oaks. The space was a welcoming one, and I was glad I would sleep among trees. Their comforting presence throughout the day had felt almost tactile, like a warm embrace long forgotten. I set to the task Sawyer had delegated without feeling the worst for it. I felt proud I kept pace with the group. Maybe the rest of the journey wouldn't be so bad. Sawyer must have noticed the smug look on my face while I was collecting wood for he marched to me in long supple strides, grabbed the sticks I cradled in my arm, and inspected them with a raised eyebrow.

"These are too wet. Look for broken branches in sheltered places and don't forget to get the birch bark to light the fire." With that, he headed back towards the camp.

"Yes, Elder Sawyer." I mumbled under my breath, somewhat annoyed to have made this silly mistake, then went searching for propitious places to find dry wood.

"My sentiment exactly." whispered Kel joining my side with a wink, white teeth flashing in his tanned face. A furtive look over my shoulder revealed glaring eyes looking right back. Uh, the man even had superior hearing. His hands clasped to his chest, he walked in a circle; no need to be told he was setting the protective spell around the clearing. My eyes took in the darkening wood, and I shivered, the possibility of danger not so far-fetched.

It became apparent from the moment we arrived in the clearing they were used to travelling together. Without so much as a word to each other, they cleared out damp leaves and protruding stones off the ground, made a fire pit in the middle, then collected small branches and large fern leaves, which was puzzling until they laid them down under our sleeping furs. Dry sticks in my arms, I stood there on the side, watching, not quite sure how to offer my help and whether it would be welcomed. Before I'd found the courage to speak out, Blaith came from behind, nudged me on the leg, then sauntered next to Kel, sitting next to Jolis, who hovered a hand over the fire pit, face set in concentration, before it burst into long and slender flames. She looked back at me after lying down by the warmth of the fire. Without questioning how I could possibly be sure what she wanted, I went to sit by her.

Kel looked up from the tower of sticks in front of him. "She likes you. She's normally a bit shy around new people."

Blaith had put her head on my lap after I sat down. I was rubbing her behind the ear. "I'm glad. She's lovely." I said, feeling myself smile. She was just what I needed, I thought, my mood improving.

Later, we were all sitting by the fire, our stomachs full of a lovely stew cooked by Jolis. Conversation was subdued, my presence evidently unfamiliar. I rose to my feet and gathered the dirty dishes. The river was a short walk away, it would give them time to talk in privacy for a while.

"No need." Veena stood at once and snatched them away from my arms. "I do that, and we don't want ye to get caught by some predator, do we?" Her smile was lopsided, a sure sign she found the idea delectable. Too weary to battle my case, I let it go and sat back down. If she wanted to do chores by herself, so be it. I only wished she could talk to me without sneering or taunting, this was getting exhausting. Their gazes pressed on me, but I wouldn't let them see how much this affected me. I would put it past me once more; however, I needed some sort of solution, and soon.

"What are my tasks exactly?" I asked. "I don't think gathering wood is much help." The three men looked at one another, battling with their eyes on whom would answer the pesky noble.

"It's help enough," Sawyer said at last. "Ye'll need to rest at camp. We're used to long treks, ye aren't."

"I'm feeling fine." I persisted; I didn't want them to treat me any differently because of my peerage. Jolis and Kel chuckled, one side of Sawyer's mouth twitched. Was that a smile?

"We'll see 'bout that in a few days' time, Faylinn." said Jolis. His back went stiff. "I mean ... my Lady." he added, the mortification clear in his voice. I narrowed my eyes at him. A small satisfaction at seeing his face redden blasted my irritation.

"My father will have your head on a stick if you disrespect me ever again." I said in the haughtiest voice I could muster, unable to stop myself. This game could be played both ways. Jolis looked at Sawyer in dismay. Kel, astute, winked at me and we burst out laughing. Even Sawyer joined in and tapped Jolis on the back. "She got ye there, mate.'

"Well, aren't we all cosy?" Veena's dry tone slashed the lightness in the air.

I refrained to roll my eyes at her behaviour befitting a youngling, then looked at Jolis. "Please stop calling me Lady, all of you. Faylinn's fine."

"At your wishes, your Highness." sneered Veena who went to lay down her mat. I gave up; this one had clearly a dragon's tooth against me. Watching Jolis and Sawyer perusing an old map, my earlier unease reappeared.

"Where are we heading?" their heads jerked towards me. "Can you show me?"

"All right." Sawyer nodded and fingered a route when I knelt next to him. Nowhere near the Forest of torments, I sighed deeply. The relief was sweet.

At Jolis's questioning look I said, a sheepish look on my face. "Dwennon said you might plan to go near the Forest of...the Cage. I've heard stories at Court. Silly I should believe them; they were told to scare children and women." I shrugged.

"Not stories." Sawyer's face was grim.

"We've been to villages that have been attacked." Kel's mood was sombre. "What we saw wasn't pretty." he grimaced. "No one knows for sure what attacked them, but some people saw large furry forms in the distance, unnaturally large ones."

"Like those wolves?"

"Yes, and that's not counting the people who have disappeared." Jolis seemed to be reliving something, something I'm sure I didn't want to experience. Ever. At that moment an owl let a shrill call as it flew above us, I became aware of branches tapping in the wind, the fire crackling within its circle of stones. My heart rate eased, thankful to nature's normalcy.

"Right, time for a much-needed lesson." exclaimed Kel as he sprang to his feet, looking as fresh as this morning. He grabbed my hand and pulled me up, all the while giving a grin that didn't bode well for me. But I was glad of the distraction. "Jolis let it slip that a rabid bear would make less noise than you did in the forest."

My gaze jumped to Jolis. I knew I had been noisy, but to liken me to a bear! His cheeks reddened, but he kept staring firmly on the fire. The coward.

"Come here man. Ye can't make those claims and not help the poor damsel." I elbowed Kel in the stomach none too gently. "Darn, that hurt." he cried out, stepping away from me. "Didn't think ye had it in ye." he added, rubbing his middle watching me with interest. Jolis was now next to us, looking contrite yet amused.

"No more lady, damsel or any other derogatory titles, understood?" I asked my face devoid of the smile that wanted to pour out.

"I won't say it again, on my honour." Kel placed his big hand over his heart with feigned solemnity.

Good enough for me, I flashed a quick smile then turned to Jolis. "Was I so bad?" A sound behind us resembling an ugly snort echoed in the clearing, I chose to ignore it.

"Well," he stroked his jaw. "Right so, but I can teach ye in no time. Sure, won't take ye long, ye've a good balance. I was watching earlier on." He was now scratching his head looking embarrassed.

I placed a hand on his arm. For all his sullen look he was gentle underneath. "That was thoughtful of you. Shall we start?" His shoulders relaxed and he gave me a short grin.

"It's mainly a matter on how to place yer feet on the ground, see? Most people walk like so, heels first." He demonstrated, his feet heavy and loud for a moment, then he continued in his normal stride, almost gliding around the clearing. "Now the trick is," he said coming back to my side. "To place the outside of yer foot down, then press the ball on the ground and at last the heel." He showed me with exaggerated slowness. It seemed simple enough. "Now yer turn."

I nodded and did as told in small slow steps; it felt awkward and unnatural. I said as much. "Normal that. It's not something ye'll get right from the start, takes lots of practice till it comes naturally." *Nothing is ever easy, is it?*

A long arm draped itself on my shoulders. "Don't despair! With all the walking we're doing ye'll be an expert in a couple of days. It'll hurt plenty without a doubt, but ye'll get there." Kel chuckled at my chagrined expression.

Jolis shook his head, and shoved the arm off me. "Oi!" exclaimed Kel in mock outrage while Jolis was leading me away from him. "Don't ye listen to that idiot. Ye'll be fine. Now let's do it again."

"I heard that." A sulky voice travelled over the fire. Jolis and I exchanged a smile then got back to work.

* * *

With each passing day, my body was heavier and achier to the point it felt I was struggling in a sea of viscous sap. I never dared complain about it, but as Veena's frown grew permanent, my steps became slower. Though nobody ever said a word against me, which they had every right to, an added weight laid on my shoulders: guilt, anger and a few other emotions played a game of tig; my mood forever changing. Yet, I kept going; determination, boneheaded as it was, overpowered the rest.

On the morning of the sixth day possibly the seventh – it was difficult to keep track – Jolis's earlier words rang true: my body was more rigid than an old tree's trunk. I could not move a limb without pain, the likes I'd never experienced, lashing through the slightest attempt of movement. The others, ever efficient, were moving through the morning routine in a smooth and flowing dance. They left me there on the floor, seemingly oblivious to my anguish. Maybe I should stay behind, I'd become the burden I'd swore I wouldn't be, and this could only get worse. I set my pride and feelings aside; getting the message to father took precedence. While swearing in my head – my teeth busy grinding – I sat up, my decision simple. Sawyer was rummaging through his bag on the other side of the fire, Veena next to him.

"Don't do it." I heard her say in an irritated voice. "She's not worth the risk." I frowned as she looked at me with pure anger, then turned to him whispering furiously. I leaned forward but the rest of their hushed conversation was lost to me. Then, Sawyer straightened with something in his hand and walked away into the woods. Veena kicked a stone and stormed off the opposite way. Kel and Jolis were eating their breakfast, silent. After some delicate stretching, which brought tears to my eyes, I joined them. I waited for the other two to come back to let them know my decision.

Sawyer appeared first and knelt next to me, a small bowl in his hand. "Drink this." I took my gaze off the dark green liquid and looked at him. "What is it?"

"For the pain." With those words he left my side to sit next to Kel. I took a hesitant sniff of the concoction. The bitter and pungent smell made my eyes water. Without delay, I drank it in one go, grimacing at the acrid taste. Soon this was replaced by a pleasant heat cascading to my stomach, which spread out to my limbs. I shot a glance at Sawyer. This spell was amazing. The pain was almost gone. So was the strain in my muscles as if an armour had been lifted off my body, leaving me light and supple. Just then Veena returned all sour faced, dampening my mood.

Later, as we were packing up camp I went to Sawyer and handed him the bowl. "Thank you," I said looking at my feet. "I feel alive again."

"No need to thank me, Dwennon thought of it. I'm just preparing it." he said with a dismissive hand.

"Thank you, nonetheless. I admit upon waking I had made up my mind to give up." I shrugged, but humiliation stuck to me. "Also, I should apologise. You were right that time, I shouldn't have come."

"No, I was wrong. Ye're doing good." I stared, bemused, at

his face. It looked strained, dark rings pulled at the skin under his eyes. "I've a few of these," he lifted the bowl. "Your body should be used to the effort by the time they're all gone." Lost for words, I watched him walk ahead unsure of what to make of him.

* * *

The next few days blurred into a monotonous routine of walking, eating and sleeping. Setting camp was a welcome change of pace although in time that, too, became tedious. Once the enforced silence while walking was lifted, Jolis and I were free to talk to our hearts' content. He'd needed a few nudges at first to come out of his shell and stop looking at me as a noble. When he did though, there was no stopping him talking about the wanderers, his family, nature. He was a wonderful walking partner. I was quite fond of Kel too. In the evenings the two of them were bickering to no end. They always made sure to include me whenever the whole group was gathered, Kel taking on the role of joker, obviously, while Jolis came to my "rescue". The other two were more withdrawn for very different reasons. While Veena avoided any conversation I was involved in, she was perfectly fine talking to the rest of them. Sawyer was another matter though, he chatted with us, even joked at times but it felt contrived, like his mind was somewhere else. I wished I knew where.

Like Sawyer said, my body grew fitter with each passing day. It was good to match their pace with my own strength, especially now I knew the truth. The last time I took the potion, his face had looked so haggard I'd asked him if he was all right. After his poor excuse of bad sleep, Veena had exploded with accusations. Everyone had looked in shock as she screamed it was my fault he had to prepare a potion that drained his energy. It was my fault he was weak. That I put him in danger for my own selfishness. With each word she'd stepped closer to me, fury contorting her face. I was looking at Sawyer for any signs she was lying, but his grim face said it all. I was sure she'd have hit me if it wasn't for Kel taking her away in the end.

"Is it true?" I asked Sawyer.

He rubbed a hand over his face and sighed. "Aye."

"I'm so sorry. Why didn't you tell me? I wouldn't –"

"Have taken them, had ye'd known. That's why I didn't say anything. I knew what I was getting into, no need to be sorry."

"I –"

He shook his head. "Don't. Veena exaggerated, I'm fine." I didn't believe him at all, but it was kind of him to say so. "Anyway, I've only given ye a half dosage the past two days." That was good to know. Still, I was sorry I'd caused him trouble.

"Regardless...Thank you." I cleared my throat. "That was kind of you." He looked at me for a moment, then nodded before disappearing in the woods. How glad was I the next day not to need it because I wouldn't have taken it no matter what he'd said.

I grinned. Now everything was back to normal. The sun was high above in a deep blue sky when rustling and heavy stamping ahead of us broke the peaceful goings-on of the forest. We'd kept to animal trails to avoid any human contact. At the sound, I rushed to a tree with a low bough and heaved myself up, fearing a wild boar was charging at us. A smooth touch so at odds with my feelings ran from the tip of my fingers to my mind. Just for a moment I was lost in the birch's essence in a daze, then things got messy, pulling me back to my surroundings abruptly.

Bursting through bushes Kel, followed by Blaith, came running towards us shouting, "Behind me". No sooner was he in front of Veena than a group of men rushed towards them, swords drawn. Sawyer shouted to me to stay put. This was no hardship because I was frozen with fear. Why hadn't I made a bow? I could have helped them from my vantage point. I'd been lazy, complacent nothing had happened.

Time seemed to pause for a second, all of them eyeing one another. Then one man lunged towards Veena, snarling like an animal. He swept his sword from above to strike her down. I held my breath waiting to see how Veena would fare, but Sawyer's big bulk moved in my line of sight. Clashing metal reverberated in the air. They were all fighting now, grunting with the effort, some of those men taunting, swearing. Where was Jolis? I craned my neck, but all I could see was his opponent half-obscured behind a tree. Blaith stayed close to Kel at all times, a low growl slipping from her bared teeth.

I looked on helpless as my four companions took arms against our attackers. Their clothes were nondescript, probably some low life miscreants. I counted four of them. At least the fight would be fair. However, the trees made it hard to move, swords caught branches and trunks instead of flesh. In a brave move, Blaith bit Kel's opponent. Thrown off, his sword plunged into a trunk. The precious seconds it took to pull it out were enough for Kel to run him through. Before the man had crumpled to the floor, Kel turned to the others looking for an opening, his face hard. The men were skilled, but no equals to the intensive practise the wanderers put their warriors through. Kel and Jolis had provided many entertaining evenings with riveting tales of fisticuffs and sword play with, to my delight, some demonstrations. This, however, was not enjoyable. I closed my eyes. I did not want to see any more of this, yet I could not escape the sounds echoing in my head. And the smells. The sweat, and that distinctive smell of blood making me queasy.

After what seemed an unmeasurable amount of time, but could have been no more than two minutes, quiet descended, the forest was as still as I was. I opened my eyes in dread.

The men laid on the ground unmoving; my group, I was glad, was unharmed. Jolis and Sawyer started searching the men's clothes. Unable to move, my eyes riveted to the prone bodies – no, not bodies, corpses – I took deep breaths. They were going to kill us. Even though I had no part in their deaths I felt responsible. *Stop it!* They were going to kill us. We had no choice. Kel came to my tree and reached out a hand splattered with fresh blood. I stared at it transfixed.

"Sorry." he mumbled and wiped it against his trousers. Once I was down, he asked the others if they'd found anything.

Sawyer lifted a heavy purse. "Full of gold."

"Mercenaries?" Kel asked. Sawyer nodded.

"Sent by Quentin?" I asked my voice unrecognisable. His grim face was self-explanatory. "How?" I was shaking my head as though it could remove all the fear, the confusion.

They were all looking at the men strewn on the ground. Jolis shrugged, "I wouldn't be surprised if he paid a bunch of them to check out the surroundings. What I don't get is why they attacked us as soon as, like they knew we were the right people. That troubles me."

"Nah," Kel said. "I reckon they're the type to attack and rob anyone on their path, extra bounty. Not an ounce of humanity those rats." He spat at the ground. For some silly reason, I had expected the guards to come after me, guards that were easy to tell apart anywhere, not mercenaries that would look like any commoners. Anyone we crossed from now on would be suspect. I shuddered.

"I need to know how to fight." I blurted out. One thing I learnt that day was I needed to be prepared for anything. Mercenaries, guards. I might not be able to kill them myself, but I would die trying. No more hiding.

Sawyer came to me then, a scatter of blood on his leather vest and his arms. He stood there for a time staring at me, his fists were clenched hard, and I could see his jaw tensing. *Is he furious at me?*

"Please," I added.

He gave a short nod, "There might not be a tree next time. I knew this..." he shook his head and went to pick his pack up.

The rest of the day was sombre, I wasn't the only one lost in my thoughts. That night, I tossed and turned on my furs trying in vain to chase away the memories of blood, of breaths being drawn for the last time. The thought they would have killed us all wasn't enough to placate my turmoil; a distant voice kept repeating it was my fault they were dead. I didn't want to let the others see how much the attack affected me. I kept my face as emotionless as possible, spoke when necessary, but something told me I didn't fool them. The deep breathing of my companions – my saviours – entangled with my dark musing. Didn't killing those men chip at their souls? Were they so used to take lives their sleep was unaffected? I felt disloyal at once. My feelings were clashing in a maelstrom of confusion. I was glad they'd killed those men, but unhappy they had to do such an unforgiving act on my behalf. I sat up, sleep far from my reach. I needed to distract myself, something to put my mind at rest.

The branches laid next to my satchel were another proof of my failings. Seconds after I'd mentioned to Jolis I planned to make a bow, he'd gone to a tree, cut some branches down, and gave them to me pleased with himself, oblivious to my inner anguish. I'd ran to the tree in panic to apologise, hands splayed on its trunk, uncaring how this might look, before thanking him. I wasn't brave enough to explain the real reason for my strange behaviour and gave him the least idiotic excuse I could find. It was a tradition in my province to thank the trees for their wood, just like the wanderers did when they killed animals. It was a bit far-fetched, but apart from looking at me curiously for a moment, he seemed to believe it.

Sitting close to the dying fire, I fed it more logs and felt a soothing warmth spread over my skin. Taking a knife from my pocket, I shaved off the bark, wood buzzing in my hands; it was a wonder how that was possible. Was a tree's life and essence embedded so deeply it left a residue after its death? Could it feel pain? I stared in horror at the now stripped branch. My heart rate slowed down when I remembered how different touching a live tree was, it felt so personal, like I was reaching parts of its innermost being and visa versa. I had recoiled in fear the first time, young, unable to fully comprehend what had happened. In time, it became natural, something I didn't question. Under supervision most of the time, I had little occasion to touch trees at court, and I guess I hadn't realised until my escape I had forgotten how this bond felt. Not far from me stood a massive oak tree, it must have lived through four or five generations. Maybe I could touch it.

"Faylinn," My back tensed. *Is it calling me?* I looked hard, the branches were swinging in the gentle breeze, nothing appeared out of normal.

"Fay?" I turned my head to the whisper on my left, not the tree then. My shoulders relaxed, belittling the racing of my heart as Sawyer sat right beside me. *Did he call me Fay?* A strange pull tugged at my heart.

"Ye looked far away." he said placing his hands over the fire. I shrugged, none of them were aware of my mediocre gift. Come to think of it, I only knew Sawyer's.

"Couldn't sleep?" His words brought me back to why I was still up. I nodded, meeting his eyes the first time since this afternoon. *Should I talk to him? Would he think any less of me?* I glanced at him and that thought evaporated in smoke. I hadn't known him for long, but so far he'd been just and fair, a good leader.

He took out something small from his pocket and started sharpening a knife in swift and rehearsed movements. Long fingers encircled the dark metal. His hands were not smooth and manicured like the dashing gentlemen who came to visit my cousin in an attempt to be in her good favours. No, they were tanned and roughened by hard work, they were beautiful nonetheless. His face was set with concentration. Maybe I was wrong and he wanted to share the fire's heat. A comfortable silence settled between us. I focused on my task and ignored the unnerving feeling caused by his closeness.

Finished carving the notch of the arrow, I placed it next to the others, picked another branch, then started whittling it into shape.

"What kind of a Lady knows how to make a bow and arrows?" The lightness of his tone suggested he didn't mean anything rude. My hands paused on the rough wood. He picked up an arrow then the bow and inspected them with a critical eye. "These aren't bad." He nodded his approval. I smiled, grateful of the compliment. "Who taught ye?"

I found myself telling the embarrassing truth of how, as a child, I had asked my eldest brother Haelan – twenty years old at the time – to teach me. He'd been adamant a girl from a noble family should not learn how to hunt, confident I would give up the silly impulse within a couple of days. Little did he realise how determined I was. For weeks I followed, haunted his footsteps, nagging him all the while, until he conceded with a large sigh and a grin on his face, declaring he didn't like stuffy conventions anyway. Of course, my parents were none the wiser – mother would have fainted had she known – but a part of me hoped father would have approved. As I kept speaking I was pleased to see a myriad of expressions crossing his usually guarded face, however it was his deep laugh that sent a jolt to my unsuspecting heart. I looked away flustered.

"Ye speak the truth?" He asked still chuckling.

I smiled ruefully. "I was but seven, lively and headstrong to boot."

He stroked his nose absentmindedly. "Not much has changed I reckon. Well, the seven-year-old part did, 'course." he said with a rasp in his throat, then turned quickly to add a log to the fire.

Confused, I decided to change the subject. I gestured at the bow he was still holding. "Do you know   how to make one?"

He shook his head, "Nah, plants and protection spells are my thing."

"I could make you one."

He lifted the bow and ran his fingers along the curve as soft as a caress. "I'd like that, thanks." he said handing it back.

I took out a scraper from my satchel, an eighth birthday present from Haelan who had it made by a reputed woodcraft man. One of my few treasured possessions. With time and effort, the wood would be as smooth as glass. Shame I didn't have anything to seal it with. As though he'd heard my thoughts Sawyer asked how I would protect the wood and whether I had anything to string two bows. He seemed genuinely interested by the process. Delighted to comply I explained how I needed to forage the woods to find something to make the strings – hemp or stinging nettles would do – and how it could take weeks to make a decent bow. Those I would make wouldn't be robust enough to last years, but we would have to make do with what I could find. He went to get his bag and returned to me. After rummaging through it, he took out some pots and a flat crinkly fabric.

I reached forward, "Is that rawhide?" I but squealed in glee.

His eyebrows raised – something he was doing a lot around me – then he smiled, "Ye're a weird one, lass." My cheeks flushed. "Pig's rawhide, good enough I take it?" he added in a playful tone. Well, Myrddin's curly beard, he sure was in good spirits tonight.

"It's perfect, and there is plenty for two." Possibly three as mine would be smaller. "You wouldn't happen to carry beeswax too?" I knew I was pushing my luck, but it didn't hurt to ask. He grabbed a dark pot and placed it in my hand; my mouth opened like a fish out of the water. "Anything else?" he smiled amused. I shook my head while opening the cork and smelled the heady scent, a reminiscent pang echoing in my heart.

"This is more than I wished for." Our eyes locked, an odd tension building between us.

He was the first to break contact, taking away with it the weird and wonderful sensation. "We should sleep."

Yes, you're right. Thank you." Not only for what you gave me I wanted to say, but for being there when I needed company. He nodded, his face intent, and I wondered if he could read my inner thoughts.

My sleep was undisturbed the remainder of the night.

CHAPTER 12

Dwennon

The deeper into the forest they walked the denser it became; the stench in the humid air clung to their clothes. The sun failed to penetrate the thick canopy of centuries' old trees, leaving the ground littered with leaves in different stages of putrefaction. Kept in constant dimness, Dwennon's thoughts turned grimly to the young man he'd taught in what felt like a lifetime ago. His eyes focused on his feet. He couldn't bear to look at his lifemate walking behind him, her skirts rustling between her small legs. She'd worked so hard to pull him away from the darkness that had gripped his heart with an unrelenting hold, to make him savour the present, that he felt uncomfortable reflecting on his old life. This was how he defined it in his mind: the life before and after the betrayal, the time before and after his shameful mistakes. Could he have prevented it? The question didn't bear asking, not anymore. But like any distressing and unwelcome thoughts you wanted to escape from, it was impossible to ignore.

A stick cracked under his careless footsteps. Less than ten yards away a deer dashed behind trees, her hooves as silent as the breeze cooling his clammy skin. *There.* He recognised the bear-shaped boulder at the top of the incline and pivoted on his heels. Leanne was red in the face, breathing heavily. He'd asked Sammy, one of the apprentice warriors, to join him, but his lifemate had insisted to care for him herself. She'd argued she was the one who took care of him for so many years, a little walk in the woods wouldn't put her off. He mused whether she regretted her decision as his gaze skimmed over her ample form.

"Not long now, my dear." he reached in his bag for the water skin. She took it with a grateful smile and took big gulps of water.

"I'm not done in yet." she grinned, gave the water back and started walking at a slow pace up the slope. That's what he loved about her; no matter what came at her, she kept that genuine smile and sense of humour. Dwennon watched for a moment the woman who'd saved both his life and heart, then leaning on his stick heaved sore muscles after her. He felt older beyond his years.

At the top of the hill shards of light pierced through the cluster of deciduous trees, growing bigger and brighter the closer they got. With a hand protecting his eyes from the blinding sun, he stepped into the circular glade. No matter how many times he crossed this threshold between forest and sanctuary a quiet reverence enveloped all his being. The magic was almost tactile. Under deep meditation one could catch a glimpse of its shape and colour. But he was too old and tired to feel the need this time. Leanne, who'd never been to The Dyads sucked a sharp breath, then with slow hesitating steps faltered to the circle of stones, placing a shaking hand on one before going to the next. Spent, Dwennon lowered himself to the ground, and watched with pleasure the river of emotions crossing her lined face: surprise, wonder, elation, and yes, fear.

Before they'd left, he'd explained how this secret place had been chosen by Myrddin and his council for its concentration of magic to form a portal to transport their persecuted kind, their ancestors, into this planet rightly named Newlands.

Nowadays, not many people knew of its existence. Hence the reverence with which she almost caressed every standing stone, how her feet glided with careful steps on the dry and lush grass. This site was monumental. Dwennon didn't know whether or how the portal could be reopened, but he certainly wasn't ready to find out. It must be kept secret at all costs from the corrupt, the greedy, the evil that had tarnished their Kingdom.

Not many people in the Northern Kingdoms understood magic came from the earth they walked on, the air they breathed in. He'd learnt this astounding discovery on his travels in the Closed Lands where it was common knowledge. Here, the majority of the populace – himself included for a long time – believed magic surrounded their planet in an invisible veil. Magic which formed within themselves while they were growing in the womb. And it did to some extent, but not the way they believed.

At last Leanne came to sit next to him. Quiet. Unwilling to break the peace and serenity this place induced. After breaking their fast with a small midday meal – neither of them could stomach more than a handful of nuts – Dwennon swivelled to face Leanne and crossed his legs, hands clenched into fists. "I want you to stay right here, no matter what happens. The boundary of the circle will protect you in case I..." He couldn't utter the word fail. He was afraid if he did, it would admit to its suffocating possibility. Nothing good would turn out if he let the deep fog of anxiety consume him.

She placed her hand on his and squeezed. "I'll be right here, dear." The look in her eyes held more than a simple promise. His heart pinched tight with untold emotions, he pecked her soft cheek, lifted his bag and sorry bones, then placed himself in the centre of the circle. With deliberate hands, he made a fire pit with stones and sticks he had spelled to contain any smoke within. The doll went on top, its slack body eerily set up in a sitting position, facing him. A bead of sweat travelled down his face, the hands holding the bundles of herbs were shaking.

He glanced towards his lifemate, the worry on her face was replaced with a quick smile and a nod of encouragement. Dwennon took a shaking breath and closed his eyes. He was the forest under a fresh blanket of snow, a baby taking his first slumbering breaths, the mellow notes of a flute. All thoughts that fed the simmering anxiety, that questioned his abilities flew to the deep recess of his mind. Peace soothed him, and with it came focus and reassurance. Arms outstretched, he began.

✱ ✱ ✱

The Black Arts were brutal on a person's essence. They ate at one's soul, one sharp bite at a time, whenever he or she performed a ritual or a spell. Like the predators detained in the Cage they were feeding off one's humanity, chipping at it until all that remained was pure evil.

> *Beware the Black Arts*
> *Guard thy soul at all costs*
> *The power of one's heart*
> *Shall prevail before it's lost*

Myrddin's ominous warning kicked around Dwennon's brain. Those were words he'd read as an inquisitive young man; words he'd wished he'd remembered sooner. Getting rid of the doll had proved to be as complicated as he'd anticipated; the safe spells he'd learnt during his apprenticeship had failed miserably. He'd chanted until his throat grew coarse, burnt the purifying herbs in a blue-flamed fire. By the time the dimness of dusk had enveloped the glade, the herbs had run out, the fire died down. He'd collapsed on his knees with both fatigue and defeat. The doll's thready eyes had seemed to mock him, taunt him about his failure. It was in that weak moment of self-pity and despair, he'd made the brave or rash decision of using what he'd sworn all his adult life never to use: an essence spell.

Only the most powerful and gifted novices were taught how to make essence spells in their last year of university. From the little knowledge he'd gathered along the years, Dwennon understood people's gifts were a slither of magic they tapped on without conscious thoughts. He didn't know how but some people could extract more of it than others.

The essence spells, on the other hand, used deliberately the planet's resource of magic at its rawest form. No one – not even Myrddin – had succeeded to harness it into a manageable form. It was all or nothing. They were a last resort only to be used by the few powerful enough to survive the sheer force emanating from the planet itself. His head swayed a little when he realised he was one of them.

He tried to move an arm but the limb, as leaden as a two-handed sword, refused to cooperate. Lifting hooded eyelids, he stared into thick darkness; his pulse spiked in fear until he saw the light of a dying fire to the far side of, what appeared to be, a large cave. How in the stars' light had Leanne carried him here? He'd warned her the spells would sap every ounce of magic and energy out of him, refusing to admit they might kill him in the process.

He shuddered, remembering the freezing blackness that had invaded his mind, the pain as hot and excruciating as a flow of lava travelling through his veins. Had it been the magic? He'd barely managed to finish the spells before blacking out, death a welcome thought. Yet, here he was. Alive. Shuffling noise informed him of Leanne's approach long before she put a cool hand on his cheek. The candle she'd brought over accentuated the bags under her shining eyes.

"Ye got me worried, love." her voice wavered. He wanted to wipe away those silent tears, but his hands stayed flat on the damp floor, useless. So, he gave her a shaky smile in the hope to reassure her. She helped him sit up against the cool stone wall, brushed his messy hair into place, then placed a cup to his lips. He obligingly opened his mouth and sipped at the herbal infusion. He recognised the invigorating taste of peppermint and ginger with a tinge of honey. After taking two more sips, he braced himself and asked.

"Did it work?"

Her kind eyes were assessing him. "Aye, dear. All this suffering was not in vain."

He closed his eyes, relief seeping into his soul. His breathing slowed. "Oh no, ye don't!" she exclaimed. Reluctantly he opened his eyes once more. She was by the fire. The loud clang of a metal pot on the fire echoed along the cavernous walls. An instant later, she came back with a bowl of the rabbit stew she had insisted to bring.

A spoon to his mouth, she said, "Eat up! Ye can't heal on an empty stomach." He knew better than contradicting her. While he chewed and swallowed his food obediently, the colour came back to her cheeks, the line between her eyebrows disappeared. After he'd eaten to her satisfaction, his shoulders relaxed, and a bone deep fatigue settled over his body. His eyes drifted shut. She laid him down with the same care she would a baby. Dwennon fell asleep with a smile on his face.

CHAPTER 13

Faylinn

The weather had been dry lately. A warm wind coming from the South had put an end to the morning chills. Odd for this period of year, but nonetheless welcome. As per usual I was collecting dried sticks and wood for our evening fire, and I had my pick of lovely, dried wood. I took advantage of the time to choose branches that could be used for arrows. The drier the better. I was reaching down to pick another branch when Jolis called my name and sauntered towards me.

I hadn't seen him all day as, since the attack, Sawyer had assigned him to scouting for added precaution. It was unusual for him to stray from the imposed routine of setting up camp, so I straightened up slowly and contemplated his face for any clues of trouble. He gave a lazy smile, "Don't ye look at me like that. All's good and well."

"Good. Don't think I could cope with anything bad after spending the whole day with those two sullen faces." I wasn't being fair, only one of them was all high and sullen; Sawyer was silent to listen for any oncoming attacks. Jolis chuckled, "Well, hope my little present will cheer ye up." He brought up what he'd been carrying, and I gaped.

The fingers of my free arm ran down the soft leather of the quiver. "It's beautiful." I breathed. My lips wobbled a moment, then stretched into a smile. I would not cry.

He scratched the back of his head. "Nah, it's nothing much. But ye can't have arrows without a quiver." I hadn't even thought of that little detail. On impulse, I dropped the pile of sticks I'd collected to the floor and hugged him, still holding my beautiful present, then let go. "Thank you. I'll cherish it forever."

"Glad ye like it, lass." He said picking up the sticks, not meeting my eyes. From my position I noticed the tip of his ears were bright red. His lack of self-confidence still surprised me after knowing him for months.

I bent down to help him and said, "When have you had time? You've been working on the pendant for your youngling."

As we leisurely made our way back to the camp he explained, "I might have had a time or two during my breaks. With nobody to talk to me, I get plenty done." A mischievous grin appeared on his face.

I swapped at his arm. "You fiend, I really miss our conversations."

He gripped my hand and gave it a squeezed. "Me too, my friend." It was my turn to grin now; it was nice to hear him call me his friend.

❋ ❋ ❋

Another two weeks went by slow and steady without any happenings. The forest coalesced into a blur of lush grass, untamed underbrush, of leaves tinted with reds and yellows. An urge to touch the trees, to feel their essence increased with each step, each breath I took. Impossible to ignore, my hands were clenched into fists tight enough to hurt; the distracting pain taking the edge of my restlessness. I couldn't risk it though. The connection was usually short and sweet, but once it had lasted half a morning. The weeping willow in question had revelled in showing me all it'd witnessed. I suppressed a smile as I remembered the visions of lovers kissing by its low branches and families enjoying a picnic by the pond.

Anyway, I didn't have time to spare during the day. Covering as much ground as possible was primordial. And evenings were split between making bows and arrows as well as learning how to fight with a knife with Jolis. I was glad he'd volunteered instead of the others: Kel was too much of a joker to concentrate, Sawyer too intense, and Veena... was Veena. Jolis was a good teacher: gentle yet firm. He would make a good father to his unborn child.

He got me started on wooden sticks rehearsing countless times the basic stances, the complicated footwork, then he proceeded onto parries and self-defence moves. Who would have thought so many things were involved in knife fighting? Despite myself I disliked the lessons. Knives were too short, too close to the opponent. Shame they didn't have any spare swords, I swear the extra length of the weapon would make the fights less daunting, less personal.

When satisfied with my progress, he moved me onto real knives; no more pretend. They lent me their smallest and lightest ones for the rest of the journey. Their weight felt strange and uncomfortable in my hands, the cool feel of metal harsh. Then it was back to the routines all over again.

It was gruelling, but worth it. During my first fight with Jolis, my body responded to his assault of its own accord: I evaded, parried, jabbed and feigned like a decent warrior. Kel's words. I even managed to get one near hit. From that point on, Jolis demonstrated with Sawyer or Kel certain complicated moves in a real fight, then in slow motion. An uncomfortable burden lay heavy on my chest every time I fought though. The chance, the thought I might one day plunge these blades into somebody's live and breathing body writhed in my stomach.

Tired and sweating from the exertion I would then sit by

the fire working on a bow or arrow while the others sparred with each other to keep in good shape. Sawyer was reticent to go to populated places, so between the four of them they shared the task of procuring fresh meat. I'd wondered at first at their decision of taking only one bow. However, the attack had opened my eyes: the wanderers' warriors favoured close combat, hence the ridiculous number of sharp instruments on their bodies. A bow, as well as being encumbering, could only be used from a distance. Still, I was convinced the bows I was making would prove useful at some point, and the worse comes to the worst they could throw them on the ground before fighting. In the meantime, our dried meat supply was thinning fast, and with Kel and Jolis backing me up, I'd convinced Sawyer to spend the next two days solely on hunting and drying the meat.

"Shall we stop to eat?" Sawyer's deep voice brought me back to the present. The sun shone high in the sky, casting blades of light through white fluffy clouds onto the forest's floor. My stomach growled its approval. Since the attack we were taking double precautions: only necessary talk while walking, and both Kel and Jolis were scouting for any unwelcome presence, human or animal. Unfortunately for me, it made for an awkward noon break. Veena talked to Sawyer ignoring my presence – my many efforts to befriend her scorned – while he listened and answered in his usual laconic way. He was more approachable in the evenings when everyone was gathered, and the protective spell set. He took his mission seriously, I mused when, finished with his food, he went into the woods with no word of explanation.

Veena's eyes took in his every movement. I wondered if her feelings were more than admiration and loyalty. He didn't seem interested, but who could tell with Sawyer. That man was difficult to read. It was possible she was so cutting with me because she believed I was to blame for getting them caught into this risky mess. That, and her views on nobles. Her behaviour was a pain, yet I couldn't fault her opinion, I felt the same after all.

"What're ye looking at?" she curled her lip, then came to stand right in front of me. "Ye think ye're so special, looking down on people like us." she spat. A familiar wave of mental exhaustion drained the good mood I had been feeling. This had to stop. I was sick and weary of her hostility. Before I could reply she added, "I saw ye that night with Sawyer,"

Ah.

"Acting all sweet and intimate, ye..." she looked behind me at the sound of crinkling leaves, eyes wide with shock. *Is Sawyer back?* No, he wouldn't make any noise. The hair at the back of my neck rose when I heard chuckles, unfamiliar male chuckles. I grabbed my knife, but an arm – no mistaking the rich black of the royal guard – snaked from behind me and grabbed my hand hard.

The man tutted, a grin on his face as he turned me round. "Nah ah ah, little one." he pried it from my hand. The knife fell in a dull thud, the sound resonating numbly within me. Then he forced me back down with a gloved hand while another guard did the same with Veena. She wasn't looking at me. Her shoulders were tense, her mouth a thin line of fury. How did the others miss them? It was lucky Sawyer had slipped away, maybe he'd heard them and managed to hide. Two against one wasn't bad odds if he had the advantage of surprise. That hope shattered in an instant when a short while after, six more guards joined us, Sawyer at sword point.

It appeared we'd been ambushed like newborn rabbits. Two of them shoved him to the ground all the while regaling their fellow comrades how they'd caught him with his pants down. Sawyer's cheeks went bright red, in rage or humiliation I couldn't tell. Probably both. After having a good laugh at their easy prey, the one with a thick moustache asked, "Where's the Lady Faylinn? What have you done with her, you rats?"

Good, my disguise was working. I ducked my head down, not wanting to tempt fate.

"What Lady?" Veena said after a short silence, her voice

shaking but docile. "We're but commoners on our way."

I dared a glance her way. Her body was shaking, her breath shallow, even her eyes held terror. Her little act seemed to do the trick. Boots shifted and the murmurs of a conversation I couldn't hear drifted to my ears. I raised my head an inch to look at the others for any clues on what to do, but Veena was watching the guards talking. Sawyer was studying our bags, contemplating. I hoped he had a good plan if they refused to let us go.

The guards came back next to us. "You're coming with us for a nice long talk about lying to Royal Guards. We know she was with you." I tensed, fighting hard to shut all emotions from my face. How would they know for sure? By now Dwennon had burnt that creepy doll, hadn't he? The air became tight around my chest. What if he'd failed? What if Quentin had hunted the doll to the wanderers and killed them all. I stared bleakly as a guard yanked Sawyer up.

"Tie him up." The one in command barked from where he was crouching, looking through Sawyer's satchel. I shook my head. I couldn't let myself drown in what-ifs and maybes, I needed to focus on the problems right in front of me. The main one being I couldn't let them take me because they would guess my trickery upon closer inspection. And I couldn't have that happen.

My mind focused on the knife resting on my left upper arm hidden by my cloak, then I recapped combat routines, but before I could so much as twitch a finger, the rattling sound of air exhaling and a falling body started a bout of chaos. I looked up in time to see Kel – high up a tree – take down another guard with an arrow while Jolis, sword in hand, was running towards us, his face dark with fury.

To my right, Veena unsheathed her sword and lunged at another man in the matter of a second. The guard darted to one side and thrust to her right. The loud clang of metal reverberated when their swords met. She was a good head smaller, but with her agility and years of experience, she was holding her own. The other guards were busy with Sawyer and Jolis. I didn't have time to reflect on why no one had come for me. I cast a quick glance to the large rock not far from me, where I'd left my almost finished bow and arrows. That had been the stupidest thing I did today. How many times had they drilled me on keeping all weapons close at hand?

I shuffled low to the ground towards the rock, which was too close to Veena and her opponent for comfort. Behind the rock, my eyes couldn't stop watching her movements. She kept shifting out of reach then closer in an uneven pattern. The guard tried to keep pace with her, tried to guess where she would strike next, but his sword only slashed empty space, time and time again. He was sweating and growling his frustration, and I couldn't help seeing him as the mouse to Veena's wild vicious cat. When at last by chance, or possibly when Veena tired of him, the guard hit her sword, he sneered down at her. "I'll enjoy killing you, you b..." His last word was lost in a gurgle. Eyes bulging, he clawed at Veena's knife sticking from the side of his throat. Before he could take it out, he toppled over.

Three down.

Quickly, I reached for my bow, but one of the shot guards had fallen on it and my quiver. I rolled his large body, refusing to dwell on touching a dead man. That would come later if I survived the next few moments. No, *when* I survived.

Bow and arrows in hands, I rushed behind the cover of a tree making sure nobody was hiding behind me. I didn't fancy any more surprises. Sawyer and Jolis were both duelling to my left with guards as skilful as them. Veena was hanging back, knuckles white on the pommel of her sword, ready to jump in the fight at any time. On the other side, Kel was still up there, but the biggest and tallest man I'd ever seen – a falling boulder would be less daunting – was sprouting obscenities at him while ramming himself into the tree. The arrow embedded in his shoulder didn't seem to affect his strength. A tearing and groaning sound followed the onslaught, and before the guard could throw himself once more at the tree Kel jumped to the floor as agile as a mountain cat. By the time he rolled to his feet further away to my right, his sword was already out.

I searched for Blaith among the trees as she rarely strayed far from Kel, but I couldn't spot her. That didn't mean she wasn't there, lurking, like Veena waiting for her time to act. My eyes went back to Kel. He was keeping his own, but in the seconds I watched them, the guard cut him on the bicep and the shoulder, my friend's blood staining his sword.

My choice was made.

On silent feet, I sneaked behind bushes and trees to face the guard. Kel was panting, sweat dripping in rivulets by the time I saw an opening; the guard's heavy blows were taking their toll. Spikes of heat shot from my weapon and travelled through my body. A buzzing noise was filling my ears; it reminded me of when I was tied up to Quentin's bed before it had blown to pieces. During the seconds I dwelt on my gift, they had circled further into the forest. I hooked an arrow and lifted the bow while I prowled closer. The men, moving in their macabre dance, lunged, swerved or parried, taking them further away from me, trees always in my line of sight. Kel's arms were shaking with each deafening impact, and I worried I couldn't help in time.

Something shifted within me then. It was now or never. Shooting the guard from where I was standing should be near impossible yet, I knew with an assurance anchored in the deepest part of my core I would succeed. In an intuitive push from within, I projected my desire into the arrow, then urged it to strike the guard no matter what. The twang of the string bit at my fingers with the release of the arrow, which flew in a straight line, passing through low branches, scraping the top of bushes before, a large tree in its way, it took a sharp bend to bury itself deep within the guard's chest. Awe was shortly replaced by dawning realisation, and my heart crumpled with his body.

I killed a man.

The lack of sound blew my despair into the bright sky above. Behind me the others, their faces red with exertion, were silent towers over the dead guards. Stepping closer, I realised with a twisted sickness in my guts I had known one of them; he'd been decent for a royal guard. I sent a quick blessing for his soul, not all of them were despicable. Blaith crawled out of shadows, her piercing eyes fixed eerily on me, catching me in their snare. Not for the first time I wondered if she had magic of her own. Sometimes she appeared to grasp situations in a way no animal should. Kel broke our uneasy bond by stepping in front of her while staring at me with something akin to wonder.

I didn't think the others saw what had happened. Would he tell them? Of course, he would. The idea somehow frightened me, and I moved away from him. Now was not the right time to discuss what had happened. He opened his mouth to ask the inevitable when Sawyer, fists grounding by his sides, thundered.

"What in Myrddin's blasted name was that? We were ambushed like novices." He faced Kel. "How come ye didn't see them?"

"Hang on there, mate." Kel stretched his impressive height, walking towards him. "There was no one when I passed earlier on," he poked Sawyer in the ribcage. "Aren't ye supposed to keep yer damn eyes open too?" Veena regarded me with a look that said I was to blame, then clipped me with her shoulder on her way to the riverbank. She started cleaning the blood on her arms, her gestures fast and efficient.

"Ye're right," Sawyer said, his shoulders hunched, his hand cupping his eyes. "I let my guard down."

"We all did," Jolis said with a pointed look at Kel. "We got too complacent and one of them escaped if ye haven't noticed, he slipped away like the snake he is. Anyway, it's renowned royal guards have magic. Who says one of them couldn't make them all invisible?"

Kel nodded, his face sombre, then hit Sawyer half-heartedly

on the shoulder. "Damn, I hate it when that lad's right." Sawyer managed a small smile and both men administered painful looking taps to each other's backs. If all arguments could be resolved like so, the world would be a better place. Veena sheathed her sword with unnecessary force. Not going to happen with her, I sighed.

"It's all well and good, but that doesn't explain how they knew where we were and why they were so sure we were with her." Veena said, jutting her chin in my direction. Kel and Jolis looked at me with confused expressions, so I related what the guard had said. Everybody fell silent.

"Unless" Veena's hard eyes fixed on me. "Ye're the one directing them straight to us." My cheeks flushed; my vision blurred for a second as anger made me dizzy. It was one thing to dislike me, but to accuse me of treachery was absurd. My fists clenched, I lifted my chin ready to speak my mind.

"I think Veena might be right." Sawyer's words drained the blood from my face, I stared at him dumbfounded, and I took an unsteady step backwards. A sense of betrayal slashed through the deep trust that had crept inside of me unawares.

"Are ye out of yer mind?" Kel cried out. "She's as good as dead if she goes back. Why would she…?" he waved his hand at the carnage.

"Oh, come on, Kel," Veena scowled. "Are you blinded by her pretty act and manners? She took us all on a wild goose chase, and the whole damn thing is probably not even true." She unsheathed a knife. "Maybe it's time for questions." Jolis came to me before she could take a step forward and placed a comforting hand on my shoulder. No words were needed. I bit my lip hard as tears burned my eyes, glad he and Kel were on my side. I couldn't look at Sawyer anymore.

"Veena, enough!" Sawyer's growl stopped her in her track, as one everybody turned to him. "I never said Faylinn was aware of it." I gasped; hands closed over my mouth. *Is it possible?* The revelation left me trembling like a leaf in a summer storm.

"Myrddin's curly beard!" Kel exclaimed, then stepped in front of me and shook his head, one hand on his chin and eyes suspiciously bright. "That's right! Maybe ye should strip right now. Must make sure it's not in yer garments, hey? I'd be happy to help lassy." he added waggling his eyebrows. I narrowed my eyes at him. Would he ever learn?

Jolis shoved him in the chest and pushed me behind him. "Stop it ye slimy eel! Is that a way to talk to Fay?" He was shorter by a head, but that didn't stop him from closing the distance between them in defiance.

Kel lifted his hands up and chuckled. "Back off shorty, just a jest. We could all do with a bit more light-heartedness, is all." Jolis growled something under his breath that brought heat to my face.

"They're not mine anyway." I said, trying to dissipate the hovering tension between them. Jolis was a gentleman, very firm on how men should act with women, and Kel's sexual innuendos, although mostly jokes, brought about his blustering overprotective nature. I gave Kel a short smile, his help was unconventional but heartfelt nonetheless, then walked to Jolis who was still fuming, his nostrils as round as a stag on the brink of a fight.

"It's all right," I whispered while rubbing my hand on his flexed arm. "I'm used to Kel's ways by now."

"He shouldn't...That's not the way..." he grumbled and threw his arms to his side. "He needs a woman setting him straight, that's what he needs."

"Like you?" I teased, earning a smile.

Sawyer approached with my satchel, gave it to me, then folded his arms waiting. The message was clear. One by one I extracted my belongings, shaking, unfolding them, double checking to find Myrddin knew what. In the end my hand touched an item, a long-forgotten item. Realisation froze the blood in my veins as fast as a freezing spell. I extracted the map and placed it on the ground. My hand was shaking.

"I'm so sorry." My voice was so low I wasn't sure they'd

heard me. I looked at them all, shame blazing my face. "I took this from the Castle when I set on my way. It's magical. I never thought…" I swallowed hard, unable to forget the deaths I had caused with my carelessness.

"A pox on it," Veena spat on the ground then faced Sawyer. "That's what ye get for taking an idiot with us. We would be halfway by now if not for her." He was staring at the map, his face as hard and unrelenting as stone, a small crease between his eyebrows. Veena's face softened at once. "I'm sorry, I shouldn't take my anger on ye. I know ye'd never have agreed to take her if it wasn't for Dwennon."

I knew as much, but the reminder stung. Old feelings resurfaced, I felt stupid and selfish to have imposed my presence upon them, a presence clearly unwanted. I shook myself out quickly of this self-made misery; I hoped it wasn't the case with Kel and Jolis.

Sawyer pushed the map with a foot. "Jolis, burn it if ye can. Fast. We need to make a move." The others stood to attention while Jolis knelt and placed his hands on our traitor. Green acrid smoke burned at my nose before it burst into flames.

My mind still reeling from my mistake and eyes fixed on the fire, their conversation barely made any impact until Sawyer said, "We need to head West now, skirt the Cage."

Panic wringing out all notion of guilt, I exclaimed. "No, we shouldn't go there, it's far too dangerous." I shouldn't have bothered talking for all the response I got. After casting a furtive look at me, they continued planning a new route, naming places unknown to me until Sawyer ended the impromptu meeting in a growl sounding like "Let's go."

Seeing the sheer terror on my face, Kel stepped next to me. "It'll be fine, we're not going in." I gave him an incredulous look. "As ye've seen we're good fighters." I shook my head in disbelief, this was way more dangerous than royal guards. They were crazy. Without thinking it through I ran to Sawyer.

"Sawyer, we can't do this, we're going to our deaths."

"And who's fault is that?" snapped Veena close behind.

I would not let her venom affect me. Taking a long shaking breath, I pressed on. "What about those villagers you think were attacked or disappeared, what if the barrier is defunct?"

"I know damn well it is, lass! I've seen what those creatures can do, believe me." The tone of his voice had reverted to that cutting edge from when we'd first met. I willed him to look at me, but his eyes stayed focused in front of us. "Even without the map the guards can easily guess where our original path would take us. They won't think ye foolish enough to venture so close to the Cage. It's our best chance."

"But we are!" I couldn't stop the whining in my voice. "Fools, if we do this."

"Ye left us no choice."

His harsh words, arrows embedded with painful truth, sank deep, deep within my heart. My feet stopped. My actions, though not on purpose, had caused trouble after trouble from the start, and here I was the only one complaining, whining like an irritating youngling. I wiped tears of self-loathing and frustration. But what else could I do? We were heading to our possible death, my fault, yet I could not find a way to make it all better. I was in over my head. Kel and Blaith both spun to look at me at the same time and gave a tight smile – well, not Blaith – before disappearing in the brush. Ever silent on his feet, Jolis stopped in front of me, serious eyes fixed on mine.

"You too? You're angry with me?" fresh tears rolled down my cheeks, losing his friendship would devastate me. "How could I have known it would give our location away?"

"Not that." he sighed in frustration. "I'm mad because ye hid that map from us. Ye still don't trust us, do ye?"

"What? No," I hesitated. Was he right? Maybe at first. But now, after weeks of getting to know them there was not an ounce of doubt in me that I trusted them with my life, even if it meant going near the Cage. "I do trust you all." My answer came too late though, he shook his head, then walked off. Panic ensued, but I followed him not giving up.

"I forgot about it. I swear. What with meeting you all, my

plans went a bit awry." He raised his eyebrows. "In a good way, I can see that now. And it was at the bottom of the satchel..." I grabbed his arm to make him stop. "It slipped out of my mind."

For a long minute, in which I hoped he could read the truth in my eyes, we looked at each other, then he reached out and tapped a knuckle gently on my head. "All right, I believe ye. Now stop feeling sorry for yerself, it's never helped anyone." My eyes fell on Sawyer's retreating figure.

"Tell him the truth."

"He won't believe me." From his growling earlier on he didn't seem open to conversation.

"Won't know until ye try." True, but I liked my head attached to my body very much so. "Trust is something that needs to be won on both sides. Sawyer doesn't give his easily, that's why he took it hard."

"You mean he trusts me?" Hope dared to show its eager face. Jolis's lifted eyebrow squashed that assumption.

I made a face. "Right." Trusted.

"Just go talk to him, Fay." He chuckled.

* * *

It took me three days of endured brooding silence, of adverted eyes to finally set things straight. His surly mood had made me reluctant and cautious at first, but the third day I was plain annoyed at his avoidance and monosyllable replies. Kel had confronted me at the first opportunity, and apart from a stern look and another lecture on trust, he'd been no different than usual. Veena was still the same, although she seemed to enjoy watching the rift between Sawyer and I.The opportunity to catch the latter alone presented itself when she went to wash the dishes and the other two were busy training. As per ritual, Sawyer was honing his weapons on a whetstone, his large hand working in a long, even motion. Blaith laying by the fire, lifted her head at my approach, I ruffled her ears before sitting close to Sawyer in order to keep a modicum of privacy. Our proximity brought back to mind the last time we sat together by a fire like this after our first attack; how different the ambiance had been. I commiserated the bond, however small, we had created that night. Granted, I had done most of the talking, but something had changed. And I wanted it back, a forlorn whisper echoed in my heart.

"I'm truly sorry about the map." I ventured in a gentle voice. His hands stopped and I could have sworn I heard a grunt escape his lips. He seemed to be doing a lot of that around me. I sighed.

"Listen, I took it when I was desperate, used it a couple of times. When I met your group, things were taken out of my hands, not to my satisfaction if you must know, and although I was, am, grateful for your help, I decided to bring it with me in case." I shrugged. I did a lot of that around him too. "I don't know why, maybe in case you all dropped me because I was too slow." He'd started on his work again, his face unreadable and I feared my words were making things worse. "Then, we went our way and with everything that happened, I forgot about it. Never thought it could pose a problem, I swear. I was careless, a barmy halfwit." Almighty stars, I was talking more and more like them. A minute possibly two passed in silence. I knelt in order to get up – I'd try again the next day – but a big hand pushed me back down.

"Stay." was the only thing he said to me.

Who knew such a small word could hold so much meaning?

CHAPTER 14

Selena

The salty taste of sweat dripped on my parted lips. I stopped then ran the wide sleeve of my work clothes over my drenched face. A faint air movement tickled my neck before a sharp pain exploded on my head.

"Ow!" I cried out, raising my arms in front of me in a defensive gesture, one I'd grown to know was pointless.

Shina, all of her 4 foot 10, stared down her nose at me, a closed fan in her right hand. "How many times do I have to remind you girl? No stopping on any account when cleaning the floor." I was sorely tempted to ask if I should barrel my way through even when the Master was entering the room – it'd happened once, and of course I'd stopped; not that he'd noticed with his head stuck in a book. I didn't ask though. One, I was too much of a coward and two, damn I feared that fan. Where did she keep it? None of our clothes had any pockets. Her greying eyebrows lifted and for one dreadful moment I was sure she could read minds. I'd have to ask Zen if it was possible. I liked him. He was easy to talk to unlike the tyrant facing me.

I kept my eyes on the floor, head bent. I'd learnt the hard way she didn't like people looking at her in the eye, a sign of rudeness according to her. "Why is that so?" she went on and

I repressed a sigh; I'd been there at least three times before, so why didn't I learn? *Because you're feeling lost a tiny voice whispered.*

Shifting my feet, I recited in a dull voice, "Irregular lines appear on the wood." My eyes wandered over the gleaming wooden floor and failed finding said lines.

"Right, now start over."

My head snapped up at the unfairness; I'd just done two thirds. My body twitched with restrained irritation. So, what if there were a few lines, it wasn't the end of the world. Mouth closed tight, I lifted the cloth from the floor, dunked it in a bucket full of vinegar, squeezed the liquid out, then made my way back to the corner of the room. I paused when she followed me.

What now?

I hated my lack of confidence, always second guessing if what I did or said was good enough. *What would a self-assured person do in this situation?* From the inside of her belt Shina unfolded a piece of cloth similar to a bandanna and motioned for me to lower my head. With deft and gentle movements, she secured it around my forehead. After a nod of satisfaction, she glided on silent feet into the kitchen.

That woman was a puzzle. She was brusque and demanding, she bugged me no ends teaching me how to clean the correct way – even Marie Kondo would be hard put – and flicking that freaking fan. Then, out of the blue she would do those random acts of kindness, which left my soft, mushy heart unable to dislike her. I was still shaking my head when Zen called from the panels looking out onto the garden.

"Don't think too hard, even Ryuu fails to fully understand Shina." he chuckled. "And he's known her all his life."

"Was she..." I hesitated.

"Like a fierce dragon when she trained me?" My eyes drifted to the panels separating the rooms, it was shut but those paper-thin enclosures weren't exactly soundproofing material. No noise, so I nodded and let a smile break out.

"That and more." he advanced towards me. "I was a bit of a handful back then." His whole face lit up with his mischievous, boyish grin.

Although I'd been living with them a mere three weeks, I'd easily made friend with Zen; he was fun, laid-back and didn't seem to mind my shyness. He reminded me of Anna in a lot of ways. One of which was the ability to talk about anything and everything, perfect for someone who didn't talk much. My heart tugged in its usual painful way whenever I thought about her or granddad.

Every day I'd tried to get back home. And every damn day I'd failed. I shoved the unpleasant feelings deep down. I still couldn't handle them.

Thank God for Zen though. He was great at distracting me. Like me he was an orphan, and the little girl inside me reached out to this man who'd experienced the same pain, the same void. Despite his never-ending smiles, his eyes spoke for themselves when he explained how, both of his parents sick, he'd taken off looking for a healer.

"I didn't go far." his smile had turned wry. "We lived in a remote part near the mountains in the East. After a couple of days in the cold... Ryuu found me, all tired and sick, and healed me. I was too worried for ma and pa to care about his weird hat. He's not one to get angry, but dragon's teeth I felt his wrath that day. Told him about my sick parents and he took me there on his horse as fast as he could." he looked up to the sky. "We were too late. Sometimes I wish I'd stayed with them until the end, you know, to say goodbye, and thank you."

"I understand." I hadn't meant to say it out loud, but sometimes words wanted to be said.

He'd looked at me for a while, stood up, then placed his hand on my head. "Yes, I believe you do." He'd left me alone, a thousand knots caught in my throat. Ever since then we grew close, he took on a big brother approach to our relationship, which I was thankful for as I'd always craved to have siblings.

I looked at him now, all traces of sadness replaced by

mischief. "I'd love to hear all that, but I have work to do, unlike some people." I raised an eyebrow. Since my arrival, Zen's house chores had gone down a fair amount, a fact he had no qualms teasing me about. When I'd asked what he did with the rest of his days, he'd vaguely mentioned some work for the Master, nothing precise though.

"Actually, I have an important meeting with the Master. I'll be away for a few days." It wasn't the first time he'd been assigned errands in Washima or the surrounding Domains. It was all so secretive, my curious mind salivated with envy.

"Oh, where to?" I feigned disinterest, and his side smile let on he knew I was anything but.

He placed an arm around my shoulders and bent down his mouth close to my ear. A rush of excitement ran through my very still spine. He whispered, "Oh Selena, Selena if only I could tell." I shoved him when he started laughing. Making his way to the master's room he waved at me. "Have fun!"

I threw the cloth hard and huffed, crossing my arms over my chest. One day I would get it out of him. A rattling sound came out of the kitchen; fearing another fan attack, I lunged for the cloth, head bent down, and started running up and down the room. Strenuous, but at least my thoughts could run around in peace uninterrupted. I reflected on my new life, which at first seemed very different. However, upon closer inspection I came to realise that I had exchanged one sheltered life for another.

In London, although I interacted with many people at Uni and in the shop, the contact was short and easy. Essentially, I'd only been close to granddad and Anna. My life had revolved around two places, two people. Here, I was stuck in one place with only one person I felt an affinity with. Shina was still sizing me up, and I barely saw the master, let alone spoke to him. Most of the time he was cloistered in his rooms or walking in his private, fenced in garden donning his peculiar hat. From what Zen told me he was one of the councillors of the Head council from the Closed Lands. It comprised of twenty councillors, five per Kingdom, and a head councillor whose task was to oversee the other councillors and made sure a peaceful balance was respected between Domains. This was as far as I knew, but Zen had promised to teach me about their culture, history and geography after I'd become accustomed to the workload. I supposed he didn't want to bombard my "damaged" brain with too much information. That didn't stop me from finding other sources.

Sometimes my jobs sent me to other buildings in the Kondo grounds, which took my breath away no matter how many times I saw it. Everyone was polite to me, yet I could detect a subtle awe and wariness in their body language. It took me a while to realise their behaviour was not due to my being a foreigner, though it didn't help things. No, as it emerged, I'd been the first person allowed to work and live in the private mansion in years, when Zen arrived to be exact. The master had refused to take anyone else, in spite of the workload, to maintain his insular hermit-like existence. No one, bar the three of us, could come and go as we pleased in the main house. That meant every single item, which needed to be brought to the house, had to be left on the front walkway, heavy crates of food included. My arms had never been so sore. Tyrant Shina or not, I was happy with the outcome. After my first week of work, I'd found out I was earning wages; something that had escaped my overloaded mind. To this point I was unsure on what to do with it, so I saved it in case the master decided to be rid of me one day.

Had I worked anywhere else, the other servants would have seen in a heartbeat that I lacked magic. Which meant I should really, really, thank the master properly next time I catch a glance of him; he'd disturbed his haven in order to protect me, I could see that.

My musings jumped to those wanderings around the estate, well to one place in particular. As I was still unaccustomed to the goings-on, Shina had entreated me with but one job outside the main house: bring dirty washing to the laundry room and retrieve it at the end of the day. Not very exciting, but I was now on speaking terms with a young woman called Leea. It had taken us a good week to speak without bowing constantly like nodding puppets as she was more introverted than I was. A lot of them were. A world apart to the loud mouths and disrespectful lot sprouting all over the UK.

One day, after a dissatisfying morning filled with many fan encounters and feeling brazen and reckless, I asked her in a loud whisper. "Why is Master Kondo wearing that hat?" Well, granted I knew about his strange eyes, and I hadn't seen anyone else with similar eyes, but with magic ingrained in their culture that didn't explain the presence of the hat.

Leea cast a quick gaze over her shoulder at the other workers, drying and ironing in the back of the room, then leaning close to me she whispered back, a mixture of wonder and fear in her brown eyes. "He's got evil eyes."

"What do you mean?" The little I saw was anything but.

"Apparently he got them from Arai, his ancestor." she glanced at the others once more, satisfied they were oblivious to our conversation she went on. "Arai was a frightening and evil mage that tried to kill Myrddin." Her eyes widened at the last word. I nodded, pretending to know who he was. "I heard from Naka, a cousin of the midwife's neighbour who assisted his childbirth, that his mother screamed when she first saw his eyes." she paused for effect. "They were blood red."

"Really? Red eyes mean evil?"

She frowned for a split second, then shrugged. Obviously gossiping was more exciting than wondering about my ignorance. "Yes, and from what I heard his mother refused to see him after that. They had to find a woman who'd just given birth to nurse him, paid her loads apparently." She pursed her thin lips. "I wouldn't have done it even if I was starving. The silly woman boasted about her riches, and what happened? She died shortly after the master was weaned on food." Her head bobbed up and down, face resolute. "Cursed. Then his father, afraid to be cursed himself, tried to throw him down the well, but the old mistress, rest her soul, banished him and his wife on the spot and brought up the baby as her own child."

"That was very bold of her." Though I doubted it'd happened exactly the way she told me. People had a way of embellishing the dullest occurrences.

She nodded vigorously, loosening a lock of black hair from her tight bun in the process. "Servants only work here because the wages are so good, and we don't interact with him. I got the work through my neighbour's recommendation. She said as long as we don't touch him, we wouldn't be cursed." She made a fist, hit it twice on her chest, then raised her hand, palm up, to the ceiling all the while looking up. "She was right; nobody died in the years I've been here."

I frowned. "You're scared of him?" She looked at me as though I was an idiot or demented perhaps, then she nodded. Hearing that rumour – no doubt it was a rumour because I'd seen Zen touching him without dropping dead the next day – those people's reactions at the healing session made more sense; I'd assumed they feared his powers. Poor master, no wonder Shina and Zen had been as closed as a steel reinforced bank door the only time I'd dared to ask a question about the hat. Prejudice wasn't exclusive to my world it seemed; they were humans after all.

After that informative chat, I took it upon myself to learn as much as possible about him, get to know the enigma under the hat. The search busied my mind, which was increasingly homesick, and it was like playing spy in a way. I started to keep an attentive ear everywhere I went, sometimes stopping a tad longer by the master's door when he was talking with Zen or Shina. So far, nothing of importance had come up. The only times our paths crossed he bowed to me without a word, yet I'd caught him many times staring at me while I was working. I didn't know how I could be so sure, but I was. I guess I was a mystery for him too with my amnesia story. If only he knew the truth of it all, even I still struggled to put it into perspective.

Room finished, I straightened a very sore back, then went onto the porch looking out into the garden to stretch my stiff body from top to bottom. The sight of a pointed hat next to the koi pond brought my previous thoughts back. He threw food to the fish, some of them jumping out to catch it, then watched the hungry fish fighting over a morsel. I wished to see his face, read his emotions. Was he haunted by the way people acted around him? Or had he lived so long with it that he didn't care anymore?

Maybe he was fine. He had a huge house, money and a powerful position, and let's not forget great healing magic. Shina and Zen for friends. What more could he ask for? It was clear he didn't like people's presence as he spent most of his time alone, and who could blame him if they looked at him like the monster they thought he was. I didn't get it though; he'd never hurt anyone, I'd asked Leea. He treated his workers respectfully and was fair, she'd said. Yet, there was still this hovering fear floating around the grounds and the Domains if what she'd said was to be believed. Even after all those years, they expected the worst out of him. Preconceived beliefs were damn hard to break it turned out.

* * *

The sun was setting when I stepped into my room and closed the panel behind me. The view from the window outlined a live painting of the garden under a multicoloured sky. It was hard to look away, but it was the first time since the day I arrived I'd finished my chores well before dinner time. Casting one last glance at the beautiful scene, I knelt by my bed and removed the book that I had hidden under the mattress. It was a pretty lame place to hide it, but the only available one in this minimalistic room.

With fingers red and sore from scrubbing pots I opened it to the usual page and stared at it. I had lost count of how many times I had said the word *Ake* over the weeks. I had read it, whispered it, even implored it. Yet, it had never worked.

Tonight, I couldn't manage to say it. What was the point? I was sick and tired of psyching myself every day to reignite some semblance of hope only to have it snuffed out in a breath. My life here wasn't bad in the least, hard work, but pleasant. It was easy during daytime to ignore the days passing by. The time and distance separating me from my loved ones. I was making new friends, and like it or not, I sometimes had fun.

Evenings were another story altogether. Alone in my rooms, it was hard to run away from the longing, the insecurities. And the guilt. God, that unshakable guilt following me with each step. How could I enjoy my new life in a new exciting place, with new people? I hated imagining what granddad and Anna were going through. They probably thought me dead by now, I'd been missing for so long. Had they, like me, given up any hope of ever seeing each other? I'd tried so many times to let go of the grief, only for it to suffocate me and keep me awake at night.

But I understood something today as I gazed at the master. No matter how many times I tried to shove my feelings of grief, of homesickness to the deepest recesses of my mind, they would always keep resurfacing under the cover of darkness, when I was at my weakest, all alone. And the more I suppressed them the more it hurt when I awoke from dreams of walking on the creaking floorboards of our bookshop, the smell of books lingering on my breath.

I had to face all those overwhelming feelings, embrace them with all the sorrow, the ugly tears they would bring. It was better to feel this pain rather than smothering all the good and happy memories, their faces, their smiles. Little things that made me believe I could go on regardless of the unpredictable fate I was under.

CHAPTER 15

Faylinn

A wooden sign was the first indication to our approach. Written in a foreboding red paint, the words "The Cage. Cross at your own risk" stood out behind the dark green leaves of an overgrown bush. Everyone stopped and stared beyond. If it hadn't been for the sign, I wouldn't have known any better. At first glance the forest looked no different to what we'd been walking through close to two months now. Yet, the underbrush was closer to the uneven ground, the trees denser, their limbs reaching high up to get a slither of light.

My eyes focused on a tree two hundred yards away from us: three slashes cut deep in its bark. They looked fresh. I raised a trembling finger towards it at the same time Blaith bared her teeth and growled at something we couldn't see. Jolis inhaled a sharp breath. "Better keep a good distance." No one argued.

We traced our steps back until the warning disappeared from our sight, then we headed west keeping the Cage to our right. The boundary was winding and swerving so much, we encountered many more such signs, some promising certain death. Each time forcing us to head further South.

By that stage, the itching to touch trees had gone out of control to a full-blown painful need. After a couple of hours of walking and having reached another sign, I relented; if it came to the worst I would tell everyone about my magic. Sweat drenching every part of my body I stopped in front of an ash. A feeling of anxiety invaded every cell of my body the moment my hand grazed the silvery bark, a feeling not so different to what I was feeling. I glanced at the forest looming to my side, it looked so dark I wondered if the sun's light was swallowed by the evil residing within. I kept walking like this after that, my hand touching, discovering these familiar yet different trees. Similar emotions, unrest and surprise at my presence, accompanied me while pulses of energy warmed my frozen body.

The atmosphere was sombre when we took a much-needed respite. No one spoke. Like me, they kept glancing all around us, their bodies rigid and alert. Blaith's gaze was focused in one direction, her ears twitching occasionally. The idea of sleeping in these surroundings unhinged me. I'd rather walk all night and put as much distance between us and this place as we could. Not for the first time I was grateful for Sawyer's ability to cast powerful protective spells. Chewing on jerky I ate slowly, focusing my awareness on my surroundings to push away my distress. Bird's chirping and fluttering wings echoed from above. I looked up. The sky was hidden behind a thick canopy from where the sun forced its way through patches of bare branches, casting us in dapples.

My food finished, I got up and headed absentmindedly to a red oak a few paces away. There was something special about oak trees, their grand presence felt full of power and knowledge, I often imagined them as the kings of the forests. And this one had me snared in its boughs. All thoughts of my companions faded in an instant; unable to resist the silent call, my hands settled on its craggy bark. A maelstrom of images imbued with strong emotions unrolled like a picture book through my mind: creatures, lots of creatures, some I'd seen in books, others so repulsive my stomach clenched in response. At last, the tree's message of "Leave or die" sent me crashing to the ground. I gaped in dismay at the oak, a shudder spreading through me. It was the first time a tree had failed to show, as strange as it sounded, compassion in my time of need. Unable to take in the profusion of information, I scrambled away fearing its low branches could reach me. I didn't think I could bear experiencing that again. My breath was short and fast, faces swam in front of me as though distorted in water. A warm hand touched my cheek, Jolis.

"She's freezing." I heard him say, then a gentle heat emanated from a second hand into the rest of my body. "Slow down yer breathing." Blue eyes came into my field of vision, they looked worried, so I did what they told me to. "Take a deep breath, and let it out nice and slow, lass." Soon after, my lungs and heart resumed their regular rhythm. Sawyer removed his hand and watched me expectantly.

"We can't stay here, it's too dangerous." I was the first one to break the awkward moment. My eyes fell to the empty space by Kel's feet, bringing back a flashback of bloody grey fur. "Where is Blaith?"

"She's on look-out." Kel cocked his head and regarded me with sympathy.

"You need to call her back, now!" I said, my voice sharper than I intended.

Veena rolled her eyes at Sawyer. "Seems our princess has finally lost it." I stood up at once and started towards her, fury was pumping hard in my blood making me reckless. I'd had enough of her persecution, I'd been unable to retaliate against my aunt and cousins, but now was different. I could fight back however hard I wanted to. Veena was watching me with an amused smile. I would enjoy wiping it off her smug face with my fist.

Sawyer's voice tore me from the violent direction my thoughts were taking. "Enough with the two of ye!" He folded his arms and looked pointedly at me. "We are not going anywhere until ye explain what's going on. Did ye sense something from that tree?" My mouth dropped open while the others stared at him wide-eyed. "Ye're not as discreet as ye think." he added in a gruff.

"And here I thought she just loved trees." uttered Kel scratching his chin.

Jolis gave a loud snort, "And ye wonder why Sawyer's the leader." Kel backhanded the other man on the shoulder half-heartedly.

I had misjudged Sawyer, he was far more intelligent and observant than I had expected a commoner to be. At once I berated myself at my condescending beliefs. Beliefs I had gained in a closed-off and biased class. I had so much to learn from the real world, from these people. I took another deep breath. It was time to tell them of my gift. I owed them that much. A far away howl cut my intention short.

"Blaith!" Kel cried out and sprinted towards the heart-wrenching sound. "She's hurt." How did he know for sure? It could be a trap set by those...things. The others looked at one another and set at a run after him.

"No! Don't go! Not in there!" my cries were met on deaf ears as they headed for the Cage. Their loyalty to one another was commendable; not everybody would rush to their worst nightmare to help a friend, be it human or animal. Acting against my better judgement, I followed them into the one place I had sworn to myself never to set foot. We were stronger in numbers. At that point, it was the one thing I was sure of. My feet made an awful lot of noise, birds flew off in outrage; I didn't care, it was too late for that. I caught up to the others save Kel, who had vanished in the underbrush in spite of having a short head start. Was that man even human? He was so in tune with Blaith at times I expected him to transform into a wolf. Body-morphers were rare, but not unheard of.

We ran, following broken branches and flattened ferns until we burst into a clearing. Out of breath I bent down, hands on my knees, as Jolis crouched over some rotten leaves. No clear tracks were visible to my untrained eyes. "He went that way," he pointed to our right. Before I could straighten, Sawyer told Veena and Jolis to go on, and we'd catch up. Unsure on how to react – I was grateful for the reprieve yet angry at my lack of stamina – I scowled at the ground, letting my emotions roll past. I didn't like the idea of the group separating, but I couldn't deny I needed the rest. After a sip of water, I relayed Sawyer my worries.

"I don't like it any more than ye do," he said once we started walking again. "I'll have Keltor's hind for it. He knows better than this." his shoulders slumped. "But I understand why."

"Blaith must be dear to him." I whispered, deeply aware of where we were heading. "However reckless his actions, they're admirable. They show a good heart."

"He found her half dead as a young pup, looked all over the place but could never find her pack." He explained. "They've been inseparable ever since." His voice held a hint of forlornness.

"I used to have a dog, Suli." I confided. "I missed her a lot when I moved to the Capital. She's gone now." I said softly while wishing Blaith would be fine. Sawyer gave me an odd look, opened his mouth, then shut it with a sigh. "We'd better hurry." He said before following the others. *What a strange man.* I stared at his powerful back, the muscles shifting under his clothes and gear; he lifted a low branch out of his way and looked over his shoulder right at me, brows raised. "Right." I said, my breath lodged in my throat, before following behind him.

As we made it deeper into the woods, the trees thinned out just enough to let warm light filter through; they loomed higher, their thick trunks cracked open or deformed. The underbrush, thronged with spiky or sticky plants, reached just under my waist. The uncomfortable thought we wouldn't be able to find an injured wolf under this mass swirled into my head until I couldn't hold it anymore.

Sawyer looked grim as I shared my point of view. "I've had the same thought, but Kel has this amazing bond with Blaith, he'll find her. My concern is whether we'll find them before running into trouble."

Maybe it was a sick brush of fate or plain coincidence, but as the word trouble barely slipped from his lips, an ear-piercing yell made us stop in alarm. Eyes wide open, we looked at each other one second before running, crazy as it was, towards the noise. Branches and spikes were tearing at my clothes and skin, but the fear pumping in my blood was all I could feel. Sawyer's footsteps soon slowed to a stop. He put a finger on his lips as he hunkered low to the ground behind a tree so huge it could have hidden all of our group. His head bent with an ear towards the noise, his face had that intensity he got whenever he was concentrating.

A sound, which reminded me of a tent's door flapping in the wind, resounded from ahead of us. I placed a hand on his shoulder to get his attention, then made a bird like gesture, raising my eyebrows. He nodded and stretched his arms wide open. My hand closed tightly around my mouth, catching a moan or a curse, I wasn't sure which. Big birds meant big beaks and big claws. We skulked closer, doing our best not to make any sound ourselves.

A man's awful shout of pain froze us in our tracks, and I read on his face the same emotion I knew was on mine: fear. Blinding, terrifying fear. Lifting my bow from around my shoulder, I notched an arrow with trembling hands. Out of the corner of one eye, I glimpsed Sawyer ease his sword free. He took a step forward, paused, then spun and gazed down at me, his face resolute. His whole demeanour screamed fierce warrior. He put a hand on my shoulder and whispered, "cover me from behind." His confidence, his reliance in me halted the shaking. I nodded, "I will."

It was near impossible to move fast and unheard with all this greenery, thankfully the flapping sounds covered our every move. An inhumane screech echoed before Veena cried out in rage and all attempt of silence was left to the wind. Sawyer ran in front of me, then stopped behind a hollowed-out tree, its black gash a telltale of a lightning strike, and put his arm out to prevent me from going any further. The flapping and screeching were deafening now, but I could still make out grunting. On one knee he peered to the right, his head shot back, and he turned haunted eyes towards me, swearing under his breath. Never a good sign. Before he could stop me, I took a peek. In a small clearing, Veena, sword slashing the air above her, was struggling to keep the most enormous flying creature I'd ever seen away from her. Her feet were crushing long grass and flowers too beautiful for this rotten place, the air from those wings bringing the lovely scent to my nose. Its screech sent goose bumps all over my body.

This was no bird: its hooked beak held razor sharp teeth, each feathered wing was the size of two men, and its talons as long as Veena's head. These were the only features resembling a bird for its head and body were human in shape and covered in dark brown fur. Dark Magic. Nature wouldn't have created anything so grotesque and repulsive. Two eyes as black as charcoal studied Veena with intelligence. It looked evil. I caught sight of another one higher up, hovering, waiting.

"Can ye aim at its head?" Sawyer's whisper snapped me out of my terror. My hand took a firm hold of the bow, lifted it and aimed as I willed the arrow to plunge into the creature's eye. Would it work? Maybe last time had been a stroke of luck. I repeated my plea regardless, I could use the hope however unreal it was.

I shouldn't have doubted my newly found ability because the arrow did as it was told, and the creature cried in what sounded like surprise before falling in a heap on Veena. I aimed my bow to the other one, but it took one shrewd look at me then soared away, sending dust and leaves in its wake.

"Clear!" Sawyer shouted before rushing to lift the vile creature off Veena who was pinned under the massive body. Before I could take one step, my eyes fell on a prone shape a few yards away to my right. My mind went blank, detached from my advancing body, ears roaring denials as I dropped the bow on the ground and knelt next to Jolis's still body. A diagonal gash ran from shoulder to leg, blood, lots of blood covered his clothes and the grass beneath him.

My hand went to his pale face, touching, prodding, wanting to see his smile, a breath, anything. Two drops of water landed on his beard, I stared at them in confusion before realising they came from me. An excruciating pain the likes I had never experienced before gushed inside of me. My friend, my dear friend. I wanted to scream about the unfairness of life, the cruelty of taking away a good man at the dawn of his life. Forty-three was too young to die, even someone with a weak gift could reach a hundred years with ease. Why did I stop to rest? If it wasn't for me, we could have saved him. My head falling on his shoulder, I cried without restrain.

Two large hands pulled me back gently, Sawyer was crouched beside me a hand resting on my back, Veena opposite us. Both were silent, tears of mourning running down their cheeks as they stared down with anguish. I didn't want to imagine the pain they were feeling. No, I couldn't. They'd known each other most of their lives, they'd had a bond as profound as siblings. Sawyer bent over and removed Jolis's smaller weapons and put them in his satchel, finally with shaking hands he took his necklace.

Before I could ponder this, he said in a shaking voice. "For Layna." His lifemate.

"We need to make a move." Veena's tough demeanour was back in place although she was still pale. I had the urge to throttle her. Didn't he mean anything to her? The fury collapsed as fast as a tidal wave. Who was I to judge? Maybe it was her way of coping with the loss; people did strange things in times of mourning. "The blood will attract Myrddin knows what." She added more to Sawyer than me. He'd been still, his wet eyes on Jolis. He nodded. I frowned, surely, they didn't mean to leave him like that.

"What about his burial? We can't just..." my words dried on my tongue at Veena's furious look.

"Didn't ye hear me? Do ye want to end up like him?" I recoiled as though she'd slapped me.

"Of course not, but we can't just leave him to be eaten by...," I croaked, the images that came with the thought made me sick to the stomach, I ran two paces and threw up. By the time my stomach had calmed down, Sawyer had arranged Jolis with his arms crossed, his sword sticking in the ground by his head.

"I've placed a spell," he spoke softly. "Nothing will be able to touch him." He watched Jolis, then in a murmur I could barely hear he said "Farewell my friend. Until we meet again." He squeezed my shoulder before stepping away.

I went down on my knees, taking in Jolis's face a last time before kissing his forehead. "Thank you for being my friend." My throat was as tight as a suffocating vine. "May you be happy wherever you are."

A sharp rustle, then loud growling pierced the grief, I reached for my bow and jumped to my feet in an instant, facing where the sound had come from. Guess all that training wasn't for naught. My self-satisfaction was short-lived. In front of Sawyer, whose back was to me, was an animal as tall as him on its four legs. Not an animal, another creature. Its head was that of a wolf, the size and strength of its long, gaping maw big enough to rip Sawyer's head off, its long and thick black fur grew sparse on its neck until it turned smooth and sleek all the way down to feline paws. I resisted the impulse to run far, far away, grinding my teeth together hard. I would not lose anyone else. *Think, brain, think.*

I scanned the small, but unobstructed clearing. I was too close. During the short time I went around Jolis to get in the right position, eyes and ears focusing on possible attacks, Sawyer was swinging his sword left and right. The beast backed away a few steps, taking in every movement, every breath. For a moment I thought it had worked, it would take flight, but instead of running away it sprang forwards in one massive leap and caught Sawyer's blade with its sharp teeth. Its vicious eyes still on Sawyer, it flicked its large head and flung the sword behind it. Two small daggers were already in his hands when I glanced at Sawyer.

Useless against a beast this size, they didn't look strong enough to get through its hide let alone its skull. Its eye though. I reached over my shoulder for an arrow, eyes never leaving them. Both were sizing the other one up, waiting for the right moment to attack. Sawyer was acting strange though, shaking his head hard repeatedly. I paused.

What's wrong with him?

Then I saw Veena, sword in hand, creeping behind the beast. It happened in the matter of a footstep: the creature lunged at a distracted Sawyer, who was not fast enough to get out of its way, at the same time I fired an arrow, the quickest I'd ever done. The arrow struck true in its eye socket, but not before the beast sank its serrated teeth in Sawyer's left leg. His yell was interrupted by the massive frame that fell to the ground, taking him with it.

By the time I reached Sawyer, Veena was weeping, "Don't die on me," cradling his head. "He's still breathing, just fainted." She told me and my throat released the breath that had been lodged in it.

I bent down and slapped him none too gently on the cheek. "Are ye out of yer mind?" Veena was now hysterical. "Can't ye see he's badly hurt?"

I ignored the shock and frustration caused by her helplessness, preferring to focus on what needed to be done. "Look here, do you know how to heal him?"

"No," she snarled at me. "But don't ye dare lay another finger on him." She lifted a hand, blood covered her fingertips. Did he hit his head? On my knees I spotted a rock the size of my fist with a drop of blood. Could this day get any worse?

"We have to wake him up regardless," I silently apologised for what I was going to do. "He's too heavy to carry to a safe place." The hand I lifted was unnecessary, he came to by himself, eyes glazed over, complaining about our noise. Veena made a throaty noise as he untangled himself from her clutch and looked at his leg.

"How bad is it?" I asked dreading his reply.

Jaw clenched, he lifted the torn leather and examined the damage, shielding us from it. Sweat was forming large droplets on his forehead. "Could be worse," he smiled wryly. "It's not bleeding lots, a good sign." He ripped the lower part of his tunic into a long thin strip and tightened it on his thigh above his injury. "Come on, let's go."

I looked at him confused. "What about your leg? And your head?"

His brow furrowed as he reached to the back on his head, the hand he removed was slightly stained with blood. "That explains the headache," he said more to himself than us, then his eyes met mine. "Head's fine, I'll deal with the leg when we're out of this damn place." His gaze fell on Jolis for a second, "We'll go someplace Kel can find us." The untold words *if he can* haunting his eyes. Bracing both hands on the ground he twisted his body and tried lifting himself up with his good leg.

"Ye stupid goat," Veena huffed and put an arm around his waist, her shoulder nestled under his arm to give him some support. My breath came out in a swift swooshing noise when I did the same on the other side of him, my back cracking under his weight. *The stars help me he is heavy.* His solid muscles strained and flexed under my arm and hand, the scent of sweat mixed with something else, something that sent dancing shivers down my spine, wafted from him. I bit my bottom lip and let go as soon as he was upright.

He stood for a moment, his throat swallowing hard a few times, before he limped, favouring his left leg, in the direction we had come from. Veena rushed to him and settled his arm around her shoulder. His silence worried me. His injuries must be bad, really bad. With quick movements, I retrieved his sword and satchel, sent another plea for Jolis before immersing myself in the tall foliage, daggers in hand.

We took turns helping him walk, eyes and ears straining for more trouble. At some point during the unnerving slow walk,

I found a thick and sturdy branch, which he accepted without grumbles as a crutch of sorts, but it was clear he was struggling even with its help. By the time we had crossed the barrier, my neck and back were aching from the strain of nerves, bags and weapons. My shoulders sagged a bit. We were out of danger. But I didn't allow the relief to sink in too deeply, Sawyer still needed tended to. Which brought a question to mind.

When I asked them where we were heading, Veena informed me there was a small hut in the surroundings. Apparently, there were similar huts scattered all over the Kingdom for wanderers to use when out hunting or in case of trouble. The bare necessities were kept replenished, with healing supplies and herbs Sawyer added.

We took no breaks, kept walking to Sawyer's pace until the sun, its rays stabbing our surroundings with its blinding light, was close to meet the ground. At last, Sawyer halted.

"Stop!" he breathed; his teeth clenched tight. I glanced at Veena, but she didn't meet my eyes, hers were fixed on him. Then he whispered roughly, "From the shadows of this world, I leave my life within yer hands." I stared at him, was he delirious?

He looked down at me with hooded eyes. "Dwennon cast a protective spell on all shelters. That's how we can go through it."

I waved a hand in front of me, though it was useless as he'd already undone the barrier. "So, without the words you just said we couldn't go through?"

He shook his head. "No, the spell is a complex one, it conceals the hut and sets down a sort of barrier. People can get past it, but they'll end up on the other side without setting foot inside.

Clever. "It sounds to me very much like a portal."

Appreciation glinted in his bright eyes. "Aye."

"How many are there?"

"About fifty of them. It took him years." I didn't doubt that. But who would have thought such a frail looking man could be this powerful? Dwennon had been the High Mage, evidently, he hadn't lost his magical prowess.

"Enough with the chatter." Veena's voice was sharp with annoyance, "We need to get you warm."

We traipsed through the forest to a small-sized wooden house, bordered on one side by a stream. The last streaks of sunlight flooded the inside the moment Veena opened the door, our elongated shadows floating on the hard stone floor. The hut consisted of a single room, a chimney embedded in the back wall, with a small pallet to the door's right, animal skins and blankets piled in disarray on top of it. Two large wooden shelves, looking worryingly bare, were mounted on the opposite wall, a couple of crumpled medium-sized Hessian bags underneath. No table and chairs.

Veena went straight to the wood beside the fireplace. I grimaced; I should have thought of that instead of letting my curiosity take the better of me. I cleared the bed for Sawyer to lay on while he was busy opening and sniffing jars. He kept a couple. Smoke drifted to our side a minute before the fire burst into small flames.

"Anything useful?" Veena stood up and wiped her hands on her trousers before walking next to him. I grabbed a couple of candles and their holders from one shelf, lit them up, then placed one on the mantelpiece and one next to the door.

Sawyer shook his head with a grim face. "Not enough. I'll …"

Veena talked over him. "I'll go and get a healer, there's that village nearby and …"

"Vee, I'm not sure ye'll find one."

"Then that town further South, unless…" she put her bag on her shoulder and whispered something in his ear. His face went rigid, then he shook his head looking, to my surprise, angry.

Veena faced away from him, fists clenched tight. "If I can't find a healer, I'll get herbs." She looked at Sawyer over her shoulder, eyes shining. "Don't… I should be back by morning."

"Be careful." he whispered. A nod then she walked out. What was that about?

A rattling noise behind startled me, I rushed to the fireplace to unhook the cast iron pot. I couldn't say Veena was inefficient.

"Don't," Sawyer's word stopped my hands. "I need to boil these." he took out what looked like rags from his bag and winced as he made to move towards the fireplace.

I went over and grabbed them. "Here, let me do it. I have to put them in the water?" He nodded. I did as told and glanced at him frowning, hesitant to ask what was on my mind.

"What?" he prodded.

I hesitated. "Well, Dwennon told me you were a healer so, why can't you heal your wound?"

He sat on the pallet, his leg stretched out and sighed. "I can't," his voice was as weak as his body. I'd never heard of a healer unable to heal themselves. *What a nasty trick of fate.* "I could do it as a youngling but then, I just couldn't." He shrugged.

"Have you tried just in case?" I asked fast as if saying it quickly wouldn't offend him as much. He looked at me with a wry smile. I took that as a yes. "Do you know why it stopped? I mean, there must be a reason."

His head bobbed in agreement, and he looked to the side. "Dwennon's got his little theory." I waited for more, but it never came. He took a couple of pots out of his satchel, then a knife and began to cut at his trouser leg above the injury.

"Put the rags in a bowl, will ye?"

I used a fire poker to lift the hot lid and take the boiling rags out. As I placed the bowl next to him, I scrutinised his wounds for the first time. And cringed. Bile burnt its way to my throat like pure lava, yet I was unable to tear my eyes away from the sorry sight. Red angry skin surrounded deep and bloody lacerations running down his thigh. It looked bad, really, really bad. When I said as much, his face twisted in a grimace. The two pots clanked against his leg when he shifted closer to the edge of the bed. "I was lucky it didn't strike further up." He continued his preparation: jars, more cloth, a needle and thread were lined up next to the wall. I felt faint at the sight of them. At what it implied. His voice was low and gruff when he said. "I would have bled to death."

I inhaled sharply. Lucky indeed. I crouched down, resting my forearms on the bed. "How can I help?"

He lifted his eyes from his perusal and studied me for a second. "Ye don't have to." he said, grabbing a rag and proceeded to clean his wounds. From the steady and focused look on his face, he could have been doing his morning ablutions. However, his skin was wan, and his hands were shaking. A slow hiss escaped from his lips and his leg startled when he poured a yellow liquid over the cuts.

"I insist." He placed the last rag in the bowl after wiping the excess liquid and looked at me for a long time; my shoulders squared under his scrutiny.

He let a sharp breath go and ran a hand over his face. "Can't believe I'm doing this." He said more to himself than me. Light blue eyes, serious eyes, held mine. "Can ye sew me up? Not sure I can do it myself. Hands aren't steady enough."

My eyes drifted to his leg; now it had been cleaned I could see the wound wasn't as deep as I'd feared. "I can." I could do this, I mentally reinforced that statement until I believed it. I'd sewn hundreds of pointless pieces of cloths, not perfectly, but at least I knew how to go about it.

Flesh, as it transpired, was nothing like fabric. The bone needle was thin, but I had to apply strong pressure in order to break the skin every time. This made for laborious work as he insisted I stitch the skin as tight as possible. I kept checking up on him whenever my bloody fingers pulled the thread tight, leaving a trail of puckered scars. It must have been excruciating, yet he didn't flinch in the slightest while I held the torn skin close together and sewed; he just took deep long breaths and dragged them out even longer. The only signs of his pain was the greenish hue to his face and clammy skin. How could he stand this much pain without shaking or making any sound?

Thankfully, he fainted halfway through. I was sitting on his calf, afraid he'd move by inadvertence, when he came to, his head lifting from the bed with a start. "Don't move." I urged him as I pulled the string one last time then cut it. I lifted my head in a slow and gentle movement, my neck and shoulders as stiff as my last tutor. His face was drained of colour, making his eyes stand out more. "Have you got anything for the pain?" I asked, stretching and rotating sore joints and muscles.

He shook his head and threw an arm over his eyes. His other hand wiggled in the direction of a small jar. "Can ye spread that on the wounds? It's for the inflammation."

I undid the string, removed the waxed leather and inhaled the pleasant smell of lavender mixed with something I didn't recognise. I put a finger in and spread the sap like texture over his wounds. His leg tensed, then relaxed as he took deep slow breaths. "There's not enough," I whispered, biting my lip when the pot was empty. "I could only do half."

"It'll have to do." he murmured, eyes closing. "Can ye bandage the wound?"

I picked the cloth and set to work as fast and as gently as I could. By the time I finished and tidied everything up, he was sound asleep. The mattress shifted when my bodyweight lifted from beside him, but he didn't stir. I lingered next to the bed, fingers playing with my bottom lip, to make sure his breathing was slow and even, before going to the fireplace where I kept busy for a while, preparing food and tea.

My back to the wall, sitting on a sheepskin, I took a sip of the stew and cringed at the bland taste. Cooking was not my forte. How did Jolis manage to make them so delicious every time? My heart gave a painful throb. The limp pieces of vegetables and meat swished and stirred from my trembling hands. I put the bowl down, not hungry anymore. The immediate worry of Sawyer's injury and finding a safe place now over, my mind latched onto the loss of my friend and the fear

Kel had met a similar fate. Turning to the fire on my knees, hands outstretched, I let its warmth settle over me. Its heat, invisible fingers uncoiling tight muscles, soothed every ache, every disquiet. The knotted vines in my stomach uncurled and slithered away. On a long exhale, I sat back down, took the lukewarm bowl in my now steading hands, and ate. I needed energy to keep watch over Sawyer in case... I refused to form the thought.

My eyes rested on him once more, on his large chest moving up and down, his breathing too fast, too shallow. How could things have gone so wrong, so fast? I pinched the bridge of my nose with my index and thumb. I was so, so tired. I could slap my old self silly for not thinking things through, for being so oblivious. I didn't regret coming though, I felt more alive than I had in years. It had been the right thing to do despite the difficulties, the struggles.

The grief, the fear, they were constant screams in my heart and soul. Yet, I thanked the stars for them, and I would thank them every damn day for the rest of my life because it showed my heart wasn't numb anymore. It twisted, it writhed with love and hope. My hands opened, palms up, on top of my knees, then closed into tight fists. I wished I didn't feel so powerless, I wished I could just embrace my flaws and shape them into strengths. *Who's stopping you but yourself*, a voice murmured from deep within.

I don't remember drifting off to sleep while my thoughts were full of the past and the future. My head shot up from my bent knees at Sawyer's loud voice. One glance at the candle indicated I'd slept a good hour. My long limbs unfurled with agility gained from combat practice. Two long steps brought me to his bedside. His words came out slurred and incoherent, but one stood out: Mother. On impulse, I sat next to him and stroked his head. Sweat had dampened his hair into golden curls; he looked so young, so vulnerable. Hesitant, I put a hand on his forehead.

It was burning hot.

I was reluctant to leave him alone, but sweat was running down the side of his flushed face, dripping on the bed. I rushed outside to gather fresh water from the spring, then back by his side, sloshing water in my haste on the floor. On my knees, I grabbed leftovers rags and dipped my hands in the bucket, the water nice and cool, then squeezed excess water before placing one on his forehead and wiped his face and neck with another one. But I knew it wouldn't be enough to get rid of the fever. I lifted the blankets and furs. He was drenched all over, his clothes sticking to his clammy skin. Only one thing to do.

I swatted at a rogue lock of hair on my brow while eyeing his upper body. "Right, I must do this." I let out a puff between my lips. "No, I can do this. The question is, how?" Not able to prevaricate any longer, I stood up and removed the blades I could see, which was a fair few. Thank the stars he'd removed his vambraces beforehand. Then, I lifted a long sinewy arm from the mattress and pulled at the leather vest with my free hand. It did not budge. Left with no other option, I placed a hand under one shoulder and the other under his knees, praying to the stars, Myrddin and whoever was out there, he would not wake up. My back gave a nasty crack as I rolled him onto his side towards me and held him against me. Sawyer gave out a low moan. My hands went back to work quickly, the vest removed, along the rest of his weapons, in no time.

With a face as red and hot as embers, I peeled his shirt off. My gaze fell on the lovely pendant dangling on his glistening chest straight away. Carved out of wood it resembled a person holding a bow and ark, the wood so shiny I wondered whether the bee wax in his satchel was meant for this pendant alone.

The tip of one finger reached out and grazed the smooth texture. An ocean of longing crashed into me and left me breathless, a beautiful blond woman with green eyes smiled in my mind's eye and I lifted my finger as though stung. *I shouldn't have done that.* My hand curled into a fist, I took a step back and squashed that small part yearning to know who she was and what she meant to him.

CHAPTER 16

Faylinn

T he first part of the night was spent between cooling him down as best as I could and collecting fresh water from the river. Once, just as I was closing the door behind me he woke up in a delirious state, bright eyes fixed on a spot next to me, face crumbling in agony. Before I could move, he reached out a shaky hand and called out to an imaginary Jolis. My heart cried in silence as he kept rasping sorry over and over again in between chattering breaths. He barely noticed my ministrations, his feverish mind lamenting the loss of a dear friend. In the end, exhaustion took over him, dragged him in a fitful and restless sleep.

Tears of frustration pricked at my eyes, a need to scream or hurl something across the room reverberated in my bones. My chin dropped to my chest, arms limp on my lap. I was another useless noble who could hardly do anything for herself let alone someone else. The old anger and bitterness over the wasted years spent at the castle resurfaced; my life would have been so different at home. I didn't doubt I would have suffered hours of insipid and pointless lessons on etiquette, no escaping those, but they would have been bearable had I learnt about history, plants, how to look after our tenants like Mara did.

Sawyer's bout of coughing extracted me from my self-pity. I glanced up from my sitting position by the bed and met open eyes. Lucid, alert eyes. Rising on my knees, I brought a cup to his lips. He took one sip and swallowed, his eyes closing for a moment. Had his fever broken? Buoyed with hope, I placed the palm of my hand on his forehead. A whimper slipped. He was still too hot. His hand reached mine and squeezed it, gaze intent on me. His lips moved, yet no sound came out. Frustration flashed in his eyes for a second before he licked his dry lips. When he opened his mouth again, I leaned close to it, finally catching the words. "Book, satchel."

I nodded my understanding. "I'll get it in a minute, you need to drink more." I urged him, refilling the cup with fresh water, which sloshed on my hand as I lifted it towards the now slumbering man.

Not good. Not good. Not good.

The words kept going in my head as I put the cup down, as I paced to the fireplace and back, hands wringing. Why wasn't the fever going down? And now that I thought about it, why was he feverish in the first place? I didn't know much about the healing arts, but something with his wounds wasn't right if he was getting worse. Left with no choice, I removed the bandage around his leg, hands slow and steady, and a shuddering cry wrenched out of me.

The wounds I hadn't treated with the salve were infected. Unsteady legs took me to the fireplace to boil more water. My movements were instinctive. Once more, I dunked cloths in boiling water, removed excess water, then wiped the pus that had started to appear on the scar. Again and again, until it was all gone.

Yet, I knew it would come back if I left it so.

Leaving the dirty cloths in a bowl, I sat down next to Sawyer's satchel like he'd instructed and found a small book. A journal. Each page had beautiful drawings of plants with detailed descriptions on location, uses and concoctions. My eyes went to the remarkable man who had spent, no doubt, a considerable amount of time writing about the medicinal properties of each plant. I didn't know whether to be impressed by his dedication and love of healing or to slap him silly for not telling me about this book sooner.

I read through it as fast as I could, indenting the pages of plants I needed. The sky was layered with undertones of light blues and silver, a slice of yellow on the horizon, when I closed the journal, at last satisfied with my findings. Glad dawn was near, I gathered water, tea and food next to the bed in the hope he would use them.

He woke up at the sound of clinking crockery, face still flushed from the fever. That time he managed to stay awake long enough to drink a few sips of water. While I brushed the sweat away and changed his cooling rags, I explained I was going to go and get healing plants straight afterwards. He nodded, eyes unfocused. I wondered if he'd truly understood what I said. Still, it was worth trying.

My hand on the doorknob, I looked back at the pallet and hesitated. What would happen if he woke up in a delirium without me? Was I making the right decision? I held on to the scream of frustration, which had yearned to rupture out of me all night long, as I rested my head on the door. None of my help had sufficed, I needed those plants to cure him, yet leaving him by himself felt so wrong. *Stop it!* He talked about the book for a good reason. And anyway, Veena might be back before me. With that last thought as my anchor and refusing to imagine Veena's reaction if she found a very sick Sawyer left by himself, I took two steps outside only to be assaulted with more worries.

How would I find those herbs and plants? Would they even be in the forest at this time of year? Panic circled in my head as I walked on the path but was struck short by a sudden idea. I rushed to the largest tree (the older the more sentient) and touched the bark, visualising the drawing of one of the plants I needed. *Please let it work, please help me.* A sharp laugh, half disbelief half gratefulness, escaped my lips as the tree showed me the way. I would never complain about my gift ever again. With the help of my unusual friends, I gathered everything I needed in good time.

The rest of the day was spent between brewing infusions, mixing lotions and giving ministrations. The latter was a challenge in itself as Sawyer, confused and disorientated, took some convincing to drink. However, I managed to make him drink the required amount of white willow bark for the fever and placed a compress of peppermint, oregano and marshmallow root on his leg to fight infection and reduce the swelling. I sat by his side on a sheep's skin, nodding off during his calm spells. By dusk these got longer; his breathing became regular, and I placed a tentative hand on his forehead. Dry and cool. A huge grin broke on my face, and I let out a quiet laugh.

"What ye laughing at?" his once fevered eyes were now their usual ice blue, although a touch of merriment softened them. I folded my arms on the bed by his head. I was still grinning when I said, "You, sir, have come a long way. Your fever's broken." I grimaced. "I need to check the wounds though." His face was still drawn and pale, but his alertness gave me hope. Without consideration, my hand tucked away a thick strand of hair which had fallen over his eyes. Eyes that were intent on me. Flustered, I went to the fire and prepared another brew. He drank it in big gulps and sighed, content.

He raised an eyebrow. "This willow bark tea?" I nodded and recounted everything (leaving out how I used my magic) that had transpired while he was unwell. I was baffled he couldn't remember a thing. He sat up, arms a little shaky, and removed the bandage. My gaze fleeted to his dangling necklace before dropping to his leg, no sign of infection.

"Ye did great, Faylinn." His praise warmed me up all over and took away some of my tiredness; I was truly glad he'd recovered. I was exhausted to my core, but a deeper confidence had blossomed within me, which in turn had prompted a sense of ease, of peace. For the first time in a long while I was proud of myself.

After I applied a fresh poultice, he put a warm hand on mine and gave it a squeeze before releasing it. I looked at him in surprise; he wasn't a tactile kind of man. "Thank ye," his eyes crinkled to the side. "I owe ye my life."

I flapped a hand in front of my face, embarrassed. "No, without your book I would have been as helpless as a pup. Really you saved your own life." I regretted my words when his body tensed, sure I had offended him. Then he burst out in a deep-throated laugh, and I exhaled in relief and, well, in a bit of a shock.

"Just take a compliment when it's given, lass. That was well thought off, and that book can't do no good by itself, right?"

"I suppose." I smiled back, body relaxing. "I'm glad you're better."

The flicker of something crossed over his eyes before he looked away fast, too fast to detect what it was.

At that moment the door flew open in a crash. A dust-covered Veena rushed in, but at the sight of our closeness she stumbled to a halt. Her face reddened under the grime, and she crossed her arms over her chest. "Guess I didn't need to get hot and bothered about ye, ye seem to be getting on just fine." Her lips were a mere line, she had deep dark bags under her eyes. I felt sorry for her; she'd obviously been worried sick about Sawyer. That bubble of empathy burst with her next words. "I haven't slept a wink to find ye a healer and look at ye two getting all cosy." She paced the room up and down, recounting all her misfortune (no healers for miles) and her woes (bad weather and inhospitable villagers). I would have felt sorry for her had her tone of voice not dripped with condemnation; clearly, she believed we'd spent the night in blissful intimacy or other such nonsense. She stopped mid step and pointed a finger at me. "None of this would have happened if ye'd stayed at the camp like everyone else wanted ye to. But no, the

Princess" she spat the word out, "Had to have her own way." She swiped an arm around her. "All this mess we're in, Sawyer's injury, Jolis –"

"Enough Veena," He didn't raise his voice, yet one couldn't miss the authority.

She faced him, her eyes furious. "What? Ye're on her side again?"

"We're all on the same side." he sighed with exasperation. "I was in a bad way, Vee, and Faylinn saved my life. Could ye ask any more proof of her loyalty?" The gaze resting on me was not one of gratitude. She looked at the hand he'd put on my shoulder, then stormed out of the room. It was then I understood the real extent of her feelings for Sawyer, no wonder she hadn't cared about my being friends with Kel and Jolis. I felt silly not noticing something so plain obvious, but if I was being honest, I'd refused to see the truth, blaming her attitude on her fierce loyalty.

"I'm sorry," he said after the silence lengthened. "She's..."

"You don't have to apologise, it's not your fault."

"No, it is. Her behaviour towards ye is rude and aggressive. I should have dealt with it earlier, but my relationship with Veena is complicated, we've known each other our whole lives. She's like a sister to me." he tilted his face towards the fire. "The night of the Great Hunt she'd convinced me to go to the next village's inn. My parents were killed that night." his voice was but a whisper. I couldn't imagine what he and Luela had been through. The great hunt had been thirteen years ago; Luela mentioned he was thirty, so he'd only been seventeen years old when he lost his parents and she even younger. The heartaches I'd complained about felt childish and minimal to what they'd endured. "When we got back to the camp later, people were screaming, the scent of ... blood was heavy on the breeze. My parents... I wanted to fight, but she held me back and we hid up a tree, watching..." he was silent for a long time, lost in the nightmare he had described. I felt numb. No one should experience such a traumatic event. I wanted to say something, anything to show him how his anguish affected me, but before I could find the courage, he went on. "I guess she feels responsible and is trying to make up for it. She's been looking out for me for a long time."

"That explains why she's so hard on me, I'm one of the people who killed your parents. I'm the enemy." I couldn't bear to look at him even though my family had nothing to do with it. The seriousness of the hunt didn't strike me until I was older, but vague memories resurfaced: father's face gone white with shock, of my sobbing mother begging him not to go. To see his brother, the king, it turned out, and make clear his anger and disgust in front of the whole court. Years later, Haelan admitted such a public display was the only reason for our family's lenient punishment – being sent up North. The richest nobles still had some power in those days. My dear uncle wouldn't have been able to kill his brother and his family without an uproar, so he'd played it safe.

"Well, that and more." he said evasively scratching his beard, his expression troubled.

A tightness pressed on my chest. "Thank you for sharing something so painful, and I'm sorry about your parents." The words tasted bland in my mouth, they were too little, too insignificant, but it was all I could find to say. He gave me a sad smile and nodded. Something told me he didn't talk about this with many people. The fact I was now one of them left me tongue-tied. The silence stretched on without either of us moving a muscle. In the hope to break the awkward atmosphere and lighten the mood, I said. "I didn't know you could talk so much at once." I rose my eyebrows in a comical way to make sure he understood I was teasing.

His relieved grin made him look boyish. "Neither did I." He said and we both laughed. "Come and sit on the bed." He patted the spot next to him. "Ye must be dead on yer feet." We settled against the wall, shoulders touching while he explained what he needed me to gather in order to heal his injury faster. Listening to his voice, I started to relax for the first time in what felt like a month, the past two days had been trying to say the least. The stars knew what it would take to find Kel and Blaith.

CHAPTER 17

Faylinn

A s it happened, they were the ones to find us. Their arrival the following day was a very different affair. Once Veena cooled off, she put herself in charge of cooking, then went about her business, mouth tightly shut. The tension in the room was atrocious. It brought me back to the battleground that was Court life. I considered every move I took, every word that went past my lips – not that there were many – for fear of starting another row. Sawyer had gone back to his usual guarded self, and I wondered if his earlier behaviour was a near death effect. Sorrow darkened my mood at the idea he'd closed off his heart again. Luckily, I spent a good part of the day looking for the extra herbs and plants Sawyer had asked for. Later that evening, Veena broke her sulky silence to suggest taking turns to keep a watch over him during the night, he didn't look like he needed it, but I preferred to err on the safe side. I did not want a repeat of the past night. Sawyer grumbled we should rest, but two won out.

We were having breakfast, an affair of thin porridge with dried nuts, when the door burst open with a cheerful, "We're back!"

Kel filled the doorway and then some; Blaith was panting next to him, a bandage around her upper body.

Relief filled me up with renewed energy and carried me to them, I ruffled Blaith's ears then hugged Kel. "Thank the stars you're all right." Tears rolled down his travel worn vest. He held me close, his chin on top of my head, until my crying stopped. When I let him go and rubbed my eyes, he chuckled, "I should disappear more often if that's the greeting I get every time." He opened his arms wide, a wicked smile on his weary face. "Veena?" I tensed.

"Ye big idiot, like I'd let ye fondle me." A corner of her mouth was raised, a big improvement. Kel went to sit next to Sawyer on the bed and tapped him on the back. "Dragon's teeth I'm knackered." I brought him a cup of tea and a bowl of porridge and sat close by, hoping selfishly that Sawyer would break the news.

"Where have ye been?" Sawyer asked.

"Found Blaith deep in the forest," Kel said between mouthfuls, he didn't seem to care about the tasteless meal. "She'd been lured by some wolves I suspect. Something was odd with their call, like if ye listen to it too long ye can't help but follow." He shook his head. "Far too unnatural if ye ask me. Anyway, found her just before some long-clawed beast finished her off.' He shuddered. "Killed it, then took her out of that forsaken place. Her wounds weren't life-threatening, but we had to stay put until she could move again." Finished with his food, he placed the bowl on the bed. "I remembered this place, hoping ye'd be waiting for us. Turns out I was right.' he smiled and rested his head on the wall. "Where's Jolis? Hunting?"

I looked down at my lap, fighting back tears burning my eyes: it was too fresh, too raw. Sawyer told him about our misadventures, his eyes were fixed on his clenched hands. He left no details out. When at last silence invaded our room, I dared a glance up. His head bent, Kel was whispering under his breath, tears dropping on the skins. I'd seen Sawyer do the

189

same thing over Jolis's body, last words for the dead warrior.

Later that evening, after a much-needed rest we were all staring at the fire when Kel asked Sawyer, "With ye in such a bad shape, did ye ask Veena…?" he glanced at me for a second, then back at Sawyer who was frowning, his frame as rigid as a statue. I looked from one to the other not comprehending, then Veena burst out, tears in her eyes.

"He refused." I was missing something important here. "Do ye have so little faith in me that ye couldn't bare yerself to me? Ye'd rather die?" she shouted at Sawyer. My head snapped back. *What?*

Sawyer ran his hand over his head, a sure sign he was embarrassed. "It's not as if I didn't have any other options." Veena's hands were firm on her hips, her defences up. He gestured for her to sit next to him. She hesitated for a moment, then moved to the bed with reluctant steps. Kel caught my attention and nodded his head towards the door. Before we stepped out, I heard Sawyer say in a gentle voice, "I value our friendship, Vee, and I'd be damned if I hurt ye in any way for my own benefit."

As soon as Kel shut the door behind him, I asked what was going on. He went to sit on a bench below the front window, dim light tickled his unruly strands of hair. He patted the space next to him and I complied, curious. He seemed to ponder what to say for a while. "Veena's magic is no secret among our group, but we like to keep it that way outside our boundaries, if ye ken what I mean." he didn't wait for a reply and went on. "Ye see, Vee's ability is somewhat taboo; it's not my place to say, but I doubt she'd tell ye." *No doubt about that.* "And ye're entwined in all this mess, ye're part of us now." He placed his arm around me, then squeezed my shoulder and my heart in the process. He let go and leaned forward, his forearms on his legs. "When someone's injured, Vee has got this terrible pull, this force to put her hands on the person and heal them."

"So, she's a healer. What's the matter with that?"

"Aye, except unlike a usual healer who only sees the physical damage, she can read people's spirit, their soul whatever ye want to call it."

"Does it mean she can do that whenever she touches someone?" In a way, it was like Luela's gift.

He brushed a hand over his face. "Nah, it's more complex than that. I think the person must be hurt. Even when it's a small physical injury she can read their soul. Mind ye, that's not quite right. She experiences their most vivid memories and emotions, these sort of things. She just can't help it. I don't know how to explain. It's as if she's sucked into their mind as soon as she touches them, and she can't move, can't do anything until whatever's wrong is fixed. It didn't bother her at first; everyone has the odd dark thought or memory, and she's a tough girl our Vee." He was quiet for a spell before he went on. "Then one day, while our warrior group was out scouting, we came across this young woman dragging her bloody body, as pale as a spectre. When Sawyer approached to help, she screamed the birds away. So, Vee took her to one side while we stood guard at a safe distance, and she healed her, no questions asked." he shifted. "It turned out that woman had been beaten up and sexually assaulted, and Veena felt every moment of it like she was the victim."

My stomach constricted and roiled. This was beyond horrible. How could she live with such anguish? As if he'd read my mind, Kel said in a gentle voice. "Vee was in shock afterwards. We stayed away from the camp and kept her in a hut, far from people. I'd never seen her like it, so broken, so weak. She tried to end her life in the river one day, after that we never left her alone. She pulled through though." He gave his head one big shake and straightened. "But she only uses her magic on rare occasions now, and only when she's sure the injured one has no distressing emotions within."

"Thank you for telling me." The way she'd blown made more sense now. "That's why Sawyer refused her help." He wanted to protect her.

"Aye, he's got turmoils of his own." He sighed and ran his hands in his hair. "Sorry, not sure I can talk about that one."

"Do you mean his parents' murder during the Great Hunt?"

His face spun to me, bewilderment lining his forehead. "He told ye about it? Himself?"

"Yes." I dragged the word out, uncertain of his reaction.

"Well, strip me naked and roast me on a stick." He chortled. "I never thought I'd see the day." He regarded me with appraisal.

Before I could ask for an explanation, the door opened and shut, the sound echoing among the nocturnal life. Veena went down the path and told us over her shoulder we could go back in, her ever present frown firm on her brow.

Kel sighed, "Veena has to let go of Sawyer, I'm surprised she lasted that long. Stubborn, that's our Vee for ye." He chuckled. "Mind ye she hasn't been waiting patiently."

A lump the size of a thick branch settled in my stomach. "She loves him." That anchored my suspicions. "Does he...?" The words stayed lodged somewhere.

"He's refused her necklace every year, but I think it's finally sunk in he won't ever love her the way she wants him to."

"Because of what just happened?"

"Mmmm, that and more." He sat back and sighed. Sawyer had said something similar earlier, but my mind felt too distracted to try to make sense of it. What had kept my full attention was the undeniable relief I'd felt at hearing Sawyer's refusal, then the sorrow that came afterwards. I'd become one of those girls pining for him. I looked up to the stars to appeal for strength. They were casting their magical light in a velvet sky; my thoughts, my emotions and my whole self felt insignificant below such wondrous beauty.

CHAPTER 18

Dwennon

The camp's familiar hustle and bustle was the best medicine a man could ask for, Dwennon thought while he hobbled among his people scattered in between trees and tents. The weaver was bent over a tapestry depicting animals in a forest, his lifemate an arm's length away was discussing with the other hunters their next hunting ground. As far as he was aware everyone enjoyed their work; it was no surprise every one of them were reliant on their magic. The age-old conundrum of whether the gift shaped one's interests and passions came to mind.

Cries of jubilant laughter preceded a cloud of running children. They twirled around him once, twice, then disappeared behind a brown tent, leaving the air behind them full of smiles and mischief. Dwennon beamed, his heart brimming with the treasures. Even the sky, a blue as intense as the summer flower with its namesake, proclaimed this would be a wonderful day.

The effect of the Essence spell had taken its toll on his ageing body, but two months on Dwennon felt reasonably well. He'd never be as fit as he used to, however, it was a small price to pay to thwart Quentin and Roldan's plans. To while away the days in his sick bed, he'd decided to write a book on how to detect and defeat the Black Arts. So, he'd jotted down the little he did know as well as pouring himself over any memoirs, spells and history books he owned; and those his companions had managed to procure at his request. So far, none of the information he'd gathered came close to the one and only book which, he knew, possessed a thorough knowledge on the subject.

As a precocious and rather bored student, Dwennon had unearthed a rare book on the Black Arts in his tutor's study, hidden under a strong veil spell he had cracked all too easily. For a few nights, he'd sneaked into the office to read it, and had been startled by what it'd revealed.

Every mage in Comraich, whether rich or poor, was taught about Arai (more commonly known as the Leech Emperor), the mage who'd created the Black Arts and had proclaimed himself, under duress, Emperor of the Southern Islands – now part of the Closed Lands – where communities seeking sun and warmth had regrouped. However, the details of what happened were thin and few. The old world and the first years on Newlands were other subjects that also had a lot of blank spots and inconsistencies, and not for one minute had Dwennon believed it was a coincidence, or that the founders were too busy to build a new life to keep detailed records, which was the official explanation. No, there had to be more.

Dwennon had felt smug with self-righteousness after he'd finished reading *Newlands' dark beginnings*, written by Myrddin himself. The whole period of Arai's ascension to power and tyranny had been scribed in detail. How Arai was from Japan, a land from the old world. How, with people preoccupied with establishing new lives in a foreign world, nobody had suspected anything wrong was going on until whispers of slaves, bound with words, working in mines, of people killed at the stroke of a Japanese symbol had reached the Council, situated in Comraich, far too late. Many had perished under his rule.

Along with the Council's decision to have a sole language as they'd failed to eradicate Arai's word spells, Myrddin had explained how he'd vanquished Arai, and hereafter his attempt to destroy any knowledge of the Black Arts. Hence the scarcity of scrolls or books on that period. What had puzzled Dwennon, and had not been in the least mentioned in the memoir, was how Arai had managed to pass through the portal into Newlands, which had held a sophisticated spell preventing anyone with even the smallest whisper of evil to pass through.

At the time of his passing Myrddin had given the memoir to his trusted friend Brayen, who in turn passed it on to his ancestors. Giles, Dwennon's tutor and later friend, had been the sole survivor of this once powerful family. That very same book laid hidden, he hoped, in his old quarters within the Royal Castle, a gift from Giles upon becoming the High Mage. And he needed to find a way to get it back.

Dwennon put a hand over his face, then rubbed the ridge between his eyebrows. His mind tended to dwell over darker things these days, he couldn't shake off the unease. If only Sawyer had made contact.

The sharp clang of metal on metal took his feet to the heat of their smith's wooden hut. Jonus was working on a horseshoe, sweat running down his ruddy face and brawny arms. He gave Dwennon a sharp nod when Dwennon sat on a stool, not far from the fire-pit. The fire popped and crackled, called him. His unblinking gaze did not waver from the flames while their warmth spread over his aching limbs. His heavy body, or was it his essence, felt on the brink of floating away. Soon, his heartbeat was pulsing in tune with the embers and his breathing slowed.

Oblivious to the world around him, Dwennon watched, as calmly as watching the sun rise, the tendrils of reds and yellows morph into white skin, long wavy brown hair and dark eyes: a girl's face. The image receded to show her walking in an unfamiliar place, surrounded by lots of people and strange closed-in carriages with black wheels. In a sudden flicker, the setting dissolved into a dragon sitting on the embers, a dark-timbered house with a slanted roof looming behind it. The dragon's mouth opened wide, shimmered into the thick haze of heat then transformed into a tree, a weeping willow the likes he'd never seen; each of its silver branches reached to the ground in overlapping glimmering waterfalls. By its side, holding her injured arm, knelt the same young woman as she looked furiously at a dark-haired figure standing over her, dagger in hand. The vision stopped as abruptly as it started. He hadn't realised he was on his feet until Jonus cried out, "Dwennon my good man, if ye care for that hair of yers, I'd step back."

Dwennon blinked a few times to clear the trance clouding his mind, took in what was in front of him, then jerked back. He was right by the fire, an arm extended to grab something, something that wasn't there anymore. He swung round and shuffled as fast as he could manage to the safety of his tent, leaving a confused Jonus behind. Heading straight to the chest, which contained his most precious possessions, he rummaged until he recovered from the bottom his old journal, one he hadn't used for a long time. His foresights were far apart and few, he could count on one hand the number of times they'd occurred. All, to some extent, useful, but this one felt very different. None of the others had ever been as vivid or as long. Taking a quill, he settled on a cushion and wrote what he saw starting with the girl's colour of hair and eyes. He made sure not to miss even the simplest of details; premonitions were not set in stone, but they always held some direction, some truth pertaining to the future.

When he'd penned everything down, he tried to make sense of what he'd seen: those strange things around the girl, the lights and foreign clothes. It had happened so fast, and his attention had been centred on the girl he hadn't been able to focus on them for more than a second. He shook his head; this was no place in Newlands. To his knowledge the only plausible theory was – and it was one that shook him to the bones – he'd had a vision of the old world, which proved to be as strange and fascinating as he'd believed it could be. The old world was a subject people always loved to speculate on, especially scholars and younglings. But first, he needed to speak with Kondo who resided in Washima, one of the Closed Lands. He'd recognised their family's emblem and beautiful home.

Under the peaceful ruling of King Cardian he'd had the privilege to travel on the merchant boat venturing the Savage Sea once a year. Only trusted people from the Northern Kingdoms were granted passage by the Head of Council of the Closed Lands. To this day, he'd never forgotten the unpleasant physical and mental assessment required to board the ship. His title of High Mage had neither impressed nor deterred the first mate; he'd received the same treatment as the other travellers. He'd spent months travelling in each Land as an ambassador trying to better the fragile entente between their Kingdoms and rebuild a trust the first Comraich ruler, King Taron, had shattered. He'd lodged for one month at Kondo's guest house, one of the councillors of Washima. They'd formed a friendship that had endured distance and time with the added help of the magical mirrors, a gift from her, they used to communicate.

After he'd recovered from Filius's treachery, she'd invited him to live in Washima fearing for his life. It had been tempting for a short while, but Leanne's undeterred smiles had won out. They'd kept in touch once a year, on the anniversary of the day they met, to celebrate their friendship and discuss mundane as well as political affairs. Dwennon took his mirror out of its hiding place and started the spell. She would be surprised to hear from him three months early he mused, a smile spread on his face at the anticipation of seeing her.

To his shock, Ryuuki, Kondo's grandson, was the one to answer his summon. Like all those years ago when he'd first met him as a young man, he was wearing a cone-shaped hat with a veil covering half of his face. He'd never had the nerve to ask why he had to wear such an inconvenient accessory. The appearance of white teeth was the only sign the man remembered him.

"Well met, Dwennon. It has been a long while."

"Well met, Ryuuki. I must admit I wasn't expecting you, although this is a pleasant surprise. I'm aware I'm contacting your grandmother earlier than our usual meeting and she may be busy, but I must speak with her on an important matter." He smiled to tone down his rudeness, it was their custom to ask about one's health before starting any form of dealings. He knew the man was bright enough to detect the urgency of his plea.

Ryuuki's hat bent down, giving Dwennon a view of the dragon sitting at its highest point. Even through the mirror, he could make out the carved-out scales, the talons and the striking colours. *Such magnificent craftsmanship.* Silence dragged on. His heart seemed to miss a beat before Ryuuki said, "My dear grandmother left us in the depth of the snowing season. I was waiting for the mourning rituals to complete before contacting you. I'm deeply sorry, this must come as a shock to you." Once more he bowed his head.

This was an understatement, he thought, the mirror trembling between his hands. She'd seemed fine when they'd last spoken, this was so sudden. For a long moment he was lost for words; tears sprung to his eyes as he recalled her mischievous face, her witty banter. His voice strained as he conveyed words too insipid to represent the sorrow of his heart, "She will be greatly missed, I am so sorry for your loss. She told me how close you both were." He wiped at his tears.

"You are very kind, thank you." Another bow. "She was a mother to me and a teacher. I miss her and her wisdom, however, she decided it was her time to go." Following the rigorous protocols his family demanded, the young man held himself together: there were no tears slipping past the veil, no tremor in the tone of his voice. "She endured much pain, but refused my healing." He confided. "You know how stubborn she was. She wanted a natural death like grandfather to be reincarnated where he is." Dwennon wasn't sure if that was indeed possible. "I hope her pain wasn't in vain and her wish came true." The hat tipped sideways. Was he reliving her last days? Dwennon sincerely hoped Ryuuki had someone with whom he could crumble if he needed to, regardless of all this pointless decorum. Nobody should repress human emotions for the sake of propriety.

"May she be in peace wherever she is." Dwennon whispered.

"Thank you for your kind words, your friendship meant a lot to her. Her health deteriorated at an alarming rate, and she couldn't bring herself to let you know of her decision. However, she asked me to relay this message, "Until we meet again, old friend." Warm tears made their way down Dwennon's contorted face, it was the last thing they told each other at the end of their conversations. A smile broke despite the grief, she was right, they'd meet again.

Ryuuki had the delicacy to let Dwennon's emotions settle before asking, "You mentioned something urgent?"

Dwennon massaged his head, hoping to take the flaring pain away. "Yes. I need to speak to your family's new head."

"That would be me."

Kondo had disapproved of her son and daughter-in-law's self-indulgent lifestyle and neglect of Ryuuki so much so she'd raised the boy herself. But to go to the extent of dishonouring the family's tradition by making her grandson the head, something far more serious than what he'd been led to believe must have taken place. Pushing his curiosity aside, he related his vision. Ryuuki was quiet for a long time, and Dwennon wished he could see his eyes to get a feel of his thoughts; eyes always betrayed what was in someone's mind if one looked hard enough.

"I must apologise, but there is something I need to verify before we continue." Ryuuki said at last.

"Of course." Dwennon exclaimed. The projected view

changed to that of a ceiling. After putting down the mirror in front of him, he stretched his legs and rubbed a shaking hand over his face. He longed to tell Leanne the sad news, opening his heart to her always made it lighter, less burdened.

"Dwennon?" Ryuuki's voice called from the object. He reached down for it.

"Here." He said while positioning it to show his face.

Ryuuki was holding one of the new and popular inventions a Southerner had created: a piece of glass with the imprint of a girl looking at him.

Dwennon straightened at once, "That's her. But how?"

Ryuuki nodded, "I thought as much. A friend of mine found her weeks ago hurt by the wayside. She seemed confused and unaware of where she was. What is most unsettling was she'd never seen magic of any kind until we found her. I assumed she had been assaulted and her mind had recreated an escape route of sorts, but what you've just told me, that curious place, nothing of the sort is in Newlands." He inclined his head to the side, the veil straight in spite of the angle. "I can only deduce she is from the Old World." Dwennon could have sworn he'd detected a slight reverence in Ryuuki's voice, and now that he could let himself think about it as a firm possibility, he could see this was something tremendous, life-changing even. How had she arrived here? He asked the same question to the younger man who held a hand up, palm facing him.

"I must ask for your patience. I wish to enquire into this matter further before making assumptions. I remember grandmother telling me about a prophecy regarding an outsider long ago." His voice trailed off, Dwennon could well imagine the distant look in Ryuuki's gaze.

Dwennon wanted to dissect every theory they could come up with, yet he didn't persist on the matter. He replied the only way he could, "I understand. I'll also look into it and keep the mirror close-by if you need to contact me."

After polite goodbyes, he tidied the mirror and went to look for Leanne.

CHAPTER 19

Ryuuki

The magic dissipated, Ryuuki placed the hat on the table next to the mirror, which now reflected pale white skin and green eyes shining like fireflies. Those fell on the glass imprint of Selena, her expression of dismay at his odd request. His cheeks flushed at the memory; the urgency of the task had smothered his shyness. He refocused on the imprint; no need to dwell on what couldn't be changed.

So, she came from the Old World.

No wonder she'd looked as out of place as a cherry tree blooming in winter. A woman in the throes of fate. Not for the first time, an urge to speak with her pulled at his cautious nature. This was curious. Something in him had stirred when he'd healed her. Instinct? Attraction? She was pretty and demure, which was to his way of thinking good attributes. And he'd found himself staring at her from afar or crossing her path on many occasions without conscious thought, like an invisible string had tied itself around their bodies and pushed him towards her. Yet, it felt more than a simple matter of attraction, and the more he thought about it the more he was convinced it sprung from magical origins. Dwennon's vision certainly struck him as a good indication she came to him for a purpose. Which he'd have to figure out. He'd talk to her; this time he couldn't get out of it. Tomorrow though, not today, not yet; he needed to prepare himself.

His mind set, he took out paper, ink and bamboo reed to write the details of Dwennon's vision for himself. He'd always been proud of his sharp memory; a man in his position had a necessity, a duty to remember thousands of names and unending mountains of mostly monotonous facts, but lately he'd become forgetful. It had started with a simple misplaced letter, albeit an important one. However, not but three days ago Zen had come to his rooms with a book Ryuuki had no recollection asking for. That had made for an awkward moment, thankfully Zen had turned it around in his usual merry way. He smiled to himself. The day he'd brought Zen home had been a fortuitous day indeed. Zen possessed the light of a hundred suns, he thought, slowly thawing the ice entrapping his scarred heart.

Rubbing fingers over the bridge of his nose, he felt the tension coiling around his neck and shoulders. At times, he resented the duties his grandmother had brought upon him, he didn't feel either strong enough or worthy of the power to care for his people. He stared at the piece of paper and sighed. Now there was this matter to deal with. He stood up, stretched his legs and back, then went to the open door; disquiet eased as he rested his eyes on his favourite place. On warm days, he loved to work in the gazebo on the lake. No one was allowed in there, so he could borrow nature's strength to do his tasks. He longed to go there right now.

A cool breeze touched his flushed cheeks in a tempting gesture, but his will, his need to find any clue about the prophecy kept his feet still. He went to the bookshelf enclosing his private collection, most of it memoirs and journals from his ancestors, including one of the founders of Newlands, Kyouko Arai. Taking a few select volumes, he sat on a cushion and pushed away all other tasks he should be working on from his mind. This was more pressing. Zen could have helped him read through the thirty odd books, however, he'd been ingrained at a young age to respect and honour his family. Sharing their deepest thoughts and secrets with an outsider – even one he considered a precious friend – would feel like a betrayal to tradition.

The light from outside was waning when he closed the book in frustration. Nothing in there either. Flicking his fingers, candles came to life casting an intimate and warm feeling to the room. As he got up, a tray of dinner left by the sliding panel gleamed in the flickering light. He wasn't in the least bit surprised he'd missed Shina's presence. She was quiet and efficient. He placed the tray on the small table for later, he didn't feel hungry. Before he could make his way to the bookshelf, a swirling dizziness overtook him. He stopped and sat down hard, eyelids tightly closed until it passed. Worry etched his face as it occurred to him this too, along with the lapses of memory, had been happening quite often the past few weeks. It might be a coincidence, but they had begun right after Selena's arrival. Frowning, he shook the uneasy feeling off. It was probably overexertion.

He hadn't intended to keep the girl in the main house; he'd learnt throughout the years to be wary of people in general and strangers especially. He'd wondered at first if she'd used amnesia as a ruse to get close to him. Yet, his unabated intuition told him to keep her close at hand, and it looked like it'd been the right thing to do.

Her arrival had uprooted his peaceful routine and fret his nerves raw. He'd postponed his martial training and mind clearing sessions to think of ways to help Selena get her memories back, and with the workload for the upcoming council meeting, he felt the consequences of those long hours bent over his desk. Now he had to search for the prophecy to top it all.

The sudden vision of a hand holding a round brush over

a piece of parchment ended his ramblings short. The hand swiftly drew an illustration. No, a symbol. As the tip of the brush pushed off the paper, his sight on reality came back. The rapid beat of his heart resonated in his ears. The hand had thick and tanned fingers. Not his own. So why did it feel as though he had been the one holding the brush? *What in the name of the stars is happening to me?*

Was this a vision? The same sort Dwennon had experienced? Ryuuki recalled some ancestors who'd had the sight, yet he'd never had the slightest ability. And now, out of nowhere... This was no coincidence. At once he went to his desk and drew the symbol until it resembled as best as he could what he'd seen. He took in the lines, which appeared to have a pattern. He didn't recognise it. An old language maybe? He rubbed the heels of his hands against his tired eyes. He would show it to Dwennon next time they spoke, he decided while placing the paper in his desk's drawer. He didn't have time for this. Taking another journal, he settled his fraying nerves then perused it while eating a cold, yet delicious, meal. As expected from Shina.

There! A rejuvenating thrill oscillated throughout his stiff body. The candle on the desk flickered with the pattern of his rapid breath, sending excited shadows around the room, which fought against the faint dawn light seeping through the panels. Hands firm on the sides of the yellow pages, he read it once more:

> As our young world rages,
> Cries and thrashes under its ill fate,
> An outsider of our own,
> Twice in the clench of time,
> Bound by an unbidden path,
> Will tip the scales,
> The stars willing,

Towards redemption.

Ryuuki read it to the point he could close his eyes and project the lines word for word, the invisible ink imprinted in his mind. His grandmother had shown him the prophecy in one of his history lessons. They'd reflected, speculated and argued about its meaning. She'd always loved a good puzzle, he smiled. The thought spread warmth throughout his numb heart inundating the ache of his loss. Like her, he'd assumed the outsider was someone from the hostile Northern Kingdoms of Newlands.

Fleeing from prosecution, their ancestors had arrived at the foot of the cold mountains up North; the land was vast and abundant with trees and fertile soil to accommodate their numbers. In time, the harsh winters had prompted the communities acclimatised to warmer weather to emigrate further South, beyond the boundaries of the Blood Desert. Then, Myrddin decided to end his life. Nobody knew for sure how old he'd been.

What ensued was a political coup by none other than his most gifted grandson Taron who'd been biding his time, it emerged, to reveal his true nature. Some scholars speculated he'd been the one to persuade his grandfather to breathe his last, if not murdered him. Ryuuki couldn't fault their assumptions. Contrary to Myrddin who had been benevolent and charitable, most of his ancestors had proved nothing but cruel and self-serving.

Failing to be selected to replace Myrddin on the High Council of Newlands, Taron built an army of his own under cover. At the same time, he used lies and treachery to turn the Northern councillors against each other, weakening their close bonds. He attacked and conquered the two biggest provinces, Comraich and Tuath, before declaring himself King of Comraich. The other smaller provinces and their councillors surrendered all powers one by one, unable to rival his army.

The Southern councillors were no fools; they knew a man

like Taron would never be satisfied until he ruled the whole of Newlands. So, they gathered their most powerful mages and scholars to discuss the best way to keep the king and his army at bay. The Blood Desert, an inhospitable landmass of thousands of miles of sand and rocks, worked as a natural barrier from the North. Their vulnerability, they all agreed, was the vast expense of shores; most of them left to the wilderness their population was so low. But to get to these shores, Taron's army needed to cross seas and oceans. The solution came on a blustering day when the waves took down trees with their sheer strength. For months, they crafted, then learnt to master how to create and control storms. The spell that summoned the waters to unleash the magnitude of a hundred storms was cast in the middle of the seas and oceans. As a precaution, they invented another spell which could detect any bad intentions coming off a person. If they'd survived the storms, whomever dared to cross the waters with sinister or evil inclinations would meet an unpredictable, yet assured death before they could so much as put a toe on the shores. Unnecessary to say, those spells had kept their Lands safe for more than two hundred years, earning them the name of Closed Lands.

Northerners were feared and despised, and the butt of many rude jokes. Most people imagined them as barbaric and uncivilised outsiders. Ryuuki knew better and felt sorry for their oppressed population, that's why he'd assumed at first Selena was one of them. However, she gave the word outsider a whole new meaning, and to his surprise, one he didn't fear at all. On the contrary, he was bursting with questions about this faraway land, where his ancestors had lived so many centuries ago. The sentence "Twice in the clench of time" caught his attention. Did she travel in time? Was that even possible? Only last month he would have considered it impossible, even absurd. But now... Anyway, why would she need to travel in time to come to their world? His head was throbbing in tune to the din of crickets. There was only one way to find out: more research. But first, he needed to sleep. Marking the page, he left the book on his desk, then trudged across to his bed, dropping pieces of clothing along the way. He was asleep the moment his head touched the pillow.

* * *

The sun, its blazing heat uncommon for that time of year, projected shadows on Ryuuki's immobile form sitting under an elm, in the ritual of mind clearing. Various thoughts and images floated in his mind, not unlike clouds in the sky: some see-through and unassuming while others rolled and flailed their dark and dense masses. The latter had made a period of his life a living nightmare; short fitful nights and migraine-filled days taking his carefully arranged routine apart at the seams. It had taken time and mental fortitude to accept what was to be. He understood that now, no point in dwelling on what could never become.

Regulating his breathing in long and slow flows, he contemplated every single thought or feeling, accepting the good as well as the bad. The air passed through his lips in a faint whisper whilst he imagined blowing those lingering black clouds away, leaving a clear blue sky in their stead.

Thirst beckoned. He opened his eyes to a placid pond mirroring the blue sky he craved for. For the first time in years, the view failed to appease his troubled mind. The stars only knew he needed a restful sleep. He grabbed a pitcher set in a tall pot filled with spelled ice that stayed frozen, served himself a fresh drink of unsweetened green tea, then drank a glassful in one go. The coolness caused a sharp but transient headache on top of the one he already had. He sighed. No point in pretending not to notice the one black cloud he'd failed to embrace, and which was producing waves of unpleasant feelings.

I must talk to Selena. Then it can all be sorted out and I'll be back to my old self. He'd known without a shadow of a doubt the cause of his unrest was the prospect of talking to a stranger, a female stranger to be precise. Yet, for days he'd pretended it could wait, his duties and research more pressing, and the sleeplessness and headaches grew to the point they never stopped. He stood up on limber legs and put his hands on his hips. He could speak to officials, people ruling Lands without getting anxious, he wouldn't let a young woman distress him so.

Mei's face flashed unwelcome in his mind. Her lovely brown eyes wide as she took in his uncovered face. The horror and fear reflected in them. He rubbed his temples at the memory, wishing it away. Even one as power hungry as she was had run away, resulting in the failure of his sole engagement. Word amongst the rich and influential had propagated like the wildfires burning in Yoruba right now. Black vicious words about him; evil eyes. No decent person could ever have eyes the yellow and red of a burning hell. It's funny, he mused, how fear brought back up utterances of a long-repudiated religion none knew well, let alone believed in. Yet, he'd been likened to the mythical Satan as a sixteen-year-old.

Suffice to say, any other engagement set forward by his grandmother had been met with polite yet firm refusals. Embarrassing as it was, this occurrence was the root of his shyness and social failings with women, the more attractive they were the worst the anxiety. A serious blow to any boy's self-esteem certainly, traumatic for one having lived a sheltered life, who'd yet to come to terms with his strange eyes. He couldn't blame his grandmother for trying; he understood now how she'd believed finding him a wife at a young age would be easier.

After the incident, the mystery of his hat was mystery no more. Rumours, tales of the Councillor's grandson carried to the deepest and most remote parts of the Closed Lands. He could have removed his hat then, what was the point in wearing it anymore? Even his grandmother, the one who'd forced him to put it on, had admitted it was futile. Despite the thousands of tears he'd shed over the hat, of the hate he'd felt time and time again, in the end he refused to part with it. It became his shield and weapon all at once. Nobody could see the shame, the bitterness, the hurt. Their attitude changed from curious to fearful. Let them wonder if he'd become as evil as his ancestor. The stars shone on him the day he met Zen. His sunny personality and non-judgemental nature had helped melt some of his cynical beliefs.

Sometimes he would wake up, bright-eyed, a hopeful outlook on life, only to have his insides twist and turn with terror the moment he attempted to leave the main house without his hat. But what if he was overthinking things and letting the fear win over common sense? Maybe people would accept him like Zen and Shina had, see past the multicoloured eyes and realise, really realise, he'd never done anything mean and terrible in his life. That he'd rather die than endanger his people. What would Selena say if she saw his face? Was her world as superstitious as his? His curiosity about the old world was the final incentive he needed; setting his hat on his head with absentminded hands he strode to the house with resolute steps.

CHAPTER 20

Selena

Bento box in hand, I strolled down a gravel path surrounded by a palate of colours: blooming shrubs on one side; irises, lilies and daffodils, which I was pretty sure only bloomed in spring, on the other. Japanese maples and different types of conifers of all sizes and shapes were interspaced within a lawn of springy clover. An artist could spend a lifetime painting it and still feel that urge to put it on canvass one more time. But since I wasn't, I took in the beauty of it all and let it soak into me. It was strange to find this peace within myself without the help of a book.

Having lived all my life in London – Hyde park had nothing on this – the healing powers of nature had taken me by pleasant surprise. I made sure to spend time in this oriental oasis every day. Most flowers were still in full bloom thanks to the Indian summer Washima was experiencing, not that they called it that way anyway. I glanced at the daffodils, and possibly magic too. The change in weather had Shina hot and bothered; she'd grumble at least once a day "it didn't used to be that way" or "what was the world coming to if you couldn't rely on the seasons." "By the way it's going, we'll soon have winter in summer." She'd thrown the bitter words over in my direction, one day, then had disappeared leaving a trail of dissatisfaction. Zen had clarified the weather patterns had taken a turn for the worst the past ten years, with extreme heat in the North of Yoruba and Washima over the spring and summer months as well as violent storms – which sounded like hurricanes – in the islands, amongst other terrifying things. Once or twice I'd almost let it slip my world was the same, although I doubted the small population in Newlands of just over forty million was at fault.

The gardens, like the rest of the grounds, were an amalgam of Chinese and Japanese design. However, magical implements like the waterproof and everlasting magical lights ensconced in little stone shrine-looking houses were scattered here and there. I usually spent my lunch break with Zen, but he was out on one of his errands, so I decided to eat outside and enjoy the warmth of the day. Before rounding a corner, I caught sight of a ginger tail peeking out of a black plant with fluffy looking white flowers. I bent down low walking on tip toes towards my target. I'd spotted him occasionally, but so far, my attempts at making friends had failed.

The tail flicked once, then disappeared the moment I reached the plant. *Shoot!* I stretched up in a huff, bumping into something in the process. The surprise impact seemed to short-circuit my brain as well as make me lose balance. Well, it was the only explanation I could find for my actions. Instead of letting go of the bento at my imminent fall, I held on to it for dear life, eyes closed as I felt my body fall towards the ground. My meeting with said ground was stopped, thank God, by two arms catching me a moment before I touched the gravel. Somebody's body was pressed hard on mine. My eyes opened in surprise, then my mouth followed suit when I looked into green eyes so intense, they seemed to be lit up from inside.

"How beautiful!" The words left my lips before my brain registered whom they belonged to. The green darkened to a deep purple. I knew I shouldn't stare but I was transfixed, under their swirling spell. Only when he straightened and we stepped apart, did I take any notice of his face, a youngish face looking chagrined. I'd wondered many times what he looked like underneath that hat and wasn't disappointed.

He was good looking in a delicate Japanese kind of way, almost feminine: features thin and appealing. He had small slanted eyes and a skin so white the sun seemed to reflect off him. In contrast, his hair was a black that could swallow the darkest of night. I blinked at the sight. He seemed equally lost on what to do. We both stood staring at each other as still as the animal statues dotted around us. A loud meow broke the spell, I looked sideways at the culprit. Not a second later the master darted for his hat, which had fallen behind me, and placed it on his head. His hands were shaking. I wanted to tell him he didn't need to wear it in my presence, but I was a mere servant in his household, and I understood why he'd feel uncomfortable around me.

Placing himself in front of me, he bowed his top body low. "I'm deeply sorry. I do hope you are unharmed." His voice cast a trail of shivers from ears to toes, which curled in my soft silk slippers. I flushed at the way it affected me, and now I'd seen the man behind the voice I loved it even more. *How embarrassing!*

Mentally giving myself a slap, I performed an even lower bow to show deference, and babbled on, a sure sign of my nervousness. "I'm the one at fault, I was crouching down to see the cat. You couldn't have seen me until the last second. I'm sorry, I should have been more careful." He was nodding his head, silent. Was he going to assign me somewhere else? I was sure some Lords punished their servants for less. From the little I had gathered about him, he seemed fair and kind, but I'd seen his eyes; he might decide to be rid of me after all. Once again silence fell between us. I shifted on my feet and glanced down at my bento still resting within my arms. How could I leave? Should I wait for him to dismiss me? I stifled a groan, I wasn't used to this silly hierarchical etiquette.

"Actually," he cleared his throat. "I was on my way to speak with you."

My body froze while my mind ran as fast as a cheetah on speed. Had I done something wrong? "Are you on your midday respite?" he continued, oblivious to my mental turmoil. I nodded. "Well, let's find a quiet place, I'll have Shina bring my meal over." He made to walk away but wheeled round as though struck hard. "That is, if you don't mind eating with me." I shook my head furiously regardless of my panicked heart yelling "I do." I was scared crazy, but somehow saying no to my employer didn't seem like the right thing to do in this case. There was no union of any sort helping me here, only my poor useless wits; I just hoped I could stay here until I understood what to do with myself.

We sat down on the clover grass under a Japanese maple. A small breeze swayed a sprinkle of dapples around us like an old-fashioned disco ball. It was strange to think I couldn't share this simple observation with the present company. My gaze went to the red stone pendant swinging on his chest as he set his bowls on the soft rug. To the unknowing person it looked like a normal stone, lovely and expensive, but normal. However, not five minutes ago I'd had the perfect example that appearances could be deceiving, even more so in this world. As we'd walked, he had taken the pendant to his mouth and spoken to Shina as though on a walkie talkie. It clearly worked. I looked on, impressed at the meal spread out in front of us. I was very quickly becoming enraptured by all things magic and a bit jealous if I was being honest. How would it feel to have magic of my own?

We ate in silence for a while until I couldn't stand the sight of his struggles to eat: the wind was catching his veil which kept getting entangled with the chopsticks.

I took a long, deep breath, then in a wavering voice said, "You don't need to wear your hat if it's causing you trouble." I shrugged my shoulders, an act clashing with my cherry red cheeks. "I've already seen you without it. And Zen said you don't wear it with him and Shina…" I trailed off. Eyes glued to my lap. *I hope I didn't affront him.* Crickets and cicadas were suddenly louder, I concentrated on their calls trying to ignore as best as I could the silent figure next to me. Movements in my peripheral vision. The master placed the big hat on the floor by his side, his cheeks held a rosy tinge to my surprise. Then it dawned on me, I was probably one of the few people he could talk to without the stupid hat. "Thank you." he said, "It's awkward to eat with it."

I sighed with relief. "Is it heavy?"

"No," he lifted his currently light blue eyes to meet mine and lowered them almost at once. "It's made of spelled bamboo. There's a well-known bamboo craftsman living in the village nearby; he can make almost anything with the plant, it is remarkable. He made the hat as light as a strand of grass."

"May I?" I lifted a hand, my scientific brain clicking into action; this was something I needed to check with my own hands.

The question seemed to take him aback for he asked his eyes as big as rice buns. "You wish to hold my hat?"

"Yes, if that's all right." After a slight shake of his head, he picked it up and placed it in my outreaching hand. My vision and sense of touch contradicted with one another. I closed my eyes and opened them again. It took me a moment to accept the absence of a weight my brain had anticipated. *Amazing.*

I gave it back unable to express my feelings. Orange eyes watched me in a contemplative way, then stared at his bowl. *Shoot!* I couldn't have made it any more obvious I didn't belong here. He took a breath, intent firm on his face, but let it out while his hand put his chopsticks down. The wait was excruciating, but I managed to eat in spite of my knotted stomach. *Should I say something?* I kept catching glances of his ever-changing irises. Far from scaring me off, I had the urge to move closer to him and take a proper look at them. How many colours did they change into? I'd yet to see a normal one, even the blue I'd glimpsed held an unnatural glint. He caught me staring and I adverted my gaze afraid to offend him.

He sighed. "I must apologise, outside my affairs I'm afraid I am a poor conversationalist." Well, we were both in that boat.

Time to end the torture. I swallowed. "You wanted to talk to me about something?" His position shifted and his face became resolute, eyes a deep purple.

"That's right. I will be forward if I may." It wasn't a question, but I nodded nonetheless, his face was dead serious as his eyes bore into me. "Are you from another world?"

I blinked, taking in his question and repeated each word twice in my sluggish brain before I was sure I had understood it right. My ears felt awfully hot; it might have been because my heart seemed to have jumped in my throat. Unsure on how to respond, I edged, "What gave you that impression?" I did not mean to squeak like that.

He frowned, not impressed with my evasiveness, then his head rose sharply as though a thought had just occurred to him. "Regardless of your answer," his words were slow, tentative. "I want you to know you are safe here. I swear it upon my honour." He added, which I mused was a big deal for these people.

I contemplated my options for a while. I could keep up with the present charade, but the lies were getting heavy and uncomfortable, especially since I was getting closer to Zen. And it was becoming difficult to hide the plain wonder I was feeling every time I had a new magical experience. Only yesterday I nearly screamed like the Harry Potter nerd that I was, when I saw dishes washing themselves in the kitchen while Shina was chopping vegetables. I lassoed my straying mind and brought it back to the present conversation. I could tell him the truth. He wouldn't have brought this up if he didn't have an inkling, or worse maybe he could read minds to a point. A cool sensation cleared my head at once, and the decision was made.

"I appreciate everything you have done for me: my arm, my

job..."

"Job?"

I caught a deep breath and let it slide through my nose in a slow motion. "It means work where I come from. As you said, I'm from another world." No reaction, just the same hard stare. Apprehension made me blurt, "I'm sorry I lied, it's just..." I thought none of you would believe me, that, or take me for a nutcase.

"You don't need to justify yourself on this account. I understand all too well." A hesitant smile escaped his thin mouth. Yes, of course he would, and right then I felt a kind of bond between us. He fell silent, lost in his own thoughts. I watched fascinated by the range of colours emanating from his eyes, it felt like watching a very bright and flickering video game, hypnotic yet dizzying. Those ever-changing eyes were looking at me right then, but I couldn't lower mine in spite of the courtesy I needed to defer. His head bent to the side as he inspected me, a line forming right in the middle of his eyebrows.

"We have lots to discuss regarding your situation. I'll summon Zen and Shina to my rooms." He said getting up in a smooth and elegant manner before talking in his pendant. He reached forward with one hand to take mine, then lifted me up as if I was as delicate as a flower at the end of its life. *I could get used to this.* He wasn't tall without his hat, only a few inches more than me. "But first, if I may?" he said while we made our way back then paused, so long I wondered if he'd forgotten what he wanted to say. I craned my head towards him.

He threw a furtive look at me, his cheeks growing pink and stuttered. "Why... why are you not... I mean, you don't seem... scared or unsettled by my eyes." His fingers were playing with the veil of the hat in his arms, he looked everywhere but at me. "Is this something normal in your world?" I couldn't fail to hear the hope in his voice, and something pulled at my heart. This man, this grown, intelligent man who had been branded like a pariah still craved to belong, to be as normal as everybody else.

"Well, I wouldn't say it's normal per se," I edged. "But lots of people dye their hair all kinds of colours, even rainbows; or they have tattoos on their skin, and piercings, they're like earrings you put on various parts of the body." Some interesting places too, but no way in heck would I tell him so.

"I find that… curious, for lack of a better word."

"How so? Back home they are so many of us, lots of people crave to stand out and be different in their own unique ways."

He nodded, "Things are different in the Closed Lands. Our magical abilities are unique to each individual, it's rare to have two mages sharing the same abilities as well as power. Yet, we thrive as a group. We have been ingrained since childhood to temper this individuality, to use it only for the good of our community, our Lands, not for personal advancement. You'll find out soon enough, people are suspicious of those who look or dress differently. Including these." he waved his hand in front of his face. "However, I do not blame them. We are all wary of curses, of the Black Arts. And for good reason. I guess you heard the rumours of my infamous ancestor?" I raked my teeth on my bottom lip, then nodded. No point in denying it. "Anyway, I can't fault them for their fear, they do look intimidating."

I did not like the bleakness dimming his presently brown eyes. Following an impulse from God knew where, I said, "For all that it's worth, I think they're beautiful." He stopped in his tracks, his features all rigid while a deep pink flooded his face and neck, a pink very similar to the one of his irises. I faced away embarrassed at my brazenness.

"Thank you, Selena." He walked on, but not before I caught sight of a smile.

I caught up to him, eager to change the subject. "I'm having a hard time believing all this hocus pocus. Curses, prophecies and all of that. Surely, they can't be real, right? Zen said there was no religion in your world, but in mine they are associated to heaven and hell, so technically they shouldn't exist here…?"

I stopped at the funny way he was looking at me.

"The absence of religion notwithstanding, they do exist. That's how I found out you were from another world." His lips pursed.

"What?"

"There's a prophecy about you."

"What?" My feet stopped as I watched him step up the walkway. This was the stuff of stories and far away myths and fairy tales. After putting his indoor slippers on, he turned around and said, "Come. There's a lot you need to learn."

Curiosity battled with disbelief. A prophecy about me, just a normal girl. But then again, my situation was worthy of a fantasy book, I couldn't fool myself any longer. My life was no longer normal. Why did I have to find that book? Was this fate? Had it been decided in spite of me long ago? I looked at the man that hopefully held all the answers and followed him inside.

* * *

Zen's half hanging mouth would have been very funny if it wasn't for the fact my mind was still reeling from my own shock.

"You're from the old world?" His voice rose to an impressive high.

I gave a tentative smile, not sure if he was freaked out. "It would appear so. Well, if this old world is really my own. I'm not from your world, but I don't know," I paused. "My one hasn't got magic of any form that I know of, so I'm not sure it's really the one you think of." I shrugged.

Zen's mouth widened in an impressive smile. "That's just… amazing, incredible." He was now on his knees, waving his hands while talking. My comment had clearly passed him by. "I've always wondered how it is, you'll have to –"

The master lifted a hand to make him stop. "In normal

circumstances I would be cautious to make quick judgement, however, on this occasion I've got sufficient proof." That got everyone's attention, and once again we all waited, silent, for the master to speak. "A few days ago, I spoke with an old friend of my grandmother." He glanced at Shina. "Do you remember Dwennon?"

"Yes, a good man for a Northerner." She said. My eyebrows rose. Quite the compliment, Shina didn't hide her hatred of Northerners in the least.

"He'd just had a vision of a young woman in a strange world before seeing this house. When I showed him your imprint, he recognised you instantly." So that's why he asked for it. I'd wondered if all his staff had to have one done.

"Right, if what you're saying is true, Earth, the planet I'm from, is what you call the old world. Did you all live there before? Where is Newlands anyway?" I caught the other questions I had by tightening my lips.

The master inclined his head. "Let me start from the beginning. Our ancestors lived on Earth many centuries past. Facts are sparse for that period. All I know is that most people couldn't use magic. Our kind was feared to the point of hysteria, even hunted." I nodded. That would be the witch hunts. "The most powerful mages convened to find a solution to the massacre. As preposterous as it sounds, they decided the best solution was to create a new world, one that would only welcome magical users. There's no records on how they could achieve such a feat, however –"

"Wait!" I interrupted, "Are you saying they made a new planet? With magic?"

He inclined his head. "That would require a tremendous amount of magic, but Myrddin, one of those mages I mentioned, was the most powerful mage ever to live." I grabbed for the cup of tea next to me. I needed a shot of vodka, or two, but you couldn't be too choosy in these situations. I rolled the flavour over my tongue: chamomile. Guess Shina knew I would need its calming effect. While I drank the master continued. "They then made a portal, the Dyads, for people to go into Newlands. It's situated somewhere in Comraich, one of the Northern Kingdoms. Again, it's unclear how mages learnt of its existence and how to open or close it. I was under the assumption it couldn't be used anymore." His eyes narrowed. "But now I wonder. Is it how you arrived in Newlands?"

I shook my head. "No, I didn't go anywhere, something brought me here. I can show you."

Surprise and eagerness made the master's face even younger. "You've got it here?"

"In my room. I'll go and get it now." I said while standing up, and doing just that.

When I came back into the room, all three pairs of eyes followed the book I was carrying. I handed it to the master who carefully placed on his lap. "I can feel its magic, but how is that possible?" He exclaimed, then leafed through it, shaking his head. "I don't know this language." Zen came over to look over his shoulder, then to my surprise Shina did the same.

"The old mistress did say our ancestors used a different language before it was prohibited." She said, her usual frown even deeper while in thought.

"You are correct. I've always wondered why." The master muttered, then he looked up at me. "What do you call this language?"

"Well, in English it's called Japanese, but Japanese people call it nihongo."

His eyes turned a bright blue suddenly. "Would their land be called Nihon by any chance?"

I nodded, "Yes, it's a country on the East Asian continent on Earth."

The master flashed a quick smile at Shina, which she did not return, however, you couldn't miss the interest in those brown eyes. "One of my ancestors claimed my line, and Shina's, came from Nihon in the old world."

"You do have the same features as Japanese people." I said and swallowed hard. "Guess this proves Earth is your old world then.' I looked at the old book. What I would really like to know is how granddad procured it.

Or if he knew what it was.

CHAPTER 21

Faylinn

We endured three days of sullen moods before relenting to Sawyer's continual insistence he was fit enough to walk. On the one condition he used the crutches Kel and I had fashioned for him during his enforced rest. While sanding and sealing the wood to a shiny finish, I infused them with my gift to take some of the pain away while he used them. I was no healer, but wounds like these had to be painful despite what he said. I hoped it would work. I was uncertain whether I communicated with the essence of the wood, like I did with live trees or if I imbued the wood with my magic.

Haelan would know. I couldn't wait to tell him about my newfound tricks. He was the most powerful and knowledgeable mage I'd ever met, though from what I'd perceived Dwennon was a close second. I remembered him spending days closeted in our library bent over Myrddin's books on magic which had been passed down through generations of Wymers. I doubted the king knew or cared we had them in our possession. Roldan would. It was lucky grandfather had given them to Haelan before his death. From what I'd heard, Haelan had been a precocious child interested in everything and anything: the ideal first son. Even though he was the son of father's first wife, mother had brought him up with all the love he deserved. I loved all my siblings dearly, but Haelan had a special place in my heart; he was my best friend as much as my brother. He'd sneaked to my rooms at the castle on occasion, bringing news of family and friends left behind. Like me, he was ordered by the king to stay at Court, though his spells of time were shorter and only once a year. To keep an eye on him and size him up Haelan believed. That's what the king did; kept his enemies close, and I often wondered if he had an inkling of Haelan's abilities. Most likely he was testing his loyalty.

The next few weeks went by in sombre silence, we kept short days blaming it on Sawyer's slow pace because it was easier than admitting we were all in low spirits, and that the broken routine was a constant painful reminder of Jolis's absence. To make the grief bearable, I spent our walks thinking about my family and imagining their faces when I arrived home. In the evenings, I spelled my bow and arrows and that of my companions when they were sleeping. I was unsure if the spell had to be cast straight away or if it would work after days or even weeks, but it was worth a try. As a test, I cast the spell every inch along the shaft on some of them, while using it only once on others; each time putting my heart and soul into the invocation. It was a tedious job and sapped much needed energy, and I wasn't even sure if my efforts would be fruitful, but hope's a gift to hold dear.

Gradually, the oaks and beeches grew into evergreens, their pungent needles casting a heavy scent to the cool wind. The never-ending forests were now slashed by long stretches of meadows. To our right, the Sky Mountains – their peaks shrouded in thick grey clouds – were the motivation I needed to keep going. We'd journeyed two thirds of the way. Autumn had fallen upon us this past week, the air was crisp, the sunlight golden. My body cosy and warm under my borrowed cloak, I was grateful once more fate had led me to the wanderers.

When our supplies dwindled leaving us with only the meat we'd caught, we decided to stay with wanderers living nearby. Our trail had brought us to the edge of a lake so wide its opposite bank was barely visible. Even the sun couldn't filter through the deep, black water. I repressed the longing for a good soak. *It's probably too cold anyway.* After weaving in and out of the forest for hours Kel came to a stop, Blaith waiting by his side, her tongue lolling out. After Sawyer took the protection spell down to let us pass, grass strewn with mud became a clear dirt path. I looked back impressed; I hadn't been able to see it from the other side. "They must have a strong mage." I said, and they nodded in unison.

"Merlo is a bit of a ..." Kel made a face, "character, let's say, but he's strong."

"Dwennon's more powerful." mumbled Sawyer, and Kel chortled. I raised my eyebrow at him, and he bent down to whisper in my ear. "Teacher's pet." I laughed. Sawyer glared at him, then walked ahead of us. Jolis had left a huge gap in the group, and my heart squeezed with bittersweet delight at those moments of lightness.

"Have you been here before?" I asked Kel as we passed a huge, red-barked tree, but before he could reply we were surrounded, or assaulted I wasn't too sure which, by screaming blond and red heads. The answer would be yes. Sawyer and Kel greeted the children with good hearted taps on the heads, Blaith licked a few faces, even Veena was smiling and bending to talk to them. I stayed back, feeling a little envious. They looked at home. I wondered if each group was different or if one wanderer could fit in and be welcome in all of them. The children herded us to the sharing fire. The camp layout was the same as their one except for the type of trees and the bright green moss covering the ground in-between tents. As we approached the flap from the biggest tent lifted to reveal an old man in a striking orange tunic and yellow trousers, his white hair fell in little braids just under his chin.

My eyes were transfixed on whom I assumed was Merlo.

"Sawyer, my good lad." Merlo said as he hugged him and tapped his backside. Thinking the old man had mis-reached – he was on the short side – I looked at Sawyer, amused, but he kept his eyes down while he ground out a hello. My eyebrows shot up when Merlo performed the exact same greeting with Kel. To my side, Veena was trying very hard not to laugh. After Merlo welcomed her from afar, interesting, his eyes rested on me.

"A new warrior in training?" When he saw my hesitation, he looked at Sawyer, who gave a slight shake of his head. Merlo's expression was one of curiosity before he smiled and opened his arms in a grand gesture. "Welcome, welcome to our humble group. Angelina, lass, show them to my tent. Ye can make yerselves comfortable and stay the night." When Sawyer started to object, he added. "I insist, I'll make other arrangements for myself." He flicked his hand towards his tent, then went to speak to someone else. Sawyer shrugged his shoulders at Kel's questioning eyes, then both made their way to the tent, Veena close by. Were we all sharing? Obviously, these wanderers had no qualms about propriety. I followed them. Outdoors, indoors, it wasn't much different.

❉ ❉ ❉

After Angelina a pretty, red-haired woman, rearranged the inside of the tent to our needs – the men's beds separated from the women's by a flimsy sheet – Veena and I noticed what appeared to be a washing room behind another flap. Wooden planks covered the ground of the partition, a small metal tub was set to the back, wooden barrels full of water beside it.

Veena put a hand in and grinned, "Hot water. Now that's a gift I wouldn't mind having on missions." I knew the feeling, we'd had to wash ourselves in river water, not exactly pleasant. She stiffened at my returned smile and frowned. "My turn first."

I crossed my arms over my chest. "I don't mind, but I want you to stop with the attitude. Unless I'm mistaken, I have done nothing wrong to you except being born in a social class you despise. And I wish you'd start considering me as a person and not a title." Locked in a staring contest, I waited for an answer, or at least some type of gesture. At last, she faced away from me and said, "Water's getting cold." My fists closed so tight they hurt; I wasn't sure why I kept trying, it was a lost cause after all.

"Fine." I snapped and left the room. My head swimming with thoughts, thoughts I didn't want to broach right now, I waited for my turn by the small indoors fire. Glancing outside, my eyes met Sawyer's, his expression unreadable. He looked away at once. Strange, I'd felt his gaze on me a lot lately. Maybe this was about the oak incident from last time, he'd had plenty of time mulling over it. The need to speak to him about it had sprung upon me many times since his recovery, but each time I'd failed to know how to start a conversation about something so private and, quite frankly, still bewildering. Maybe that's what those looks were, he's waiting for me to make the first step. With renewed vigour, I promised to myself to tell them all next time we were alone.

After lunch everyone, bar Veena, were gathered around the sharing fire. With a satiated belly, my mind was wandering towards that soft looking bed I'd left my satchel on. Maybe I could rest for a while. We'd agreed to leave early the next day, some extra sleep would be sensible. As I got up and stretched, a blinding light enveloped the whole camp then faded, leaving me momentarily blind. Silence settled among us.

What was that?

When my vision cleared up, I approached Sawyer who was whispering to Merlo, and caught the elder's final words. "... been breached." He then stood on a log and shouted, "Under cover now!" Everyone stood up as one, parents gathering their children, then headed to my left where I assumed was a safe place. This behaviour felt rehearsed. No one made any noise, even their feet were muted by the moss. Had it been put there for such purpose? How often did they have to hide?

My mind reeled at the idea of guards killing innocent and peaceful people for money. I knew King Filius still held wanderers' hunts once a year, but it never had felt more real than right now.

"Where was the breach?" Sawyer asked. Three weathered faces, all elders, turned to him. "About a mile to the South." A white-haired woman pointed her finger. "They'll be upon us soon." Frowning, Sawyer took my arm and pulled me far away from the fire and took me to where Kel was crouching with Blaith behind a stack of logs next to the healer's tent. "Too late to retreat." He looked grim as on par with his words I heard shouting and crying. Some of the wanderers were walking back to the fire, heads down, looking scared and defeated. Tall burly men wearing the Royal insignia held their swords outstretched.

Royal guards.

My hands knitted together in a painful grip; I glanced up to see Kel and Sawyer sharing a pregnant look. Finally, when the wanderers they'd caught were settled on the ground, a blond guard with a red dragon sewed on the left side of his tunic, a commander, dragged Veena, her hands tied to her back, next to Merlo by the fire.

"Damn." Kel whispered to my right. I dared a glance at Sawyer whose eyes were taking in everything, probably searching for a solution. He pursed his lips and swore. "We're outnumbered. I can cast a spell to create a commotion, and if the stars wish it some can escape, but..." He faced Kel, "When the spell's in place, ye take Faylinn and run as far away as ye can."

Kel was shaking his head, "No mate. Not leaving ye with all that shite."

"Ye have to take her somewhere safe, if we all stay here then the prince has won. Don't ye see?" His voice was getting too loud, and I shushed them both. I peeked round the logs, nobody had heard a thing.

"I'm not going anywhere." I said with gritted teeth. "Kel and I can shoot at the guards during the commotion; they won't know what's hit them if they think we're someplace else. Can you do that?"

He thought for a moment, nodded, then added, "but ye have to promise if I tell ye to run, ye run, no protest." he paused. "Both of ye. I'll be close behind." Kel and I shared the same grim expression and nodded our acceptance. At that moment, the commander shouted. "We're looking for a Lady named Faylinn, we understand she was taken by force by some of you scum." I gasped. They were here because of me. A sharp guilt stabbed at my soul; I'd caused this. The beautiful children that had been so full of life only this morning were distressed, peaceful men and women taken at sword point. It was all my fault. A warm hand settled on my shaking one, and I bit back a sob.

"Ye're mistaken, she's not here." Merlo was shaking his head.

The commander backhanded him. "Silence, old man. We know she's here." Sawyer and Kel craned their necks towards me frowning, their eyes hard. My throat went too tight to breathe.

"How is it possible?" Kel whispered, Sawyer shook his head, his hand firm on mine to keep me still.

"If you cooperate right now, we'll let you live, if not..." he placed himself behind Veena and held his sword to her throat, another guard mirrored his action with Merlo.

Nobody spoke.

"The more you wait, the more people die." He nodded at the guard next to him. He flicked his sword so fast blood sprayed people crouching on the ground; a dreadful gurgling sound emanated from Merlo, whose body was thrown to the side before the guard grabbed a young man by the hair. I was up past our cover, shouting, "I know where she is," before I'd realised what I was doing. A "no" echoed in my mind, I looked over my shoulder, and mused in a dreamlike state how this was the first time I'd seen Sawyer look so petrified. I smiled at him, trying to convey a reassurance I wasn't feeling in the least and walked to the commander.

Swallowing, I said in a broken wanderer's accent, "I can lead ye to her, but ye have to promise to let my people go." May Myrddin bring me luck, I hoped my plan would work. It wasn't good, but it was all I had.

He scowled, "How do I know you're telling the truth?"

"She is." A dark-haired woman, wearing a blood red cloak over her black tunics, sauntered to where we stood: a Warrior Mage. My legs were shaking. Quentin had spared no expense to find me. Warrior Mages were the highest ranked amongst the guards, endowed with powerful magic befit for war, they could take down a group of men in an instant. How many were there? I cast furtive glances around me alarmed, but couldn't see any more of them. I needed to lead them someplace else. The commander eyed me doubtfully, then said with a gesture of his head, "Go on."

I watched Veena trapped in his arms, her face as pale as the fresh snows of the Sky mountains peeking to our right. I couldn't read the expression on her face. "Promise to let them all go, safe." I added knowing full well the conniving nature of such men. "Starting with her." I pointed at my companion.

He glanced at the Warrior Mage for confirmation and let her go. Veena whispered a "thank ye" as she passed me by. I hoped my group wouldn't follow us, I had enough deaths on my conscience as it was, yet a selfish part wished they'd save me out of this mess. *Pull yourself together, girl!* I wouldn't be a silly damsel in distress. Not anymore.

The commander barked at me, "So? Where is she?"

Stuttering, I pointed to the right of the camp where I knew nobody would be. "Hiding over there."

He shoved me hard on the shoulder, making me lose my balance for an instant. "Take us there."

"Wait!" the Warrior Mage exclaimed. "She's lying." I froze mid-step and kept my head down. My luck, she was a truth reader.

Someone gripped my arm hard, turning me round. The Warrior Mage was inspecting my face, her mouth rising to the side. This didn't look good for me. "Hold her." She directed the commander, then she took a handheld mirror out of her bag. I stared in recognition. My father owned two of those, they were spelled by a long dead Mage to communicate with someone who owned its twin. They were rare and expensive as no Mage in the past hundred years had been born with the ability to spell mirrors. Holding it by the handle, she touched a finger to the glass while muttering something; a purple mist shrouded its circular shape. Quentin's face materialised in a scowl. "I hope this is important Maylard." My body instinctively jerked backwards, but hard muscles prevented me from moving.

"I believe I've found her, your Highness." Her voice didn't hide her satisfaction.

"Show me." The commander pulled me closer while Mage Maylard thrust the mirror close to my face, I watched with disgust Quentin's mouth widen in a wolfish grin. "My dear cousin, so good to see you alive." He waited for a response, but I refused to grovel at him. His eyes were roving over my face and hair with interest. "Do you really believe your little disguise would fool me? I'd recognise you anywhere." With a predatory gaze he chuckled, "Maylard will bring you to me. I can't wait to show you what's in store for you." I bared my teeth at him, short of growling like Blaith, but his attention was already directed to the woman next to me. "I want her with me by morning."

"Understood. What do you want us to do with the wanderers?"

"Kill them all. The less there are of them the better." The mirror dulled, reflecting the satisfied look on Maylard's face. The people closest to us had heard Quentin's last words, and a wave of gasps, whimpers and exclamations spread their fate amongst them. I stared at their terrified faces, tears running down cheeks that should be smiling, not fearing death. I didn't realise my whole body was shaking until the commander ordered me to stop it.

I couldn't.

Emotions, a flood of emotions so strong I couldn't tell them apart, had taken over me. My skin tingled all over. My mind instinctively reached out to the trees around us. But what could they do? It wasn't as if they could up and walk and hit them on their heads. When the commander called for the Fire Mage to come quick, I saw red. The tingle changed into a painful pressure deep inside my soul; voices, thousands of them, called out to me, "We're here, join us." they all repeated. Who? How? I closed my teary eyes the pain was too much. Strings of light appeared in my mind's eye coalescing, shaping into a ball of vibrant green. I touched it with a finger. A loving warmth engulfed me and the pain receding to a trickle, then nothing. My eyes opened physically and metaphorically: I knew what to do.

Lifting my hand, the ground beneath our feet rustled, shook and cracked; huge roots lunged at the guards. Maylard screamed to the commander still holding me as roots climbed up her legs. "Do something!" She hacked at the thick roots with her sword, every cut she made closed itself almost at once. The commander, who had stood frozen behind me, yelped suddenly as he pushed me towards her, then ran. Before he could get very far an arrow struck him in the chest. The sound of creaking roots was deafening, my focus slipped. I took a deep breath and centred my attention where it was needed: I wanted to imprison them all, not kill them. I willed the long boughs of the tallest trees to lower themselves down and form a tightly entwined wall around the camp, but only the trees I was looking at responded. The guards that had evaded the roots bypassed my sorry attempt. Sweat broke out on my forehead. A movement to my right startled me, I jumped back. A blade swished at the place I'd been standing. I flicked my hand at the guard before he could attack me again. A root shot out of the ground right in front of him and struck him in the chest before withdrawing just as fast. I stared frozen.

Chaos reigned around me: screaming and panicked guards were slashing at the roots holding them still while the unaffected wanderers were dodging to run away. "Watch out yer right!" Kel shouted from behind me. I darted to my left without hesitation. Maylard, who had managed to extricate herself, lunged at me with a dagger, I caught her arm inches from my chest. She was strong, but I was stronger thanks to my months of training. I pressed two fingers into her wrist, and she cried out in pain, the dagger embedding itself into the ground. Belatedly remembering my own, I yanked it free from its scabbard as her hands lifted high above her head, her blue eyes narrowed on me. *Damn, she has another gift.* I made to move, but a blue light struck the mage from behind; smoke drifted up from the blackened moss where she'd stood. Shaking my numb brain, I searched for the origin of the attack, then rubbed my eyes hard at my discovery.

It was a trick of the light, it had to be, he couldn't possibly be here. But no matter how much rubbing I did my sight didn't change. Haelan was standing a hundred yards away, smirking at the dumb look on my face. It was then, as he strolled towards me, I realised the battling had stopped: guards wearing my father's insignia, a blue phoenix, were holding Quentin's men at sword point. Where were the roots? Clumps of moss were raised at a funny angle here and there, the only evidence of the roots' part in our defence. Even my partial wall was gone, the boughs once more sweeping up. A few warrior wanderers, weapons in hand, were looking up at the trees with reverence in their eyes. I understood all too well.

The moment Haelan was close enough, he crushed me with his strong arms, murmuring reassurances. Something inside of me broke down then, and I wept unrestrained like the little girl I thought I'd left behind. I felt, for the first time in months, safe. After all tears had dried, and I couldn't ignore the world around me anymore, I let him go but kept an arm around his waist, our hands entwined. I jumped slightly when I saw my companions right next to us. Sawyer's stare fixed on the intimate gesture before meeting my eyes, his were shuttered when he asked, "Ye all right?" I nodded, mortified they'd witnessed my emotional downpour. He exhaled long and hard before thundering. "What ye did was…" His face had turned bright red.

"Reckless, stupid, dumb-witted are the words you're looking for?" Provided my dear brother. Kel burst out laughing and patted me on the head, relief clear on his face. Healan grinned at me. "That's my Fay, all right." He rustled my hair, then scrunched up his nose. "Not too keen on this boyish look of yours."

I raised an eyebrow at his long blond mane at present tamed with a leather string; when free, the curls were so dense they sprang in all directions around his head. "You should talk, sheepy head." I hit him softly with my elbow in the chest and he chuckled. Sawyer was scowling at us, and my eyes fell on Merlo behind him, my mood sobering. Following my gaze, he excused himself and went to the old man, Veena and Kel at his heel. Blaith sniffed Haelan's leg, then followed.

The last of Quentin's guards were laid or carried away where I didn't care to know. I had no sympathy for such people. Wanderers were trickling back into the camp in small groups, the warriors gathered the bodies of their fallen comrades around the fire while families watched, crying in silence. Four of them dead, four deaths that wouldn't have happened if it wasn't for me. I gulped down a sob and squeezed Haelan's hand hard. He seemed to read my mind, as usual. "Their deaths are on Quentin's hands, not yours." I wasn't so sure, but I nodded regardless, it was easier to agree. We moved back to watch their ceremonial dirge, hand in hand. Some of his guards were close to us, their demeanour sombre; I was glad to see friendly faces amongst them. My father had made sure to employ good people, no matter their lineage.

By the time the mourning ceremony ended, the camp was enveloped in shadows, the sky shades of light blues. A chill had descended upon us, and I was grateful to see two women feeding the sharing fire. After the bodies had been swaddled and taken away – Haelan had instructed his men to bury the enemy's casualties far away from the camp – the wanderers dispersed, eyes red, shoulders slumped. The elder woman, whom I assumed had taken the position as first elder, encouraged them on their way in a calm and soothing voice. "Normality will help heal our torn souls." She said, albeit hollow of conviction. Nobody contended her words or burst out in anger at life's unfairness. They looked broken, yet resigned. Their behaviour confirmed what I'd suspected: this wasn't an uncommon occurrence. My heart squeezed painfully when my companions came to sit with me looking torn and mournful once more. I stayed silent, words of comfort escaping me. Our sorrowful party was uninterrupted until Haelan, who had gone to speak with the elders, joined us for supper.

"We'll leave first thing in the morning." He said. I looked up from my plate, catching Sawyer and Kel's startled faces. I hadn't had time to think about what would happen next, of course Haelan would take me home. Would my companions come too?

"Would ye care tell us who ye might be? It's obvious ye two are close, but we've vowed to take Faylinn to her father, and that's what we're going to do." Sawyer said resolution written all over his face. Uh, oh, that little detail had slipped my mind.

Haelan glanced at me in surprise, he hadn't missed the lack of title, then scrutinised them all before replying with a lazy smile. "I beg your pardon, I'm Haelan Wymer, Fay's brother. I'm reassured she was in such good hands and I'm grateful for the support you've shown her. I can't wait to hear how this came about." He shook their hands while they introduced themselves. It felt surreal seeing the two different worlds I'd been living in collide so. By the end of the evening's serious, but nonetheless pleasant, conversation, Sawyer's posture was less tense, he seemed to like my brother I was pleased to notice. It had been decided we would all go as planned to my home and speak to father. Haelan's face had turned a deathly white when I'd related what occurred with Quentin, the delicate details to his ears only.

"Thank the stars you had your wits about you. Quentin though, the wretch, the..." He clenched his fists. "Wait till I get my hands on him." In the dim light his eyes looked black with deadly intent. I'd never seen this side of him, never really believed he had it in him.

Then he smiled ruefully. "I'm the one to blame for their discovery." He sighed, a hand covering his eyes. In that gesture alone I knew he felt responsible for the deaths of those innocent wanderers. "When Sunlark and I realised you weren't at the castle anymore we told father. He sent me to Court early with some silly excuse to the king. When –"

"Wait!" I interrupted. "How did you know I wasn't there anymore?"

"Now don't get mad, Fay." He said looking uncomfortable. He lifted with one hand the necklace around my neck, the one father had given me on my departure to Court. "It's spelled." I opened my mouth in outrage, but he shushed me before lifting a similar one on his chest. "They're twin necklaces; our grandfather, the old king, had them fashioned for his queen. He wanted to be sure she was safe at all times." That shut me up, unsure how to feel about it. "Father took it severely when mother insisted they send you instead of Mara." The corner of his mouth rose in a wistful smile at my dumbfounded expression. "He loves Mara dearly, but he feels closer to you. You're just one of the boys." The others laughed as I swatted him on the head. "Seriously though, he agreed to let you go on the condition mother gave you her necklace, therefore forfeiting her safety in the process. As I was also called to Court on a regular basis, he gave me his." I was left speechless. All those years shut in my misery, I had failed to consider the loss and guilt my parents felt upon sending their child away into the viper's nest.

"What about Quentin?" Kel asked stroking a slumbering Blaith, her whiskers twitching. "How did he find us?"

Haelan stared into the fire for a long moment, the crackling logs filled the silence like a warm blanket. He sighed, "I made an unforgivable mistake in my hurry. When I arrived there, the king had barely noticed your absence," he looked in the distance, his face hardened in disgust. "And the queen said you'd probably ran away with a servant." My mouth made the shape of an o, but it stayed lodged in my throat. "Well, you did a brilliant job at playing the empty-headed companion, so much so they didn't even care about letting us know you'd disappeared."

Just a replaceable subject. Sharp resentment of this forced imprisonment blurred my vision for a second. "Anyway, I became suspicious when Fiona went along with their silly theory, she knew you better than that. I was planning to leave the next day when she slipped a note into my pocket, telling me about your bruises. I was in your room when I contacted father with our mirrors to tell him what I'd learnt, then he gave me the words to see where you were through the pendants."

"Wait," Sawyer interrupted. "Why didn't ye do that in the first place?" I agreed, why lose so much time at Court?

"Father's orders. Through the necklaces' bond I could feel something wasn't right, but that you were alive. I couldn't be sure though; it might have been stolen. You didn't know how special it was, which I can tell from this experience was a gross mistake on our part. We should have trusted you with the knowledge, and for that I am sorry." His eyes searched mine. I squeezed his hand in support and was rewarded by a small smile. "The spell to locate the twin necklace is difficult, the further the person is positioned the more draining it is, so it was a last resort I'm afraid. I'll show you how it works."

He took my necklace and went 100 yards away, placed it on the ground, then came back. Still standing up, he murmured something. A dry noise, like a clap of thunder, resounded. Over us hovered a magnificent blue eagle, it stared at Haelan for a second before flying towards the necklace in two flaps of its wings. Just then the stone set in Haelan's pendant brightened, the air above it shimmered and the image of all of us gathered next to a green tent materialised before him.

Incredible. In a way it was similar to the map I had stolen from the castle. Haelan spoke to the pendant again and the eagle flew high, giving us an overall, if dim, view of the camp. How clever. My companions, wide-eyed, were obviously sharing my sentiment. "I caught sight of you and the wanderers a week's away from here. Unaware to me, one of Quentin's lackeys had been following me to your room and saw everything. I would have been oblivious if it wasn't for Fiona." He grimaced. "I had been foolish enough to leave the door ajar. Anyway, my guts told me I needed to get to you fast. I went back for the guards I'd left in the forest and came for you, checking the pendant when needed."

I fiddled with the helm of my tunic. "How did you get here so fast? And for that matter, how did Quentin's men find us if what you saw was another place?"

"I might have spelled our horses along the way." I opened my mouth to ask what kind of spell exactly made horses run the equivalent of weeks on the road in just one but thought better. I would ask him at another time. "As for Quentin's men," he continued. "In the pendant's image, his lackey saw where you were at that stage, and he couldn't have missed the fact you were with wanderers. I reckon he deployed several troops to search for wanderers living in the area." I frowned, it didn't quite add up, the commander had claimed he knew I was here. Haelan pressed his finger on the stone, and everything vanished. He sat down with a sigh. "I guess I'm still recovering from the last one." Stretching sideways I kissed his cheek and thanked him for his timely rescue, though the words felt neither strong nor sufficient for what I felt.

"Am I forgiven for not finding you fast enough?" he was

smiling, but I knew him too well to misread the signs of uncertainty radiating through him.

"There's nothing to forgive."

He swallowed while nodding his head; his green eyes were shining and mine shedding tears as he reached out and hugged me again.

The others were talking amongst themselves, earnest faces cast in flickering shadows; I studied them, enjoying feeling cosy and safe within Haelan's arms while wondering if the rest of our journey would go smoothly.

CHAPTER 22

Faylinn

Despite being surrounded by a large party of armed men on horseback, I kept glancing at the main road over my shoulder, expecting for trouble to find me once more. Haelan's confidence in our security soon alleviated my misgivings at such a direct defiance against Quentin. My brother was anything but meek and with his weapons' training and powerful gifts I had no doubt of his skills. Our last leg back home went smoother and faster, but it had been a long while since I'd ridden on a horse. By the end of the first week of hard riding my leg muscles and sore bottom were screaming at me, and I was convinced I would never walk straight again. The wanderers were faring as poorly as I was, when asked Kel confirmed their warriors didn't use horses often as they were too conspicuous. I welcomed the pain though, if it meant we would arrive in the safety of my home in good time.

One night after supper, Haelan asked me to show him what I'd learnt from my fighting training, claiming it would help stretch my aches and pains. I wasn't convinced but complied begrudgingly. When we were both spent, me especially, I dragged him to a log away from prying ears and filled him in on my newfound magical abilities.

He whistled as I finished. "I'll have to check in my books if there are records of similar gifts." Even in the dim light of twilight I could capture the bright fervour in his eyes. "This is no mean feat, Fay. That's..." he shook his head. "Astounding."

I snorted. "Nothing compared to what you can do."

"Well," he scratched his beard, a feature all the men were sharing as there was little time to rest let alone shave. "I wouldn't dismiss it, nonetheless. You've got great potential."

I twisted my mouth. "If you say so."

"We'll experiment with it when we're back home, then you can have a good think about what you want to do with it. You're not tied down to that sleazy lot anymore. Father won't send you back... regardless of what King Filius says." He added at my sceptic face.

My fingers fumbled with a leather strap. He was right, I needed to think hard about my future, something I thought I'd lost the right to. It was like the cage I'd been trapped in had opened to many different paths and I didn't know which one to choose. The matter though, would have to wait until the issue with Quentin was dealt with.

As our third week started, the familiar landscape of a valley surrounded by rolling hills of evergreen forest filled my heart to the bursting point with joy. Straining my eyes on the patches of pasture scattered amongst the trees, the white blotches became roaming sheep grazing the long grass. The pungent smell of pine needles mixed with damp soil was redolent with happy memories; even the cold breeze on my face was a welcome sensation. Home was near, I could almost see it from our vantage point.

"If you want a warm bed tonight, get cracking." Haelan shouted and I whooped with laughter as he galloped down the hill. Everyone was in good humour, even Veena was laughing. My chest squeezed with pain as Sawyer's eyes rested on me and he smiled. At first glance he didn't look any different from the day we'd met, but if you looked hard enough you could see that somehow along the way, he'd become more relaxed, less strung-up, lighter I wanted to say. I could feel Veena's eyes scrutinising me. Since that last incident with the Royal guards, she had been less hostile with me, or it might be due to the fact I had an ally in my brother, and a formidable one at that. Still, I couldn't wash away from my mind the longing glances she occasionally cast Sawyer's way. We weren't so different in that regard.

The smile I gave Sawyer felt brittle before I pressed my knees to my horse's flanks. When he took off at a gallop, I secretly hoped the wind of my face would brush away all thoughts but that of home. Haelan gave me an enquiring look as I caught up with him. Despite an age gap of twelve years, we had this strong connection between us, and more often than not, we could read each other's mind. Sunlark jested we were magical twins.

And right on cue, when I was close enough that only I would hear his words, he said, "Good man, that Sawyer." My cheeks burst to flames. "And a good leader at that."

"Mmm hmm." was all I could come up with. Damn him for seeing through my muddled feelings.

"Father would…" I cut him short with a raised hand and glared at him. "Not father's affair." I whispered between my teeth, afraid to be heard, then shoved him in the chest. One thing had become clear on my journey, life was too short: I would choose my own path.

He shrugged, eyes alight from within. "All right, all right firecracker, I shall say no more."

I huffed, then trotted away from him in search of a corner to regain my calm.

❊ ❊ ❊

Late afternoon the uneven clusters of cottages brought tears to my eyes. I'd imagined them in my head so many times it felt unreal seeing them in all their splendour. Sensing my change of mood, Haelan reached out and squeezed my shoulder in support. At the front of our group of riders, I took in the smell of damp grass and of fires burning the autumn's chill. Although our horses were walking at a leisurely pace through the village, their numbers created quite a ruckus. Many curious heads peeked from inside warm cottages to see what was disturbing their peaceful sanctuary. At the sight of Haelan and his men, they rushed out, children in tow, and waved their hands or hats in welcome; my brother greeted them with equal warmth.

Roofs and windows were in good shape, garden walls sturdy, even the roads were well-kept in spite of the abundant rain we got in these parts. I spotted Mrs Pots's Inn, its shutters still a bright yellow to catch the eye of weary travellers she'd told me once. The market square was full of people ambling between the different merchants, their chattering noise didn't hide our approach, every single head craned to look at us. Upon recognition, they too waved and greeted our party. Everyone looked happy and healthy. Pride for my father warmed me up all over, he obviously took great care of his people, and was loved for it. Past the last cottage, the road took a sharp corner, then ascended a steep hill. My hands grew sweaty and slippery against the leather of the reins.

Home was near.

Along the way, I rediscovered familiar woods, its inhabitants shying away from our party, waiting in terror for the noise to subside; fields where sheep and goats were roaming among scattered trees and boulders. At its peak our family manor stood in its grandeur. It had been an age since I beheld the sight of my favourite place, my safe place.

We stopped in the courtyard by the main entrance. Everyone dismounted at once, happy to stretch after long hours on the road, but I stayed still, taking in everything around me. The new roses climbing over a trellis by the front doors, the new larger stables.

One of Haelan's men reached a hand towards me. "My

lady." I took it absentmindedly and slid down the horse, which he walked to the stables. The front doors opened and dogs I'd never met ran towards us, barking their greetings, their tails wagging as they walked between our legs. My ears were ringing, my chest felt constricted. This was home, yet not home anymore. I clenched my jaws hard, but before emotions could overwhelm me a piercing scream echoed around us and back, horses neighed and shifted at the unnerving noise. I watched, beaming, as my beautiful sister and mother rushed down the stairs, legs constrained in their heavy gowns. Soon, two sets of arms enveloped me, keeping me trapped. I didn't know whether to laugh or cry at this infusion of love. The latter won out. A muffled "What did you do to your beautiful hair, young lady?" made me choke with laughter.

"Welcome home, big sister." Mother and Mara let me go, and I gaped at the brown-haired young man before me. This couldn't be my youngest sibling. The last time I saw him he could barely reach my shoulders. Riogan chuckled at my astonishment and gave me a tight hug, Sunlark close behind ruffled my hair and did the same. He hadn't changed much unlike Riogan, the perks of being mages; our prime years were long and youthful. My eyes settled back on Riogan. It hit me then how I hadn't seen my family, apart from Haelan, in more than five years. I'd been so focused on surviving at Court then away from it that I had failed to reflect things might be different here. But if I was being honest with myself, I'd put all thoughts of them in the deepest recesses of my mind. The only way to keep sane.

A drift of pipe smoke and ink wafted to my nose, I turned round, expectant: Father, his hair in its usual disarray, though white now dominated his brown locks, strode towards me a grin on his handsome face, arms wide open. Like the little girl I'd forsaken, I ran the rest of the way and threw myself at him. Things might have changed around here, but that feeling of being home felt the same. "My little one," he croaked and inhaled deeply. "How I missed you so." Inclining my head, I saw his eyes brimming with tears, mirroring my own. He stepped back but kept a firm arm around my shoulders. The guards and horses had gone, leaving my companions standing behind my family. Introductions were made, dogs included, before we all went inside.

We were led to the sitting room where Lucy, our cook, served tea and small sandwiches to our famished party after giving me a quick hug. Tucked into my favourite couch between mother and Mara, who was holding my hand, I told my tale – my adventures Riogan called them in the end – with the help of Haelan and a formidable looking Sawyer. To be fair, all three were sitting stiff-backed on their seats, scrutinising the interior and looking uncomfortably out of place. Our household might not be as opulent as the Castle I reminded myself, but to them we were rich. By the time we'd finished, my whole family was pale and shaken.

"I've no words to express..." father swallowed, face contorted with guilt and distress. "What we've put you through..." he glanced at mother who was crying, a handkerchief muffling her sobs.

A small bit of satisfaction at their pain poked its nasty head up, I severed it; it wasn't their fault. Never had been.

"I blame the King. You wouldn't have sent me away if not for him." This was the truth. "Don't cry mother." I placed an arm around her frail body, my arm muscles firm compared to her delicate frame. A sudden feeling of pride in my new strength surprised me.

Father stood up. "I need to think things through." He looked at the opaque sky out the window. "In the morning, after a good night's sleep we can discuss what to do next." He bowed at Sawyer, Kel and Veena. "I don't know how I can ever repay you for saving my daughter's life." He quieted their effusions with a hand, kissed me on the cheek, then left the room mumbling words to himself. All three of them were looking at me with confused expressions.

"He gets like this," I said in way of explanation. "Whenever a problem lands on his lap, he likes to shut himself off until he's got at least the outset of a plan. Anyway, he's right. We'll be able to see things better after sleeping in a real bed. I don't know about ye all, but damn I missed a good old bed." I grinned, and they seemed to relax at the idea. They'd never complained, but that didn't mean they enjoyed sleeping in the outdoors. Kel had admitted to me yesterday it had been the longest they'd been away from home.

That last statement seemed to arouse mother from her misery, she rushed out the door, taking my siblings with her, to get rooms ready for our guests. Not before Haelan whispered in my ears before quickly walking away, "Lovely accent by the way. I'm sure mother will approve." I watched his retreating figure. What was that about?

"Your family's real nice." Kel provided to break the silence. Our scenery was so at odd with what we'd been through, I could tell they didn't know what to do with themselves.

"Aye," agreed Veena. "Not bad for nobles." She shrugged her shoulders at my surprise. "Nothing but the truth Lady Fay." A corner of her mouth crept up for a second.

"Thank you, I'm glad you think so." And I meant every word; it was high time they realised not all nobles were greedy and self-serving. "Make yourselves at home, and please let me know if you need anything at all." I hesitated. "I'm truly grateful, I wouldn't be here without the four of you." My voice ended in a whisper. My thoughts full of Jolis. They all smiled sadly, their stares turning inward.

* * *

After an early breakfast the next day, my eldest brothers, my companions and I crowded father's office. The mahogany furniture, the family paintings and even the plant mother had insisted he kept to liven up the room were in the same place, not so much as a misplaced ink pot.

Father was sitting at his desk, his favourite pipe in hand which he lifted towards the door. "Faylinn dear," His brow was crinkling. "You don't need to be here. Your brothers and friends here" he pointed at them. "Can help me with the finer details I'm sure. We're going to discuss uninteresting matters for a young lady." The slight was unintentional, yet hurtful. Everyone around me stopped moving, I caught Veena's frown and felt an odd satisfaction she now had a full front view a lady's life wasn't all rosy and sweet. The irritation brewing under my skin wanted to explode, but I knew very well father would not tolerate what he called a pity tantrum. I decided to choose a different approach.

"If you mean how to get allied with the wanderers to be rid of that useless king and his offspring," I crossed my arms in front of me. "I've plenty to say about that. I believe I've been subject to those uninteresting matters more than ye lot gathered up together, don't ye think?" Father cringed. "Language dear." I rose my eyebrows at Haelan who made a face. Was my speech so different? It's true I'd picked up a few locutions here and there from the wanderers' dialect, but it wasn't that strong, was it?

"Faylinn, what you've achieved is tremendous and brave, and no words can relate how proud I am of you. However, you are home now and no longer need to be involved in these affairs."

Colour flooded my face. Those were pretty words implying I should behave like a woman befitting my class. Mortification and disappointment in father warred within me.

"Lord albus, for what it's worth," exclaimed Sawyer. "Fay... Lady Faylinn has been essential to getting this intelligence. She grasped the situation head on and faced the challenges we encountered with courage and wit. Among the wanderers, these are prized qualities. She more than impersonated a warrior, she became one. My companions can vouch to that."

My throat felt awfully tight, and when Kel and Veena both nodded their agreement tears sprang to my eyes. Oblivious on how much his words meant to me, Sawyer continued, "I believe it should be her prerogative to decide whether she wants to take part in further talks or not." My father's eyebrows had furrowed, yet approval and something close to astonishment, for he wasn't shown to be wrong often, were glinting in his shrewd hazel eyes. Sawyer's features were as implacable as ever. No wonder he was chosen to be an elder if a powerful noble failed to make him quake in his boots. He returned my grateful smile with a sharp nod.

Father's expression turned stony as his gaze travelled between Sawyer and I. At last, he sighed. "It was wishful thinking on my part that your love of adventure had tempered down. Well, make sure you tell your mother I have tried my very best or I won't hear the end of it." He chuckled at my grin, then instructed us all to sit down

It was decided father would send appeals to trusted allies: noble friends he'd kept contact with and the elders from wanderers' groups that stayed in our province. Sawyer would contact the rest of them. Haelan dispatched messengers recalling all our guards to the estate. A meeting point between allies would be appointed after their responses. They all agreed it was pointless making concrete plans before knowing exactly who would join us. It was frustrating being unable to act straight away, but father had made a valid point: The king would never believe his younger brother over his son, thinking it a stratagem to oust him from his throne, and we would all end up at best in the royal dungeons for treason. Furthermore, as it stood, we would be slaughtered by the Royal army. Reconnaissance, as we'd all agreed, was the first step. Yet, I had the nagging feeling we needed to act now.

Belatedly, I handed father Dwennon's necklace with the news of its owner. His eyes, and everyone's, were fixed to its magnificent pendant. I knew the feeling, and with much restraint I rested mine on father, who sat still for so long his regard vague, I feared he'd forgotten our presence. At last, with a long breath he tore his gaze away, pupils dilated. I made a mental note to ask Dwennon about the pendant and its history.

Seeing my expectant face, he said. "I remember it, it's still as enthralling as ever." I couldn't agree more. "I can't believe he survived. Filius made a real fool out of us. I'll send Dwennon a letter straight away." He started gathering another sheet of paper and grabbed a feather.

"There's a quicker way ye can contact him." Father's eyes rose to Sawyer's and nodded for him to continue. "Haelan mentioned you held an enchanted mirror, Dwennon has one too." Sawyer glanced at his friends' startled faces and added. "Only the elders know of its existence." I wondered about the need for secrecy.

"If it's not a twin of my one," father was shaking his head. "Then I can't reach him. It would need –"

"A secret incantation." Sawyer interrupted. "I know it."

Father's expression lightened immediately. After Sawyer whispered to him the secret incantation, he took his own from one of his drawers. Curious, I stepped behind father, next to Sawyer who had stayed at his insistence. Dwennon's frowning, wrinkled face filled the mirror in an unflattering manner.

Father gave a short laugh. "Dwennon, my good man, how glad I am to see you looking fit and well, but Myrddin's trembling bones, you're still as ugly as ever."

Dwennon, after a moment's muted shock, grinned, his face becoming as craggy as centuries-old bark. "Your Highness, still as impertinent as I remembered." After further greetings between the old friends and a rebuke from father about Dwennon's secrecy, father explained why he'd called.

Dwennon's shoulders visibly relaxed when he saw Sawyer then me in the background. "You have no idea how relieved I am to see you my boy. You too dear child." Sharing his happiness, Sawyer shed his usual mask and smiled at his mentor. "A messenger told us what happened at Merlo's camp."

He continued, taking away that faint smile with his words. Sawyer then filled him in on what occurred in the Cage and Jolis's death. Dwennon's face fell and fighting back tears he asked the location of his body.

The following conversation was short but to the point, Dwennon was of the same mind as father. However, he wasn't sure whether all wanderer groups would join our cause. I couldn't blame them. They'd suffered enough under the hand of the Royals. With luck, the first snows would hold off a while longer. Meanwhile, everyone was expected to regroup, gather weapons and supplies while waiting for a meeting date. The few spies father kept at Court would be notified shortly. After Dwennon bade farewell, everyone else left the room.

I stayed in my seat. When the door closed behind a puzzled-looking Haelan, father looked up from his writing. "What is it, dear?"

"The villages in our province look well-attended to and thriving. The wanderers were telling me how unhappy people were in the Kingdom, the taxes too high, how lots of families could hardly feed themselves. I am pleased to see it is not so here."

Father frowned, "Yes, the last time I went to Springbay people were visibly poorer with many parts of town no more than hovels. I'm surprised you were unaware of it."

I smiled wryly, "I wouldn't know, I was confined to the Castle the whole time, remember? And whenever we travelled in carriages, the queen kept the curtains drawn as she didn't want to cast her haughty eyes over common folks." He swallowed hard and looked down at his folded hands. I shouldn't have been so blunt, I berated myself, but some things needed to be said. "The wanderers have opened my eyes on many things I'd only heard about in lessons or rumours." The chair creaked as I shifted forward. "I've experienced things nobody should, it's changed me, father. I can't unsee the wrongdoings of our Kingdom, and I certainly can't sit around anymore pretending everything is all right. I want to help set things right for everyone like it was during grandfather's reign."

"You and Haelan both." He exhaled; worry drawn on his face.

"For good reason father. Look at what you've achieved in Highlands! From what Haelan told me all villages are the same as River's edge; people are well looked after, happy. That's how the whole Kingdom should be. You should be king, not that hedonistic good for nothing brother of yours or any of my cousins, they don't care one bit about their subjects." He was smiling at my vehemence, and I frowned cross he didn't take my words seriously.

"I'm honoured you feel that way Faylinn, but if someone had to take the crown, it should be Haelan. I'm a bit ashamed to admit it, but he is the one behind all of this." He spread his arms around him with emphasis.

"What? But you're the baron."

He made a face. "Soon it will be only in name, my dear child. I sometimes spend time on the accounts and visit our tenants, but my health hasn't been so good since you left." He wouldn't meet my eyes, and now that I took a close look at him, tell-tale signs of lack of sleep marked his handsome face; he'd lost weight too, even his hair was thinner. Before I could interrogate him further, he went on. "Your brother has come up with many ways to help our people; he's a born leader through and through." His eyes shone with pride. "He commands our soldiers, sees to the villagers' needs in a weekly assembly he's created in which everyone from the province can attend. The list of what he's accomplished is a long one. He should be the bearer of my title; however, we don't want Filius to have wind of what's occurring."

Although learning about father's bad health sat in my stomach like a heavy stone, I could tell he didn't want to talk about it. I'd question my siblings later. I focused instead on the pride I felt for Haelan, yet worry gnawed at me.

"Won't someone rat to the king though? He should be more

cautious. In fact, I'm surprised nothing has come up yet."

"If you respect those less fortunate and treat them right, they'll repay you in kind. Our people are fiercely protective of Haelan and our whole family. They will be with you too." He added before the thought had formed in my mind.

I left the study unsure on where my place in the family would or could be; they were all actively working towards the wellbeing of our people, they all had a purpose. Sunlark was training new recruits. And in charge of a troop specialised in helping villages in the event of natural disasters and unforeseeable events, such as fires or storm damage. Mara and mother helped the poor and the sick, and Riogan was training to be a healer. His gift had been late to manifest. He could see the sickness in people, but unfortunately that was the extent of his powers. Unlike mage healers, he would have to use herbs and plants to heal people and animals. One never stopped learning such lore Sawyer had confided after I'd returned his book and complimented his work.

As for me, I'd spent ten years moaning and sulking at my predicament and acting like an idiot. Squaring my shoulders, I set off to find Sunlark and my companions: time to train harder.

CHAPTER 23

Faylinn

Sweat was dripping from my forehead unto the training tunics I'd borrowed from Sunlark. Ignoring my tender muscles, I wiped it off in an absent-minded move and focused on my opponent's feet. Jolis had taught me that most times it gave away the direction of the next attack.

"Take a quick glance or ye're giving yer game away." The sharp details of the memory, his warm eyes, his voice, took me by surprise. "See, keep yer opponent real busy?" He'd demonstrated while feinting to my right. "Just so." I'd barely noticed anything, and I was looking for it. "Gets more complicated if your opponent knows the trick though and uses it against ye."

"Like pretending to go one way to catch you?" I'd asked with a simpering smile, doing exactly that, but Jolis, of course, had caught on and parred my attack." His laughter reverberated in the walls of my heart.

I thrust my wooden sword to the right, but the blow came to the left and hit me with the flat of the blade. I groaned in frustration. Green eyes flecked with yellow stared down at me in mirth. With a smile as wide as a thief's who'd found the castle's treasure room, Kel remarked, "If ye're trying to watch yer opponent's steps don't let it be so blatant sweetling, a flick of the eyes here and there is enough." I glared at his smug face. He wasn't even flushed, and we'd been at it for an hour.

I huffed, "I'm no good at this."

"Of course, ye're not." Came the reply from someone else I'd failed to beat. "Ye just started learning to fight." Sawyer raised a blond eyebrow. "Ye can't expect to be any good after a mere couple of hours here and there." He lifted his hands in front of him in mock apprehension as my glare fixed on him. "Just saying, but ye're doing good, right Kel?"

"Right, right, tremendous." They shared a look between them, and I slapped them both on their arms while laughing. The tension and pressure we'd shared on the journey had vanished after a couple of days; we'd achieved our goal, and now we had people, a large group of people, to take strength from. The issue was out. I didn't know about them, but I felt freer than ever. I took a swallow of the water skin Kel handed me and asked Sawyer if he wanted to fight me next.

"Afraid not," his look turned pensive. "Lord Albus asked for our presence in his study at once."

"Oh," I studied his face for any signs. "Did he say why?" The last three days since our arrival had been very quiet, father didn't expect any response until the end of the week.

"No, but a messenger burst through yer front door not but fifteen minutes ago." I chewed on this piece of information while we made our way, hoping it would be good news.

That last wish was not granted as father announced to a roomful the king was on his last legs from a mysterious disease that baffled all Royal healers. He held the message high and brandished it like a sword. "The queen and crown prince have already succumbed to it."

Everyone was still, absorbing this surprising turn of event. "I see I'm not the only one in shock," father went on pacing and turning behind his desk. "How in Myrddin's grand soul did I not foresee this…like father like son." He shook the paper in his hand for emphasis, the action not unlike a cantankerous old farmer cursing children for stealing his juicy apples.

Haelan got up from his chair, took the message and perused it all the while frowning. "Obviously Quentin is less of a fool than I thought, I was hoping his arrogance would give us more time. Then again, Roldan might have understood the precariousness of their situation and convinced him to take action before we could." he looked at me. "You did seem to think they were far more friendly than they let on at Court."

I nodded. "What about Gwynn?"

"No mention of her." father, now sat on his chair, sighed. "I assume she's sick too otherwise her death would have been proclaimed." He placed his head in his hands and massaged his temples, eyes seeing right through our small assembly. I held no love for Gwynn, but it irked me her health was of no import to the spies because under Comraich's law no female could rule the Kingdom. An archaic and pompous law if you asked me. Prolonged time with wanderers had certainly opened my eyes to the strength and aptitude of my sex. And matters of equality.

"We can't let him go unpunished," ground out Haelan. "I despised the lot of them, you can be sure I shed no tears at their early demise, but he shouldn't be able to do away with his family without repercussions, Roldan too."

"Aye," agreed Sawyer. "And who knows what they'll do next. We should act now. They won't expect it."

Kel nodded, "Probably thinking we're all shaking in our commoners' boots. The way Fay described him Quentin seems arrogant, too much so. It might come to our advantage if we move now when the Court is in shock."

Father seemed to share their opinion for he said, "I agree we should act. However, we mustn't let our feelings overpower our judgement. I say we assemble as many soldiers as we can, wanderers included, close to Springbay. There, we can gather all the intelligence we need to make a sound and solid stratagem. Rushing into things would only serve our enemy. Any complaints?" At our complete silence, he continued, "I'll contact Dwennon right away. Haelan, Sunlark, gather all the soldiers we've got. I'll send messengers to those already heading our way with their new destination and to trusted inns to hire horses."

"Father!" exclaimed Haelan, "You know very well I can spell the horses to run like the wind." I flinched and felt my companions stiffen, he'd showed us for a short while his little ability, as he called it, on the way home. The expression "Run like the wind" was not an understatement; it had taken me days to untangle my hair, and I still sported the sores on my inner legs and other uncomfortable places.

"No, no, dear boy," father shook his head rather faster than necessary. I hid a smile with my hand. Guess I wasn't the only one not relishing the experience. "We can't have you exhausted before we get there."

Haelan only managed a short "But," before father interrupted, "That's final! Anyway, the rest of you, get ready for a long ride. And Faylinn, please break the news gently to your mother." I nodded not looking forward to the task. "She'll be upset you're leaving so soon."

I stared. "You're letting me go?"

He smiled sadly. "I didn't think I could stop you." He was right, I had made up my mind. I flew into his arms and squeezed. "Thank you for understanding." The sound of my voice was muffled in his shoulder.

I was not one to prevaricate, but I hoped mother had gone to the village on her daily errand, leaving me time to collect my thoughts. I was granted no such luck. Although we had Lucy, mother liked to help making dishes, especially desserts which were her speciality. She was chopping carrots, Mara by her side peeling them; the atmosphere was merry and amicable when I stepped inside.

Mother put her knife down when she saw my troubled face. "Bad news?" she asked, a slight tremor betrayed her composed countenance. Lucy went to prepare some tea at once while we took seats around the table, the vegetables all forgotten. Try as I may, the news I was bringing came as a deep shock; no gentle way or words could ease the ramifications. Mara looked paler, if that was possible, and her eyes were rimmed with unshed tears. Mother blotted at hers when she said. "Your father and brother are still set on going I take it, you also." Not a question, but I replied anyway.

"Yes."

"At least Sunlark has the sense to stay." No need to mention he'd wanted to go, but Haelan was the one to convince him to stay with a small guard and protect our people. "You and your brother, you're just like your father," she whined. "Ignoring what pain you inflict on others for your beliefs, good or bad. Selfish and foolish the three of you. Haelan I can forgive, for it's his duty to protect our province. But your father is sick, and you, open your eyes Faylinn, you're a lady, not one of them." I guessed she meant the wanderers. She had been all civility itself and treated them as important guests, however, I had not failed to notice her frowning disapproval whenever I interacted with them.

I took her anger full on, let it strike with words she didn't wholeheartedly mean and would later regret. She hadn't changed one bit, I sighed inwardly, always letting her emotions prevail over her rational thoughts. We were quite similar on that count, and some people, my brothers came to mind, liked to point out our hair also shared a similar shade of auburn. I waited patiently, for I knew she'd come around. Mara got up and placed her arm around mother, then said in a wavering voice. "Come mother dear, we need to help make food for their travel." To my utter amazement she did as told whilst muttering under her breath and refusing to look or speak to me anymore. Well, some things had changed for the best I reflected while I hurried to my room to pack once more.

The next few days were short in sleep and unending in tasks. Preparations kept the whole household busy from the moment the night sky bled into greys and blues. Swords were struck, arrows fetched, spare leather shaped into armour; supplies that were kept for the long winter days wrapped in saddlebags. Not one soul was left idle until men training outside could no longer perceive their opponents. Only then did we stop for a well-earned rest. Father and Haelan kept longer hours than most, spending a good part of the night in deep talk.

The day after we'd heard of the king's death they held an assembly in the meeting hall, a building next to the village square. Hundreds of people residing in the nearest villages took attendance. After they'd explained the situation with Prince Quentin and reassuring them they would do their best to protect Highlands – he was not popular around these parts – they asked for the villagers' help making weapons, clothes and food rations for their army. I watched, sitting to the side, this gathering so different from the opulent ones among nobles. Not one villager complained. On the contrary, some of them asked to join the soldiers and the three blacksmiths had a row of volunteers willing to help day and night. These were people who didn't live in big manors, didn't have much money to spare, but they'd shown more loyalty and kindness than I'd ever seen amongst my peers. Jolis's words rang true then, "Trust works both ways."

CHAPTER 24

Dwennon

"**D**wennon!" The hammer Dwennon was holding froze mid-air and dropped to the ground; he stretched to his full height, bones and ligaments creaking in the process. Turning around from the tent he was erecting in their makeshift camp, he caught sight of the running woman who'd called him. She stopped in front of him and bent down, hands on knees, panting. Her face was red from exertion. Small and thin with an average face, she was dressed as a commoner, all traces of her warrior training toned down. She'd been chosen along Leope to mingle with commoners in the Capital. While buying essentials for the camp, they were to catch any talk or whisper going around on the Royals and Roldan. He went to his satchel to retrieve his waterskin before giving it to her. After a long drink she straightened, rubbed her mouth with a sleeve. "That's better, Ta!"

"What news Sara?"

"Ye won' believe this. We might not be needed after all." Her eyes were bright, betraying her excitement.

Dwennon's white bushy eyebrows shot up. This was not the announcement he'd anticipated. He pointed to a log by a tempting fire. "I'm all ears, child." He said, walking towards it. On soft steps, only their warriors could achieve, she followed him then spoke after they'd both sat down.

"The whole Capital is agog with the execution taking place this week's end." Dwennon, who'd been warming his chilled fingers, straightened at once. "There're posters everywhere; Prince Quentin is to be executed for treason. We got a few of the more prominent merchants chatting. Nothing useful in all, one of them had a brother in the Royal Guards. Apparently, they've been ordered to keep quiet, so he couldn't tell us anymore than what we knew."

"Roldan?" enquired Dwennon.

Sara raised both shoulders. "No one knows, it's all been hush hush up at the castle, more so than ever. But there's already bets among the populace on who'll be the next king. Ye won't like this." She grimaced while tilting her head to the side. Dwennon's original amusement at people's entertainment morphed into uneasiness. Sara's eyes had sharpened. "Roldan is predicted to take the throne. But get this, everyone we've spoken to said they bet on Albus Wymer or his oldest boy and didn't understand why Roldan would even be added to the betting list as he's no claim. So, we decided to say good morn' to the betting master. Even Leo, who can sweet talk just about anyone in giving up their dirtiest secrets, couldn't get the man to give us the sightliest morsel."

No doubt Roldan's purse had helped in the matter, thought Dwennon. He probably thought having his name next to Albus and Haelan would make the commoners assume he had a right to the throne through some obscure law. He forced his jaw to relax. "I don't like this. I don't like this at all." He got up and placed a hand on her shoulder. "Thank you both for your work. I need to think." His voice trailed away after him as he weaved his path through the camp. They'd chosen a large depression deep in the forest north of Springbay. The moment he'd set foot on the ground, he'd walked the perimeter necessary for the number of people expected to put up the shielding spell he used the most. Sawyer would expect it, for the rest of them, scouts were on the look-out for friends as well as foes.

Wanderers from different groups were catching up with one another while putting tents up or attending to their equipment. Their laughter and banter failed to put his mind at rest. Lost in his thoughts, Dwennon's foot tripped over a protruding root, he stumbled then fell on his hands and knees in thick mulch, which had cushioned his fall. The impact inundated his senses with the essence of autumn, he took a deep breath, savouring it all. Nature always had a way to calm him down, keep his mind focused, keep him grounded. He chuckled to himself while wiping his hands on his travel-dirty cloak. Kawana, a warrior from the northeast, rushed to his side and offered Dwennon a hand, which he took with good nature. The inconveniences of old age didn't affect him like it did some people. Why fight the natural circle of life? Why resent something you couldn't stop? It was pointless.

"Anythin' broken?" Kawana swept his eyes over Dwennon once he was up. If a mountain could talk, Dwennon mused, it'd have the same low and gravelly timbre as Kawana's. The man was huge and brawny with a stern expression, rivalling Sawyer's, honed through decades of hard training. Yet, Dwennon knew his heart was as big, if not bigger, than his size.

Dwennon felt fine, but he patted all over his body to satisfy Kawana's scrutiny. "All in one piece! Thank you Kawana." The large warrior's chest deflated with relief. "Can't have ye hurt before things get interestin'." He tapped Dwennon on the back then lumbered back to what he'd been doing.

A new wave of anxiety swamped Dwennon. After his meeting with all the elders living in Comraigh, he was aware many of his people were hoping to take things further than removing Quentin from the throne. He'd caught whispers of taking the monarchy down for good. Despite the revelation of his past life as the High Mage, or maybe because of it, none of the elders had been willing to help Albus or Haelan to the throne, bar those who'd resided at some point in Highlands,

Albus's province. Too small a number. They belonged to a long line of cruel and tyrannical kings, his old friend King Cardian was the exception to the rule, they'd unanimously decided. They didn't know the last of the Wymer princes, they didn't trust them. Yet. And although they were willing to meet with them upon Dwennon's insistence, he feared they had only agreed to form an opinion on their potential future enemies.

Dwennon placed a hand over his mouth and stared into space, not seeing anything in front of him. Now they had Roldan to deal with. He'd foolishly hoped it could wait until after Haelan was made king. The small satchel he was keeping on himself at all times shifted, igniting an idea. Being careful where he was stepping, he found a quiet place in the trees, took out his magical mirror, then spoke out the spell to reach Albus's mirror. By his calculations, they should be a day, maybe two, behind them. Not long to wait, but he needed to warn them.

His reflexion frowned accusingly at him. And then what? It said, the mirror stayed still, his mind didn't. He'd sworn to himself he would fight till the very end to patch old mistakes. He couldn't move on with this weight on his conscience. Yet, he had to admit to himself he felt too old, too slow. He was the High Mage no more. His powers were still intact, but his body was having trouble keeping up with it. Destroying that doll had taking its toll on more than his physical form, his mind wasn't as quick and sharp as it used to be. He didn't feel fit to make life-endangering, life-changing decisions anymore. He'd seen that very same understanding in Albus's eyes, that very knowledge that time, life was spiralling out of control. Their days were numbered.

That is why he placed all hope on Haelan. If he was being honest with himself, he liked the idea of Cardian's first grandchild to be king. The little he'd seen of the man had shaken him to the core. Haelan looked nothing like his grandfather, yet his smile, his mannerism, even his way of interacting with people was all Cardian. He would become a great king, the greatest of all, he could feel it thrumming in his old bones.

CHAPTER 25

Dwennon
&
Faylinn

The acrid smell of badly clogged up drains and horse manure as well as the stench of sweaty bodies tightly pressed together shouldn't have cut Dwennon to the heart. The memories of the once beautiful and thriving Capital interlaced with the dismal truth of his senses. For many reasons, not all sentimental, he hadn't set foot in Springbay ever since his near-fatal escape. He'd put his old life behind him including the subjects he'd sworn to protect. What would King Cardian think of his actions, or lack of? His heart squeezed with renewed determination. He would do anything in his power to thwart Roldan's plans.

The cowl of his heavy cloak hung low over his face. Albus and Haelan, three steps before him, were similarly clad, the thick fabric hid the bulk of their weapons. Dwennon had the bare essentials for close combat. Which was laughable as he had neither the strength nor the endurance to fight even the youngest and least experienced guards. His younger self would have been ashamed of such weakness, he shrugged the thought away, not quite sure where it had come from, he'd already made his peace with the undeniable truth.

His gaze settled on the tall, hooded figure navigating the crowd ahead of him. He'd taken Haelan aside for a long conversation after their arrival. The others, Sawyer in particular, had watched, eyes brimming with curiosity, as he'd ushered him away from ears with some inane excuse. He'd wanted to confirm what his inner self had sensed when he'd known him as a boy. They'd talked of the Kingdom, of his family, of the future. Haelan was dead set on putting his father on the throne, not himself. When Dwennon had asked him why? He'd looked at Dwennon with a straightforward expression in his deep green eyes. "I don't deserve to be on the throne, not yet." He'd replied.

In that moment, Dwennon had recalled something Faylinn had mentioned to him once. "My brother Haelan's words are a window to his soul. He says it as it is. The only time I've caught him lying was done out of kindness or compassion. He doesn't pretend, dupe or betray." She'd paused there. "Mind you, life at Court doesn't count. Anyway, he's genuine to a fault." His openness might cause him some trouble in the future, Dwennon reflected, if he wasn't careful. There were plenty of ill-intentioned people out there capable of harming him. Dwennon wiped his runny nose on a sleeve, a handkerchief would look out of place. He shouldn't be so negative, it was clear Haelan was astute enough to pick out his friends from his foes. Moreover, he had a trustworthy entourage. Yes, Haelan would make a good king.

They reached the corner of the market square they'd chosen to watch the execution from and confront Roldan if he made any attempt to take over the throne forthwith. Albus's bulk went in front of the baker's shop as planned, Haelan's continued past the clothier, the butcher and stopped in front of the inn; he turned to look at Dwennon, then nodded before continuing further along in a diagonal line to a spot where he'd have a clear view of both platforms. Dwennon shuffled his feet to where Haelan had indicated. Amongst the men and women standing shoulder to shoulder in front of the inn, he recognised some wanderers and some of Haelan's men. All in place. The side of the execution stage was in front of him, it was empty bar the executioner and a solid lump of wood, its top concave in the middle, dark stains from past beheadings visible. Its presence caused his guts to fold and unfold upon themselves; he'd escaped that very fate. He shifted his head towards the field of eager faces and searched in vain for Sawyer and Kel. Worry shadowed his every breath, his every move. He prayed to Myrddin's spirit to protect them all.

* * *

A shove to my right sent me toppling into a young mother carrying her youngling, I muttered excuses at her glare and readjusted the hood of my brown cloak. The streets of Springbay were heaving with people. Be it commoners or nobles, every one of them were heading for the same place. Feet trampled over feet, elbows pushing and pressing, driven by curiosity they cleared a path towards today's attraction. The old marketplace was as resplendent as I'd heard, its vast and flat expanse was square in shape, shops three stories high made from the grey stone abundant in our Kingdom stood as tall as oaks. Right at its heart, the glorious bronze statue of Myrddin surmounted a large circular fountain made of white marble. King Filius had employed countless mages specialised in metal to get rid of it, yet there it was; a monument to our history and hope, I liked to believe.

As I was jolted left, right and from behind, amazement failed to part with me: how could thousands of people choose of their own will, and with excitement no less, to be squashed thus for what was to me nothing more than a barbarous act? Scattered among these unsuspecting people were my father and Haelan's men and the wanderers, dressed in inconspicuous tunics under dull cloaks hiding their weapons. It was a strange feeling to be accepted as one of them. Spotting them ahead of me, I forged a path towards Sawyer and Kel, initiating along the way a course of verbal abuse from the people I had pushed none too gently.

"Never seen so many people in one place." I said out of breath as I joined them.

"Public executions of a noble are rare." Sawyer said. It didn't explain why so many of them were fighting to get the best view; killing someone, justified or not, was a terrible and life-altering deed, as I well knew, not something to cheer about. I cast a disgusted glance around me. How they could bring younglings to see someone's head be severed from its body was beyond me, it was far too gruesome. My lips pursed in disapproval. If it wasn't for the fact we knew Roldan would attend, I wouldn't be here, my hatred for Quentin notwithstanding.

As soon as we'd set foot, unsteady ones on my account, at the camp Dwennon had informed us about the turn of events. Our spies' ominous absence cast an uneasy atmosphere amongst the troops, everyone was sombre in spite of the good news Quentin's horrendous crimes were accounted for. None of us liked the lack of relevant information, yet a plan had to be made. It was straight to the point: kill Roldan. Who indubitably, was trying to get the crown for himself, and put father on the throne. It had sounded easy enough I thought, looking around me. How were we supposed to fight with no room to move and without endangering townsfolk?

"We're here as support, remember?" Sawyer answered my worries in a whisper close to my ear. "Haelan, Dwennon and the other warrior mages are taking on Roldan; the archers will strike the guards if they so much as move." I resisted the urge to check if they were in position on the roofs and in the windows surrounding us. Oblivious to my thoughts, he continued, "People will run for protection, away from us. We'll point them in the right direction."

I nodded, stomach still unsettled, but reassured our people would be strategically placed all over the market square. Hopefully they would protect the innocent from harm, although I bore no idealistic misconceptions as to expect no casualties. As much as the scheme has been discussed and prepared, there was no guarantee events would run smoothly; gifts could be volatile and unpredictable weapons.

The heads of every prominent noble family were sitting, stiff-backed, on upholstered wooden chairs on a small stage to one side of the market square. Not for the first time, I wondered why they were listening to Roldan without protest. I remembered quite a few opportunists cunning enough to vie for the throne for themselves. It all seemed too effortless, too ordered.

The three of us positioned ourselves at the entrance of Parade Street leading to the Castle; it had the advantage of having a clear view of both stages. As the mournful lament of bells announced the anticipated event, a tightly closed formation of Royal guards – every one of them tall and brawny with their shields up and swords drawn – marched from Parade Street towards us. We were crushed in a surging wave to the right as people fearful, yet awed, hastened a path to whom I presumed to be Roldan hiding at its core. Of medium height and frame, neither thin nor bulky, the word average fit him to perfection. Shame it didn't apply to his magic. I watched them pass us by, eyes narrowed. In an ideal world only good and worthy people would be bestowed with strong magic, it seemed fair and right. However, as it had been proved countless times our world was anything but.

A commotion to the front brought my gaze to the main platform. Quentin, hands tied behind his back, was held by two fierce-looking guards. Had they brought him with magic? Commoners were throwing rotten vegetables at him; he was pale, his usual arrogance absent, and in its place was pure terror. Appalled to feel a slither of sorrow for him, I brushed it off reminding myself the years of bullying, and not to forget the murders of countless people. This type of twisted show didn't sit well with me; the setup, the way people craved death. Yet, the humiliation and fear he must be feeling at this moment was well-deserved and more of a punishment than the lenient death awaiting him. Nonetheless, the real matter was he wouldn't hurt anyone ever again. A hush settled over the crowd when the formation climbed the stairs to the main stage and stopped in the middle, a safe distance from Quentin. Guards parted, revealing the small and elegant form of my cousin Gwynn.

My mouth went slack, half-opened, I was left speechless; the others were also frowning in confusion. Had she survived the poison? She did look unwell. Her face was haggard and of a sickly hue. Despite this she held herself with a regal bearing, bringing back to mind the many hours we'd been forced to walk with a heavy tome on our heads, however ill we might be.

I placed a hand on Sawyer's arm, his head bent down close to mine. "What now?" I asked, a frantic panic was creeping and erasing every order Haelan had given me. "We can't continue as planned, she'll get hurt." I might not like my cousin, but that didn't mean I could passively watch her getting injured or worse, killed. "Roldan is not even here."

He grimaced, "Look again." My eyes roved over the nobles' stage, Roldan was sitting in the front row, his smug face fixed on Gwynn. When did he get here? Maybe he was the one who'd brought Quentin. "We wait for the signal, as planned." There was a hardness in his voice that brooked no arguments. A dizzying surge of emotions swayed and ebbed in the blink of an eye, my lips pressed with reaffirmed resolution.

Gwynn's strident voice bounced and echoed against the closed-in marketplace. Yet, not a whisper could be heard among the people anymore; close-by a baby contorted in his mother's arms, his face was an angry red, but no wailing pierced this unnatural quiet.

Magic.

Sawyer's mouth moved, but his voice was muted, he gestured towards the nobles. I scowled at Roldan. The manipulations were already taking place. "My good people of SpringBay," Gwynn resumed, "I stand before you today to avenge our King, our Queen and Crown Prince. It is with deep shame and sorrow I have to admit their deaths, their murders, were implemented by none other than the king's own blood, my own blood." She paused and placed a shaking hand over her mouth.

Before me was a Gwynn I'd never met; I couldn't reconcile the upset, almost broken, woman standing before me with the contemptuous and apathetic one I'd lived with. Their death must have devastated her, her social standing gone in a matter of days. Her composure regained, she declared, "Prince Quentin planned the murder of our family in order to claim a throne that didn't belong to him, he used cowardly and deceitful means. Means that show his true evil nature." She turned to the nobles and curtsied. "I am deeply grateful to the High Mage for his wit and support in dismantling this devious attack on our Kingdom and saving my life in the process." He bowed at this honour. "I stand before you today to sentence Prince Quentin to death by beheading for treason. I stand before you today as your new Queen. Proceed." She watched Quentin as she said those last words and turned sharply, the hem of her dress near floating as she went to sit next to Roldan. *Queen?* The laws instated during the reign of King Taron, the first Monarch of Comraich, precluded women from taking the throne.

* * *

The sudden clang of bells struck deep. Dwennon hated that

sound. People to his right were turned away from the stages and shouted profanities to a bundle of guards marching their way towards the side of the execution stage where Dwennon was standing. Quentin, head and shoulders slumped low, was dragging his shackled feet in the middle of the group. As he lumbered up the stairs, his eyes, intense with fury and fear, were cast to the floor. His lips were pressed so tight together they'd lost all colours. His jaw clamped hard when the commoners started throwing rotten vegetables or eggs at him. One of the guards pulled on his chains hard and dragged him next to the executioner in full view of the swearing people. At another onslaught of rotten food, Quentin stepped back to avoid the brunt of it. The guards at his back shoved him forward, smirks twisting their large mouths.

Dwennon watched from the perimeter of the platform, conflicted. Quentin's execution shouldn't be used as some morbid spectacle. Taking someone life, no matter if they were good or evil, shouldn't be easy, nor should it ever be taken lightly. All the people who had died by his hands were present within himself, in a part he refused to shut out or ignore. He believed in accounting for his own actions. Some might think the guilt, the responsibility he carried was a sort of self-inflicted martyrdom. He inhaled the putrid air and grimaced. Maybe they were right. The stars knew many of those he'd killed had been black to the core, they didn't deserve a smidgen of regret.

His gaze flew from Quentin to the stage set out for the nobles and presumably Roldan, catching mid-way to the small female form of Princess Gwynn standing a few yards from her brother. How had he missed her arrival? His head shot in Haelan's direction; unable to make eye contact he turned and tried to get Albus's attention. A feat futile with those dratted hoods, Dwennon cursed under his breath. None of them had predicted this turn of event. What next? His hands itched to say in the sign language used by wanderers' warriors. Again, pointless as Albus didn't know of it. The urge to push forward towards Haelan in order to talk to him was momentarily halted by the sudden absence of any noise.

The thick pressure of magic thrummed in his ears. Powerful magic coming from the platform furthest from him. His eyes focused on the person responsible. Roldan. Sitting with the nobles. Nothing from his calm demeanour could betray he was the one behind such intricate magic. Absorbing Gwynn's speech and its implications, he squeezed his way beside Haelan before remembering they couldn't communicate. Frustration spiked through the shock. Queen. This was a coup of sort, an unusual one. Taking a quick glance at Haelan, Dwennon observed his tensed jaw, the rigidness of his back. The boy turned, the sun caught the inside of the hood, his eyes were swimming with anger yet resolution. He gave a sharp nod to Dwennon and to Albus over his shoulder, then threw his hood down.

The signal.

Well half of the signal as the whispering spell Haelan had intended to use was now worthless. Dwennon hurried back to his designated spot ignoring the elbows jarring numerous parts of his body, crushed feet. The unleashing of the mute spell overwhelmed him all of two seconds before he remembered what he was about. With Roldan and Haelan in his field of vision, he started chanting in his head his strongest protective spell. He felt it stretch over Haelan, then Albus widening over and around all their brothers in arms before a slither of magic found its way back to him. Its settling took all of two breaths, yet as Dwennon focused back to the world around him the air had turned as thick and charged as in a dry storm. The boy! He snapped his head to the side for a better view. Between Haelan's fingers were red tendrils of magic. The more he pulled and weaved his fingers in a deceptively random pattern the darker the tendrils became. By the time they turned the colour of long-fermented wine Haelan opened one hand, palm up.

Dwennon, his task completed, could only watch in awe

the raw power emanating from the sphere resembling a spool of yarn. Quick as lightning, the spool shot out towards Roldan, burning its way through a shielding veil Dwennon had failed to feel let alone see. The veil slowed Haelan's magic enough for Roldan to push Gwynn to one side before he jumped backwards. Dwennon's eyebrows shot to his hairline. The apprentice had outdone his master. He felt rattled and rather inadequate. His mistake had cost them the element of surprise. Before Haelan could attack a second time, Roldan had cast a visible net of protection around himself, his arms were circling above his head, gathering a dark mass of roiling magic. Behind Dwennon arrows, some aflame, shot straight into the veil, which flickered and pulsed under theirs assault but held true.

Dwennon had a moment of clear, terrifying lucidity. As quick as his scrawny legs could take him, he hurried back Albus's way. Why had they left him without a strong mage? No, the question was how could Roldan possibly know Albus was here? They'd made sure he looked no different from any other commoners surrounding him. Dwennon cast a furtive look at Roldan; his eyes didn't give a thing away, yet Dwennon knew the worst would happen and he would be too late to reach Albus. Pulled to the side by a wave of scared and fleeing people, he struggled to stay on his feet. He tried to throw a second spell over Albus and the people around him as he feared his first one wouldn't be enough under Roldan's ruthless magic, however someone bumped into his shoulder, breaking his concentration.

The spell failed.

Terror in his eyes, in his bones, he watched the bolt of darkness strike the building right behind Albus and his guards. Dwennon cast a quick holding spell, wrapped it around the building; he felt himself sway under the pressure as though he was holding on to the building with his bare hands. The spell snapped. Dwennon dropped onto his knees. An ear-splitting rumbling and groaning preceded the shop's collapse, the deluge of stones and timber crushing all who were unfortunate enough to be nearby.

* * *

A grotesque live painting depicting chaos erupted all around me. Some people's neck were taut from shouting, screaming, their features a whirlpool of emotions. Some purple in the face and throwing their fists at the nobles, while others were crying with what I could only assume was happiness at being rid of oppression and blinded by hope in Gwynn. Yet not a single sound escaped from our muted prison. Gwynn ignored the commotion amongst the crowd, her eyes fixed firmly on the planks.

In the next instant all sounds were unleashed, deafening the marketplace, my ears. The announcement of Quentin's imminent execution went ignored as commoners all around us were reeling with the startling news. My eyes were on Gwynn and Roldan; even as the axe collided with Quentin's neck, she kept her gaze adverted, hands clenched in her dress. She looked pitiful like a frail mouse within a cat's paws. There and then I knew what to do. I turned to the others to tell them my intentions, but an ear-splitting crack in the air cut me short. Light as bright as a thousand stars struck down, blinding me for a moment. The black spots cleared from my vision. Everyone around me had frozen, petrified, in place, a few rubbed at their eyes. Then, people started running and shoving left and right in panic, their children tight bundles against their chests. I struggled to stay put. A burnt smell reached my nose at the same time I realised the seat where Roldan sat, not but ten seconds ago, had turned into a black pile of ashes. The man himself was standing behind scattered chairs, their occupants having fled, arms high above his head in a foreboding move. Gwynn was in the far corner hiding behind a massive Royal guard.

Did I miss the signal? Kel grabbed me by the shoulder; Sawyer and Veena, who had appeared from the stars knew where, were directing people away from the battle. Kel shook me gently. "Ye all right?" An arrow, its tip in flame, flew over heads and struck one of the chairs. Roldan jumped back as it exploded.

I blinked away the haze in my head. "I don't understand, Haelan's signal… I didn't hear…" I stopped at his rueful smile. *Silly me.* One group of our men was taking on the guards, the others unseen, but I knew they had a perfect view of the stage and more precisely Roldan. He grabbed my hand and followed the throng to join the others. I was determined to help Gwynn. She didn't know what she had got herself into; Roldan would take advantage of her weak constitution and use her like a royal puppet or worse. I would save Gwynn one way or another.

I directed my companions to an empty spot by a shop's facade and told them as much, but their faces, as rigid as granite, didn't inspire approval. At another time, it would have amused me how the three of them shared equal frowns and arrested looks. The ground trembled under another onslaught. Sawyer broke the staring contest and surveyed Parade Street. "Can't, she already slipped away with a ton of guards," he narrowed his eyes. "Heavily armed guards."

I huffed, "Never mind that, I'll talk to her at the castle."

He crossed his arms, muscles bulging against his warrior clothes, knives in place, and the short bow I'd made him resting against his chest. When had he taken his cloak off? A glance at the other two showed similar outfits. Ugh, that was a trick I needed to learn. "Too dangerous, Lord Albus' instructions were clear, ye stay out of trouble, not run towards it."

I growled he was so infuriating. I knew father had put him in charge of supervising me, but he should know by now I wasn't some defenceless woman. "I know how to get in there unseen." I tried to abate the fire within me. "I can even reach her rooms without a soul knowing about it. I'll be quick, I swear, just long enough to tell her what I overheard, and I'll be out of there. We'll be the only ones to know." My unfeigned confidence unsettled him for a moment, I swear I could see the possible problems unravelling in his mind. "Gwynn might even decide to go with us until Roldan has been dealt with. Look at it as a rescue mission for a real damsel in distress." The hardness in his eyes had diminished, I'd even caught a twitch of the mouth.

"She did look unwell." pointed out Kel. I mouthed a thank you to him when Sawyer turned to the fighting by the stages. Royal guards were strewn on the ground arrows embedded in their armour. Roldan, encircled by a black shimmering light, was making signs with his hands reciting what I assumed was a powerful spell. I turned around impatiently, we needed to move while he was distracted, any minute he could decide to flee.

Sawyer held my stare again and exhaled, "Ye sure she'll believe ye?"

I shrugged. "Only one way to find out."

He turned to his friends. "Ye two, stay here and help. I'll go with Fay."

Veena frowned, "Ye sure ye don't want back-up? She tends to breed trouble." She pointed at me with an accusatory thumb.

"We need someone here who knows where we are." The words *just in case* were left out, yet hung heavy above our heads. As if I looked for trouble, no sir, it was the other way round; trouble always seemed to find me. *Not this time*, I comforted my unsettled nerves, the passages would be safe while Roldan was kept busy. I pulled at Sawyer's arm. "Come on! Enough prattle. The entrance is behind the..." My last words were muffled by another ground shaking blast before a building crumbled into mere pebbles, a building where father was supposed to be.

"No!" A scream unlike anything I'd ever heard wrenched

the following stunned silence, I started towards the wreckage. Father! I needed to know he was all right. A dense mist was slithering past my footsteps, creeping up at a steady speed when Sawyer ran in front of me and placed his hands on my shoulders; I swatted them, but they were as immovable as magical binds.

"Ye can't go there."

"I must, what if he's injured? I can't just let him...What if they all..." I swallowed.

"Yer people are there, have more trust in them. Dwennon and Haelan together are a force to be reckoned with; Roldan won't stand a chance." His certainty melted my unease. I chanced a glance over his shoulder, the view was thwarted by settling dust.

"You're right." The words were wrenched from my tight lips. "Let's go."

❊ ❊ ❊

Breathing in the settling dust of the debris, Dwennon choked and coughed while waving a futile hand in front of him to see the damage. Another booming crack echoed around the market square. Dwennon ducked. Ears half deaf, he caught sight of Roldan hiding behind the thick leg of his platform, throwing random attacks at Haelan, who'd advanced yards away from Roldan now that people had ran away.

Out of the corner of one eye, Dwennon caught rapid movement. Far too shocked and struggling to adjust to his impaired senses, he barely managed to turn towards the silhouette running towards him. He squinted. Dark clothes. Not a guard. When Kawana's strained face became clearer, Dwennon let the air he'd held tight in his lungs rush out. "Let me clear this," Kawana gestured at the gritty cloud encompassing them. His left hand swished to one side, the air cleared at once. Dwennon coughed a few times more then cast his gaze between Haelan and their people fighting Roldan and the Royal guards, and the pile of broken stones.

Kawana made the decision for him. "They're all right. We need to recover our people's bodies." No trace of hope any of them could have survived. If he remembered right, there had been four of their men positioned close to the shop. As they approached, more wanderers joined them from their shadowed hiding places. Dwennon recognised the few who had been tasked to stay back and only come out to help their wounded or carry casualties back to camp. One of them had the gift of levitation, she ordered them all to stand back while she picked stones as heavy as five men like they were flowers in a meadow. Dwennon's concentration turned inward, his spell was fraying under Roldan's offensive; Haelan's protection was the most damaged. Eyes on the boy, he projected another layer, extended it far and wide until it was big enough to be folded over him in a thick skin. The boy had to survive.

Satisfied, he spun around and started. A few yards to his right, a large broken stone crashed on a precarious-looking pile of rubble. His gaze flew to the wanderer. What was her name again? Macy? Lacy? He'd only met her in passing, but his inability to remember her name shafted. Leanne had noticed he wasn't as sharp as he used to. She hadn't broached the subject with him, it was the frown he'd caught too many times for his liking that gave it away. She was waiting for him to admit what was going on, what he wasn't so sure now that he was ready for.

Running footsteps behind him trampled on his thoughts, a flash of curly blond hair fluttered past him. "Father!" Haelan's voice cracked with fear. "Where is he?" Dwennon joined him beside the others gathered around the first body they had recovered. Someone crying leaned down and closed the dead woman's eyes. He picked her up, met Dwennon's anguished eyes before moving away towards camp.

"Haelan," Dwennon managed to rasp to the boy removing stones by hand. "I'm sorry, the blast was too strong, my spell crumbled with the building, it took me by surprise, I couldn't _"

Haelan turned haunted eyes towards him. "Any chance any of them survived?" Dwennon was speared back to a time when Haelan was just a boy on his grandfather's lap, giggling when he pretended to drop him, then slapped back to the present world. So much pain. He managed a small shake, his chest stiff with the pain he was inflicting. Haelan's face twisted, fat tears tore down his face, he wiped them away with his sleeve before straightening up. "We need to be quick. Roldan has managed to give me the slip, expect more guards very soon." He turned to the woman still lifting stones as fast as she could. "Nancy, I don't know what we'd have done without you." Ah, that's right, her name was Nancy. "Can you work on the right while the rest of us focus on the left?"

"Good idea!" She replied, her hand directing another large stone away from them. "Let me know when ye need shifting a big one."

That said, everyone rushed to form two lines at separate points, hands passing stones in swift and economical motions from one to the next. Amongst the casualties twenty-one were commoners. No children, thank the stars. Each body was laid down to one side under an opaque shield keeping animals out until people would come and seek their missing relative or friend. Albus's inert body was one of the last recovered. They decided to carry their comrades to camp in a tight formation with their strongest magical warriors at the front and Haelan, Dwennon and Kawana keeping the back. Eyes red from unshed tears Haelan kept glancing over his shoulder at the empty market square.

"They'll have made it to camp." Dwennon whispered close to his ear.

Haelan gave him a wan smile. "You're right. I've just got this nagging feeling something's happened to her."

Dwennon knew too well not to dismiss such feelings, they often held truth. "Sawyer has her back."

Haelan met his eyes dead on. "I hope you're right." So did Dwennon.

CHAPTER 26

Selena

The swaying cadence did nothing to take my mind away from the fact I was sitting metres high on a horse, well maybe not that high, but too high for my taste. Zen patted my arms encircling his waist as tightly as a harness moulded to a climber's bottom. "Ease up, will you?" he chuckled. "I do care to breathe." I unclasped my hands and relaxed my grip even though every neuron in my brain warned me against it. Tension gathered in my shoulders and neck. "Aah, that's better.' he exclaimed, 'Told you before, Sunshine is lovely and docile. She's a good girl, she is." he tapped her with an affectionate hand. "Not one to go rampaging, little Sunshine. Now, my horse Starburst is another story." He laughed at some secret adventures, no doubt.

I forced my gaze onto the scenery in front of us, too afraid to look down. The spectacular colours of autumn in full swing were blazing against a deep blue sky. Miles of deep forest extended before our high vantage point, hinting at more rolling hills and valleys. "Why did you take this horse if she isn't yours?"

He tsked, "It's not this horse, it's Sunshine." I hid a smile against his back. One thing I'd come to learn in the months since my arrival was that Zen was horse mad: he loved them, cared for them and talked about them to the point I now had developed a fair understanding in all things equine and equestrian. I wasn't ready to ride one by myself though. He'd asked, cajoled, pleaded, but still I held my ground, literally, on this one. I knew I would have to learn soon as it was the most reliable source of transport in this world. How I missed cars.

"I wanted to take Starburst, but Ryuuki objected." he grumbled.

Ryuuki

Even I was allowed to call him that, it's amazing how fast our friendship had grown, same with Zen. Back home, I struggled to place coherent words when meeting people, and although I wasn't too bad with the students from my Japanese course, I'd only been able to be truly myself around Anna. I'd always felt self-conscious about my looks, my personality, afraid I was lacking in both, and people would get bored of me.

Yet, with these two men I didn't feel judged. They accepted me, clumsiness and quirks included, wholeheartedly, even Shina in her own odd ways did. I was sure there were plenty of people like Zen and Ryuuki in my own world who'd passed me by. My little adventure had forced me into lifting my eyes from my books and understanding that people were as vulnerable as I was. A budding confidence was taking root within me although getting rid of my shyness would take some time and effort, old habits and all that. The boys loved to push me to express myself. After Ryuuki had gathered us all in his study and told the others about my origin, the prophecy – my prophecy – he'd looked at me, eyes unwavering, and asked. "What's on your mind?"

How could he tell? I smoothed a hand over my forehead, yes, I was frowning. This had to be a misunderstanding, I couldn't be the one in that prophecy. How could I free a world?

Ryuuki, who was sitting on a dark blue pillow in front of us, placed a hand on mine, at once I felt a warmth spread through the tips of my fingers. My fists eased their grip on my trousers.

His soft creamy voice removed the rest of the tension. "In your own time. I would like you to share your thoughts, please."

I lifted my head as he took his soft hand away, enthralled by the honey hue of his eyes until he looked away. Zen gave me an encouraging nod while Shina, hands crossed elegantly on her lap, waited, no judgement on her face. Deep in my chest, through the echoes of my heart I could sense the acceptance of these people I'd barely known three months.

"This can't be about me. I'm nothing special and certainly neither brave nor strong enough to save your world." I was shaking my head. This was all ludicrous.

"Child," the gentleness in Shina's voice surprised me. "One thing I've learnt from the ninety years I've been on this planet is that everyone, each in their own way, is special. Who we are makes us special. Do you understand?" I did and didn't, but I nodded nonetheless. She went on, "It could have been someone else who found that book, but it was you. It is your fate. You have to embrace it." I stared mutely at the floor.

"Selena." Zen's voice was lacking his usual playfulness. "I know it's a lot to take in, a new world, a new way of living, and now this. But we are here for you."

"Zen is right." Ryuuki smiled gently. "We will do our utmost to help you. From Dwennon's vision I already garnered you have to seek the Silver Tree hidden in our midst."

"The Silver Tree?"

He turned to the low table behind him and took a large light-brown leather book. Ryuuki opened it to the page with a red ribbon divider before handing it to me. One page contained a watercolour painting of a willow tree, its long branches a silver colour. The opposite page was written in a beautiful cursive script.

"The earliest records of the tree are two hundred years old, but the scholar who wrote this book believed it's older. He saw it for himself, hence the picture, others who have found it say it's lifelike. The tree's location is a mystery. Magic has shrouded its surroundings and whenever someone finds it, they forget how to get there as soon as they leave. Grandmother was convinced only good-hearted people could find it. I hope she's right, who knows what unsavoury people would do with its power? Anyway, not many attempt the journey nowadays."

"Why so?"

"Well," Zen joined in. "A lot of men have disappeared over the past decades. I think I could count on one hand the number of men I know who found it. It took one of them many seasons. It's a long and dangerous journey for sure."

"It's possible they perished along the way." The master's hand was set on his chin, his gaze lost to himself.

One thing they said struck me. "Why only men? Is it not possible for women to find it?" That would be my luck to have to look for a misogynist tree.

Shina had the nerve to cackle. "Why girl, you do say the silliest things sometimes. Of course women can find it. We, however, are less predisposed to boast about it." I frowned, unsure I understood right. "Lots have found the tree, but only their family and close friends know the truth of it." She lifted her chin, eyes proud. Obviously, someone in her family had done so. Or had she?

"What's so special about this tree?"

The master nodded at Shina, confirming my previous thought. "Grandmother explained she felt a guiding hand in her quest and upon seeing the tree she was compelled to touch a particular branch. However, I've also heard tales from other people touching a single leaf," her chin went down, resolute. "Never the trunk though."

This didn't answer my question however interesting it all sounded. "What happens when they touch it?"

"They get rewarded with an artifact." She said in a reverent tone, then stopped to my utter annoyance. Not everybody knew what they were, I could have huffed in frustration. Did I have to ask for every detail?

Before I could, the master explained. "They're magical objects that enhance someone's power. They can be passed down through blood lines, however, they don't work on all descendants, only one per generation. My belief is that you need to get an artifact yourself. What baffles me though is why." It took me a second to click.

"Maybe the artifact is for a mage coming with me?" I ventured. It was the only plausible reason I could think of. It made sense really, as I would need magical help to find the tree in the first place. Ryuuki nodded but didn't look convinced.

Looking at the vastness of the land surrounding me, I felt lost. How was I to find this elusive magical tree? Ryuuki assured me I would feel it deep inside of me. I was dubious. Only last night, I tossed and turned in bed trying to detect something, anything: a feeling, an incline or a gut instinct. I'd only felt an itch and a blooming headache. We, meaning Ryuuki, Zen and I, were set to go soon after Ryuuki had settled his affairs and duties with the Council as much as he could; he would have to delegate loads to his assistant who lived in the Capital.

A jumble of feelings clashed with one another in my head, scattering me into an emotional mess. This crazy sounding venture pulled at my inner adventurer, but I was tired from starting a new life, tired of not knowing what to expect in the future. I needed time to accept I might never go back home. Never see granddad and Anna again. What were they going through? Were they still looking for me? I wished I could reassure them. More often than not I felt torn between wanting to be with them and making a life for myself here. True, I didn't know much about the Closed Lands, but I loved it here. All this magic, the good weather, the clean air. Sometimes I wasn't sure I would go back home if I had the choice. Anna and granddad's face dripping with disappointment showed up once more in my mind. My stomach turned. I felt like an ungrateful and callous granddaughter and friend.

The din of the busy street we were progressing on drowned my dilemma. Women with baskets over their arms called out to the rider before us, horses going up and down the cobbled road forced chatting passersby to retreat in sunken doorways. Zen waved and greeted a few of them like old friends. At a stable, he dismounted in an agile and practised motion first, then put one hand on my waist. Impatient to get down, I grabbed the pummel with one hand like we'd practised many times, lifted my right leg high over the horse – the last horse did not like getting kicked – and slid down on the firm ground. Stretching my wobbly legs, I let go a long breath. Would I ever get used to riding a horse?

"Was it that bad? I'm hurt at your lack of trust in my equestrian prowess." One quick glance at his twitching lips and I knew he was joking. "I assure you I am a fine rider, the best in the region in fact." He threw his arm wide in a grand gesture. The stable hand who was taking Sunshine away guffawed at his outburst.

"You big idiot!" I grinned. I could never resist laughing when he spoke all posh; it was his way of teasing Ryuuki and his perfect manners.

Out of the building I realised the tension had left me, my problems forgotten. His joking and laid-back behaviour might make him appear like a bit of an idiot when, in fact, he was sharp-eyed and a compassionate and caring person. *I'm glad I met you,* I wanted to say. Zen, already at the end of the street, exclaimed with a waving arm to hurry up. *Another time.*

Sweet smells wafted all around me. My feet, and hungry tummy, led me to a baker's stand which held both familiar and strange creations. I felt like a child again when Zen asked me what I wanted and I pointed at what looked like a doughnut, a favourite of mine. Zen chose a sort of bun in the shape of an S, all the while asking the baker how his family and business were doing. After paying, he handed me the warm doughnut, I bit into it straight away. My taste buds rolled in ecstasy as we started wandering towards the stall he had business with.

It was a strange feeling being in this historical movie-like scenery. Vendors, squeezed close to one another, were shouting their wares or haggling with customers who had to dodge other customers and their baskets on their way to another stand. Tables bursting with fruit, vegetables and jars of delicious looking jams and honey, cages rattling under chickens' unnerved feet and livestock, scattered in small made-up pens, took up the best part of the market square. The smaller section, though, was the one to hold my attention captive. I tripped over Zen's foot when he stopped.

"Oops, sorry." I mumbled, my eyes still cast over my shoulder in the direction of the magical stalls, more precisely to a man waving, flicking his fingers while in front of him threads entwined and interlaced to form a beautiful forest green cloak with patterns I couldn't decipher.

"Go! Have a look around." Zen said, giving me a slight push. "I'll catch up with you." He didn't have to tell me twice. After making it through the crowd of villagers, I reached the stall where the tailor, if you could call him that, spread his arms wide then clapped them once; the fabric fell neatly folded onto the table. The show was over. I looked with longing eyes at the beautiful green cloak; little willow trees sewed with a brilliant silver thread embellished the hemline. *How fitting.* My hand went to the purse I'd tucked inside my belt then froze. Ryuuki was generous with his wages, I'd saved quite a good amount. While I mentally argued with myself on whether I should buy it, the tailor shuffled closer and exclaimed, "One silver coin for a pretty thing like you, unless you've something to barter?" He raised thick eyebrows, eyes sparkling. Trade was the norm, be it for food, clothes or magical services. Shame my only contribution so far was cleaning, but I could part with a silver.

I shook my head. "I'll pay." His shoulders seemed to deflate a tad, and I bit down a smile. Zen had mentioned people around here loved a good haggle. After giving him a shiny silver coin, he came around and placed the cloak across my shoulders. He stepped back and nodded to himself. "Just the thing! Good day young lady!"

My hands forever stroking the smooth material, I explored

the rest of the market, a smile on my face. These people were not much different from those I'd seen in the Broadway market in London. Their clothing, like Ryuuki's household, were a mixture of oriental clothing, long Chinese style tunics over baggy trousers, Japanese hakama and yukata with leather sandals or slippers, or long flowy dresses. No silly high heels in these parts, thank God.

Further away from the hustle and bustle, I spotted a bookstore. Dodging left and right people carrying baskets and linen bags full of wares I went to the shop's window. The few books on display all looked the same: silver titles on brown leather. *I wonder if they've got novels.* Out of the corner of my eye a movement distracted me from my perusal. I turned my head to the right and saw a large bulging chest within arm's reach. Unease crept up my rigid spine, I craned my neck. What I saw did not reassure me in any way; the eyes that were looking down at me were strange, almost vacant, a trait I'd witnessed on druggies too often for my liking. They were enclosed in a very round and ruddy face, topped with greasy looking hair. Not the type of man I wanted to find myself with. His mouth was open in a dumb looking way, saliva made a trail down his chin. I stepped back, maybe he wasn't quite all there in the head. One big meaty hand reached out towards me, and I freaked out.

I turned and ran away as fast as I could in the opposite direction. Taking the first street appearing in front of me, I didn't think about getting lost or the fact I would have been safer within the crowd. I listened to the fear screaming at me to put as much distance as possible between us. I took a left turn then a right, I never stayed on the same street for very long. Wooden houses and cottage-looking ones were scattered at a distance when I finally slowed down, short of breath, the centre of the village a distance away from me. The town wasn't very big, I had reached the outskirts already. Glancing over my shoulder I saw him right down the path lumbering towards me. I'd gone back on the main road without realising it. Faint music sounded to my right, following the catchy tune I took the alleyway right next to me, then went to hide behind a barn at the rear of what looked like a pub or an inn. Two men with glasses half full were leaning against an outbuilding thirty metres or so from me, they laughed between themselves while their gaze washed over me.

"Hi there sweet thing." One of them called out. "Want to join us?" He raised his glass with a wobbly arm. Another prickle of alert woke up and I cursed my bad luck for running in the wrong direction, surely the other man wouldn't have assaulted me in the market. Now I had left one problem for a bigger one. I stepped back only to bump into something hard. Before I could react a hand grasped my arm, the touch cold even through my sleeve. I turned around in an attempt to dislodge it, but the handhold was as tight as steel handcuffs. I expected to see the weird guy from earlier on. To my surprise a smaller man held me in his clasp.

His mouth twisted in a smile that did not reach his bleak eyes. "Looks like you're a tad unwell, love. Why don't I take you to me house there?" He nodded towards a pretty wooden house, too pretty for the likes of him. His face was pleasant enough, but his breath stank of alcohol, never a good sign.

I forced a smile then declined as politely as I could muster, my mind busy working out ways to unhook his unyielding grip. "My friend will be looking for me by now. I must go." No sooner the words left my mouth than he twisted my arm hard, back taut against his chest. The cool feel of a blade settled on my cheek.

I whimpered.

This was not the kind of adventure I wanted. I surveyed my surroundings, now desperate to see that big guy, hoping he would fight this one off while I would leg it as fast as I could. He wasn't there though.

The man at my back gave me a shove forward. "Come along now," he chuckled. "Let's have a good time with my mates." To my horror the other two men unfolded from the shadow they had hid in and started towards the house. I dug my heels deep in the dirt path, then stopped as the blade was pressed harder against my cheek. "No funny moves, love."

Shame consumed me. I could not recall any of the self-defence I'd learnt in an after-school class. Why hadn't I paid more attention? Shaking as violently as a feather caught in a storm, my sight went blurry with unshed tears. My head a dizzy and sluggish mess, I tried to make coherent thoughts, but they evaporated like puffs of steam as soon as I focused on them. Sweat was dripping down my forehead and back as images of what was about to happen flipped through my terrified mind.

He pushed me harder. I only half registered the movement because my ears were now screeching in a high pitch, deadening everything around me. I could neither see nor hear and my whole body felt as though it'd been left in a sauna for a whole day. Amongst the blur, I thought I heard Zen calling out to me from a distant place. That couldn't be right though. How would he have found me? My free hand was clawing at my throat and chest in a futile attempt to ease the heat on my skin. It was getting unbearable, suffocating.

Then something strange happened: smoke penetrated through the haze, smoke that was far too close for comfort. My body felt so hot. Could I self-combust from sheer terror? A chilling scream pierced through like a muffled siren in my impenetrable fog, then I blanked out.

CHAPTER 27

Ryuuki
&
Selena

Eyelids heavy with the sums of trade figures Ryuuki took a sip from the steaming cup on the table then shifted his legs to a different position. He'd poured over his estate books since early morning and most of the warm day had passed him by unawares. He longed to be out, in his garden to be precise. Yet, it would have to wait another day. He dismissed the fact he'd told himself the exact same words every day for the past week. That last pile by his left elbow assured him he would be done settling his affairs on the morrow.

The green tea failed to give him the boost of energy he needed to work proficiently. Weariness had settled on his bent neck and his shoulders were stiff. Getting up, he grabbed a plate of rice balls from the tray Shina had placed on the side table for noon break. Hours ago, he mused, watching the sun on its descent. Just then, the sight of a delicate blue bird shattered his waning resolve to keep on working. A walk through the garden while eating would help him revive his spirit numbed by numbers. No sooner had he crossed the walkway and chewed on a rice ball than his pendant flashed. Only two people were connected to it. Shina being on the premises, Ryuuki had no trouble predicting who was calling him. Placing his hand on the stone he greeted Zen and waited for the lively voice of his friend.

"Ryuuki...' Zen's voice was out of breath and strangely high. "This is bad, I need your help at once."

Ryuuki dropped the rice ball that was halfway to his mouth, the food he'd just eaten an iron anchor sunk into his stomach. "Where are you?"

"The barn behind the Black Bear inn. Hurry, I don't know what else to do for her."

There could be only one person he was referring to: Selena was in trouble. He ran past the main room telling Shina in a breeze where he was going, then rushed down the front stairs. He was vaguely aware of his servants throwing themselves out of his way or watching him, eyes wide with surprise. At least it wasn't fear he could read this time, it felt like an improvement. The thought nearly made him laugh. Maybe he should run like a madman more often.

He'd done lots of strange and new things since that woman came to live with them, things he'd never dared to have imagined, not the least exposing his eyes to a woman so soon after meeting her. Her naive acceptance and, if he was not mistaken, admiration had been a lovely experience. For the past few weeks he'd forgone his hat completely inside his private residence – as he did so prior to her arrival – and never once had he felt embarrassed doing so in her presence. When they'd happen to meet, she would bow her head in deference but always looked him in the eye when speaking to him. He loved that about her, she wasn't afraid of him.

The stable hands jumped and shook at his brusque commands. While they saddled Firebolt his mind pondered in furious waves what could have happened, what could have gone wrong as they'd only gone to the market. Could someone have realised she wasn't from their world? Even so, they were used to travelling peddlers from around the other Domains. Her accent and manners shouldn't do more than raise a few eyebrows. Foot in the stirrup he lifted himself then settled on his fastest horse. He couldn't conceive what had taken place, but at least he would get there fast. The stables were situated judiciously next to the main gate, he pressed his legs gently against the horse's flanks. Used to his owner's touch and movements, Firebolt walked into the courtyard, passed the gate and took off at a gallop.

Through a flurry of dust and dirt their path joined the main road where villagers and traders were travelling at a slow pace. The sound of his arrival drew curious glances over shoulders or pointed fingers. Everyone gave way in a rush except a small boy waving a grubby hand at Ryuuki with enthusiasm. His mother turned around, beheld his fast-advancing form and tugged the child in her arms while rushing to the side screaming. Firebolt could easily jump over a child without harming him, but deep down he knew it wasn't the horse that had set her actions in motions: his hat did.

This hat was as bright as a beacon for all the attention and repulsion it directed at him. Irritation and sadness slackened his grip on the reigns for a while. How he wished people's reactions and thoughts towards him would stop affecting him so.

"These people are not worth your sorrows." A voice said in his head. Not his own. The ring to it sounded strangely familiar; something, a memory maybe, pulled at him as though he should recognise it. "They can't see past their normality-seeking noses." He cast a quick look at his pendant. Not this. The voice laughed then. "All in good time, boy." It said before the laughter died down. A shiver raised the skin on his warm arms. Who was that? Unease shook him, he didn't like the tone of that voice. However, his mind had to focus on what was to come as the first cottages outside the village appeared over the rise.

Slowing Firebolt down to a trot, they made their way to the inn; white smoke was coming out from behind the building. Around the bend, the scene that greeted him was not the one he'd expected: Zen was throwing a bucket of water on Selena, an unconscious Selena, while the innkeeper held another one next to him. A stable boy nearby then took Zen's empty bucket and ran to the well. What in the stars was going on? As Ryuuki slid down the horse, he noticed amongst the gawking villagers a big burly man watching from a distance, Tirus, the other pariah around here. Despite his bulk and strange behaviour, the man was harmless. He'd fallen out of a tree as a young boy and had never been the same since; no healer had managed to undo the harm, Ryuuki included. Why was he here? Things were getting more and more peculiar by the second.

Hurrying towards Zen and the innkeeper, he said. "I asked you to show her the village, not drown her."

Mid-action Zen turned to him and heaved a sigh of relief. "Praise the stars you're here." His shoulders lost their tension, but he kept pouring water over Selena. When his friend moved to the left Ryuuki noticed another unconscious form on the floor. Before he could move towards the man, Zen cried out. "Don't bother with him, a leech deserves to live more than this pile of manure. Tirus saw him assault Selena and came to get me, well, dragged me because I could make no sense of his gestures. Anyway, that whoreson had a knife to her throat when we got here, then she just…" his voice pitched high again with the timbre of his distress. "I didn't know what else to do."

Ryuuki placed a hand on Zen's shoulder and projected a tendril of soothing energy. "You did well, my friend." He peered over his shoulder at Tirus, contemplating why he was the one to get Zen. He longed to ask the big man but knew any questions would be received with a blank stare. Tirus didn't like to talk. He knelt down next to Selena. Her skin was flushed and clammy, his hand, which was close to her cheek, could feel the heat radiating from her. He touched the tip of a finger on her forehead for a second in spite of his gut feeling telling him not to then recoiled: it was burning hot. Several prods to other parts of her exposed skin gave similar results.

"She's cooler than she was." Zen opened his right hand; angry and painful looking blisters covered his palm. Ryuuki grimaced as he stood up then waved to Zen to pour more water. His eyes settled on the man on the floor. "Have you checked him up?"

"No." he said with gritted teeth. "Don't know if he's alive and I don't care."

Ryuuki crouched down next to the man and examined his clothes. The fabric of his tunic was marred with black as though burnt, a strong smell of smoke hung in the air. He looked at Zen in alarm. "Did he catch fire?" Now that he looked at Selena's clothes hers showed similar signs.

Zen looked at him confused. "Yes, they both did, didn't I just tell you?"

Ryuuki bit down on his irritation hard. "No, you stopped at that man assaulting her."

Zen rubbed a trembling hand over his face. "Sorry, that shook me up some." He waved Ryuuki over while instructing the innkeeper to keep putting water on Selena. Away from prying ears, he said, "When we arrived, Selena's face had this unnatural red colour and she looked scared out of her wits. I called her name, but she didn't seem to hear me." He shook his head then nodded at Tirus. "That was weird, he was mumbling about beautiful rainbow colours around her, clapping hands and getting all excited. Next thing I know, Selena put her hand on that ratbag's arm. He jumped back, screaming, but she wouldn't let him go. And just like that they both caught fire." He looked down then scratched his head like he always did when stressed. "I know she did it, the fire I mean. She looked in some kind of trance and the air around her was all wavy, you know, like on a hot day."

The revelation left Ryuuki speechless for a while. As though coming from a dense fog, one line of the prophecy resurfaced.

"An outsider of our own", he whispered. Zen's head shot up, eyes alert.

Ryuuki kept his voice low, "What if she's a mage, we know not all of them made it to Newlands. It's plausible she's a descendant of one who survived the hunts." Zen looked equally terrified and excited. "Let's get her home."

The journey felt like a burning eternity. On Firebolt, Selena was propped against his chest, his arms keeping her from falling. A heavy blanket, borrowed from the inn, protected the horse while their clothes were the only barrier between them. The dampness of her charred clothes combined with her body heat created an acrid smelling mist all around them. His eyes watered. Coughing didn't help with the mist choking his nose and throat. Upon arrival at the stables, the hands hurried over to them, eager to do their master's bidding. Ryuuki rose a hand to keep them at bay. He dismounted, all the while keeping a hand on Selena's swaying form, then took her in his arms. Without so much as a word, he made haste to his house, fearing his clothes would catch on fire at any moment. The pain didn't break through the cloud of apprehension and uncertainty. Shina, ever so efficient, was on the walkway waiting for them.

"Get some ice for the bath!" He called out as he ascended the front stairs. Her eyebrows raised at the form of Selena's slumped body. She didn't say a word. She went straight to the cooking room, sliding doors open for easy access on her way. The silence was pressing, a heavy presence on his soul, his heart. He couldn't talk. The implications of what was going on were tremendous, forming the words would only make it more real. First and foremost, there were more important things at hand; he forced himself to focus on healing her. And regardless, there was no point in letting all the questions flood him if nobody could answer them. Settling Selena on a chair, he started to undo buttons with one hand while holding her with the other, the pad of his fingers smarting under her touch. Zen, only a few steps behind him, came forward to help, wincing whenever his skin came into contact with her burning flesh. Shina tutted at what she saw when she entered the room. After throwing ice in the tub and filling it up with water, she extended a hand towards Selena.

Ryuuki pushed it away. "Don't touch her, we'll do this. We can't have all of us covered in blisters."

"What are our times coming to?" She grumbled.

"Enough!" Ryuuki roared. Both Shina and Zen jumped at his outburst, he rarely rose his voice. He took a calming breath, feeling ashamed of himself, and added, "She's burning. We need to make it stop."

The last of her outer clothes gone, she was left in her undergarments. This would have to do, he thought, urgency licking at his hands. He ground his teeth as he held her close within his arms before lowering her down gently in the tub; red welts marked his pale skin when he let go. The water hissed upon touching her skin, a cloud of steam rose from the tub and enveloped them. The room became too hot, too humid, their clothes, their hair hung limply and a tinge of sweat clung to the air, reminding Ryuuki of a summer storm.

His mind pondering on how to proceed, Ryuuki barely noticed Shina going out the room and coming back with more ice, which she added to the water with her bare hands. After the bucket was empty, she knelt on the opposite side, eyes watering with worry. "Poor girl. What happened?" Feeling guilty at shouting at her, he explained the best he could, Zen providing his input every now and then.

"She's one of us?" Shina's tone was sharp.

"It would seem so. One way to be sure though." His eyes narrowed and focused on the woman that had taken apart his safe routine, burnt it into smoke, he mused. "Hold her still if she moves."

The ice had melted, the water was lukewarm, Selena's skin had returned to her normal creaminess. Laying his hands, palms flat, on Selena's upper chest, he closed his eyelids then went into a meditative place he could only achieve when healing. Sounds and throbs of her life source ran from his hands to the tip of his toes, he could feel her energy pulsing in a mad dash. He waited patiently for lines and shapes to take form, for colours to steep in his mind; like a gifted artist her body was drawn to perfection, down to the smallest cells if he wished to focus on them.

To his surprise, every sinewy and sharp form radiated with different hues. Normally a person had one or two, on rare occasions three, specific colours attached to their body: their magical essence. This magical essence was the root of their magic, their gifts. People with a red magical essence tended to be gifted with the element of fire, a blue essence had an affinity to water. He's observed many colours, possibly not all of them, and although the majority of the people he'd healed shared the same colours, the shade, the brightness and which part of the body the essence was focused on differed with everyone. To this day, he'd not met two people sharing the same magical essence. Until this day, he'd never have believed what he was seeing could be possible. Selena's magical essence was beautiful: a rainbow swirling, twirling in an embracing dance around and within her. It was absolutely mesmerising. He'd never seen so much power in anyone. A rainbow. Wasn't that what Tirus had said? How fascinating, it appeared the man's ability was to see a person's magical essence. He put the knowledge aside for now, it might come in handy one day.

Ryuuki searched for the cause of the heat, but his grip on her kept slipping from where he wanted to concentrate. A tug, a force pulled him towards something else. Instead of fighting it he let himself be taken. Mental turmoil broke down his defences, at once images broke into his mind: memories, emotions he would never be able to forget. Her hopelessness became his, her fear, a mass of roiling dark clouds gathering energy, was waiting for the right moment to implode within her, within him. No, not me, he called out. *I'm Ryuuki, a healer.*

The pain subsided with each beat of each word, then vanished.

The only time he'd attempted to mend a soul, Tirus's soul, he'd been nearly pulled, trapped inside of it. His mind had been broiling with confusing, flashing images as well as a maelstrom of violent emotions. Ryuuki, afraid for his sanity, had given up in the end, unable to put the pieces back together. Selena's, however terrifying her wild emotions were, still held a structured pattern. He picked at the memories swirling in her head and inspected them carefully for a time. With intuition that came from his healing ability and meticulous care, he grasped those needing his immediate attention and conveyed feelings of peace, warmth and safety.

After a time, he was left with memories of people and roomfuls of books impregnated with sadness and longing. He projected his private residence. *Home, your new home.* After a beat, Shina and Zen's faces along with his own, his eyes as colourful as her own essence, replaced the old memories. A loving feeling enveloped him, he basked in its warmth, a sun's rays to his heart. It was humbling that she'd come to care for them, himself included, in such a short time. As he withdrew from her, a touch of something, an emotion perhaps, grazed him but it was gone before he could grasp what it was.

* * *

Warm water was lapping my body in pleasant waves, soothing my sore muscles. Did I fall asleep in the bath? I opened my eyes at the same time I sat up. A heavy thud and pain lanced in my head as I collided with something hard. My tear-streaked gaze focused on the unexpected object. *Oops, not an object.* Ryuuki straightened up, rubbing a hand over his forehead.

"Sorry," I mumbled. Then realisation hit me hard, water sloshed over the bathtub when I quickly crossed both arms over my breasts, which were fully covered. I looked down in surprise (yep, I was in a bath full of water in my underwear) then up at the three faces staring down at me.

Awkward.

I scratched my head as the familiar scene reminded me of my first day here and I waited for an explanation, for there had to be one if their shared frowns were any indication.

"You nearly burnt to death, but what you care about is your state of undress?" Ryuuki was incredulous, a look I shared with him.

"What do you mean 'nearly burnt to death'?"

"You don't remember?" Zen lowered himself down next to me, sparking a memory. My brain went into overdrive at that moment: Zen, the market, that strange big man, then the events at the back of the inn fought with one another to make themselves known in my achy head. I ran a hand down my face, my breath rugged. Clearly, I was missing something. Last thing I knew I was being held by that guy, the acrid taste of smoke on my tongue. "Did he try to burn me?" I asked although the idea didn't make sense, he'd wanted to rape me. I shuddered.

Ryuuki shook his head, looking uneasy and even apologetic. That didn't bode well. "You did."

I frowned, the movement stinging like thousands of little needles. "I don't understand."

Ryuuki knelt and grabbed the edge of the tub, his fingers white under the grip. As he opened his mouth Shina interrupted. "Master, the girl needs time to recover. Surely, another time for explanations would –"

"Not make things any easier." He answered while his eyes, a pure dark grey, held mine. The old woman remained quiet after that. "Selena, what I'm about to tell you may be hard to grasp. It will affect your life in ways which you'd never imagined before. It is a gift as well as a burden. If we had more time I would rather wait until you recover before telling you. However, you must know now in order to survive. May I?" I wanted to see Zen's or Shina's expressions to have an incline of their thoughts, a clue, anything to reassure me this wasn't as terrible as Ryuuki's tone implied. Even the colour of his eyes was somber, but his stare held mine with an invisible grasp.

One part of me craved to find out what had happened, how I'd gotten in the tub in the first place. The other though, crouched down low, hands over ears singing la la la like a child blocking out unwanted voices, scared of what fate was yet again throwing at me. But one thing life had taught me was that ignorance did not make anyone any happier or safer, and neither did it solve nor remove the problems. I had to face it head on. I nodded my acquiescence, not trusting my own voice.

"What nearly burnt you and that man, was you, your power to be more precise." He paused; his face grave although the glint in his eyes betrayed his excitement. "You're one of us." *What?* I glanced at Zen who was grinning, at Shina, then back to Ryuuki not quite believing the implication of his words. "I felt it, saw it with my mind's eyes. You are a Mage, Selena, the strongest I've ever seen."

CHAPTER 28

Faylinn

We set off at a run behind the fleeing crowd. Doors opened and banged closed. The stomping of feet drifted away. The closer we approached the outer wall enclosing the Castle, the wider the streets became. In these parts of town only small groups of nobles, wide-eyed and pale, rushed to their elegant houses. Despite the seriousness of the situation, my eyes roamed everywhere around me, thirsty to take in every single detail. Nothing looked as I'd imagined it: the commoners' quarters were more desolate, dirtier, smellier than I could ever imagine, not a tree in sight, only brick touching brick with the odd alleyway separating clusters of crumbling houses. How the king had let people live in such poverty without shame nor guilt was beyond me. On the other hand, not so far nobles resided in large and clean streets; trees lined the road on both sides, and flowers, cascading down windows, lit up the austere and tall houses.

Keeping the wall in view, we rushed through the indistinguishable streets until the pebbled road turned into a dirt-packed track, not long after that we reached the forest bordering the back of the Castle's grounds. I ran to the nearest tree and gave a mental image of the hidden door beseeching its help; in response it showed me the quicker path to find it.

"Quite the useful trick, that one." Uttered Sawyer, not in the least out of breath. I'd revealed to everyone my unusual gift at home one evening when we were gathered for dinner. It'd been liberating to confide how it had evolved the past few months to something that made me proud and useful. I didn't know if someone out there had a similar ability, it happens of course, but I didn't care, I felt unique, lucky to have it. I wouldn't change it for Myrddin's gifts.

"Yes, I'm amazed I never thought of communicating with them in that way before." I pressed hard on the sharp pain in my side, peeved at my lack of endurance. My mouth twisted to one side. *It's running for you every day, girl, if you want to keep in shape.*

Soon afterwards, panting like an old and frazzled dog at the end of its life, I reached a familiar ivy climbing on what appeared to be a mound and went to tear at it. For the life of me I couldn't understand how it got so dense so quickly. After a second, two strong arms moved me out of the way and went to work; a scalding comment about being strong enough to do the work regardless of my gender flew right past him. Stewing in my own temper while sitting down for a much-needed rest, I grew ashamed of the way I had barked at him. Knowing Sawyer, he'd noticed my struggles and took the task of uncovering the door as a silent kindness. "Sorry about that." I mumbled to his back.

He glanced at me over his shoulder then resumed pulling the vine away from the door. "I'm used to yer temper by now." I gave a chuckle, I deserved that. He was quick, within moments we were in the damp and dark passage. I swore. Sawyer's deep laugh echoed around us.

"Been round us too long, lass." he said and went back outside.

"Never heard you swear."

He came back with a thick branch of ivy. "Doesn't mean I don't." Even though his face was cast in shadows I could hear the playfulness in his tone, and I chuckled. A soft whistling emanated from him just before the leaves lit up in a bright green.

"Ooh, useful trick." I stole his earlier words. My head shot up with an idea and I rushed outside to get another one.

Back next to him, he looked at me inquiringly. "One should be enough. We..." he said, and I held my hand up to make him stop, which a distant voice in my head found ironic. Eyes shut tight, I concentrated on the small branch in my hand; I opened myself, merged with it and willed it to light up. I opened my eyes with anticipation.

Nothing.

I shrugged. "Never mind." I threw the ivy on the compact earth. "It was worth a try."

I could feel his eyes boring into me and decided I was too much of a coward to meet them. He swung the branch in front of me, I took it and started up the passage at a quick pace. Nothing seemed to have changed I was glad to notice; my footsteps from months ago were imprinted in the layer of dust. Here and there were little impressions and scratchings, but nothing man-made. As the path inclined and the ceiling lowered to a neck-bending height, the air turned stale and closed off. I drew slow breaths and fixed my stare on what was ahead, it would do me no good dwelling on the fact we were under tons of hard compact soil with no direct escape. Strange, I'd not felt this oppressiveness last time, maybe I'd been so focused on my future freedom anything else had paled against it.

Sweat ran down my back at the speed we were keeping up, we should be able to half the time it normally took me to walk this path. At the first intersection, I took the way heading to the west wing where Gwynn's rooms were situated. Sawyer's steps were as discreet as ever, but I could feel his heat radiating right behind me.

A slither of his breath curled on my bare neck, causing a delightful shiver to run down my spine. "I take it ye've been down here many times." He whispered at the next intersection when I went towards another path to our left without hesitation.

"Whenever I could. Got lost on many occasions though, so I devised a system of sorts." I stopped and pointed to a rough engraving behind him. He stared at the gross picture of a crown with a G underneath and nodded. "The royal quarters? Cute drawing." His eyes were dancing. I lifted mine to the ceiling and lead the way again.

My feet stopped a few yards before Gwynn's rooms, then turned towards Sawyer. I whispered. "Her rooms are just around the corner. I want you to wait here."

"No!" his stance was as clear as fresh morning air. I knew he wouldn't yield.

I lifted my arms up in frustration. "You don't understand. If she sees you hovering behind me, she'll think she's under attack and will call the guards." His face didn't so much as twitch, I persevered. "I need to talk to her woman to woman, she won't see me as a threat."

"That's what I'm afraid of, but...." He deliberated for a long moment, then agreed none too happy. As I turned around, he called out in a whisper, "Wait. I'll stay by the door. Call out if ye need help." I nodded and was about to go but he added, "And ye should have this on hand." He lifted the bow at my back and held it before me. "To be on the safe side." I frowned. The bow wouldn't be exactly the picture of a peace offering. He pushed it forward and I relented, placing my hand on the shaft. A trickle of anger, not my own, jolted across the palm of my hand and invaded my senses, I met Sawyer's startled gaze as a burning fear, followed by fierce love and longing alighted my whole body like red hot embers. The bow scattered to the ground as we both let go at the same time, our eyes locked on each other.

"What..." My next words were silenced as Sawyer's hands grabbed my arms and pulled me towards him, a second later his lips were on mine. Hard, desperate. This was not a tender kiss the likes I used to dream of receiving in my young goose years, this was a kiss full of repressed feelings and passion. A world away from the soft one I'd received from an apprentice gardener when I was fifteen; it'd been lukewarm, pleasant. Not this one. This kiss unlocked sensations, feelings I didn't know I possessed. My hands snaked up his shoulders and neck into his newly cut hair. In some distant awareness, my lungs were working furiously, my head was dizzy, my legs barely supporting me. I didn't care. All I could focus on was the softness of his lips, the intoxicating smell of his. I pressed my body close to his instinctively. He groaned and deepened the kiss. I lost all sense of time. This was where I wanted to be. Yet, an uncomfortable awareness tugged at my mind, one I couldn't grasp. I didn't want to grasp.

To my dismay, I moaned in protest when he wrenched his mouth away. His forehead resting on mine, he looked at me as open as I'd ever seen him, his chest heaving in sharp bursts. I was amazed he kept so much fire under his serious facade, but the shell had cracked it seemed as he caressed my cheek with a shaking hand and gave me a smile worthy of shattering stars into dust. We didn't talk, I didn't think we could, and besides no words were needed, we'd shared our most intimate feelings.

It was enough.

When our breathing settled at last, he bent down to give me a quick kiss. "Ye better go. I'll have yer back." The intensity in his eyes screaming he always would. I nodded, suddenly nervous. The elation was deflating.

We shared one last look before walking around the bend. After a furtive search, I found a smallish knob and pressed it. When my hand met the wooden panel, I ignored the sharp sting the timber sent me and found myself in between silk and gauze dresses. Gwynn's closet. It was huge, I could stretch my arms on both side and still not reach the end of it. One hand still firm on my bow the other pushed one of the doors a crack. This was the dressing room: white marble, streaked with black in a pattern similar to smoke, covered both floor and walls, I spied Gwynn standing in front of a lady's dressing table fashioned with an oval mirror at its centre; she poured water in a dish and bent over it. This was as good a time as I would get to come out. Thankfully the doors did not creak. I tiptoed a few paces behind her, waiting for her to see me. Eyelids closed, she took the towel to her right and patted her face. To my enjoyment, she jumped and gasped when she saw my reflection in the mirror. She turned round wearing a speculative look, or was it calculating? Unease pooled at the bottom of my stomach.

"Well, cousin, I didn't expect to see you again." I did not care for the way she was appraising me, mouth raised in a sneer. Gone was her wobbling lips and now that I could study her up close, so was the pallor of her skin, her cheeks were rosy. In fact, she looked the healthiest I'd ever seen her. Was she cured of her illness? I took a step back. This had been a bad idea, a whirling sense of urgency screamed in my head I'd been wrong, so very wrong.

Taking another step back, I said trying to buy time. "I wanted to check up on you." It wasn't wrong.

She raised an eyebrow, "Are you saying it has nothing to do with those people trying to kill Roldan?" Interesting that she cared. "Some of my guards spotted Haelan at their side." She cocked her head, waiting for my response.

My teeth sank into the inside of my cheek, unsure on what to say. "You can't trust him." I exclaimed in the end. "He was conniving with Quentin to kill you all." I waited to see if she would pretend ignorance. I was no longer in doubt of her involvement, but I needed to keep her talking in order to escape.

"I am overcome with gratitude. Do you mean to say family love brought you to rescue me?" she asked her voice mocking, taunting. "Somehow I am doubtful you shed any tears when you heard the King and Queen were dead."

"Of course, I didn't care a dragon's tail, this country is well rid of them." I shut my mouth in a snap. Damn. Getting her angry wouldn't achieve anything but trouble. I moved back. "Look, before I ran away, I heard Quentin and Roldan discussing the murder of the king. Roldan has now betrayed Quentin. Don't you see you're the only one left in his way to the throne? And when I saw you today, alive, I thought I had to tell you what kind of a man he is. He's got his own agenda; you can't trust him." I reiterated.

She burst out laughing and asked in a singing tone. "What do you say, dear, shouldn't I trust you?" I gasped. My hand lifted the bow while the other reached for an arrow, but hands forced them down and kept them in a strong hold. *Curse it! Where did he come from?*

"You should choose your companions better, dearest."

"Unhand me at once." I ground out. He let go but took my weapon and threw it on the dressing table, striking pots and brushes with its velocity. Roldan moved to Gwynn's side then appraised me. "That won't do you any good." His eyes pointed at my hand hovering over my hidden knife. I scowled and took it out anyway. He chuckled, "I can see what Quentin saw in you after all. Feisty, aren't you?" His fingers flickered and the knife flew to the floor, too far away for me to reach. I tried not to look as panicked as I felt. Why hadn't I listened to the others? It was out of the question to call for help, Sawyer would be dead the second he entered the room.

Gwynn bristled. "I want her dead now." She screeched like a mad woman. How could anyone at Court have missed this? They'd played us all for fools. Could Sawyer hear any of this? I regretted not asking him to wait among the dresses.

"Hold that temper of yours, I'm afraid I am quite spent. They took me by surprise, and I was outnumbered. I had to retreat." Shame he'd managed. He was rubbing his temple, his eyes on her, so I took another step back.

"You do look wan." Gwynn ran a hand over the side of his sharp-boned face and readjusted his cloak in a loving gesture, so at odd with the Gwynn I'd lived with. I took another step backwards, but Roldan noticed and struck like a snake, grabbing me by the arm.

"Not so fast, Lady Faylinn." His hand felt like ice, my whole arm was numbing rapidly. He turned his head to Gwynn. "You should keep her for a while, she's got more magic than she lets on. Like her brother as a matter of fact. You can steal her magical essence for a while, my dear, she should last longer than your puny handmaids I suppose." What was he talking about? The calculating evil in his eyes terrified me, this man had to be killed today no matter what. The weight of the knife at my back reassured me, I'd have to plan this carefully. I could do this, I said to myself trying to calm my fraying nerves. "Her brother, though, would make a more interesting catch. You could try some of those manipulating spells we found in the book." his eyes narrowed in reflection before settling on me. "Yes, a powerful man that brother of yours. Your father, however, not so. Shame." He shook his head in mock sadness. My body went hot then cold in a second. Father. Had anything happened to him? No, I took a calming breath, he was trying to unsettle me because he was weak.

"Never mind that, how did you get in here?" His question took me back to the problem at hand. I held my lips tight, head bent forward, while trying to work a way out of this without getting myself killed. He cursed, then shoved me to the floor. "I told you we should have checked the whole castle to find those damned passages." He shouted at Gwynn while moving towards the closet, his head was turned over his shoulder as he spoke. It took two seconds. However, two seconds were enough for Sawyer to burst through the doors and release an arrow. Roldan, quick as lightning despite being battle weary, raised a hand to create a magical shield. Like that fateful day I'd killed a man to save Kel, the arrow hissed past the shield protecting Roldan's front, made a sharp turn before striking his heart from behind. The shield vanished a moment before Roldan collapsed, blood pooling on the marble floor.

My enchanted arrow. I watched, stunned, Roldan's dead form. I couldn't believe it had worked for Sawyer, and after so many days.

"Guards!" The piercing scream echoed in the room as Gwynn lunged towards Roldan and took him in her arms. Heavy footsteps were fast approaching. Sawyer grabbed my hand, and we dived through the dresses, the panel, which we didn't bother to close; Gwynn's muffled yells of "I'll have your heads for this" floated down the passage giving me wings.

We ran as fast as we possibly could in a tight enclosure, arms, hips grazing or hitting the walls as we made turns at full speed; ran until we were by the rotten door. Only then, did we stop a moment to close it and fetch an old fallen trunk, Sawyer had spotted on our way in, to brace it against the door. We took off again, fear of discovery abating with every step. When at last we stopped to rest because I couldn't possibly breathe any faster and my legs were burning from the effort, Sawyer informed me he'd used a spell to wipe our footprints away. I could only look at him in amazement. No wonder he was an elder so young. I'd been so focused on running for my life, no other coherent thoughts had crossed my mind. To be fair, I reminded myself, I'd never received the training he'd had.

Later, as we slunk through the forest towards our camp, he took my hand and asked, "Ye did something to that arrow, didn't ye?" I told him of my experiment with all their bows and arrows, on the off chance an event like this might happen.

He stopped me in my track and squeezed my hand, "This is an incredible gift. Just imagine how it could help weaker people, anyone to defend themselves."

I made a face. "I'm not so sure. It was appropriate with Roldan, but what if it gets in the wrong hands, children..." I shivered at the thought.

He frowned, lost in thought. "Did ye ask it to kill?"

"Yes."

"That means ye could just incapacitate in the same way. Order the arrow to strike one limb for example." My eyes widened, of course. "I know wanderers would be mighty eager to strike a deal with ye." He played with a strand of my hair absentmindedly.

I nodded. "I could have them colour coordinated, red for a kill, green for a small wound..." Ideas cramped my tired mind, but I was ecstatic. This felt right, I could help father's army defeat Gwynn. It shouldn't be too difficult now Roldan was dead. Sawyer smiled at the look on my face then took me in his arms and held me tight for a while. Belatedly, I thanked him for saving my life.

His smile grew crooked. "Guess we're even now." The laugh on my lips died down as his hands settled, as soft as young beech leaves, on the sides of my face, and he showed me how thankful he was we were both alive.

A throat cleared somewhere ahead of us. Sawyer's taunt body was shielding me before I could catch my breath, then relax.

"Well, well, well, ye two took yer sweet time about it." Kel was resting against a tree, his arms folded over very dirty clothes. To my dismay, Veena was right next to him, her features shuttered. I glanced at Sawyer. He gave me a reassuring nod and took my hand to join them.

"Haelan asked us to find ye two, we've all retreated to the camp." Sadness dulled his usually merry eyes as he met my own. I knew then Roldan's claims had been true.

"Father?" I croaked, "is he..."

He shook his head, his gaze downcast. Not him! Not father! "I'm sorry Fay, he was crushed under a building during that lightning attack." The one Sawyer had stopped me from checking. My heart had felt it then, I just hadn't recognised the signs. Head down I let the tears take over. Was this how it felt every time you lost someone you loved? Like a limb was ripped from you. The pain, the hollowness in one's heart. When I took a rattled breath, two arms crushed me against a hard chest and encircled me in a safe and supporting cocoon, as though I was going to shatter any second. *Was I?* Father's death was like a sick jest of life, I'd just been reunited with him, and now he was taken away from me for good. The picture of a smiling woman flashed with a sob.

Mother.

I wiped my eyes and nose on a handkerchief, my pain would be nothing compared to what she would feel, she had lost the love of her life. We would all have to take care of her, father would have wished for it. I needed to be strong for her, for Mara and Riogan, who was far too young to lose a parent. When at last I calmed down enough to operate, I took Sawyer's hand and started walking.

CHAPTER 29

Faylinn

Trees surrounding the camp shed leaves all around me, casting feelings of love and sympathy as they caressed my skin in their fluttering path. Their support was as important to me as the warm hand holding mine. My heart cried with love, a love I didn't know I held and a love I'd lost far too soon.

Injured and tired looking men sprawled on the ground while their brothers in arms and the few healers who had travelled with us attended to them. Others were taking down tents, folding, tidying, taking apart what had been raised but a few days ago. Halfway through camp, Haelan rushed over to me, eyes rimmed red with sorrow. No sooner than Sawyer let go of my hand, his strong arms enveloped me in that safe bubble I always felt with my big brother. It lasted a fleeting moment, but already I felt stronger, ready for what laid ahead of me. He directed me to our tent. No words were expressed, yet I understood what I would find.

However, expectation and readiness were worlds apart. After the flap fell behind the two of us, a wail of anguish escaped my trembling lips and my legs buckled. Healan was my strength, his arm supporting me with ease. A pallet was set in the centre where the fire had been only this morning.

Father's body laid down under the opening of the roof in order to show him the way to the stars and to our ancestors. The dim light could not hide the terrible state father was in. Blood, congealed with time and mixed with dust, covered half his face, striking a sharp contrast to his white skin. His clothes were torn, revealing gashes and broken bones. I went down on my knees and ran a hand across his head, tears running down my nose, my cheeks, but I didn't swipe them away. Let them drain my sorrow. Yet, how I knew grief was a long and deep well impossible to dry up; you never fully recovered from the loss of a beloved one.

Haelan placed a hand on my shoulder then put a bucket full of water down; I took one of the cloths on the handle, he the other. With quiet reverence we undressed and washed father. Haelan reset with gentle hands the broken bones, took away cuts, bruises and blemishes until father looked undamaged and peaceful. The extent of his abilities never seized to amaze me. I knew he was doing this for mother and Mara, but the apologetic look from his green eyes told me he wished he'd done it before to spare me too; I squeezed his hand in response as words failed me. He was a good man my dear brother, and I realised at that point I would do anything in my power to put him on the throne.

With father finally dressed and looking almost like his old self, we couldn't avoid anymore what needed to be done. Haelan cleared his throat and wiped his nose on his sleeve, shoulders slumped with weariness. "We leave at sunup." I nodded, eyes still locked on father, I wasn't ready to let him go. He put his arms around me from behind, his chin on my head. "I'll leave you alone to say your goodbyes." I retracted from his embrace shaking my head, I couldn't, it was too soon. Haelan held me by the shoulders and forced me to look at him. "Fay, you have to. You have to let him go or his soul won't be able to move on." I froze, then buried my face on his chest. I'd heard of roaming souls, unable to pass into the afterlife. "Do this for him. I know it's difficult after you've just been reunited with him." I broke down again. How could he always read me so well? He was right, I knew it, so I wiped my tears and said a wobbly, "All right."

"You know," he added after a while, still holding me. "Father never forgave himself for sending you away. Our spies were giving frequent reports, and he grew more and more guilty knowing how they treated you. After you couldn't visit us anymore… there was always this sadness about him, as though an important piece of his heart was missing, and it was. He loved you dearly, Fay, he loved us all, but you're the one he longed for each and every day." Something big and uncomfortable felt lodged in my throat. "Every time I came back from my duties at Court, he used to press me about everything and anything Fay," He chuckled memories blooming in his mind.

I stretched up and planted a kiss on his cheek, "Thank you." He looked at me hard for a moment; satisfied with what he saw he retreated to the flap. Before he went through, I forced myself to say, "Wait, Roldan is…"

He held a hand up. "Don't worry about that, I'll have a word with Sawyer." He nodded then left me by myself.

I went to father's side once more and sat down, watching the sharp features of the face I loved so much, taking in every detail. The straight nose and the generous mouth I had inherited, the white hair clashing with his youthful face; I took them all in, never to forget. During my forced imprisonment with the Royals, I'd resented him. Brooded about his inactions, his abandonment, sure within myself Mara was his favourite daughter. My mouth twisted. How stupid of me, as I was wallowing in my own misery, not to see beyond my own problems; how selfish of me to think I had been the only one affected. Yet, I'd kept on loving him. How could I not? He had been my support, my beacon for so long, only now its light had gone. But not what he's taught me I asserted to myself, refusing to part on pessimistic words. I wouldn't be the woman I was if it wasn't for him and for this, I was thankful.

I rose up on unsteady legs and bent over to place a last kiss on his forehead.

Farewell, father, I love you.

* * *

We slept under the stars that night, our things packed, ready for a quick departure at the crack of dawn. With Quentin and Roldan dead, Haelan, who was now the rightful heir to the throne, had decided to retreat. My brother was a scholar, not a fighter, he couldn't try to claim the throne without weighing, discussing every aspect of the situation. His need to grieve might also have influenced his decision. Father's tent was the last to be taken down; we put him in a covered carriage one of Haelan's guards, under disguise, had bought from a farmer. We wanted to be as inconspicuous as possible, but neither of us could bear carrying father on top of a horse unceremoniously.

It was with the pinks and yellows sweeping over the edge of the light blue sky that we started on our way home. Most of the wanderers parted from us at the camp and bade their goodbyes and promises of future correspondence along the way. While others, Sawyer's group essentially, stayed under the pretence of additional protection. I cast a glance at Sawyer riding next to me, relieved he was by my side. *Then what?* I couldn't help wondering about the future, our future to be precise. I needed to be with my family for my own sanity as much as to help them. There was no doubt in my mind that Gwynn would punish me for Roldan's death and take Sawyer with it, the threat in her voice had been carved with pure loathing. I chased the unpleasant thought away. My eyes settled on Haelan at the front of our large group, back rigid, strands of curly hair flying free of his leather tie. One look at him this morning was enough to deduce that, like me, he'd hardly slept, yet he'd directed his men and wanderers, giving orders and instructions like a true leader. No one argued or questioned what he said, all of us certain in the fact that what he did was the best for us, for the Kingdom.

The pace was hard and unrelenting. We slept in close groups under waterproof canvass sheets tied to the trees to stave off the plummeting temperatures at Haelan's insistence. His argument was they could be put up and removed much faster than tents and that we couldn't waste time on comfort. I struggled, every one of us was exhausted beyond measure, but I understood the urgency. We rode most of the day, always on our guard and expecting an attack at any moment. Sawyer and Dwennon had placed a protection spell over us all, but Haelan refused to ease up.

"We have to keep going, I can feel it in my bones." He said one day when I pressed him about it, pointing at the weary riders and horses. "I don't like the look of this." He cast his head up to the permanent louring grey clouds that had been following us. Now that he mentioned it, there was something strange about them, streaks of red surrounded the dense mass. "We'll be safe after we leave the Sky Mountains behind." he assured me, "Dwennon believes the same." If the two of them agreed on this, I could only trust their judgement.

By the time we rode past the Sky Mountains the light in the sky felt brighter, the ever-present gloomy clouds had evaporated over us in a mist, taking the unease I had felt with it. The morning after, I woke up the most refreshed I had felt since the beginning. I even felt myself smiling over breakfast as I was sitting with Haelan and my usual group. In fact, everyone seemed in better spirits.

"I feel like a great strain was removed from my mind. I feel better." I exclaimed when Sawyer asked why I was smiling so much.

"It's those clouds." Dwennon said. One fleeting glance around our circle revealed Kel and Veena were the only ones sharing mutual confusion. "Those clouds were anything but natural." He specified.

"What was it?" Asked Veena, taking the words that had been forming on my lips, Haelan had been unable to tell me.

He shook his head. "I'm not sure, but I could sense an ill intent."

Sawyer nodded his agreement and added. "I think they were trying to find us, but the protection spell eluded them."

"How can you be so sure? They were over us the whole time, maybe following us and whoever sent them knows where we are." I said.

"No, I don't believe so." Haelan shook his head. "I had four of my men ride away from us, two to the East, the others to the West for two days. The cloud was covering the entire sky. They spoke to villagers along the way, all of them said the same story, it started the day after Roldan died." His face was grim, a look that had replaced his usual cheerful appearance.

"I don't like this." Kel threw a branch on the fire and poked another one absently. Blaith, sensing his uneasiness, rubbed her head against his thigh. He was stroking her on the head as he added. "With the High Mage gone, who could yield so much power?"

My eyes met Sawyer's in shared understanding, I'd decided to wait until we were safe in our home to reveal the truth about Gwynn, but I couldn't keep the disturbing news any longer. "Gwynn," I whispered.

Haelan frowned. "Can't be, she's been weak and ill for as long as I can remember, and her power is solely centred on water." His mouth formed a comical O. "Water, clouds are made of water." He shook his head in denial. "Not possible, it would require a lot of power, too much for her. Anyway, why do you believe she did it?"

My mouth twisted on one side. "When I went to rescue her and got caught, Roldan said something strange, that she could steal my magical essence for some time or something along those lines. I don't think he thought I would be able to escape, so he spoke about it without any care." I ground my teeth. "And

I don't think it has anything to do with her gift."

"The Leechings." Dwennon. said, and I nodded. The group fell silent for a long time, everyone lost in their own anxious thoughts.

"One thing I don't understand," Kel interrupted our musings. "How come the cloud stopped at the Sky mountains."

"My theory is that she didn't have enough reach beyond that point." Dwennon speculated. "Still, if she is behind it, she's got tremendous power. And from what Faylinn just told us, not solely her own."

My head shot up in alarm. "More power than Haelan?" His eyes were fixed on the ground as though he was scared to look at me.

"One can never tell if the Leechings are involved, Faylinn." Dwennon's gravelly voice was sombre. "But one thing is for sure, whatever power she gains from it, she cannot hold on to it. It is not part of her and is therefore transient. From what I've read, the practitioner needs to recover from the onslaught of using it."

"I remember you saying something about its bad effects if you used it." I looked at Haelan. "Have you read about the Leechings?"

"Nah, you know me. I'm too much of a Myrddin worshipper for that kind of stuff. But there was something in one of his memoirs about a male Mage who went mad in the end from practising it. Can't remember his name now."

"Arai." Dwennon provided for him, "He was the husband of one of the creators of our world."

Haelan's face lit up. "That's right, and now we're talking about it I remember I have books on the subject in one of my hidden places. Grandfather asked me to hide them somewhere nobody could find them; he was worried they would get in the hands of someone not solely interested in history. Needless to say, I never looked at them, the idea repulsed me."

Dwennon's face broke into waves of wrinkles. "This could be a tip in our favour, boy. Splendid indeed!"

* * *

The dawn air felt frigid on my face, contrasting with the hot tears gliding down my cheeks. People from all over the province were present to pay their respects to father. The family cemetery, situated in a glade nestled by ash, aspen and oak trees, resembled a patchwork of white and midnight blue, the mourning colours of our Kingdom. The white stood for rebirth, the blue for the Great Unknown. Both colours represented an affiliation to a belief of the afterlife. Until the accidental discovery of past lives by a Soul mage, it was believed once dead, every mage went to a spiritual world only magic users could reach, and where we kept on living for all eternity. As nobody could corroborate this theory, that world had been dubbed the Great Unknown. Nowadays, reincarnation worshippers were more common. Plenty of them went to consult a Soul mage in order to access memories, usually ones of great impact, of past lives hidden in the deeper parts of their souls. A spell benign enough, but which could alter your life forever. For my part I didn't care how I lived in a past life or who I was, what mattered was the present. The people I loved and cherished, the Kingdom I wanted to rescue so badly.

A strangled sob by my side burst the bubble of my wandering mind and crashed me back to the cruel present. Mara, clutching my hand hard, was crying her heart out. My own tears seemed to have dried up, replaced by numb acceptance. I'd had time to grieve on the way back home; I squeezed her hand. Garlands of blue flowers rested on and around an unexceptional stone plaque, father's name was engraved in beautiful flowing blue writing, his favourite colour, hence the blue flowers.

Mother gave the parting words as was due from the mage's

mate, Haelan and Sunlark at her side in the event she would flit away on the breeze. She'd spent the past two days in bed, alternating between wailing and catatonic stupor. Haelan, now the head of the family, had taken the task of planning father's parting ritual; he had even prepared the parting words to send father's soul into its next life. However, to our utter shock mother, her frame looking dangerously frail and her face the exact colour of her mourning dress, had come down to the breakfast table that morning, legs unsteady, but her will resolute into sending her love away forever. No one had said a word as we watched her lead the procession to the family cemetery.

As the hand, which had been around my waist since we'd left the house, squeezed me gently I looked up from the blue flower in my hand into Sawyer's eyes.

"It's yer turn to send him away." He murmured and kissed me on the forehead. These past days he'd been my lifeline, the deep root that kept me grounded to the world around me and not wither away within myself. I stared ahead of me, at mother and my siblings sharing the same red eyes I was no doubt sporting; three flowers were already placed on the mound. I took a step forward, and Sawyer's hand slipped away, its warmth replaced by cold realisation today would be the day father left us for good. Laying the flower with a shaking hand I wished to the stars he would choose to be reincarnated into a human again. I didn't know the alternative, but I couldn't imagine this world without him.

Joining the others, I threaded my arm in Haelan's. "Do you think he will want to be reborn as a baby?" I whispered in his ear after he'd kissed my cheek.

He inhaled in a quick burst, a deep ridge forming between his eyebrows. I looked down. I shouldn't have asked; it was too soon to talk about it.

Pulling me backwards away from people, he murmured, lips barely moving. "Always straight to the point. What gave you the impression he'd tell me?"

"Look, I know it's private, not something I should be asking, but..." I held my words as some people stared at us frowning. Damn them, couldn't they leave us alone?

Haelan stepped in front of me, blocking their nosey gazes. "Fay, it's fine. I understand why you're asking. It's the same reason why I asked him the very same question when his health was declining."

I gasped. I did not expect that. Haelan had always been in awe of father, more so than me or my brothers and sister, always wanting to be as good a man as he was. That's why he'd always been respectful, even strait-laced with father; I couldn't imagine him asking such a personal question, and yet. I regarded my brother with new eyes, and yes, a different kind of respect. I wasn't the only one who had changed.

"What did he say?"

Haelan stood silent for so long I wondered if my words had floated away in the breeze. "That even if he lived three hundred years, it wouldn't be long enough to satiate his curiosity." His mouth stretched into a smile.

Fresh tears fringed my eyelashes, a striking clash to the smile which now illuminated my face. Whether or not I would meet him again was irrelevant, knowing he was out there would be enough for me.

CHAPTER 30

Faylinn

Sawyer's chest was heaving in short spells, matching my own; sweat glistened over the contours of his tanned muscles, flexing with exertion. My eyes stopped just above his belly button, cheeks afire. I could stare at this view all day. Who knew men's bodies could be so beautiful? Passing a large hand through his wet hair, he stared at me, smirking.

"Eyes always focused, lass."

"Oh, but they are, big lad." He laughed at that and sauntered towards me as gracefully as his big bulk could let him. He sheathed his sword, a wicked smile lingering.

I loved that we'd reached the stage where we could banter with each other. Despite the unpredictable future, he seemed more relaxed, more open with me since that kiss. As if the rope of tightly wound-up emotions weighing on his soul had finally snapped, taking with it all the pent-up guilt and frustration, all the tension he'd been carrying for years. He'd slowly opened his heart to me. Every day we spent hours together talking of everything and nothing. It was a whole new experience for me, not only was he willing to talk to me, but he also seemed genuinely interested in what I was saying. In many ways it was similar to my conversations with Haelan: unreserved and equal. Yet, it was so different baring my soul to someone who wasn't part of my family, someone whom I'd fallen in love with. The more we stayed together the more a nuance of expectation hung between us. It was almost palpable, a tension brewing, one that was present right now, one as thick as a willow's foliage in the summertime.

He gently grabbed a fistful of my hair in his hand and bent my head up so I would look up at him, his body was barely an inch from mine. I swallowed. I knew I shouldn't have flirted with that big mouth of mine, but the mischievous and daring part of me, the one that rarely came up for breath, had spoken without my brain's approval. Right now, the latter screamed to run away from the big tantalising man while the other craved to throw itself in his arms. It was in those moments I wished I'd had more experience with the opposite sex.

"I can see my student is far from focused." Sawyer whispered. I swallowed again, saliva catching in my throat as his free hand travelled in a shiver-inducing path from the side of my forehead, over my cheek and down to my chin, which he cupped in a caress. His mouth barely above mine he added, "Maybe a different kind of lesson would be more to yer taste." Tearing my eyes away from his, they settled over the small scar on his left shoulder.

How could an offer I'd been hoping for longer than I would ever admit make me feel so young and scared? In all my dreams, I'd been confident and bold. In reality, here I stood not knowing whether I wanted this or not, whether to run away or not. Was this thing between us even serious for him? Was I just another girl?

"I'm not sure what I said that upset ye, love."

I shook my head and said, "Nothing, I'm just..." I caught myself then, unwilling to show him this weak side of me. However, he wasn't one to give up and persisted, hands firmly grounding me in place, a sure sign he would not relent until I gave up and confided my fears. I sighed in resignation but prevaricated nonetheless. "Unlike women wanderers, we don't, ah, fumble between the sheets before our bonding."

His left eyebrow twitched. "Is that so?"

"So," I stopped the movement of my foot scraping the dirt and cleared my clogged-up throat.

Sawyer cut in with, "Is this foolish rule instated by noble men by any chance?" I nodded. "Men that are repressing women to the state of no more than puppets?" His eyes were now blazing. I opened my mouth to refute his claims; father wasn't like that. All the women in my family were valued members. Yet, unlike men, we were still expected to stay pure until bonding. He had a valid point. One I'd realised a while back. Which reminded me I wasn't being honest with him.

"I don't mind." He whispered.

"What?"

"We can wait to … fumble between the sheets." He smiled wickedly.

"What? No!" His eyes rounded in shock for a second, then he laughed at the horrified look on my face.

"I'm sorry, I wasn't being honest with you, that's not really the issue here. Living by your rules for a while made me realise I wanted more freedom for myself, including the freedom to be intimate with my chosen mate." This was excruciating. I swallowed, cleared my throat and swallowed again. Words then spilt out in a jumbled rush. "I'm nervous, of course I am. I've no such experience, yet I know you do. I wish wholeheartedly I could take the situation like a wanderer, take it as a life lesson, but I can't be so carefree about this." The long silence that followed was agonising, his hands on my shoulders had tightened for a second as I spoke, his face had closed off almost at once. I looked down after that, unable to confront the intensity blazing behind his stare. Small particles of dust were twirling by my boots, transported by the crisp breeze, then swooped away with a sharp gust.

Then, he spoke so softly I looked at his lips not to miss a word. "T'is true, I've been with women in the past, but none were more than a mere fleeting fancy. Nobody from my group, mind, as I didn't want to commit. Does that bother ye?" I stared at him hard and decided to be truthful. If there was any chance we were to start something solid, I wanted our relationship to stand on trust and communication. Still, I felt quite silly as I said, "I can't say I like it. What I'm trying to explain very badly is I don't think I could do this if the opposite party's heart is, ah, not involved." I held my breath, unsure on how he'd reply.

He was staring at something above my shoulder, lost in his thoughts. "I'm not proud of some of my past actions, I'm not this upstanding leader Luela seems to see me as, and I don't think I'm worthy enough to be with ye, but..." I took a breath and was about to tell him how wrong he was on all accounts, but he cut me off with a finger on my mouth. "But I want to stand by ye however long ye'll let me, and I'll try my damn hardest to be deserving of ye. Since I met ye, something happened to me, I feel different, lighter," he rasped his embarrassment away. "What I'm trying to say is nothing in this world will make me give ye up 'cept one word from ye..."

I watched the tense muscles of his neck, his fixed gaze on me. Here he was, his handsome features set in a frown, his feelings – uncertainty, apprehension and love, yes, this was clearly love – bursting out of him without the usual restraint. Just like that all my silly misgivings evaporated in a mist of oblivion. I blinked hard, but the tears escaped regardless. Like him, something at a level I didn't understand had changed within me, he'd had an impact on me from the start. Even when he'd been cold and reserved, I'd unconsciously found myself searching for him with my eyes. Tongue tied I could only nod, a tremulous smile breaking amid the tears, then a laugh as I watched Sawyer's face grow from surprise to concern, then relief. His face suddenly close to mine he whispered, eyes heated, "Care for our next lesson now?" My heart did a funny twirl in my chest that left me breathless. I took his hand and led him to my bedchamber.

❋ ❋ ❋

The next morning, I stood in the kitchen doorway watching a scene I couldn't get enough of: Mara and mother, their hands deep in dough, were talking with my friends who were having breakfast. My brothers were nowhere to be seen, no doubt preparing for the retaliation we'd been expecting for the past two weeks. So far life had gone back to a steady tangent, fields were ploughed, animals cared for; life went on as usual in spite of the unpredictable future. Some things had changed though, now every household in our province was fully armed, guards were watching our frontier and places of refuge had been designated and protected by Dwennon's spells.

I took the only available seat next to Veena. She gave me the basket half full of sweet buns as her response to my greeting. The room was blissfully warm thanks to the massive wood stove taking most of the wall behind me. The weather had a bite to it today. The farrier told me yesterday snow would fall within a week, and I could well believe it.

I sipped at my hot tea, casting glimpses at Sawyer over the rim of the cup. He caught me looking and gave a small wink of acknowledgement. We'd stirred in the early hours, skin touching skin, the past night a sweet dream. We'd decided it was for the best not to be caught together; mother was still fragile, and although she didn't seem to mind my relationship with Sawyer – I guessed she had lost hope of me behaving like a lady – she would have one of her fainting spells if she knew it'd reached that stage before our bonding. Therefore, with some reluctance I'd let go of Sawyer and watched him get up, naked and not one bit embarrassed about it. He took his sweet time getting dressed, then after one last kiss left me daydreaming in bed. I shifted in my chair and placed a hand on my cheek. Sawyer, ever so observant, sent me an amused look. Time for another thought, if my burning cheeks were any indication.

A shadow hovering in the hallway made me pause, the silhouette stayed put for a long moment before taking slow steps closer. One look at the ghostly appearance of Haelan in the doorway snuffed the easy mood in a heartbeat. The sombre set to his eyes was to understand he had bad tidings; the paleness of his face and the thin line that replaced his jovial smile put me on edge. His mouth opened as if to speak then closed, shaking his head he sat down, shoulders slumped, in the seat Sawyer relinquished. He looked every one of us in the eye. His silence was torturous, I wanted to shout to get on with it in order to tame my growing restlessness. Instead, I stayed quiet, hands held together in a painful grip on my lap.

"I've had news from my men in the Capital," he sighed. "Terrible news." He took a long breath, then let it go sharply. "Our dear cousin has doubled taxes in order to raise a bigger army so she can rid the Kingdom of wanderers, and anyone proclaimed unlawful by herself. Vermin, she called them, that threaten the wellbeing of our Kingdom." My eyes shot to my friends; their faces had turned a reddish hue of anger, shock seemed to have muted them.

"I don't understand." Only a whisper escaped my lips. "How did she find out the wanderers helped us?"

Haelan shook his head grimly. "I'm not sure she did. It's possible she recognised Sawyer's outfit when he killed Roldan. However, I'm inclined to believe she wants to make a show of power to keep both commoners and nobles in their places."

"Am I to assume we belong to that unlawful category of hers?" Mother's voice was tremulous. Haelan put his hand in his hair, gripped it and let go in one abrupt motion. He took a deep breath. "I shouldn't need to remind you mother, Gwynn was aware of my presence at our reprisal, and she blames Fay for Roldan's death. In that light, our whole family has been cut off unceremoniously from the Royal family. We are nobles no more, dear mother, we are but traitors, betrayers, any name you fancy. If it wasn't for our people's support and Dwennon and Sawyer's protective spells we would be obliged to go into hiding." The gentleness of his tone had taken the sting of his words. Since father's death mother had been more absent-minded, like she wanted to ignore reality. Perhaps she did. "Thankfully," Healan cast a quick glance at Sawyer with a small smile. "She couldn't find out who you were. Although I bet her guards are on the lookout for someone of your description."

"This does not worry me my friend, I expected as much." said Sawyer, leaning against the wall.

Veena moved her chair back in a scrape and folded her legs and arms. "Those taxes though, surely an increase didn't go smoothly with people."

Haelan nodded, "Riots are breaking out all over the Kingdom. The unlucky ones that are caught are flogged until they promise their allegiance; those that don't are thrown in the dungeons. There are also tales of people vanishing, and not just commoners."

"Nobles?" squeaked Mara, her lovely face wrought with worry, a slender hand at her throat.

Haelan reached out and squeezed her hand. "There's something not right, I've this gut feeling there's more to it than killing opposition. I might be wrong... but I'll send some men to look into the matter at any rate."

A strange conviction took hold of me. "Could she be stealing their magical essence?"

Haelan stared at me, a startled look on his face. "Myrddin saves us all! I hadn't thought of that, there's so many of them. How could she?" The implications were frightening.

Kel surprised us all by standing abruptly. "I want to be part of yer men on behalf of the wanderers." A pregnant look passed between Kel and Sawyer.

"I'm all for it," Veena announced. "Been feeling too cooped up here and all. No offence." She looked at my brother and mother.

"Aye, count me in." The man of my heart spoke softly. My eyes closed with a wave of dizziness. I blinked them open. This shouldn't hurt as much as it did. I'd suspected. Many times I'd caught him staring in the distance with a troubled expression; sometimes I imagined the wind was calling him back to his people. I wasn't an idiot, he didn't belong here, his people needed him as much as I did. Maybe more so. He had stayed so long for my sake, I understood that now. To my shame, my first impulse was to cry, shout at him how could he leave me so. Yet, the intensity, the unmistakable love in the eyes boring into me tempered the emotional storm before it could thrash out.

"How soon?" I was proud my voice didn't give away the anguish that was slowly drowning me.

He looked at his companions and asked. "Day after next to yer liking?" They both nodded their agreement. Two days, barely. I got up and walked out the room.

✻ ✻ ✻

The following day, as the sun finally met the horizon on its descent, I walked to the family cemetery. Time had passed as swift as a falcon diving towards its prey. Preparations for my companions' departure had kept us all busy, forcing a distance between Sawyer and I that I resented, and which unleashed dark thoughts and emotions I was ashamed of. Haelan, my best friend, my alter ego was harried to exhaustion with affairs far more important than the matters of my heart, and I couldn't bring myself to burden sweet Mara. So, I sat down by father's tomb and let the flow of my torment take over the tight restraint I had put on my feelings since I'd learnt of Sawyer's impending departure.

By the time I finished the place was dark, as though my words had soaked the world in a dismal atmosphere. Despite the fresh air, the warmth of the ground kept me snug. Maybe it was my silly imagination, but I liked to think father was enveloping me in his protective embrace. As my internal monologue ended, so did my tears. I'd needed this time to contemplate and accept all my worries and fears for the future; I didn't feel ashamed of my feelings, I was young and inexperienced still.

Without so much as a sound or warning, a large shadow

settled down right beside me. Our touching knees had my heart pumping harder than if I'd sprinted to the spring at the end of our property and back again. An enclosed candle holder, which Sawyer had placed on the grass, lifted the gloominess and cast a small area in orange light. For a while we stayed like this staring away from each other. The wind picked up. Naked tree branches knocked and creaked in an eerie tune above us. No words were uttered, no limbs moved. Yet, one quick glance revealed that my partner's lips were moving, albeit in an inaudible whisper, his gaze firmly set on father's tomb. Was he talking to him? As soon as that thought cleared itself up, Sawyer turned me around to look at him. I stared, love and heartache clashing over each other in my chest.

"Let..." his finger ended my desperate plea.

When he was satisfied I wouldn't speak any more, he retracted his hand and reached behind him, unhooked his necklace and tied it around my neck. My breath caught in my throat, and tears – these ones welcomed – made their reappearance once more.

"So?" He raised his eyebrows. I burst out laughing. Only Sawyer could propose bonding in one word and make it the most indelible and romantic moment of my life.

"I accept your proposal, oh Sir of few words." I took his head in my hands and kissed him long and slow.

When we separated for breath, his eyes were lit up with joy and amusement. "Good."

On our way back home, arms around each other, we decided to keep our bonding secret until he came back, both agreeing it wasn't the right time for the announcement. My family, mother especially, needed time to adjust to the changes in store for us.

"I'll tell Haelan though." I turned my head to Sawyer. "Even if I don't say anything he will guess, he knows me too well."

"Ye two are very close." I could listen to his voice all day, shame he didn't like to talk much. "I'm glad ye've someone like him to talk to."

"Will you tell Kel and Veena?" I asked curious how he would handle the situation with Veena.

"Aye"

"That way you'll have someone to grumble about how much you miss me and how stupid it was to leave me behind?" I cocked my head with a smile.

"Aye, that and more."

"More?"

"Mmmm." He threw one of those impish smiles.

I swatted my hand on his chest and said in a high voice. "You wouldn't dare."

He chuckled and kissed me hard. "Now, who's got a dirty mind? Course I wouldn't."

"What then?'

"Oh, just a little surprise for our reunion."

I knew better than ask what it was, the fact he was thinking about our future was enough for me. We were at the back door, the warm light of a candle set on the wall casting our shadows behind us. I whispered, "Any chance of extra lessons from my very talented teacher?"

He took me in his arms and bent down so his mouth was right by my ear. "If said lessons include having ye in my arms until dawn, love." he kissed me. "I'd be delighted."

The sounds of barking to the side of the house pulled us apart. Skylark and Riodan, two dogs in tow, were walking purposefully towards us. "Come on you two," Skylark said when he reached the door. "Lucy has prepared a parting feast." When the door opened, the mouth-watering smells and chatter brought a smile to my face in spite of the feelings the word parting had provoked. I was relieved Sawyer would spend the night with me, it wasn't much, but I was happy to take any second to breathe him in, to feel his skin on my skin. Those memories would be my sole consolations on those long days and nights ahead of me.

There were no goodbyes the next morning, only whispers of love and hope.

ACKNOWLEDGEMENT

To my husband, Matthew, thank you for spending hours brainstorming ideas, for critiquing the first drafts and pushing me to keep going.
To my daughter, Ren, for inspiring me and making me happy every day.

To my beta reader and wicked sister-in-law, Tiffany Patterson, thank you for noticing those pesky typos and answering thousands of questions. To my first reader, Jo Hynes, thank you so much for your input; it gave me hope.

To my editor and friend, Erica Millett, a big thank you for your hard work, your invaluable opinion and making this work in spite of the time difference.

REVIEW

Thank you for reading A Spell of Trouble. If you enjoyed reading my book, I would very much appreciate it if you could take a few moments to write a review of it on Amazon here or Goodreads here. Your feedback and support are very important to me. Thanks!

CONTACT THE AUTHOR

If you have any questions, or just want to say hi, please contact me through my Facebook Author page:

https://www.facebook.com/I-C-Patterson-105660322115462

Or join my Mailing List on my website to get updates on future releases:

https://icpatterson.wordpress.com/

Printed in Great Britain
by Amazon

22251455R00199